Nightfire

Nightfire

A Protectors Novel:

Marine Force Recon

Lisa Marie Rice

AVON

An Imprint of HarperCollins*Publishers*

NIGHTFIRE. Copyright © 2012 by Lisa Marie Rice. All rights reserved. Printed in the United States of America. No part of this book may be used or reproduced in any manner whatsoever without written permission except in the case of brief quotations embodied in critical articles and reviews. For information address HarperCollins Publishers, 10 East 53rd Street, New York, NY 10022.

HarperCollins books may be purchased for educational, business, or sales promotional use. For information please write: Special Markets Department, HarperCollins Publishers, 10 East 53rd Street, New York, NY 10022.

FIRST EDITION

Designed by Diahann Sturge

Library of Congress Cataloging-in-Publication Data has been applied for.

ISBN 978-0-06-180828-9

12 13 14 15 16 OV/RRD 10 9 8 7 6 5 4 3 2 1

*This page is fondly dedicated to my good friend Judith Edge,
the sharpest knife in the drawer*

Acknowledgments

As always, a big thank you to my agent, Ethan Ellenberg, and to my editor, May Chen. Thanks as well go to Amanda Bergeron, always ready with a helping hand.

Chapter 1

San Diego
January 4, early morning

"Harder," she moaned. Mike Keillor gritted his teeth, started moving faster, harder. The cheap, filthy bed creaked so much he was afraid it would come apart. *"Harder,"* she insisted. The woman under him was red-faced, glassy-eyed, teeth clenched hard as his hips slapped against hers.

"More," she hissed. When they'd come stumbling into her filthy apartment, drunk and kissing, she'd said she wanted to be held down during sex. So he was holding her down, big hands clenched tightly around her wrists. She bucked up against him, hard, pelvis banging against his, and moaned again.

That was pain he heard.

Startled, Mike stopped moving inside her, lifted his hands. Her wrists were red, starting to swell. He could see his finger marks.

God.

He had big, strong hands. His father's hands. Tough, sinewy hands. Hands that could hurt. Hands that had hurt this woman.

Mike had his father's hands, but he had never seen his father touch his mother or his brothers with anything other than gentleness and tenderness and love.

His father's hands had hurt this woman.

And she liked it.

This was sickness. Madness.

Horror boiled up inside him.

Mike pulled out of her, rolled over and ran around the tiny apartment looking for a toilet. He pulled open the door to the closet, to a minuscule kitchenette, and finally found the door to the bathroom. He flung up the seat with a loud thunk, barely making it in time to throw up into the brown-stained toilet.

He vomited the six whiskeys with beer chasers, the plate of greasy fries he'd used to anchor the alcohol, and above all he vomited up the fact that he'd been fucking a woman he hurt and who *wanted* him to hurt her.

Michael Keillor didn't hurt women. Ever. The thought that he just had kept him hovering over the filthy toilet, one hand braced against the dirt-streaked tiles, as he coughed up bile.

"Hey!" A sharp fingernail poked his naked back. "You shithead! You left me hanging. Fuck's 'a matter with you?"

Mike had no idea. He stared into the godawful brown-streaked toilet that hadn't been cleaned in months.

What was the matter with him?

Good question.

What the fuck was he doing here?

Even better question.

His dick was down, the rubber hanging limply off it. He pulled it off, threw it in an overflowing wastebasket.

"Hey, you motherfucker!" She thumped his back, hard. "I'm talking to *you*!"

Mike turned to face her.

He had no idea who she was. He didn't remember her name. Maybe she hadn't told him. Maybe he hadn't asked.

The bar had been dark and loud and they had communicated mainly by her hand on his crotch, rubbing his dick. Five minutes after he'd first set eyes on her, they'd been staggering out the door to this apartment a block away.

She wasn't a working girl. She hadn't asked for money. All she wanted was a fuck.

And for him to hurt her.

He could see it now, the fine scars crisscrossing her face, two knife scars on her naked chest, old and new bruises. She'd been hurt already, a lot.

She was scrawny more than thin, as if not only she didn't eat enough, but what she did eat was crap. Mike outweighed her by more than 120 pounds. She'd picked him up in a bar, a drunk and powerfully built man, and now she was provoking him.

She slapped him, then stepped right up into his face, features twisted in a sneer, mouth blurry with smeared lipstick. "You hear me, you asshole? You fuck me till *I'm* done, not till you're done. And go puke somewhere else, limp-dick asshole."

Mike simply looked at her, breathing down another spasm of bile.

She watched him, dark eyes bright with anticipation. She'd just challenged him, insulted his manhood.

There was a script for this, a set sequence of events, one she was waiting for, *trembling* for. He was supposed to start whaling on her, beating her bloody. Right about . . . now.

She expected it. Wanted it. Was quivering for it. And if he could read female arousal right, and he had years of experience at it, she was getting off on the idea of being beaten up. By him.

Mike couldn't breathe.

He needed to get out of here, fast. Needed to get out of this disgusting bathroom, out of this disgusting apartment, out of this disgusting life. Now.

She was standing in the doorway to the bathroom, blocking his way.

Mike reached out to close his hands on her shoulders. Under his big hands, her bones felt like bird bones, barely covered by skin. She shivered, an uncontrollable movement of excitement. The game was about to begin, and man, she was so up for it.

But instead of flinging her against the wall, Mike simply lifted her slightly off the ground and gently put her down a foot to the right so he could get out of this damned bathroom and get to his clothes before what was roiling in his stomach could come up and out again.

He was pulling up his jeans when he felt her push his back. "You son of a bitch!" she screamed. "Where the fuck you think you're going, huh? You're gonna stay right here and get the job done, you bastard."

Mike looked around for his boots, hearing her screeching voice as if it came from a distance, like a fly buzzing and batting against the windowpane.

He found his boots—one under the bed, one lying on its side under a rickety, splintered chair. He remembered tearing them off. He'd been in a rush to get his clothes off, get them into the bed. Not because he'd been consumed by lust, he now recognized, but because he wanted to start fucking before the smell, and the filthy mess he could see even in the dim light, turned him completely off.

Now that he'd puked up most of the alcohol and was semi-sober, he realized he'd been right to hurry because what he saw was enough to switch his dick right off.

He was a Marine—even if he'd been SWAT with the SDPD and was now a partner in a thriving security business with his brothers, once a Marine, always a Marine. Marines were neat and organized. This awful hovel looked like rats nested here. Clothes flung everywhere, not one thing folded. The bed had been unmade last night, sheets filthy and stained. The whole place stank of sweat and sex and despair and—oh God—now that he was paying attention, a space was cleared off a table, with a mirror and a razor blade and some white powder that had scattered.

Shit. Fuck. Oh fuck.

A cokehead. He'd fucked a cokehead. Half fucked a cokehead.

She was screaming abuse at him, kicking him, trying to pummel him with her fists. Mike was tempted to just stand there and let her abuse him because he deserved it.

He was thirty-five years old. He'd been a soldier and a damned good one. He'd been SWAT, the best on the force. And now he was a partner in one of the most successful security companies in the country.

He was one of the good guys.

So what the *fuck* was he doing here with a cokehead? One with mental problems, too. What was the *matter* with him?

He tuned back into what she was screaming.

"—ing asshole, what the fuck do you think you're doing, you fuck-head, you can't even keep it up, I thought I was bringing home a man but I was bringing home a faggot who can't keep it up . . ."

Mike tuned back out as he put on his jacket. If there had been anything even remotely funny about any of this, he'd laugh. His big problem in life up to now hadn't been keeping it up, but keeping it down.

Sex had always been a sort of refuge, a way to turn his head, his feelings off. Like running, only more fun. Sweaty brainless exercise.

This—he didn't know what this was. It wasn't sex. It wasn't fun. It was a glimpse into a dark part of himself that scared him shitless. A dark part that inevitably led to a black, dank future made up of filthy holes like this one, touching rock bottom over and over and over again.

Her screams were louder now that she realized he was actually leaving and she wasn't going to get fucked or beaten up.

Shit. She was making a terrible racket. Someone was going to call the cops and wouldn't that be the perfect end to a perfect day? Have his old cop buddies forced to haul his ass down to the cop shop.

His buddies in law enforcement knew he wasn't capable of hurting a woman. Some of them even knew that his company, RBK Security Inc., secretly helped battered and abused women escape from their tormentors and set up somewhere else with a new life. Their own underground railroad.

But this woman showed signs of long-term abuse. If she screamed rape, they'd find his DNA on her if not in her and they'd be honor-bound to take the whole sorry show down to headquarters and get the D.A. involved.

Sam and Harry would have to come bail him out.

There'd be an inquest, maybe a trial. RBK's name dragged through the mud.

Jesus.

Mike shut the door on the screaming woman and looked around. If the apartment was bad, the hallway was worse. Every other lightbulb was burned out and the whole place stank of piss. His feet stuck to the streaked and filthy linoleum. Now that the woman behind the door had stopped screaming and was only crying, Mike could hear another woman yelling behind a door further along the corridor.

The place reeked of sickness and violence and despair.

He made his way down the stairs, head down, holding his breath. Someone had puked on the landing on the second floor. He didn't know what depressed him more—this sad dump or the fact that he'd been so drunk stumbling up the stairs, his brain in his pants, that he hadn't noticed anything.

Pushing open the street door and coming out into the clean chill night air was like a calm hand stroking him. He finally breathed in as he checked out his surroundings.

The entire street was bad news. The few functioning street-lights showed abandoned houses, human beings curled up on the sidewalk, one old geezer on a porch step drinking out of a paper bag, another one in lumpy rags, pissing against a wall, most of it splashing on his shoes as he missed.

It was probable that all the alcohol in Mike's system was now making its way through the San Diego sewer system, but it wasn't worth the risk being caught out in a DUI. He'd leave his SUV where it was. It had a tracking system if anyone stole it, and anyway, he was insured up to his eyeballs. Tomorrow he'd have Barney drive him in. Tell him some lie about being on a stakeout. Barney wouldn't even question it. He thought Mike and Sam and Harry were gods.

Mike snorted at the thought.

He looked up at the night sky, clear, a few bright stars penetrating the light pollution of the city night. When he went camping, far from the city lights, he could see a billion stars at night.

When was the last time he'd been camping? God, he couldn't even remember.

And what was he doing here, in this godforsaken part of town, fucking a semi-deranged woman? A woman who wanted him to *hurt* her? Mike had fucked a lot in his life but he'd always steered clear of the crazies. The druggies and the married ones and the crazies. Iron rule, never broken, until now.

What was he doing?

He knew what he was doing. Running away from Sam and Harry and their families, that's what.

Sam Reston and Harry Bolt. They'd been boys together and now men and they were closer than brothers. They'd all three of them grown up without families. Sam's mom had thrown him away like garbage when he was a newborn. Harry's mom and baby sister had been killed by his mom's methhead boyfriend when he was twelve. And Mike—Jesus.

He rubbed his chest. How could it still hurt? The loss of his family had gone down twenty-five fucking years ago. He was a man. A Marine, a cop, a security expert. A sniper, one of the best there was. Tough as leather.

And it still fucking hurt.

Home. He needed to get home.

Why was he here and not at home? Well, besides the fact that home was big and empty, with nothing there for him, he'd seen his sisters-in-law give each other a Look.

The whole Christmas season they'd all eaten either at Sam's place or at Harry's place. They all lived in the same building on Coronado Shores, where Mike had a large empty space he sort of called home because there wasn't another one, so that was It. Home by default.

Sam's huge apartment and Harry's slightly smaller apartment in the condo had both been transformed into welcoming havens by their wives. It was a toss-up which was nicer. Sam and Nicole's place was huge, their housekeeper was a fabulous cook, and as an ambassador's daughter, Nicole was a gifted hostess.

Four floors down, Harry and Ellen's place was a little smaller with no in-house cook, though Ellen had a little band of fanboys who happened to be restaurant chefs and they vied with each other to send her gourmet meals. At any given time, they could be eating dishes prepared by chefs of the top restaurants in town.

There was another great thing about dinner at Harry's. His wife was one of the finest singers in the world and dinner was often followed by little impromptu concerts that would have any music lover weeping with gratitude.

And the kids. Jesus.

Mike would walk barefoot over hot coals to play with Sam's little girl, Meredith. Merry was adorable, bright and beautiful. She loved her Uncle Mike, and man, he loved her back. Another little girl was on the way and they were all looking forward to her. And Harry's little girl, Grace—she was only three months old and she already smiled when she heard his voice.

So it was real easy to fall into the habit of eating three, four and, now that he thought of it, even five nights a week either at Sam's or at Harry's. And of course the weekends they all hung out together. Barbecues on the terrace or takeout pizzas and beer and ball games.

This year was the happiest Mike had ever been since his family had been slaughtered. He'd even lost a little weight because he was eating better, on a regular basis. Real food, too, not crap bar food.

His sex life had taken a hit, but if you held a blowtorch to his bare feet and pulled his fingernails out, he'd have to admit that he was more than a little sick of the bar scene and the impersonal sex that went with it.

So he was happily living through his brothers' families, though that wasn't the way he thought of it. Not until last night.

He'd spent New Year's Eve at Sam's house, playing with Merry, they'd all spent New Year's Day together at Harry's and the night after that at Sam's. When Mike asked about today, there'd been a flash between Ellen and Nicole and Sam and Harry. One look containing a thousand words.

Who was going to take on the problem child? The one who couldn't get his act together?

Eve was tired because she'd given her annual Christmas concert and it took a lot out of her and over the Christmas season had recorded a CD that was going on sale in March. Plus Grace was teething and both she and Harry had bruised rings around their eyes from sleepless nights. Nicole was three months' pregnant, suffering from morning sickness, and had a big important translating job she'd taken on over the holidays and was working on from home.

That was when it hit Mike like a blow to the head—they wanted to spend time on their own. Each family wanted to spend an evening alone, each in its own space, relaxing. The only one without a family to go to was Mike and they'd sort of taken up the burden of providing a surrogate family for him.

He burned with shame when he realized how often he simply took it for granted that he'd be welcome, any day he wanted, any meal he wanted. Feeding off the good vibes Sam's family and Harry's family gave off.

Mike Keillor, vampire.

He'd resolved to stop sucking at the teat of his brothers' families and take care of himself. Starting now. This evening, he'd opened the fridge, seen bright glowing emptiness except for two six-packs of Anchor Steam, and had headed downtown. Looking for something to eat and something to fuck.

Well, that'd turned out real well, hadn't it?

Mike had an excellent sense of direction. He'd been top in his class in Scout/Sniper training and he'd made Force Recon. The map in his head turned, he turned and started walking.

Walking became a slow trot, because he wanted to escape from his thoughts. And he wanted to get away from this part of town. It was depressing, borderline dangerous. The streets were dark, filthy. Pathetic bundles of clothes covered in cardboard huddled hard between the sidewalk and the building walls, hoping for a little leaked heat.

He ran past a rusted drum. Inside, a fire had been lit, rough hands warming themselves over the fire. The glow cast an orange light up grotesque, lumpy, misshapen faces, the faces of men who had abscessed teeth and cuts that were never treated. One man opened his mouth in a feral animal snarl, rotted teeth like black tree stumps in his mouth.

A methhead, just like the one who beat Harry's mom and his little sister to death. Harry was just now getting over that, thanks to a wonderful wife and a little girl, both of whom he desperately loved.

Mike ran faster. He wanted to get away from here, away from everything that was here, from the darkness and the pain and the sorrow. He'd had so much of that in his life.

Why could he never escape it?

He was running flat out now, that pounding rhythm that took him out of himself, sweating out the toxins from tonight and the memories of all the nights he'd gone tomcatting in dives, waking up in snarled, sweaty sheets with the woman du jour, trying to remember her name even when his hangover was so catastrophic he could hardly remember his own.

He wanted to forget all of that as he ran and ran and ran. It was more than fifteen miles to Coronado Shores, not counting the ferry, a distance he'd run daily in boot camp, carrying fifty pounds of gear. And when he seized up with stitches, that old bastard Ditty, his drill instructor, screamed right into his ear that pain was weakness leaving the body.

Ditty was right, of course. D.I.s were always right. All Marine D.I.s were God.

On and on and on. His head lifted when he reached the ocean, the clean briny smell of it in his lungs. He'd sweated out the stench of the woman's room and their sick sex. Now the only thing he could smell was his own sweat and the sea. The sky over the city behind him was now a slightly lighter shade of black and, ahead of him, he could start to distinguish the line where sea met sky.

He stopped at the ferry landing, running in place so he wouldn't lose his rhythm and kept it up even when the ferry arrived and he boarded. It was so early there were few people to stare at the crazy guy hopping up and down. When they landed, he ran straight off.

He was pouring with sweat by the time he ran down the sidewalk to his building, the last condo on Coronado Shores, fumbling in his pocket for the keys. Ruiz, one of the four night guards of the building, saw him and remotely unlocked the big two-story glass doors.

Ruiz had been there a couple of years and he'd seen Mike come home in every single state there was—after nights of drunken sex and after nights of undercover work. Drenched in sweat from a long run in jeans, a tee and a bomber jacket was nothing. Ruiz simply nodded to Mike as he slowed to a walk and crossed the huge lobby.

Upstairs, his apartment was exactly as he'd left it earlier tonight—no, last night—in a restless rush. Clean, because a cleaning lady came in once a week and because he was Marine-neat. He didn't have too much stuff anyway. Bed and couch and entertainment center and a kitchen that he never used.

Antiseptic and empty.

He stripped out of his sweat-sodden clothes, dropped them in the laundry basket and headed for the shower. He stood under the big showerhead, leaning with both hands against the wall, letting the steaming hot water sluice over his back for a full half hour. By the time he got out, the sky outside the window was pearly gray. He walked out onto the long deck overlooking the Pacific and looked out over the view he loved.

This morning the vast cobalt blue ocean with its lacy morning waves didn't instill the deep calm it usually did. He clutched the iron balcony, standing there with a big white towel around his hips, watching the sky become lighter and lighter.

Unlike Harry, Mike never had trouble sleeping. Before getting married and plunging into Harry Blissworld, Harry had gone for three, four nights at a time without sleeping, something Mike had never really understood.

Now he did. He felt no sleepiness at all. He felt like he'd never sleep again. He watched the sky grow brighter, the ocean becoming ever larger and he felt that his life was like the ocean, going on and on and on, yet never changing. He had a glimpse of his own future in the water.

On and on.

Trying not to bug Nicole and Ellen too much. But seeing as much of his nieces as he could, because he loved those little girls. It seemed to him that the only thing he had to look forward to was watching them grow up, from the outside looking in.

He felt restless, almost aching for that fight the woman had wanted. He didn't want to fight her, he wanted—shit. He didn't know what the fuck he wanted. He knew only that if he'd come across some gangbangers in his long run across town, he'd have welcomed a really good, rough fight.

He was good with his fists. Was a fighter, always had been. There wasn't any number of men he'd back down from. Bring it on.

Hooah. Yeah.

Bullshit.

Something deep in his gut told him there wasn't any kind of fistfight that would calm whatever it was that was boiling inside him.

Finally, when the sun had lightened the entire sky, he went back inside to get dressed for another working day.

Chapter 2

Chloe Mason sat in the very elegant waiting room of RBK Security Inc., which was in a very elegant building in very elegant downtown San Diego.

She'd spent a lot of time in plush designer surroundings, but she was still impressed with the large room, which managed to be both beautiful and designed for comfort and efficiency.

It also had another quality she was very familiar with. Everything in the room, from the color palette of light earth tones to the lush, healthy plants to the expensive couches and armchairs, the interesting but not shrill modern artwork, was designed to calm and to soothe.

It was still the Christmas season, but the office didn't have the usual loop of nauseatingly familiar carols playing, which many found grating and stressful, particularly if they were in trouble. Rather, the Christmas spirit was honored by soft medieval madrigals playing in the background. Instead of killing a tree, the company had put up a colored light sculpture that was both intriguing and beautiful.

She'd spent all of her childhood and a good deal of her adolescence in and out of very expensive medical clinics and that mixture of good taste and reassurance was one she was familiar with.

Even the receptionist was soothing. Chloe had walked into this highly successful office and asked to speak with one of the partners. In American business-dom that just didn't happen. She knew enough of business etiquette to know that.

And yet she hadn't made an appointment. She'd propelled herself here from Boston without even thinking of making one, excited and terrified and hopeful, in equal measure.

So she'd walked over to the elegant U design of the reception counter and quietly given her name to the slender, sharply dressed receptionist with beautiful silver hair cut by someone who knew what he was doing.

The receptionist hadn't blinked at the unexpected request. She simply looked up and asked whether the appointment was urgent.

Urgent? Was it urgent? Maybe, maybe not. Though if Harry Bolt was who she thought he was, it was more than urgent. It was life-shattering.

So she simply nodded, throat too tight to plead her cause.

"Okay then," the receptionist had said, tapping on her touch screen. "It's a busy morning for Mr. Bolt, but I'll do what I can." She looked up again, eyes searching Chloe's face. "Would one of the other partners do? Mr. Keillor has a free hour this morning."

Mr. Keillor would be Michael Keillor, former Marine, former SWAT officer, current partner. She'd read his bio on the RBK website and seen his unsmiling photograph. He looked smart and tough and capable, just like all the partners. If she had security problems, he'd probably be just as good as Harry Bolt.

But her problems didn't have anything to do with security.

She shook her head, hoping the receptionist wouldn't take her inability to speak as discourtesy. And while she was at it, that the receptionist wouldn't notice Chloe's shaking hands.

The receptionist didn't, she simply touched the screen again.

"Okay, I can clear you for Mr. Bolt at nine-thirty, if you don't mind waiting."

Chloe had waited all her life for this moment. Another half an hour wouldn't make any difference. She managed to choke out a *thank you* through her tight throat and sat down to wait on one of the incredibly comfortable armchairs that dotted the enormous lobby.

So many emotions swirled in her chest that she couldn't feel any single one in particular, just a huge pressure so powerful she could barely breathe. She wanted *so much* for—

And she stopped herself right there. Wanting didn't make things happen. If there was one thing her life had taught her, it was that. She could want so fiercely she thought she would explode and it wouldn't make any difference at all. It was impossible to understand what really could make a difference. Fate? Perhaps. Randomness? Maybe. Wanting? No.

So she sat back in the extremely comfortable and attractive armchair and . . . disappeared.

It was her trick, harshly learned throughout her childhood. Bad things happened to her when she got noticed. She'd learned very early to sit back and become unnoticed. She didn't become literally invisible. It's just that she could turn off all the subconscious signals humans sent to one another, so that no one noticed her.

She sat there, unmoving, saying nothing, and observed. Observed the other people waiting for one of the three partners. There were three men in the room, all middle-aged or older, all visibly rich and powerful. Businessmen, who wanted RBK to help them in something or with something. Two were sweating so badly a slightly acrid odor rose above their expensive colognes. The other sat in Male Mode, knees apart, clasped hands between them. He radiated anger and aggression.

Chloe didn't dare look at him. Though she'd perfected the art of blandness, she knew through bitter experience that an angry male took even a chance meeting of eyes as aggression.

She turned her head toward the entrance door so that he couldn't even pretend to think that she was staring at him, and watched as the sliding door swooshed open.

A man walked into the waiting room and all male eyes swiveled to him, watching his progress across the lobby. The three rich-looking men might think that they were alpha males in their own environments but they weren't. Chloe knew many rich men who thought their money gave them top dog status anywhere, anytime. Often it did, but not always.

This man, striding across the room, was the alpha male. He'd be the alpha male in any grouping, rich man, poor man, didn't make any difference.

He wasn't tall but he was immensely broad—wide shoulders, thick arms, strong neck. A bodybuilder but without that body-builder waddle because he clearly built onto muscles that were already there. His movements were fast, precise, powerful. The strongest man in the room, hands down. And he'd be the strongest man in the room in most rooms.

Michael Keillor. The K in the RBK. He wouldn't be billionaire-rich but he didn't have to be. He was wealthy, successful, domi-nant. Enough by any person's measure.

He scanned the lobby as he walked by, eyes dwelling for a moment on her. He didn't break his stride, but Chloe knew he was studying her. She met his eyes, fiercely blue, very intelligent, impersonal and cold. Suddenly he blinked, the coldness vanished and something happened, but she didn't know what.

When he walked in, he'd launched himself across the room as if it were just a way station as he arrowed toward the offices vis-ible behind a glass-plated sliding door, but now he detoured and stopped for a moment at the desk, elbows on the counter, leaning forward to talk to the receptionist.

The woman looked startled, then shot a glance at Chloe.

Her heart gave a painful beat in her chest. He was discussing *her*? Why? Did he have some inkling of why she was here? How could he? No one on earth knew why she was here. Not even old Mr. Pelton, the family lawyer, knew, because she hadn't approached him yet.

Time enough for that if she was successful. Not that Mr. Pelton would ever approve.

No. Her mission here was completely secret.

So why was Michael Keillor discussing her with the receptionist? It was . . . it was unnatural. Chloe wasn't used to being the focus of anyone's attention. She didn't remember learning the art of passing under everyone's radar. It had always been there and she'd perfected it over the years.

She never dressed outrageously. Her clothes were expensive but low-key, never too trendy. She was always clean and groomed, but never flashy.

All her life, people had taken one look and simply forgotten her in an instant, walking on by. Chloe didn't want attention. Not out of shyness, but because she was afraid of it. Since she could remember, attention had meant danger. If someone looked at her too closely, her heart began pounding, an instinctive and totally uncontrollable reaction.

Michael Keillor nodded at the receptionist, took another look at her that had her hands sweating, and disappeared through the sliding glass door into the offices at the back of the lobby.

Nine-fifteen. The appointment with Harry Bolt was in a quarter of an hour if he was a punctual man.

Chloe sat back to do what she did best—wait. It seemed almost her entire childhood—what she could remember of it anyway—and adolescence had been spent waiting. Waiting for the scars to heal, waiting for the casts to come off, waiting to recover from the last surgery, waiting for the next one. She was the goddess of waiting. If there were a Ph.D. in waiting, she'd have been awarded one years ago.

She knew exactly how to prepare for a bout of waiting, how to breathe shallowly, slowly, how to distance herself from her body, how to will herself to stillness.

In college, she'd read up on a number of behavioral and mind-control techniques and found that she'd taught them all to herself instinctively, without knowing they existed.

Chloe could outwait anyone. Just sink right down into herself until she needed to come back up.

But right now, it shocked her to realize that none of her techniques worked. Her breath was rapid, almost panting. Her heart trip-hammered in an anxious, uneven rhythm. Her palms were sweaty. There was no way she could will herself back into her well of calm. She kept clutching the manila envelope on her lap over and over again, until the edges were sweat-stained and crumpled. Another sign of huge stress, together with the feeling that there was no oxygen in the room.

She had waited her entire life for this moment, without knowing it. And now that it was here, she wasn't prepared. She would never be prepared. She'd thought and thought about what she would say but nothing occurred to her. Her mind was empty, hollow and shiny with panic. She didn't even know if she could talk, her mouth was so dry.

Think, Chloe! she told herself sternly. She'd done so many hard things in her life, surely she could do this?

What to say? How to tell if she should even say it? Maybe she'd talk to the man and realize that she'd been insane to rush across the country for this. Maybe—

"Ms. Mason?"

Chloe turned, heart pounding. "Y-yes?" she stammered, sliding forward to the edge of her seat.

The receptionist gave her a kind smile. Considering how up-scale this office was, the smile was purely gratuitous. Most recep-tionists and secretaries in successful big-bucks enterprises were haughty. Certainly Mr. Pelton's was. In all the visits to her lawyer's offices, Chloe had mainly seen Mr. Pelton's secretary's nostrils as she tilted her head up to look down her nose.

"Mr. Bolt is free to see you now. Third door to your right down the corridor." She pointed to the big glass doors next to the recep-tion desk.

Oh God, this is it!

Panic keened in Chloe's head as she slowly rose, hoping her knees would support her. It was a very real fear. Both her knees were complex creations of plastic and steel and they were as deli-cate as they were high-tech.

Everyone's eyes followed her as she made her slow way across the lobby, which suddenly felt as huge as the Gobi Desert. The glass door ahead of her was so clean it glowed. How was she sup-posed to—ah. It swooshed open at some invisible command.

Inside the corridor, the feeling of luxury was even more power-ful. The doors were shiny brass, with no doorknobs, only built-in flat-screens to the right. The rooms must be enormous because it felt like she walked for ages down the gleaming parquet corridor simply to get to the third door on the right.

Here, too, she was met with a wall as blank as her head. She simply stood there, clutching a purse and an envelope tightly, waiting for the next step. Any thoughts or plans simply vanished from her head. She felt as if she were walking on some kind of uncontrollable path where she could stumble only forward and never turn back.

She stared at the shiny brass door, looking blankly at her reflec-tion, mind emptied of thought for a heartbeat, two. Then there was a whirring sound, a click releasing some invisible mechanism, and this door too slid open.

Chloe stood, frozen, on the threshold. She'd been dreaming of this moment all her life, thinking she was insane because it happened only in her dreams.

When things remained as hopes and dreams you could decide how they turned out. And though not much in her life had turned out well, in her dreams this always had. It had always ended in laughter and joy.

Only in her head, though.

Which was notoriously unstable.

Chloe trembled. Stepping into this room might mean stepping into a new and better life. Or it might forever trap her behind the invisible but oh-so-real wall she'd lived behind all her life.

It felt as if her entire existence were hanging by a thread, by a step.

"Ms. Mason?" a deep voice said, and she gasped in air. She'd been holding her breath for almost a minute without realizing it.

Across another vast room, two men were standing, as gentlemen did for ladies. One was Michael Keillor.

She didn't want him there. Her business was exclusively with Harry Bolt, and if her business ended badly, she didn't want anyone else to view her humiliation. But a lifetime of training made her hold her tongue. She didn't even remotely have the courage to ask him to leave the room.

The other man was . . . was Harry Bolt. Chloe eyed him hungrily. Much taller than Michael Keillor and almost, but not quite, as broad. Dark blond hair, light brown eyes. Familiar-looking eyes.

Her heart was slamming against her chest so hard she wondered if they could hear it.

Chloe was used to observing and interpreting body language, but there was absolutely nothing to read here. Both men were utterly still, both were utterly expressionless.

She had no way at all to gauge their feelings. No way to figure out how this would end.

Shaking, with a feeling of doom interlaced in her heart with wild hope, Chloe stepped into the room.

She's scared shitless, Mike thought, glad that he'd horned in on this meeting. This Chloe Mason had specifically asked for Harry Bolt, but once Mike had seen her in the lobby, he knew he had to be here, too.

Because this woman was clearly one of the Lost Ones. A woman in trouble, on the run from some violent asshole. And shit, it made him angry all over again that there were monsters in the world who could beat up on women.

RBK mainly dealt with corporate security. In the lobby waiting for RBK's very expensive services, there'd been two CEOs and one head of security for a Fortune 500 company. Mike had read their files, knew what their problems were and knew how to solve them.

Those three men alone probably represented about a million dollars in business this year for RBK.

Chloe Mason represented nothing, because RBK policy was not to accept money from women on the run. If anything, RBK often provided the women with a little nest egg to see them through that first difficult year.

On average, after the first year, they were safe.

After last night, Mike really, really wanted to make a woman safe. Wanted to help a woman, particularly a woman like this, soft and gentle and completely undeserving of the sick fuck who'd forced her to come to them.

This morning Sam was staying home with Nicole, who had bad morning sickness, so the corporate honchos would be divided between him and Harry. Stuff he and Harry could do with their eyes closed. All three of them had an instinctive understanding of security risks—their entire childhoods had been security risks—and they had been trained very hard and very expensively by Uncle

Sam to learn how to deal with risks. It was a question of knowledge and reason.

But with their Lost Ones, the trembling and broken women who showed up on their doorstep because RBK was their last chance before falling into the abyss—when dealing with them, you used both your head and your heart.

Though the woman in the lobby had asked to see Harry, Mike instinctively knew she was his. He had to be the one to help her.

Not because she was beautiful, though she was. Astoundingly beautiful.

But because she looked so lost, so alone. She was slightly built, with pale skin and pretty, delicate features. A slightly overlarge mouth, huge light brown, almost golden eyes.

Her clothes were expensive. So were her shoes and purse. Expensive, elegant, discreet. This was a lady of taste and of breeding and she looked rich.

Didn't matter.

He and his brothers had seen a lot of everything pass through their doors. Women who'd been beaten up by low-life drug-addict husbands and lovers, sure. But also wives of lawyers and doctors and even a senator. The rich weren't immune to the joys of beating up on women and children. If anything, they were able to hide it better, and for longer.

The police were also more willing to turn a blind eye.

The rich wives who ended up as one of RBK's Lost Ones sometimes tried going to the police, but their husbands often wielded enormous power and were able to get away with things poorer men went to jail for. The wives of the rich fucks were just as beaten down as their poorer sisters.

This woman, this Chloe Mason, belonged to the rich, there was no mistaking it. And not the new rich, either. She had that understated elegance of someone who didn't need to make a splash, someone for whom good taste came naturally.

From head to toe she was groomed and lovely. But there was something underneath those pretty, expensive designer duds that was a little less lovely.

She moved slowly, exactly like someone who'd been punched hard, in a place covered by clothes. That was a little trick fuckhead men who liked beating up on women and kids learned. Their rages might be uncontrollable, but boy, they knew enough to reason it out and punch where it wouldn't show. Last week a banker's wife had come in without a visible scratch on her. Except, of course, for a ruptured spleen that had required eight hours of surgery six months before. It had followed broken ribs and a punch to the liver so hard the liver had sustained damage.

Shitheads knew what they were doing, all right. Even in a fucking rage they knew enough to cover their tracks.

Someone had done something like that to Chloe Mason, who moved so very carefully, as if she would fall down if she didn't watch it.

Oh man. Who could do that to someone like her? Who could do it to any woman or child? But especially to Chloe Mason, with her soft skin and gentle features and slender build?

He glanced at Harry, expecting him to say something, then glanced again.

What the fuck?

It was like Harry was frozen. He simply stood there, staring at her. Not in a sexual way. Like Sam, Harry loved his wife fiercely and absolutely. He had zero interest in other women since his marriage. But something about this woman riveted his attention. And blocked his tongue, because he wasn't saying anything.

Harry knew as well as Mike that these women needed reassurance. They did not need a male staring at them. Particularly a tall, strong male. That kind of staring came off as aggression and women like Chloe Mason had had a bellyful of that.

Mike elbowed Harry in the ribs, to no effect. Okay, so Harry was out for the count. It was up to him.

"Welcome, Ms. Mason," he said gently to the frightened woman slowly crossing Harry's office. Since Harry wasn't moving, Mike walked around the desk and approached her slowly. No sudden moves, just nice and easy.

She stared up at him and he had to jerk his gaze away because he was staring, too, just like his idiot brother Harry.

Damn, she was . . . she was lovely. The old-fashioned word was exactly right. Nowadays beautiful was the technical term used for a woman who worked on herself, got herself some surgical enhancement, who stood out because of the way she was dressed and was made-up.

Chloe Mason had a different kind of beauty, made up of perfect skin, delicate features, soft blond hair, huge golden eyes, none of that, as far as he could see, enhanced.

So that's what she'd look like in the morning. After sex.

Mike squelched that thought immediately, ashamed of himself. The last thing this woman needed was a man she looked to for help coming on to her.

She was looking up at him anxiously, then back at Harry, clutching a purse and a big manila envelope, visibly worried because his fuckhead brother had his head up his ass.

Since she looked like she was about to fall down, Mike chanced it and placed a hand under her elbow, as gentlemanlike as possible, though he wouldn't object to carrying her to the client chair.

No. Not going there, he told himself sternly.

Women who'd been beaten up had antennae that quivered when men were around and in their space, because men in their space was a situation that often ended badly. He didn't want Chloe Mason to have even a moment's anxiety because of him.

So he did the opposite of what he'd done walking, then running, through a bad part of town last night, trolling for trouble.

Last night, his entire body had been one hand curled up in the universal *come and get it* sign, two bad-ass drugs in his system—alcohol and testosterone. A potent mix that got lots of men into trouble, true. But Mike had been trained by the best to meet trouble head-on when it came his way. He'd bristled with aggression last night. Aggression was his friend, always had been, had saved his life countless times.

Aggression and sex were his constant companions.

But not now.

Now he needed to dial it all down, reassure this beautiful woman, not frighten her.

"Ms. Mason," he said, nodding his head at the two client chairs in front of Harry's desk, "please take a seat."

He had a naturally deep voice, slightly rough due to the drinking last night. She stood looking at him, swaying slightly, and for a second he wondered how badly she might be injured. Man, if someone had injured her so badly she could hardly stand, he was going to find out who and quietly, privately, beat the shit out of him.

"Ms. Mason?" he repeated, keeping his voice gentle.

She ducked her head. "Yes, of course. I do apologize. I've—been under some stress lately."

It was the first time he heard her voice. It was as soft as the rest of her, with a musical quality. And a faint British accent.

She was English? Mike dropped his hand when she sat down, then rounded Harry's huge desk again.

She sat perched on the edge of the client chair, one of the most comfortable chairs in the world. By definition, RBK clients were in trouble, and the company wanted them to be comfortable while they talked it out. Chloe Mason didn't look comfortable in that chair, she looked tense as hell.

Silence. Harry was still . . . frozen. Goddammit. What the fuck was wrong with him?

Mike waited a beat, two. Finally, he broke the silence.

"Ms. Mason. Welcome to RBK Security. My name is Mike Keillor and this is my partner, Harry Bolt." He shot a glance at the silent statue that was his partner and refrained from rolling his eyes. Had Harry gone back to his pattern of sleeplessness with his little daughter? Was he in a waking coma, or what? "I know you asked for an appointment with Mr. Bolt, but we often work on . . . cases together. Before we begin, can we offer you something, a cup of coffee? Or tea?" Thinking of that accent.

"Yes, thank you so much." Her words came out in the rush of loosened tension. "I'd love a cup of tea."

Right call.

Mike waited a second for Harry to move, to wake up, to fucking get with the program. Finally, he pushed the button to Marisa, their receptionist. "Marisa, do you think we could get a cup of tea in here?"

Ordinarily, Mike wouldn't ask Marisa to do refreshment detail, but she was the mother hen of their Lost Ones. Marisa'd been a Lost One herself, and had the scars to prove it. She was a fabulous employee, hardworking and loyal. But for the battered women who made their way to the offices of RBK, Marisa went all out. She pampered them and mothered them and protected them fiercely.

"Yes, sir, right away."

The little interlude relaxed Chloe Mason.

Telling their story was a real ordeal for some women. They were all somehow ashamed, though how they could possibly be ashamed of ending up as someone's punching bag was beyond Mike. This moment out of time was a respite for Chloe. Her breathing pattern evened out. A little color came back to her pretty face.

The door to Harry's office slid open and Marisa walked in with a tray. She'd done them proud. A big teapot, three cups, milk and home-baked cookies brought in by Sam's wife, Nicole, baked by their housekeeper.

"Harry." Mike looked at his brother, barely refraining from

poking him in the side with his elbow again. "You want to pour?"

Harry started slightly, as if he'd actually been asleep and had suddenly woken up. "Sure, ah. Sure." His gaze locked onto the woman's face. "How do you take your tea, Ms. Mason?"

She smiled gently. "Dash of milk, one teaspoon of sugar, thank you."

It was the first time Mike had seen her smile. She was clearly under enormous stress, probably terrified, and yet the smile was genuine, blinding. And transformed her face from quietly lovely to otherworldly beauty. A real looker. She didn't catch your attention the first time or maybe not even the second time, but when she did catch your attention—watch out.

Mike felt a tug somewhere in his chest he didn't ever remember feeling, like someone was pulling at a hook.

They were going to take care of this lovely woman. Keep her safe, take her away from danger.

And then, well—forget about beating the guy up. Mike was going to find the fuckhead who'd hurt her and kill him.

Chapter 3

Chloe drank her tea, the cup making a light tinkling sound as she put it back on its saucer. Her hands were trembling slightly. Did the two men notice? Probably. Both of them were watching her very carefully.

Odd. In her experience, men didn't have great powers of observation. Most men were so wrapped up in themselves they barely noticed the outside world unless it impacted them in some way.

These two men seemed observant, however. Which is what she wanted, of course. She wanted to be listened to, to be *heard*. By Harry Bolt, though, not Michael Keillor.

The only thing was that, right now, Michael Keillor seemed to be the most responsive. Harry Bolt just stared at her.

Both men were completely opaque to her, which was unusual. She could usually get a pretty good handle on people within the first few minutes. There were so many tells—body language, their eyes, the way they were dressed, their tone of voice, the language they used. Even the way they breathed. At times, she thought she could read people's auras, though she didn't have any training in that. Just a lifetime of observation, on the outside looking in.

It was impossible to read these two. Their clothes were non-descript. Good quality, comfortable, not particularly fashionable. Expensive work clothes for busy men who dealt with the world and didn't sit behind desks.

They were giving her a lot of space and time. She was using way too much of it.

Her hands fell to her lap, started worrying the edges of the big manila envelope that held her past. And perhaps her future.

"Mr. Bolt," she began.

"Harry." His voice was very deep, almost as deep as his partner's. "Please call me Harry. And this is Mike." He nodded to the powerfully built man next to him.

Something deep inside her quivered at the sound of Harry's voice.

"Mr.—um. Harry. I lied. I lied to your receptionist. I told her I only needed a few minutes of your time. But I'm afraid it will take longer than that. I'm really sorry I didn't make an appointment." Her hands clutched the edges of the envelope as she made an offer she hoped he'd refuse. "I can make an appointment now and come back later, if this inconveniences you."

"No problem." He sat back in his big office chair, eyes never leaving hers. He reached out and pressed a button. "Yeah, Marisa. Cancel my appointments for the next . . . hour?"

His partner, Mike, leaned forward, too. "Marisa, cancel my appointments, too."

"An hour for Mr. Keillor as well," Harry said decisively, and lifted his finger from the button. "So, Ms. Mason, we're both free and you can take as much time as you want."

Okay. Okay. Chloe stopped herself from rocking back and forth in anxiety. Where to begin?

At the beginning, of course.

"I had an accident," she began slowly. "A very bad one, when I was small. I don't remember anything about it. But as a consequence, most of my childhood and my early teens was spent in and out of hospitals. By the time I was fifteen, I'd had fourteen surgeries."

Both men winced. "I'm sorry to hear that, Ms. Mason," Harry Bolt said.

"Chloe, please." She tried on a smile but could tell by the feel of her facial muscles that it was weak. "I, um, I didn't tell you this to gain your sympathy." She didn't like talking about it at all, and never told anyone except medical personnel. It had been bad enough living through it. People she met could wonder why sometimes she moved stiffly, but she didn't feel obliged to tell anyone anything. "The reason I told you is that my—my health problems ate up my childhood and teen years. My injuries were so severe that several times the doctors gave up on me. Apparently, I am alive by a miracle. The side effect is that whole chunks of me—of my history—are gone. I can remember very little, in fact, other than long stays in the hospital and rehabilitation in a succession of clinics. I didn't even attend school until I was fifteen. There would have been too many interruptions. My, um, my parents arranged for private tutors to come to me in the hospital. I was fifteen by the time I could stand and walk and even think of leading a normal life."

She studied Harry Bolt's eyes, then switched her gaze to Mike Keillor. It was a toss-up as to who was paying her more attention. She'd rarely been on the receiving end of such intense male scrutiny. It seemed to her that they were listening carefully to her every word and, perhaps, even to the words she wasn't saying.

She took a deep breath because the minefield began now.

"I never thought to ask my parents what happened. My parents were very . . . distant. That's the only word that really works." Until the man she knew as her father got all-too-close. "My, um, my father inherited a great deal of money and then he and my mother founded a highly successful real estate business. My mother used to come to visit me a couple of times a month in the hospital, but later she got caught up in the company and didn't have much time. In the end, she came about once a month to visit. I needed such intense rehabilitation between surgeries, they found it easier to leave me in long-stay hospitals, instead of ferrying me back and forth. They could afford it."

And just like that she was pinged back to long, pain-wracked years in luxury clinics, completely alone. The nurses her only human contacts as they rotated in and out of ICU.

She'd longed desperately for the love of her parents and it was never there. It was just this black hole into which she uselessly poured her love until she learned to stop it.

She'd waited eagerly for her mother's visits, every time, all through childhood. Never learning. The visits always followed the same script. Her mother would arrive with an expensive present or two, sit on the edge of the visitor's chair with her coat on, ask how Chloe was feeling, not listen to the answer, visibly quivering to get away, bolting after a quarter of an hour. Often leaving Chloe in tears until she simply gave up on making her mother care for her, because it just wasn't going to happen.

"My parents were these—these distant people who showed up now and again. My mother more than my father. I saw him just a couple of times a year while I was in the clinics. And then finally, when I was fifteen, there were no more surgeries scheduled. The doctors said I was as well as I was ever going to be. I was released, free to go home. My parents had moved houses several times. When I got out of the hospital, I was taken to a home I'd never seen before, in a part of town I didn't in any way know. A bedroom had been set up for me by an interior decorator. That first week was incredibly strange, as I was in a brand-new setting with parents I barely knew."

"Where was this?" Michael Keillor asked quietly.

"Boston."

"And yet you speak with a slight English accent."

So far, Harry Bolt hadn't spoken much. There was no doubt he was listening, though. Chloe had the feeling he was listening intently with every sense he had, not just hearing. And yet, though she had Harry Bolt's full attention, it was Michael Keillor who was asking her questions.

The reason she spoke with a faint English accent, which she'd picked up subconsciously, was hard to explain, in every way there was.

She sat there, trying to put the words together. This was so *hard*. It was a moment of her life she'd tried to understand, tried to forget, tried to forgive. Nothing worked.

Chloe took in a deep breath, watching the two men. She was taking up their time but there were absolutely no impatience vibes coming from them. She was familiar with people's exasperation with her when she needed time to think about what she was saying. One of her many, many failings.

Only she didn't feel it was a failing here. Both men were watching her, listening carefully to her, allowing her to talk at her own pace. She was all too familiar with people's body language when she had to think over what she was saying. The impatient huffs of breath, leg-jiggling or foot-tapping. Looking up at the ceiling, looking down at the watch, doodling. She'd seen it all.

She wasn't seeing it here. She was seeing two men hearing her out with no signs of anything but interest.

And since they were, she didn't stammer. It came out as smoothly as if she were discussing the plot of a movie she'd once seen.

"I'll come to that. When I was finally released, because there wasn't anything else medicine could do for me, it was summer and there was no school. I was actually ahead two grades because about the only thing I could do in the hospitals and clinics was study. I found it . . . hard, being home. My father acted very strange around me and my mother—my mother acted strange when he acted strange. They were both very strange, though I didn't have much to compare them with.

"I couldn't figure anything out. We had these strained conversations about nothing at all. They never asked me any questions, I never asked any of them. They were both gone a lot because of business. It was a little like being back in the hospital, only I was dressed and could go out if I wanted. Then one day, my father came home early." Chloe closed her eyes. She'd had endless therapy but the memory could still jolt her out of her serenity. In an instant, she was right back there, living it, not remembering it.

A sunny day in Boston, hot and humid. She'd found a whole wardrobe of pretty summer dresses in her room, an unusual gesture of kindness from her mother. She'd spent so long in the hospital gowns and track suits; the pretty clothes delighted her.

Being outdoors was still a novelty for her, a treat. The feel of the sun on her face and the breeze in her hair a shocking delight, even on a humid Boston summer day. She'd had on a sundress with spaghetti straps and no bra because really, why wear a bra when your breasts were like two small teacups? The house had a garden, one she delighted in exploring. A Mexican came twice a week to do the heavy lifting in the garden. Mr. Martinez. Diego. Old and kindly, willing to explain to her what he was doing. Telling her the names of the flowers in both English and Spanish. She spent hours in the sunshine with him without ever thinking that maybe she was interrupting his work.

Coming in from the garden that day with a fistful of asters, flushed from the sun, she came across her father staring at her intently.

He walked right up to her, looming over her. He'd been a big man, very tall, and he used his size and height to intimidate everyone around him. Certainly her mother was often intimidated, as were the cook and the maid and the few dinner guests they sometimes had. He intimidated her all the time, which she dealt with by rarely being in the same room with him.

Without really realizing what she was doing, something she recognized only in hindsight and after painful therapy, she had avoided him as much as she could. Walking out of a room the moment he entered, keeping furniture between them, stepping back when he approached her.

Her skin crawled if he got too close to her. Once, as she brushed by him, the hairs on her forearm rose.

That day, there was no walking away from him. He cornered her, big hands against her shoulders, pressing her against a red damask-covered wall.

God, she remembered the instant panic, full-blown, almost outsized for that specific moment, as if this were a situation she'd already faced. Chloe had even sometimes wondered if she was in some way psychic because her nightmares were and always had been of being with her back to a wall and having a huge man attack her.

She'd had every variation of that nightmare, over and over again. And that afternoon, it became reality.

"Did he?" Mike Keillor's very deep voice was low, harsh. The skin was tight over his cheekbones. He'd said something and she'd only caught the tail end of it.

Chloe blinked. "I beg your pardon?"

"We've heard a version of this story a lot of times." He glanced at his partner without moving his head. "Did your father rape you?"

Chloe bowed her head. It was that obvious? She looked like a woman who'd been raped by her father? Oh God. She'd worked so very hard not to seem like a victim and yet here was this man, who had only just set eyes on her for the very first time, and he'd pegged her completely.

"No," she whispered, looking at her knees. "Though he tried." *Backbone, Chloe.* The voice of Sister Mary Michael sounded in her head, calm and strong.

Calm. Strength.

She lifted her head. "I fought back. Which was dumb, because
he was a really big man. I should have run. But I didn't." She remembered every second of it, vividly. Rage had come ravening up,
from some completely unsuspected place inside her, black, blinding rage, an emotion she'd never felt before, certainly not like that.
It had been as overwhelming as his blow. "It was ridiculous. My,
um, my father was six-two, almost three hundred pounds. He
backhanded me. To shut me up, I guess, because I was screaming
while I was trying to hit him, hurt him."

She'd known in an instant what was going on. Though she
hadn't had sex, had never kissed a boy, had never even touched a
boy, she'd read enough, and anyway, instinctively, she knew. Knew
that his red face, flaring nostrils and wild animal scent meant trouble. It had come from some place deep inside of her. Through her
reading, she even knew what the tent in front of his linen trousers
meant. An erection.

She'd gone into overdrive, kicking and screaming, grabbing a
brass candlestick and bashing him in the face with it. His look
of astonishment would have been comical if she hadn't been so
desperate. Weak, sick Chloe, fighting back. She'd shocked even
herself.

Her rebellion hadn't lasted long, though.

"He broke my arm," she said. "It had been operated on recently
and it broke easily." Cheap at the price, because he'd stopped dead
in his tracks and stared at her, cradling her visibly broken arm.

Harry Bolt suddenly looked sick. Mike Keillor looked furious.

"My mother walked in and, without a word to my father, took
me back to the hospital, told them I fell down, and left me there
overnight. The next day, cast and all, I was on a flight to London,
where I was enrolled in the Sacred Heart School for Young Girls,
where I boarded for the next three years."

Chloe smiled. She had no idea if her mother had checked up

on the Sacred Heart, if there had been some kind of parents' site giving ratings of schools for foreign girls, or whether her mother had simply thrown a dart at a page of choices. Whatever, she'd struck pure gold. The years at the Sacred Heart, under the stern and loving care of Sister Mary Michael who had become the mother of her heart, had been the happiest of her life, hands down. The nuns had been warm and welcoming, the other girls from all over the world had provided friendship, and she'd felt at home for the first time in her life.

"I stayed in England, went to university at University College London. When I graduated, I found a job back at the Sacred Heart, teaching English. I never saw my parents again. My mother and I emailed from time to time, and sometimes she talked about coming over to London, but she never did."

She'd sent money, though. Hundreds of thousands of dollars, which Chloe had dutifully banked, spending as little of it as possible. She liked pretty clothes but she didn't need a huge wardrobe. Her tastes were simple and the account grew and grew.

She glanced down at her wristwatch. She'd been talking for half an hour.

"I'm really sorry," she said, looking up. "I know I'm taking up your time but I needed to say all of that, so you'd—you'd understand."

Again, it was Michael Keillor—Mike—who spoke. "Oh, we understand all right," he said grimly. He shot Harry a hard glance. "Don't we?"

Harry Bolt shook his head. Not the *no* gesture, it was more like shaking himself awake.

Okay. So far, so good. Chloe's hands started shaking again because . . . it was time. Her life was going to split in two. If this went well . . .

Don't go there. Think of something else.

But somehow her usual trick of damping expectations wasn't

working. Hope had caught her heart in an unshakable iron grip. While recounting her past, she'd used the old distancing trick, talking about herself as if recounting the story of a remote acquaintance.

Now the story grew closer, more personal. Possibly with a terrifying ending. Possibly with a joyful one . . .

She leaned forward a little and so did the two men. Like a group of conspirators, hatching a subversive plot.

"As I said, I never saw my parents again and we communicated rarely. So . . . I had no idea that they'd died in a car crash. On the eighteenth of April of last year. It took my, um, my father's lawyer almost a month to track me down. It was end of term at my school so I flew over to—to settle my parents' affairs."

The crumpled envelope on her lap felt like it was filled with bricks. Heavy, lumpy, cumbersome.

The closer she got to the heart of it, the harder it was to breathe. Something squeezed inside her chest. She watched Harry Bolt's eyes, light golden brown, watching her.

"My father hadn't left me anything in his will, which didn't surprise me. However, my mother outlived him by three hours and she was his sole heir and I was her sole heir, so the entire estate came to me. Settling the estate was complicated, but I had lawyers and time and a place to stay—their house. Since I was there, I explored. It was a brand-new house. Yet again, one I'd never seen. I put it up for sale but you are probably aware of the fact that the real estate market is weak. I didn't really care if it sold or not. I gave notice at my school because this was important. I spent all my time sifting through papers and books and objects, trying to get a handle on my parents, trying to get a handle on my past. I took my time because it seemed to me that it was an opportunity to find out things that had puzzled me all my life."

She stopped and simply breathed. Her entire life arrowed toward this point and she, who thought out everything so carefully, who tried to anticipate all problems, had no idea what was coming next.

"There was a safe, a big one, like one of those safes in the movies. There was no way I could open it. But the lawyer told me I had a right to have it opened. He gave me the name of an expert. A man who'd done time as a safecracker and was now a 'security consultant.' A man you hired to crack into safes, legally."

She smiled faintly at the memory. Luigi Zampilli, a short fireplug of a man with the hands of a neurosurgeon. Ten thousand dollars and the safe was open in five minutes.

The two men were staring at her. It was getting harder and harder to speak. She finished her tea to moisten her throat, wishing she could fast-forward to a quarter of an hour from now when she'd told it all and knew what the reaction was.

"Inside—inside the safe were several hundred thousand dollars' worth of Treasury bonds, ten pounds of gold ingots, the title to a number of properties I had no idea they owned . . . and a black box full of documents."

With a shaking hand, Chloe placed the manila envelope on Harry Bolt's desk and stared at it. Her life in an envelope. She lifted her eyes to his, so like her own.

"I was adopted," she said finally, swallowing heavily. "I had no idea, none. When I saw the adoption certificate I felt like someone had hit me on the side of the head."

She'd been so shocked she simply sat in an armchair throughout a long day and night, sifting through her memories, letting them fall like the elements of a kaleidoscope into a new pattern, one that made more sense to her, where the old one had made no sense to her at all.

Adopted. She was adopted. By parents who hadn't wanted her. That had emerged clearly from her "mother's" diary.

"There was only the certificate of adoption, which was exclusively in my mother's name. But as it turned out, the woman I thought was my mother was actually my aunt. I was my mother's sister's child. My, um, my biological mother had been a troubled girl, in and out of rehab, until she finally ran away from home in her late teens. It took me several days to piece this information together, mainly from a secret diary my mother—my aunt—had kept, and from newspaper articles about my real mother's arrests. After my biological mother ran away, the trail went dead. So I hired a private detective. It took her almost six months to track down . . ." Chloe started trembling, looking at Harry and then Mike, then back to Harry.

Something was happening with Harry. He had barely spoken. His eyes were almost radioactively bright. The skin over his cheek-bones was tight, deep furrows bracketed his mouth.

"Track down where I came from," she ended in a whisper.

Emotion grabbed her throat. For a long moment, she couldn't speak, could barely breathe. Could only stare at Harry.

No point mentioning the thousand false starts, disappoint-ments, dead ends. Chloe's birth mother had been erratic, men-tally ill, with an unerring nose for violent, unstable men. Addicted to every substance going. The reports of the woman's past made Chloe sick, but she kept digging. Because the truth was better than this . . . this nothing. This huge hole in the middle of her chest and of her life.

Her P.I., Amanda Box, was a young, savvy woman. A former cop who'd quit because her boss had harassed her. She'd sued, won, moved on. And understood Chloe instinctively. Amanda had worked tirelessly for Chloe. It was very possible that without Amanda's ferocious tenacity, Chloe wouldn't be here, about to . . .

She gulped.

She watched Harry carefully, heart in throat.

The thing was, she didn't know Harry, didn't know anything about him. Had no idea how he would react.

This could end so badly.

She felt as if she were holding her heart out to Harry, literally. A small, pumping muscle, quivering with hope, in her outstretched hands. Dripping blood.

He could slap her down, break that heart, in an instant.

However much Chloe sternly told herself not to hope, she couldn't help herself. It must have been all over her face. It was imprinted in every cell of her body. Wild, outrageous hope that this would end well. Hope of a kind and intensity she'd never felt before.

She hadn't hoped this hard for anything, not even when the doctors had told her she might never walk again.

"Did you?" Harry asked, thick ash brown eyebrows drawn over the bridge of his nose. His voice sounded hoarse. "Did you track down where you came from?"

Chloe nodded, eyes never leaving his. Trying to read something in his light brown eyes and failing.

"Yes. Um." Her throat was dry, palms wet. "As I said, it took my investigator six months. The investigator followed my biological mother mainly through her troubles with the law. My—my mother went west, to San Diego, got married to another drug addict who walked out on her when she was pregnant with me. I was the second child. The first was a b-boy. When I was five, m-my mother's boyfriend killed her, wounded my brother, hurt me. Badly. That was the—the 'accident.'"

Chloe leaned forward, hands flat on the desk, so filled with nerves she could hardly sit still. Pressure was rising in her chest like steam. Slowly, so anxious she could barely feel her hands, she slid the envelope over to Harry Bolt. The room was utterly silent. The noise of the thick paper envelope crossing the desk sounded loud.

"It's all in there. The P.I.'s report, the marriage certificate and the birth certificates of both me and my brother. The death certificates of my mother and her husband, my father. My mother's husband's name was Michael." She swallowed heavily. "Michael Bolt. They ha-had two children." Chloe was sweating, felt deep distress and this awful, singing hope. "Christine Bolt and—and Harry Bolt. I was born Christine Bolt." She met the light brown eyes of the man she was now positive was her only living relative. Her throat tightened. It was almost painful speaking the words. "Harry . . . I think you're my brother."

Harry rose suddenly, face pale, jaw working. *"Crissy?"* he whispered, voice raw.

From somewhere deep inside her, a place she had no idea existed, lost but not forgotten, came the answer. *"Hawwy?"*

Chloe burst into tears.

Chapter 4

Holy. Shit.

Chloe was in Harry's arms, crying so hard she was having trouble breathing. Harry was bent over her, holding her tightly, crying, too. Mike had never seen Harry cry, ever. Not even when he'd come back from Afghanistan almost dead from terrible wounds and it had hurt him to breathe.

"I can't believe this." Harry pulled away and held Crissy—Chloe—by the shoulders, tears streaming down his face. "Oh my God. Is it you? Is it really you?" He didn't wait for an answer, just pulled her into another bear hug.

He didn't need to ask. The resemblance was there, something almost tangible, which was why he'd been so frozen. Harry's heart had been frantically sending him signals his head couldn't accept.

They were brother and sister, all right. When you knew it, you couldn't miss it. Male and female, yin and yang, but the same stock. It was amazing to Mike that they were clearly siblings and yet Chloe was so feminine and Harry was all male. But there it was—the same coloring, the same color eyes, even the cast of their faces was the same.

The Keillor kids had been like that. Three young brothers, clearly siblings, looking so much like their dad, but with a bit of their mom in there. A family, visibly bound by blood. His heart gave that familiar kick when he thought of them. He suppressed it, pushed it right back down again.

Harry and Chloe were making a lot of noise, words coming out so fast they were garbled, hard sobs, sharp laughter.

Sam stuck his head in, frowning, looking ten years older. Nicole had had a hard time expecting their first child, Merry, and she was having a hard time with the new one, too. Sam's nights were as sleepless as hers.

"What's all this racket—hey!" He gaped at Harry and Chloe, clutching each other, crying their hearts out and laughing, at the same time. It wasn't every day he saw his brother Harry holding on to a woman and weeping.

Mike could almost see the gears moving in Sam's head. Slowly. Sam was having problems processing the scene, unusual for a former SEAL. SEALs aren't easily surprised and don't usually have problems processing things. Sam must be really sleep-deprived.

Harry lifted his head, joy all over his wet face.

He grinned at Sam. "Sam, meet my sister, Crissy." He looked down at her. "Or do you want us to call you Chloe, honey?"

Chloe glowed, like a little sun. "Chloe," she said softly. "Please."

Sam blinked, shook his head, as if the idea were too big for his brain to contain it. "Crissy? But, but isn't she . . ."

Dead. He'd been about to say dead. Chloe turned fully toward Sam. Once that idea that Harry and Chloe were brother and sister was in your head, the truth was right there, on their faces. Unmistakable. The truth made flesh.

"Oh my God," Sam breathed, eyes wide. Seeing it.

"Yeah." Harry swiped at his face. "Yeah. Wait till I tell Ellen. And Grace!" He looked down at Chloe. "Honey, you have a niece. A beautiful little niece. Grace Christine. Named for you."

Chloe's face crumpled again, her shoulders shook. She buried her face in Harry's now-wet shirt, sobbing quietly.

Sam walked in warily. Though he'd been married more than two years now, for him a weeping woman was still the equivalent of a block of C4 with the detonator in and the timer counting down. But before he reached them, Marisa rushed into the room.

A weeping woman. Marisa was hard-wired to react. She came in bristling, shooting filthy glances at Harry, Sam and Mike, men who'd dared make one of her women, one of the Lost Ones, *cry*. She put her arms around Chloe's shoulders, glaring ferociously at the three men. Marisa weighed one-twenty dripping wet and was fifty years old. But none of them, highly trained former soldiers that they were, would dare take her on when she was in protective mode.

"What's going on here? What did you men *do* to this poor girl—" she began furiously, getting right up into their faces.

"She's my sister, Marisa," Harry said at the same time. "Come back from the dead."

Marisa's face went utterly blank. They never talked about it, but everyone in the office knew Harry's story. Knew that the loss of his little sister had been a tragic hole punched through his heart all his life.

"*Mamma mia,*" she whispered, reverting back to the language of her childhood. She pulled away to look Chloe in the face, holding her by the shoulders. Eyes flicking from Chloe to Harry and back. "*Mamma mia.*"

"*Davvero,*" Chloe said unexpectedly, smiling, wiping away the tears that were streaming down her face.

Marisa whooped, kissed Chloe on the cheek and did a little jig. Mike stared. No one had ever seen cool, calm Marisa so excited, so joyful. "*Una sorella ritrovata!* A lost sister! Found! And she speaks Italian!"

"*Solo un poco,* very little." Chloe smiled, wiped her eyes again. "I studied it only for a year."

"Hey, what's going on?" Two beautiful women stuck their heads in the room, looking puzzled. Nicole and Ellen. Ellen had probably been working with Nicole on her accounts. Besides singing for them, Ellen kept the books of Nicole's translation agency and of RBK. Mike always thought that was a great twofer.

Ellen rushed over to her husband, seeing the tears running down his face. "Harry!" She sounded more shocked than worried. "What's wrong, darling? Are you hurt?"

This last was said slowly, as an afterthought, because though he was crying, Harry clearly wasn't hurt. He started laughing and wiped away some tears, though more fell.

Chloe turned to smile at the two women, hope and light in her golden eyes. Mike had never seen anything so luminous. It was as if she had a light source glowing inside her. Her smile was heartbreaking, the smile of someone who wasn't used to happiness.

"Come here, honey," Harry said to Ellen. He opened one arm, the other around Chloe. When Ellen was by his side, in his embrace, he kissed her cheek. Ellen and Nicole were no dummies. Both of them were looking at Chloe, then Harry, then back at Chloe. Understanding that something was up, but what?

"Honey," Harry said to his wife, then gave a sort of laughing cough, as if whatever was in his chest was too big to express but had to come out. "I know you're going to find this hard to believe, but this is . . . Crissy. My sister. Back from the dead. Only now she's Chloe." He threw his head back and laughed again.

Both Ellen and Nicole gasped.

Mike was barely paying attention to them, to Sam and Harry. He moved closer. He couldn't help it. Chloe was light itself and he was helplessly drawn to it, to her. There was some kind of aura there, something he'd never seen in anyone else before, something that drew him in without any volition on his part. His legs moved without him willing it, his entire body moving toward the light, moving toward something it had never seen before and instantly recognized as something it craved.

Harry was holding Chloe and Ellen in his arms. Everyone was talking all at once, the noise level amazing. Marisa had drawn away from the group and was wiping her eyes, smiling. Sam bent down to her.

"Marisa." With any other woman, Sam would have maybe laid a sympathetic hand on her shoulder. They were all affected, Marisa as much as anyone. But Marisa didn't like being touched by a man. She still had scars from her husband's touch.

She stood ramrod straight, was back to her prim and proper persona. She nodded her head soberly at Sam. "Mr. Reston."

Sam looked at Harry, in a knot of happy women, Chloe, Ellen and Nicole, all of them talking loudly and happily, then met Mike's eyes.

Sam had clearly made a decision. He turned to Marisa. "RBK closes for the next two days. Full pay for all employees. Cancel all appointments for today and tomorrow, with apologies. We open again on Monday." When Sam looked at him, Mike nodded his approval.

Oh yeah. Finding the sister you thought long dead—yeah, that qualified for a holiday. And when that sister was Chloe Mason . . . hell yes. Celebrations were definitely in order.

"Yes, sir. Thank you, sir." Marisa's voice was bland, but there was a rosy blush under her olive skin. She'd caught the Bolt happiness bug.

They all had.

"Well, then Wordsmith closes down, too," Nicole said, smiling. Her translation agency was across the hallway from RBK. "I'll subcontract out my own translations for the next couple of days. I can always check on things from home. This calls for a real celebration. And you, Ellen—" She looked sternly at Harry's wife, a notorious workaholic. Sometimes you had to pry Ellen from the spreadsheets of Wordsmith and RBK with a crowbar. "No accounting. None. I don't want you near a computer until Monday."

Ellen laughed. "Absolutely! Are you kidding? Working when I have a sister to welcome to the family?" Ellen was hugging Chloe. "Oh man," she said. She had that rosy blush, too. "Wait till you meet Grace, Chloe. Your niece. You're going to love her. This is so great! Another aunt for her. Nicole can share aunt duty!"

"I love aunt duty." Nicole bent down to kiss Chloe's cheek. She was much taller than Chloe and Ellen, and moved a little awkwardly, her belly starting to get in her way. "But I'll happily share. And I can't wait for you to meet our daughter, Meredith. Merry." Nicole smiled at her husband, then Harry. "This is so great. I have no words."

Which for Nicole, a professional translator, whose stock in trade was words, was really something.

His brother's wives were great. Mike knew both his brothers realized how blessed they were. Two beautiful women, particularly Nicole, who had a blinding kind of beauty, with that Snow White ivory and ebony thing going on. Though Ellen was a looker, too, and a world-class singer. Sam and Harry were lucky men because their wives were not only gorgeous and smart and talented, but also loving. They'd both created happy homes for his brothers, given them constant, unwavering love and beautiful children. Neither Sam nor Harry had ever had a happy home, and they lapped it up.

But neither of the women could hold a candle to Chloe. Mike couldn't keep his eyes off her. He edged closer to see whether he could pick up on whatever it was that surrounded her. There was some kind of force field around Chloe, something he couldn't in any way define or explain but that was as strong as a tractor beam.

Nicole had a cell phone to her ear, snapped it closed. She clapped her hands. "Okay, everyone, listen up! Manuela is going to start cooking lunch for us just as soon as she stops crying. So we can take this show down to Coronado Shores. Chloe, where are you staying?"

"With us," Harry and Ellen said at the same time. "No question," Harry added.

Chloe was looking overwhelmed with joy. Mike had been bowled over by her in the office lobby, this pale, anxious beauty. Now she was glowing with happiness, eyes gleaming with tears of joy, cheeks flushed. Absolutely irresistible.

"Oh!" Chloe covered her mouth with her hand. "I don't mean to impose! I booked a room at the Del, you don't need to put me up, for heaven's sake. You have a small child and . . ." Her voice trailed off when she saw that Harry and Ellen weren't even listening to her. Ellen absentmindedly gave her shoulders a squeeze while talking to Harry about beds and space, then turned to give Chloe another kiss on the cheek.

"This is so exciting! It's the best Christmas ever!"

"No, really." Chloe stepped back, just one tiny step, but it was the first step back anyone had taken. Her hands clasped in front of her and she pulled them apart. A sign of distress.

Harry glanced at Sam and at him and they drew closer, closer to him and to Chloe.

It was a look they'd shared all through their adolescence in a brutal foster home, a look they all understood instinctively, down to the bone. Harry wanted Sam and Mike to have his back. It was a call both Sam and Mike were incapable of resisting. They'd have Harry's back no matter what. Mike would willingly take a bullet for him, and for Sam, too. He loved them.

He'd walk into the jaws of death for both of them.

Coming closer to Chloe, something he wanted desperately, was a no-brainer.

Harry took Chloe's hands in his, carefully. Harry had big strong hands, they all did. They were all careful not to hurt women or kids with their hands.

A hot flush of grinding guilt shot through Mike at the memory of holding down the cokehead during the fuckathon last night. Hurting her. She was a whack job, true, but she didn't deserve even one second of pain from him.

It was a memory that shamed him, made him feel unclean. Unworthy, of his brothers, of their wives. Of Chloe.

"Chloe," Harry said gently, watching her face carefully, "you need to understand something really important. We're all your family now. Sam and Mike and me, we're like brothers. More than brothers. We'll have all the time in the world for me to explain why, but for now—all you need to know is that they are your brothers, too. Together with Nicole and Ellen and Merry and Gracie. We're all one family. Yours."

Chloe burst into tears again. Mike could see that she couldn't contain her emotions, which made sense. When she'd told her story, he could hear a longing for connection in her voice. Almost feel her yearning. He'd had his family until he was ten. He knew what it was like to yearn. She'd had it harder than he had because she'd never known family except for the first years, when Harry protected her. Years she couldn't remember.

Sam bent to gently embrace her. Sam was tall—six-three. He had to bend down low to her. He kissed the top of her head. "I'm your brother, too, Chloe. It's just like Harry said. Nicole and Merry and me—we're your family now, too."

Chloe smiled up at him and swallowed, the muscles in her long, graceful neck moving. She swiped at her face. "Thank you, Sam," she whispered.

Sam stepped away for Mike.

Mike put his arms around her. Somewhere along the way, she'd shed her coat. She had on some silky thing, a ruffled blouse in a delicate pink—the color of her flushed face.

She eased into his arms. She fit so perfectly, just slotted right into him.

The hug with Sam had been clumsy. He was so much taller than she was, and she'd moved stiffly. The embrace had been genuine but awkward.

But with Mike, she just moved naturally into his embrace and just as naturally his arms closed around her.

Time stopped, telescoped.

The room disappeared. Harry and Sam, Nicole and Ellen—gone. No more.

There was no noise, nothing. Just Mike and Chloe, in his arms.

Mike was shorter than his brothers and Chloe's head fit naturally, perfectly, right against his shoulder, at exactly the point where all he had to do was tilt his head to rub his cheek against her soft golden hair. Bend down just a little more to kiss her.

Mike felt heat all along his front, like being covered with a soft, warm blanket that was silky, too. And smelled like heaven. Something fresh and warm.

He was supersensitized. He could feel the short gasps of her excited breath against his neck. His hand was so big it covered a good portion of her narrow back and he could feel her rapid heartbeat against the palm of his hand. The quick heartbeat of joy.

Mike had fucked hundreds of women, but he'd never felt anything even remotely like this. A mild electric shock as he held her raced through him. Everywhere he touched, it felt as if he'd never touched a woman before. Never felt such silkiness, such warmth. Never felt as if she'd moved her body into his like magnets of opposite poles meeting. A force that was unstoppable, natural, utterly right.

She rested against him and he wanted to keep her there forever, but when he felt himself harden, he moved away subtly, mentally rolling his eyes.

Goddamn. His dick had never known how to behave itself.

Oh man, way to turn this moment into something that belonged in the dives he frequented when he got his black moments.

He couldn't really blame his dick, though. His dick was right to move. He felt it wasn't getting erect so much as trying to get closer to her, close to all that silk and gold.

His dick would get closer to her eventually. Close to her, *in* her. Oh yeah. Only not right now.

Her hand was still in his and it took real willpower not to bring her fingers to his mouth. She had beautiful hands, fingers long and slender. A pianist's hands though he had no idea if she played or not.

He could almost feel her fingers against his lips, so strongly he had to drop her hand and step back, muster a smile.

When he pulled back, Chloe did, too, and smiled back up at him. "A brother," she whispered.

Mike didn't answer, didn't reassure her that she'd just found another brother.

Because what he was feeling right then wasn't brotherly at all.

Chapter 5

Chloe received more hugs that morning than in her entire life-time. It was magical, beyond words. Beyond even her imagining—and she'd done a lot of imagining on sleepless nights, staring at the ceiling, wondering what it would be like to have a family.

Wonderful, that's what it was like.

It took her a second to sort the women out. The small, pretty redhead with the slight southern accent was Ellen, Harry's wife. And . . . and her *sister-in-law*. And she had a *niece*.

Chloe had never, ever thought she'd have a sister-in-law or a niece. Blood relations. The thought made her shiver.

And then Nicole, Sam's wife. Beautiful and warm and welcoming. And since Harry said Sam was like a brother to him, well then, apparently Nicole was a relative, too.

Then there was Sam, very tall, as tall as her brother Harry, only not as good-looking. He actually looked rough, exactly the kind of man she'd shy away from, instinctively. Tall, strong, rough-looking men automatically spelled danger. This was a message that came to her from some place so deeply embedded in her heart and mind and sinews that she had never even questioned it, until now.

Notwithstanding his appearance, Sam seemed like a good guy. Though he looked like he could pick you up and smash you against a wall without breaking a sweat, the truth was, he made a real point of being gentle with her. He'd hugged her with almost exaggerated care, the way you'd hug a frail grandmother. There wasn't anything he could do about his rough voice, but he did seem to try to modulate it for her.

And he loved his wife, as much as Harry visibly loved his.

It was there every time he looked at Nicole. It didn't seem like a sick love, either, the kind Chloe now recognized had existed between her adoptive parents and had undoubtedly existed between her biological mother and her drug-addict husband and boyfriends.

No, this was the real deal, and she could see why because Nicole was absolutely gorgeous and nice. Tall, slender except for the small bump of pregnancy. Long jet black hair, riveting cobalt blue eyes. And completely natural, without a trace of that complex, instinctive sense of competition beautiful women often had around other women. She'd hugged Chloe with genuine warmth, looked Chloe straight in the eyes without even a thought to her clothes or bag or shoes, and then kept a friendly arm around her friend Ellen's shoulders as she smiled at Chloe.

The body language could not have been more clear. For both women. *Welcome. We are eager to be your friends.*

Mike Keillor—he was another story. Not as tall as the men he called his brothers, but seemingly twice as broad. He had the strongest shoulders and arms she'd ever seen on a man. A bodybuilder but without that bodybuilder stiffness and clumsiness. He simply looked . . . strong. Firmly planted on the ground, unstoppable, invincible.

It was a little harder to think of Mike Keillor as a brother.

The hugs of the two men, Sam and Harry—officially now her *brothers!*—and their wives, had been warm and brief. In the rush of excitement, she could hardly tell who was hugging her. Like plunging into a warm ocean, with lots of waves lapping at her.

But when Mike hugged her, time stopped, somehow. She was instantly aware of everything, all sensations separate and discrete. Each one unusual. Each one exciting.

The feel of him. That was what affected her so much. Harry and Sam were so tall she had to stretch up awkwardly to place her hands on their shoulders, up on tiptoe, brief hug, falling back onto her heels. The hug over almost before it began because hugging someone so tall was awkward.

Mike, now—Mike was the perfect height, taller than she was but not too tall. And the strength of him. Wow. She had never in her life touched someone as strong as he was. Like embracing a man of steel. Superman, only without the leotard. Superman, only shorter, broader, but with—yes—piercing blue eyes and yes, that lick of dark hair over the forehead that just made you want to reach out and brush it back. She'd had to clench her fists not to do just that.

He smelled wonderful, too. Clean, utterly male.

For just a moment, instead of a hug, it had been an embrace. He'd simply rolled her into himself, put his arms around her and held her close.

She'd loved it. That was a huge surprise. She didn't have to reason it all out, like she did with most of her interactions with people. *Should I do this, say this, and if I do this, what then? Is this normal, should I be feeling this, will they look at me oddly when I do that?*

Her usual exhausting head games when dealing with people. She had no natural sense for it, had always been bad at it.

Maybe it was all those lonely years in the hospital, or having parents who never interacted with her. Whatever it was, sometimes Chloe thought that everyone in the world except her had been handed an instruction manual at the beginning of their lives and knew what the script was, whereas she was perennially in the dark.

It was better once she was at Sacred Heart and afterwards, at university and out in the work world. But still, it seemed to her that she had no social instincts, only painful lessons learned in harsh schools.

But that moment with Mike—that moment out of time—it had been sheer instinct. They fit together so perfectly. There hadn't been even a split second of awkwardness. In a second, she was held against him, his arms around her back, his head close to hers.

In that instant, something stilled inside her. Her constant inner monologue stopped dead. She had no thoughts, only feelings, rushing in, overwhelming her.

Strength, heat, safety. Arousal.

Wow.

Mike moved away, and a lucky thing, too, because she was entirely incapable of it. She actually felt bereft when he stepped back. The whole front of her body felt cold, missing something vital. She stood still and looked in his eyes, those bright blue eyes, wondering if he had a clue that something momentous had happened inside her.

He was looking serious. She had no idea what his normal expression was but right then he had looked deeply into her eyes, as if he could walk around inside her head. His face had been tight, a slight tic fluttered in his right eyelid. Chloe simply couldn't look away.

Time stretched . . .

"All right!" Harry clapped his hands and Chloe jumped, the entire room zooming back into focus. Harry and Sam were closing up shop, shutting down computers, putting paper files away. Her brother smiled at her. "Chloe, we'll swing by the Del, get your stuff, and get on home. Your room will be ready by the time we get there, but we'll be eating up at Sam and Nicole's." He stopped, looked at her with a frown. "You're looking shell-shocked," he said gently, picking up her hands. "Is all this too much for you?"

His hands were so warm. Chloe smiled up at him. "It is a little overwhelming. But in a good way." She tried to still the trembling in her throat. "I'm still finding it hard to believe that I found you. That I have a brother."

He bent and kissed her forehead. "I know what you mean. At least you had some time to get used to the idea before you came here. I was blindsided." He pulled back to look down at her. "But now, you know what? I feel like you've been there all along, it's just that I didn't know." He swallowed heavily. "And now I do. It changes everything."

"Yes, it does." Tears prickled. She gave a hollow laugh and swiped at her eyes. "At some point I'm going to stop crying, I promise."

"I'm not, not for a while, anyway." Ellen came up and kissed her cheek again. "I don't have a family, either, outside Harry and Grace. So for me it's like finding a sister. We're all so happy." She spun around in the room, hands up in the air. "And now we're going to *party!* Let's get out of here and get home!"

"Here." Behind her, Mike's bass voice. Chloe turned, startled. He was holding her coat up. She slipped into it. His heavy hands rested, briefly, on her shoulders. It felt good, really good. Events were swirling around her, almost too fast to follow, making her dizzy. His big hands grounded her, slowed everything down, made everything real.

"We'll be there in about half an hour, forty minutes." Nicole was talking into her cell, and snapped it shut. "Manuela's still crying, but she's also cooking up a storm and she is going to be very angry if everything gets cold. You do not want to make Manuela angry."

"No, ma'am," Sam said fervently, and winked at Chloe. "Without Manuela I'd never eat. Ouch," he said mildly when Nicole elbowed him in the ribs.

She smiled sweetly at her husband, narrowing her eyes until only a cobalt blue slit gleamed. "Another crack like that and I know what else you'll never do again."

Sam mimed horror and zipped his lips.

Chloe laughed and then barely refrained from clasping her hand over her mouth. Old habits. Her mother—her adoptive mother—had frowned on laughing in public. But she wasn't here, would never be here again. Everyone smiled when she laughed and Sam winked at her again.

"Okay!" Harry twirled his finger in the air. "Heading on out. Chloe, you're coming with us."

"I'll come with you, too, Harry," Mike said. "Barney is picking up my SUV. I left it in Logan Heights last night."

For some reason, Harry and Sam shared sharp glances. Before she could puzzle out what it meant, a strong hand closed over her elbow. Mike, at her side.

They moved out en masse, crossing that enormous lobby. The clients had all departed. Several of the secretaries were standing, putting on their coats. They filed out, calling out cheerful good-byes.

There was a happy atmosphere in this company, Chloe saw. Her brother had created something good, together with Sam Reston and the man still holding her elbow, Mike Keillor. They had created an atmosphere of harmony, as unmistakable as that created by her nuns at the Sacred Heart.

Chloe had felt her heart lift, even that first day. A new girl, a *damaged* new girl, from another country. Shy and unused to much contact with people. The transition to London had been so fast she'd barely had time to dread it by the time she'd arrived and discovered she didn't have anything to dread.

Just watching the way the nuns treated the girls, the way the girls interacted with one another, it had been such a joy. No coldness, no withdrawal, no hidden cruelty. Just happiness and serenity.

That's what she was seeing here. The body language of people who worked in a successful environment and who worked well together, in an atmosphere of respect.

Next to her, Mike looked so serious. Harry was beaming, Sam had his arm around his wife's waist, bending down to her and smiling. Only Mike wasn't smiling. Harry and Sam seemed somehow uncomplicated next to Mike. Reading their body language easily, in Sam and Harry Chloe saw two contented men, happily married, loose and relaxed.

Mike was harder to read. He didn't look particularly happy but he didn't look unhappy, either. He was just serious. And close by her. Like her shadow, always in proximity. Anyone who didn't know them walking out of the company offices and heading down the big corridor would have assumed that there were three couples.

Harry and Ellen. Sam and Nicole. And Mike and her. She was a slow walker, but he kept pace with her exactly, as if that were his normal speed, when actually she'd seen his normal speed when he came in, zipping across the huge lobby area in a couple of seconds.

She had never been so conscious of another human being's presence. He was so large it felt like he had his own gravity field around him. She had to work, and work hard, to keep from looking at him and—surprisingly—from trying to get even closer. He still held her by the elbow, not a hard grip but one she imagined she'd have to make an effort to break.

Not for anything in the world would she want to break his grip. She couldn't even begin to imagine wanting to. His grip felt wonderful.

So here she was, walking down the corridor, having somehow acquired four new family members, and the fifth—well, he didn't feel like family so much as a man interested in a woman, utterly focused on her.

God, who would have thought such a reversal of fortune could happen in only a couple of hours?

Two hours ago, she'd walked this same hallway, sick with anxiety, trembling with piercing fear and tenuous hope. Completely alone in the world, without a compass or even a heading.

On her way over in the taxi, she'd game-played how the encounter would work out. When she allowed the tiniest chink to open inside her to let just the smallest ray of hope beam inside, she'd thought that maybe, just maybe, she and Harry could . . . what? Maybe have lunch together? Talk, certainly. She'd imagined it would be awkward, but she didn't care. She'd been doing awkward for a long time now. All her life, in fact.

And she'd try to dance around the big 800-pound gorilla—why didn't their mom's sister adopt both of them?

Chloe discovered the answer to that in a diary kept in the safe, tucked away among bank statements as if even in a safe, it wasn't supposed to be read. In it, Lauren, her adoptive mother, described what she found after the authorities had tracked Lauren down as the sister of Carol Bolt née Tyler, deceased. Lauren had reluctantly flown, alone, to San Diego, the new bride of a man she was slowly beginning to realize had sick desires and a tendency toward violence. But he was rich and powerful and Lauren wanted that. Craved it.

Unwilling duty brought Lauren to the Open Clinic in San Diego, which she'd noted with distaste in her diary was a "poor person's hospital." Chloe could almost feel Lauren's hostility rising off the pages like steam as she wrote of seeing Christine, her niece, a small bundle, heavily sedated, almost every bone in her body broken, lying barely alive, a tiny lump on the hospital bed.

Then she'd gone to see her nephew. A tall, big boy. As strong as a man, and dangerous. He'd already killed a man. She'd watched from outside as he'd raged violently, hurling dishes at the wall, screaming his fury at the world.

No contest. Her husband could possibly tolerate her adopting a little girl who probably wouldn't live. A big strong man-child who was violent? No way.

Chloe understood very well that Lauren had condemned Harry

to social services. Lauren had refused to rescue Harry, refused to take him home with her.

Harry so far had been nothing but happy that Chloe had survived. Still, she'd been perfectly prepared to accept his bitterness that he hadn't been rescued along with her.

She'd been ready for anything—from tepid acceptance to anger. She'd even have accepted it, in exchange for just seeing him. Just knowing that there was someone else in the world she was related to.

And if he held her at arm's length, she'd understand. Maybe they could meet once a year and with time, over the years, maybe some of the awkwardness would pass, if he wasn't too angry. Maybe they could exchange Christmas cards, the occasional email.

She'd have been grateful for the smallest crumbs he'd be willing to offer.

Not in any way had she allowed herself to imagine what had actually happened—full, immediate, warm acceptance into his life. Being instantly folded into his family. Into an *extended* family because, unlike herself, Harry had managed to forge strong relations. He'd created an actual brotherhood.

That extended family now included her. A couple of hours ago, she'd had nobody. Right now, it appeared she had Harry and Sam and Mike. Ellen and Nicole. Merry and Grace. And another little niece on the way.

And a partridge in a pear tree.

Mike looked down at her, bright blue eyes so very observant.

"I'll bet you didn't think you'd end up eating lunch at a brother's house today, did you?" He kept his deep voice low, only for her.

She smiled. "You're reading my mind. Do you have psychic abilities?"

Mike snorted. "No, of the many things people have called me, psychic is not one of them. It's just that you looked so scared and anxious when you came. And now you look happy."

She looked up at him, amazed at this instant connection she felt, such a rare thing for her. "I was feeling anxious and now I am happy, so you called it."

Mike nodded his head forward, where Harry and Ellen and Sam and Nicole had already stopped at the elevator. The cab arrived with a ping and they filed into it, shiny brass internal walls reflecting them so that they looked like eight happy people instead of four. Ellen whispered something in Harry's ear and he laughed.

"You can't possibly be happier than Harry right now. And Ellen and Sam and Nicole." He waited a beat, his hand tightening slightly on her elbow. "And me."

There was no comeback to that one.

Harry was holding the elevator door open with one big hand. "Come on, honey," he called out to her.

No impatience, just eagerness.

Chloe made people impatient sometimes and there wasn't much she could do about it. She simply couldn't move too fast. Walking was a complex miracle for her. It had taken her years and years of effort. She just couldn't go much faster than a slow walk. If she did, if she tried to hurry, she sometimes fell down. It had happened a few times to her intense humiliation, and once she'd broken a bone that had been broken before. The doctors had told her she couldn't afford to break it a third time. Better to walk slowly and absorb the impatience of others.

But Harry wasn't impatient, just happy. Mike wasn't radiating impatience, either. He looked like he could run a four-minute mile. Every line of his body spoke of power. Walking at her pace must have been excruciating, but you wouldn't know it. He matched her slow pace, step by step.

In the elevator, Mike dropped his hand and Chloe nearly jerked with consternation. It was as if an electric current running through her had been switched off. She missed it so much it shocked her.

"I wonder if we can convince Manuela to make her blue corn tamales?" Harry asked, with a sidelong glance at Nicole.

"Maybe," she smiled. "Or maybe not. Manuela has her favorites, she has like this little celebration menu going and I wouldn't want to mess with that." She turned to Chloe. "It'll be interesting to see what Manuela's menu is for celebrating the arrival of a long-lost sister."

"O Happy Day, O Happy Day!" Ellen sang, voice clear and beautiful in the enclosed elevator, like someone ringing a perfect bell.

"O Happy Day," Sam rejoined in a massively out-of-tune bass.

"Yesss!" Harry pumped his fist, kissed his wife's cheek, then Chloe's. "Women's clothing, lingerie, hats, cosmetics and . . . *sisters*!" Harry mimed an old-fashioned elevator operator calling out the items on a floor.

Everybody was giddy, Chloe included, by the time the elevator made it down to the subbasement level.

"See you at the homestead," Ellen called out as Sam and Nicole peeled away toward their vehicle. "We'll swing by the Del, get Chloe checked out, and then we'll come up."

Nicole's shiny black hair belled out from her face as she looked back at them, Chloe holding her group back, as usual. "Okay, guys, champagne starts popping in an hour. If you're not there we'll just have to drink it ourselves."

"We'll be there," Ellen called out. "Make sure it's French! The real deal! None of that wimpy California stuff!"

Nicole didn't turn around, just held up her hand and waggled her fingers. Her husband held the door open for her, helped her in, then rounded his vehicle and took off before Chloe's group was even halfway across the garage.

How humiliating. Harry and Ellen and Mike were keeping pace with her, crossing the vast expanse of the garage floor like a party of snails. Chloe tried to keep her voice steady as she smiled weakly.

"I'm, uh, I'm sorry I walk so slowly. Go right on ahead." She looked up at Mike. "You, too. I'll get there."

He shook his head, turned to look her straight in the eyes. In the dim light of the garage his blue eyes glowed like twin rondels of sky. His face was drawn, tight, serious. "Chloe." He picked up her hand and tucked it into the crook of his arm, watching her face carefully, as if to make sure she understood what he was saying. "Right now there isn't any place I'd rather be than right here with you."

Chloe blinked.

Oh. Wow.

Chapter 6

Chloe was embarrassed that she couldn't walk fast. Mike's heart painfully turned over in his chest at that.

Chloe had survived something few people would have. She'd been brutalized as a little girl, had spent nearly a decade in a hospital, been operated on fourteen fucking times, was alive by a miracle and . . . she was *embarrassed*?

Harry had killed the motherfucker who'd whipped Chloe against a wall as if she'd been a rag doll, otherwise Mike would definitely go look the guy up himself. Have a word or two with him.

See how he liked pushing around an ex-Force Recon Marine, ex-SWAT. See whether the fuckhead might find it a little harder to smash a 220-pound man who was an expert in close-quarter combat against the wall than a 40-pound little girl.

Yeah, Mike would look forward to that.

The underground garage of the Morrison Building was huge. Harry's allotted parking slot was way the hell over on the other side of the building.

Harry and Ellen were halfway there, Harry checking every minute or so if Chloe was following. She was.

Harry didn't have to worry because Mike was on it, and just as soon as humanly possibly he was going to be on *her*.

Mike would have sworn that last night had put him off sex for a while. A long while.

But nope. Sex came roaring back, it was in his head, buzzing in his veins, pooling blood between his legs. He fought off an erection—if the past twenty years of industrial-level fucking had taught him anything, it was the ability to control his cock—but he could feel the heaviness between his thighs, a concentration of sensation and heat.

It was different from the usual, though. If he weren't so goddamned distracted by Chloe, he could try to figure out what it was about her that was so different. Right now, though, he only had enough blood in his head to know to stick close.

Harry and Ellen were in Harry's Tahoe by the time they made it to the vehicle. Harry started the engine. "Hop in, honey!" he called, and Mike saw Chloe suppress a wince.

Mike loved Harry. There was an old saying—to love like a brother. Mike loved Harry more than like a brother but that didn't mean he didn't want to kick his ass right now.

While Chloe had been trying to explain how she didn't remember him because she'd been so badly injured a good chunk of her life had gone, lost in years in hospitals, Harry had barely been listening. He'd been frozen, a big message buzzing in his head he hadn't known how to process. And once Chloe dropped her bomb, Harry's senses had been completely blitzed by joy.

Chloe's problems had completely flown under Harry's radar. Not Mike's. He'd seen from the start that it was hard for her to move fast. Chloe hid it well, was probably used to hiding it all her life, but it was there and she was ashamed and Mike vowed right then and there that she would never be ashamed again.

Chloe looked dismayed when she registered the enormous step up into the Tahoe. Without a word, Mike easily lifted her onto the seat. When he got into the other side, she smiled at him. "Thanks," she said softly, leaning over, the word only for him.

Oh man. Her smile. How could she turn even more golden when she smiled? Mike suspected she didn't smile much. Well, life hadn't given her that much to smile about. He knew all about that.

Ellen turned around in her seat. "Chloe, I can't wait for you to meet Grace, though she might be a little fussy. We think she's starting to teethe."

"How old is she?"

"Three months."

"Great kid," Mike offered.

"Yes, she is," Ellen smiled. "She looks just like Harry, and"— Ellen tilted her head, red hair shifting on her shoulder—"now that I'm looking more closely, she looks a lot like you, too."

"Oh!" Chloe held up her hand. "I don't want to cry again."

"Turn on the waterworks all you want," Harry said, glancing in his rearview mirror.

Ellen pulled out a Kleenex, dabbed her eyes and handed the packet back over the seat to Chloe. "I'm really glad I didn't put mascara on this morning, otherwise I'd look like Raccoon Mom."

Chloe laughed. "And I'd look like Raccoon Aunt." She shook her head. "I'm an aunt. I can't believe it."

"You'll believe it in"—Ellen checked her watch—"about half an hour, forty minutes. Depending on how long it takes you to pack."

"Not long. I didn't pack much. I didn't think I'd stay for more than a couple of nights."

Silence.

Harry met her eyes again in the mirror. "You're staying for more than a couple of nights, count on it."

She would definitely stay more than a couple of nights, Mike thought. If he had anything to say about it, she'd stay permanently. There was a small apartment a couple of doors down from Harry's place. He'd have a word with the building manager. Harry'd be good for the rent.

"Here we are," Ellen said, and they swerved into the Del's huge parking space. The enormous, rambling white circular building rose all around them, red turrets gleaming in the sun. "Chloe, do you want me to come up with you and help you pack?"

"No, thanks," Chloe began.

"I'll go up with her." No way was Mike going to let her carry a suitcase down. "No problem."

Chloe turned to him, surprised. "That isn't necessary—" but she was talking to the wind. He was already at the backseat door on her side. He slid it open and watched as she put a very pretty foot out.

Damn, these SUVs were high. Not meant for chicks in skirts, no sir. As he had before, he put his hands on her waist and lifted her down. She was featherlight and soft between his hands. Touching her was pure pleasure. Man, it took effort to open his hands and let her go.

Maybe it was that light, flowery perfume she wore. Messed with his head. Paralyzed his hands.

Mike reached to slide the door behind her closed, catching Harry's gaze in the rearview mirror.

He and Harry knew each other very, very well. To the point that words weren't necessary.

That's my sister, the look said. *Take care.*

Mike's own look was eloquent. *I know. I will.*

The Del was huge and extremely busy in the holiday season. Considering she had left a dark, chilly, snowbound Boston, Chloe truly understood the attraction of San Diego. It was almost summer-like here, with buttery sunshine and the promise of warmth in the air.

Tourists were everywhere—sunburned, happy and reckless. It was a family hotel and kids scampered underfoot.

Uh-oh. A gaggle of businessmen, of the big variety. Happy and relaxed in garish golf clothes, laughing and bantering and paying no attention to anyone else as they moved in a pack, right in her path.

Chloe tensed. She was about half the size of many of the men and experience told her they wouldn't notice her until one of the men jostled her. Given the size of some of them, like refrigerators, any jostling would hurt.

They were coming toward her like a big, multipart freight train. Chloe prepared to scramble to get out of their way when she felt Mike at her side move slightly behind her. He had one huge hand on the small of her back, the other gripped her elbow lightly, and they breezed through the businessmen without a scratch.

In fact, the group parted like the Red Sea as Chloe and Mike sailed their way through. Mike kept hold of her and they made it to the front desk without incident even though they'd moved through more hordes of happy, oblivious, suntanned tourists.

Amazing. He'd steered them unerringly through what to her was a terrible obstacle course. Of course, to someone like him, it wasn't an obstacle course at all. People naturally noticed him and made way for him, the alpha male.

It was so incredible, that feeling of sailing through people. Even through that pink-hued rubbery wall of businessmen, which for a moment had frightened her and at any other time would have had her scrambling to veer course.

But she hadn't needed to. Chloe had felt utterly encased in a bubble of protection, the feeling so rare that she cherished it.

In a moment, they were in the vast, cool, wood-paneled atrium lobby of the Del, gorgeous and a little dark after the bright sunshine outdoors. Chloe stood for a moment, blinking as her eyes adjusted.

Mike steered her to the front desk, where Chloe told the elegant man she was checking out. Originally, she'd booked for three nights, thinking that even if things went badly with Harry Bolt, she might take a day or two to visit San Diego. Depending.

Never would she have imagined *this*—her delighted brother waiting for her outside with his equally welcoming wife, and an insanely attractive man standing so close she could feel his body heat, completely focused on her.

"Yes, ma'am," the man at the desk said to her request to check out early. His name tag read Ronald. "I hope everything is okay?"

Chloe blushed with happiness. "Everything is fine, Ronald. I've just decided to stay with . . . with my brother for the next few days."

Oh God, how good those words felt. She was staying with *her brother!*

"Must feel good to say that out loud," Mike mused, and she looked at him, startled, surprised all over again at how perceptive he was, this über alpha male.

Everything about him screamed macho, from the outsized shoulders and arms to the hard face with bright blue, piercing eyes. Above all, he simply had this incredible macho aura, a being that oozed male pheromones.

It was usually a perfect recipe for cluelessness, at least in Chloe's small experience of macho men. They rarely noticed anything outside themselves, which was why Mike was such a surprise. He'd seemed to be tuned into her from the first moment he'd set eyes on her.

"Yes," she said softly, "it does feel good. And not something I'd ever thought I'd say." She turned to look at him, full on, and fell right into those bright blue eyes.

She couldn't have moved if a bomb had gone off a foot away.

"I'm glad," he said softly. He had a deep voice with bass tones that reverberated in her belly. "Really glad you're here."

What could she possibly say to that?

"Your key, ma'am." Chloe was disoriented, out of time, out of space. It took her a moment to connect the elements of the man at the front desk holding out a card. When she simply stared at him—and it had been an effort to wrench her eyes away from Mike's—he put the card down and slid it across to her, probably thinking she was mentally incapacitated. "For checkout?"

Chloe flushed. All these emotions, all of them strong, finding a long-lost brother who came with an extended family, including children, reacting so strongly to Mike—they were so outside her personal experience she was having problems coping.

"Thanks." Mike pocketed the key with its holder.

"It's in the Resort," the clerk said helpfully. "Let me show you." He whipped out a map and traced the route with his index finger.

"Got it." Mike took her arm. "Come on, honey, let's get you packed up so we can go home."

Honey. Home. Oh God.

Another gaggle of men stood between them and the walkway. Supersized middle-aged men in sportswear, crossing their path obliquely. Chloe stiffened a little but needn't have bothered. Again, without even being aware of it, the men parted for her— for Mike, actually. They would never even have noticed her. Mike navigated them through without any difficulties at all.

She was so unused to being looked after, to being protected. Such a strange feeling—to relax totally while among people. She was usually on her guard against so many things.

The Del was huge and there was a lot of walking to be done. It was pointless for Chloe to try to hurry—she'd only trip, perhaps fall. Though falling wasn't actually an option with Mike at her side. He seemed to be hyper-aware of her, matching his steps to hers exactly. He'd actually offered her his arm, as if they were at a Regency ball in Bath. She took it, marveling at the warm, steely feel of him under her fingers. It seemed to her that if he were any-where near her, she could never fall down.

Such a delicious feeling. Chloe loved walking, but it didn't love her back.

Most of the fifty bones she'd broken had reknit fairly well, but the fact was that she wasn't entirely in control of her own body. An orthopedic surgeon had once explained to her that she had lost millions of proprioceptors—tiny feedback devices in the body that help humans keep balance. Walking involved intense attention to where she put her feet, to making sure she didn't trip over things that others would automatically correct for.

Never with Mike by her side, though.

Down crowded corridors, over thick uneven brick walkways, over grassy swards, they made their way without incident. When they stopped at her door, Mike slotted the card key and opened it for her.

It was a lovely room, with a sea view she'd paid an extra $150 for. There had been no way of knowing what she'd find at RBK. She'd been determined that if seeking out her long-lost brother ended badly, she'd at least have a pretty room that looked out over the ocean as a consolation.

"Nice room," Mike said, strolling in, looking around.

"Yes, it is," she agreed, delighted that it wasn't going to have to console her. "It won't take me but a minute to pack."

"Take your time." Those bright blue eyes fixed on her. "You weren't planning on staying long." It wasn't a question.

"No. I, um. I booked for three nights, as I said. If—if it didn't turn out well with Harry, at least I could look forward to doing some touristy things here in San Diego. When I left Boston, there was a foot of snow on the ground and subzero temperatures."

"Well, you're not going back to Boston for a while." Mike watched as she pulled open the one drawer into which she'd put her underwear, nightgown, two sweaters and a pair of lightweight wool slacks. Not many things. "You'll want to do some shopping. Harry'll be good for it. Hell, I'll be good for it."

Chloe turned, nightgown in her hands, frowning. "I'm not too sure I under—Oh!" She blinked in surprise. "You mean Harry would pay for new clothes. Or you would." She blushed. "I could never accept that. And anyway, my parents left me a lot of money." A ton of it, in fact. The amount still astonished and, in a way, shamed her. She didn't deserve all that money. "As a matter of fact, that was one of the reasons I came here to find Harry. I wanted to offer him half the value of the estate I inherited. It's only right. We're siblings, he should have half."

Though nothing could ever compensate Harry for having been left behind, abandoned.

Mike walked over to her, smiling. "You want to give Harry money? Good luck with that. As a matter of fact, I'll bet you dinner at the Crown Room, right here at the Del, that he won't accept a dime from you. Won't even entertain the thought."

"And what would I bet?"

His eyes held hers. The light off the ocean outside her window lit up his blue eyes until they were the color of the ocean itself. He smiled. "Dinner at the Del."

"So . . . no matter who wins, we have dinner here?"

He stepped closer. "Yeah, that's about the size of it."

Though he wasn't as tall as his oversized "brothers," Mike Keillor was still taller than she was. She had to tilt her head back a little to keep looking into his eyes.

He was so close she could feel the heat he emanated. So close he filled her field of vision, blocking everything out but him.

"Shake on it," he ordered.

Her hand lifted without any volition on her part, as if it were the hand itself that wanted to be held by his. He gently grasped it in both hands, instead of the impersonal handshake she'd been expecting. His hands were as hot as a furnace. Slowly, watching her every second, he brought her hand to his mouth and—oh my God—kissed it.

Something inside her, something she'd never even suspected existed, pinged to life. Heat, excitement . . . *desire*. Her hand started shaking in his, utterly uncontrollable. She wasn't in control of anything here—her hands, the expression on her face, her own desire.

It was like being on a raft without oars, tumbling down a raging river. All she could do was hang on. And she did.

Her fingers curled around his hand as he tugged, pulling her willingly closer to him.

Oh, everything about this was just so delicious. Chloe wanted to remember this exact moment for ever. The drapes opened onto a delightful balcony overlooking a stretch of white beach and beyond, the endless Pacific, the sun shining off the waves so brightly it was as if the ocean were filled with silent fireworks.

There was a vague, happy rhythmic sound that was the waves in the distance, overlaid by a little girl's laughter and the dull thwacking of a tennis ball somewhere. She could smell lemon polish, brine, some flowering plant outside the window . . . and Mike.

Every sense she had was heightened, her entire body turning into one huge receptor. Absolutely every sensation her body was receiving was delectable, particularly the desire.

Oh my. She'd read about it, endlessly. Listened to friends talk about it, thought about it, but never understood it.

Now she did. Now she could see why women dated and sometimes married completely inappropriate men, because if for even a fleeting moment it was possible to feel this, it was worth it.

Her entire body was warming up, fast. A wave of heat moving through her, warm and alive. She could barely breathe from the heat and excitement. She could feel every single muscle in her body, feel her heart thudding, all her extremities tingling.

Desire melted her insides, spread heat between her thighs.

When Mike pulled her so close her breasts met his chest, her vagina contracted. A strong pulse, unmistakable. It had never happened to her before but she recognized it immediately. Without any input from her head at all, her body was readying itself for him.

But what astonished her, excited her, delighted her was that extraordinary feeling of being *alive*, the life force pulsing through her, and she recognized how dead she'd felt most of her life. Somehow always at a remove from the living.

But not now. Now she was alive in every cell, connected to the earth, as human as they come. This was frightening, exhilarating stuff. She knew beyond a shadow of a doubt that this didn't come from her. She couldn't make herself feel this way. She'd tried, but it had never worked.

It took Mike Keillor, watching her carefully out of those oh-so-blue eyes, potent and strong and so very very male. He was the reason she felt so incredibly alive.

The thought would have frightened her if she'd had even a minimal capacity for fright, but she didn't. She felt alive, and strong, ready for anything. Able to move mountains. A force of nature.

Mike watched her carefully as he moved his head down, slowly, looking deeply into her eyes, trying to gauge her mood, whether she was going to object.

Was he kidding? Object? When she craved this kiss so much?

Everything about this was brand-new. An excitement so intense her breath was caught in her lungs, all that male power concentrated on *her*, when she was so used to being utterly invisible to men.

And the showstopper. Her own desire. Something she'd never felt before, certainly not at this level of intensity. Everything in her was quivering with anticipation.

And then—it happened.

Mike lowered his head to her, his eyes watching hers, then

dropping his eyes to her mouth, the gaze so powerful it was as if he touched her mouth with his fingers.

He brought his mouth to hers, briefly, and she felt electricity crackle, was surprised lightning didn't flash.

They both jerked a little, as if what had happened was unexpected. It was certainly completely new to Chloe, but then she wasn't really an expert.

Mike lifted his mouth and looked down at her. His eyes narrowed, his face somber, as if he'd just received a shock, perhaps an unwelcome one.

Before she could say anything, pull back because it seemed clear he wasn't happy with the kiss, he bent down again and there was nothing tentative about this kiss. He simply opened her mouth with his and explored it.

Another wave of heat went through her. She leaned against him to get as close as possible and it was like leaning against steel. The first time his tongue touched hers Chloe shuddered.

He must have felt something, too, because he tightened his strong arm around her back and, lifting her, walked two steps to the wall.

There was no discernible change in his breathing when he lifted a full-grown woman, one-armed. The change in breathing came a few seconds later, after her back thudded against the wall and he moved closer to her, as close as the wall was at her back, without ever lifting his mouth.

The kiss became heated, pure sex—sex with their mouths and not genitalia, but it was just as hot, just as exciting, and it had the same effect on her vagina. Each stroke of his tongue made her clench tightly between her legs, a reaction she was utterly unable to stop.

Not that she wanted to. She wanted him even closer, though that wasn't possible. Her arms around his neck tightened and she lifted herself up to his mouth, craving the feel of him everywhere.

She felt his every breath through her mouth, against her breasts as that incredibly wide chest started bellowing.

A foot stepped between hers, then two. His thighs somehow opened hers up and then his entire groin was plastered against hers and . . . oh God.

Right against her belly she could feel it. Feel *him*. Big and thick and hard. What was happening to her every time his tongue touched hers, was also happening to him. Where her vagina contracted, his penis moved, became impossibly longer, thicker. He was grinding against her, mouth to mouth, chest to breasts, groin to groin, setting off a friction that ignited her inside. Each move he made inflamed her more and more.

Her eyes were so heavy she couldn't open them. Though she'd like to see his face, there was no question of opening her eyes. Her body didn't want to see him, it wanted to *feel* him. Feel all that massive strength and heat, concentrated on her, feeding his heat into her.

The kiss went on and on and on, as she moved into a place without time, where there was just an endless now, glowing with heat.

Mike reached down to the hem of her skirt and placed his hand on the outside of her thigh. His hand was so huge it covered an amazing amount of skin. The skin of his palms was rough, she could feel the nylon catching as he slowly brought his big palm up and up.

His entire body jerked when he realized she wore thigh-highs. Chloe had always hated the tight restriction of panty hose and was glad of it now because when his hard palm moved up over the lace at the top of her stockings, he touched her bare flesh and she shivered, goose bumps breaking out all over her body, which was crazy because she was also steaming hot.

At the feel of bare flesh, he stilled, and lifted his mouth. Oh God, was she supposed to open her eyes? Because it was so hard to do. Almost impossible. Her head felt loose on her neck. She was upright simply because there was the wall at her back and Mike Keillor at her front, otherwise she'd fall down.

She opened her eyes when a second passed without Mike kissing her. It wasn't easy. Her lids lifted slowly, as if lead weights were attached to them. All she could see was Mike's face filling her entire field of vision.

He was watching her closely. Maybe to see if she'd object to him touching bare flesh?

Foolish, foolish man.

Chloe lifted herself up a little and placed her mouth on his. Mike drew a deep breath, the air coming from her own lungs, then plunged into her. It was the only possible word to describe the feeling that he possessed every inch of her.

He pulled back a second. She wondered why when cool air brushed her thighs. He'd pulled up her skirt so that when he leaned back heavily against her, she could feel every hard inch of him.

His hips pressed hard against her, thighs opening hers until somehow, as if by magic, as if by some heavenly alignment, his penis was right against her vagina, opening up her lips, rubbing against her . . . *there.*

She whimpered, the sound lost in Mike's mouth. She was entirely his, completely without willpower or volition. His mouth ate at hers, his shoulders curved in to her like some powerful wall of flesh. He moved his hips against her in short, stabbing movements, hands lifting her hips against his.

He gasped, tilted his head, tongue moving deeply in her mouth. She could feel the heat of his penis through his briefs, his trousers and her own silk panties. It burned, his penis hot, moving fast, moving exactly where all her nerves were so raw it was as if he'd switched on an electrical current right . . . *there.*

She was on some vast ocean of pleasure, warm and honeyed and filled with joy. And then the ocean rose, lifted, became a huge wave coming at her, closer and closer, faster and faster . . .

She gave a cry that was lost in his mouth as her body exploded in a burst of heat coming from her thighs, but spreading fast throughout her entire body, her vagina contracting sharply in uncontrollable pulses so strong and sharp they were almost, but not quite, painful and spread through her, down to her fingertips and toes.

She'd shot way out into outer space and came floating back down slowly, in swooping motions. Everything that had been a heated rush slowed and cooled. Gravity reasserted itself, she felt the floor under her feet again. Eyes closed, she sighed.

Amazing. Everything about that had been just amazing. The best experience of her life. As a matter of fact, nothing else had ever come even close.

Mike lifted his mouth from hers.

She sighed again and opened her eyes and received a shock.

Mike did not look happy. He looked as if he were in pain.

"I'm sorry," he said tightly, and her happiness disappeared, just like that. Like flipping a switch.

"You are?" Chloe whispered, appalled.

He was *sorry*. Well, what was she supposed to do with that? He was sorry he kissed her, made her climax? It had been the happiest experience of her life and he was sorry?

Oh my God. What had she done wrong? Had she misread the situation? But—but he'd been the one to initiate the kiss. Had she responded . . . badly? Inappropriately? Too strongly?

How horrible, because it was one of the few times in her life when she didn't overthink the situation. She didn't even think at all. Her head hadn't been involved in any way. Pure instinct had taken over, something that rarely happened to her. Never, actually.

Well, she already knew her instincts were off, didn't she?

Even more horrible, there was nowhere she could go with her embarrassment. Her back was to the wall, literally, and Mike was plastered against the entire front of her body. She couldn't move an inch. At least she could lower her eyes . . .

A strong, rough hand cupped her chin and forced her head up. Mike was looking puzzled. "You're not sorry? I took it from zero to a hundred in a second."

"Sorry? How could I be sorry?" she blurted. "That's never happened to me before. It was wonderful."

Mike blinked, astonished.

Chloe knew perfectly well that was not the kind of thing a full-grown woman should say to an adult male. She didn't date much—actually, she didn't date at all—but she read and she listened to her few friends and it was de rigueur after the age of eighteen to be experienced.

But Chloe had never really learned how to dissemble. She had no knack for it at all. The words had simply popped out of her mouth and it was too late to retract them. Too late to pull some kind of sophisticated comeback to cover her dismay.

Well, you got me off nicely, thank you. Good orgasm, definitely an A, maybe an A+. We should do that again sometime, when we're in the mood.

Mike said, his voice rough, eyes locked on her mouth. "Jesus. If you're not sorry, if I don't have to apologize, then I'm *really* not sorry. As a matter of fact, if we don't go now I'm going to do that again, very soon. Only we'd both be naked." He lifted his eyes to hers. "But we have all the time in the world for that, don't we?"

Even more than the raw almost-sex against the wall, his expression now was the sexiest she'd ever seen. This handsome, incredibly male man was entirely focused on her and sex was most definitely on his mind.

He was utterly aroused, and she didn't need the huge column of his penis against her belly to know that. It was imprinted in every line of his face. The cords of his neck protruded, a red flush stood out under his tanned skin, his jaw muscles were clenched. His eyes were narrowed, chips of blue fire between the lids.

He stared at her, unblinking, then lowered his head.

Oh, fabulous. More of that was on the way. You don't miss something if you don't know it. But now that Chloe had experienced that incredible blast of energy that somehow left her lax and warm, she wanted more of it.

Sex made the world go around. She'd known that intellectually, because sex was everywhere recognized as one of the most potent forces in human affairs. It moved mountains, apparently. Lifted up teen idols, brought down presidents, inspired great works of art, moved hearts to murder.

Chloe had always thought of herself as immune to all that, just one more sign that she was destined to spend her life on the outside, looking in.

But Mike had yanked her forward. Zapped her out of her safe space. Now she'd felt even a little of its power, once wasn't going to be enough. Not by a long shot.

Today she'd crossed some kind of invisible line. Found a brother, maybe found a lover, and joined the human race.

His lips touched hers, just barely, and already she was quivering with eagerness, nearly breathless with expectation.

A loud ring made them both jump. Mike lifted his head, frowned, bewildered.

"Your cell phone," Chloe said gently.

"Christ," he muttered as he pulled a very fancy cell phone out of his jacket pocket and glanced at the display. "Yeah. Yeah, Harry. Coming down right now."

He looked down at her, a corner of his mouth turned up. "Later."

"Later," she agreed happily.

The entire clan lived in a gorgeous high-rise that anchored the end of a stunning white sand beach. Chloe was astounded at the sheer beauty of the place.

Nicole and Sam's apartment was on the top floor, Harry had an apartment on the fifth, and Mike had a smaller one on the fourth floor.

When they walked into Harry's apartment, a smiling Latina—the niece of Nicole and Sam's housekeeper, Manuela, she was told—came out of the bedroom carrying a small bundle in a soft pink and cream blanket.

The baby was fussing, crying and wriggling.

Ellen rushed over, took the baby from the young woman and cradled her, murmuring softly. The wails grew heartbreaking.

Harry put his hand on Ellen's shoulder and looked down at his daughter.

Chloe couldn't help it. She stepped closer, touching the soft blanket, then cradling the child's head in the palm of her hand. The wailing quieted, the tiny feet stopped kicking.

You'd need a wrench to tear her gaze away from the baby to focus on Ellen's face. "May I?" She meant—*May I touch her?*

And Ellen, without a second thought, transferred the tiny bundle to Chloe's arms, not realizing that Chloe had never held a baby before.

The baby fit into her arms perfectly. A small, warm, living bundle, the tiniest human Chloe had ever seen.

She cradled the baby in her left arm and pulled away the blanket from the baby's face. When she looked down, she felt her stomach swoop, her lungs constrict, her heart plunge instantly into love. The whole world just melted away, the only real thing the warm little creature in her arms.

From a huge distance she heard Ellen's voice, a little choked. "Chloe, meet your niece Grace Christine. We call her Gracie. Gracie, meet your aunt Chloe."

Chloe stared down at the tiny, perfect face staring right back at her. It was astounding to see the little face so very like her own, the color of her eyes exactly like hers—a light brown that looked almost golden in the sun streaming in through the huge picture windows.

All the doctors had told Chloe that she could never have children. Her injuries had been too severe, bone fragments had severed her Fallopian tubes. She had been told this from childhood on and it was as much a part of her as her eyes and hands and feet.

She would never have children.

So she had never, ever thought she could hold in her arms a beautiful little girl who looked just like her. A dream so impossible she'd never even had it, never even thought of it.

And yet, here it was. A tiny miracle, in her arms. Grace.

Gracie wriggled a little, kicking madly, then suddenly settled, eyes wide open and fixed on her face as if upon a star. Chloe watched her perfect little face, and to the end of her days would swear that Gracie smiled up at her, a large, gummy toothless smile that simply clenched Chloe's heart in an iron grip, never to let go.

And Chloe knew, beyond a shadow of a doubt, that she wanted to be as much a part of this little girl's life as her parents would allow. And judging by the pleased look on Harry's and Ellen's faces, that would be a lot.

Gracie's crying wound down to gentle cooing as Chloe rocked her. She lost track of time, forgot they were expected upstairs for a meal, forgot that she should settle into her bedroom, forgot everything as she stared into Gracie's beautiful golden eyes, stroking her cheek, marveling that human skin could be so soft, drowning in the waves of love going back and forth between her and her niece.

Suddenly, the utter silence in the room caused her to break away from Gracie's magnetic gaze and look up. Harry stood with his arm around Ellen, whose cheeks were wet. She, Harry and Mike were staring at her, Mike with a laser-like intensity.

"What?" Why were they looking at her?

Ellen swiped at her cheeks. "Gracie's been fussing and crying for days now. She stopped crying the instant you held her in your arms. You have a natural way with children, Chloe."

Wow, how wrong could a woman be? Chloe had no way with kids, none at all. She'd never been around kids, knew nothing about them. Everything she'd done with Gracie had been pure instinct.

Like with Mike.

She blushed to the roots of her hair, bending over Gracie so they wouldn't see.

A cell phone rang and Harry's deep voice answered. "Yep, introducing Gracie to Chloe. Yeah, they liked each other. Coming right up."

He clapped his big hands together. "Okay, guys, Sam is sucking up all the champagne and Manuela's food is getting cold. Chloe, honey, you can get settled in here after lunch. Is that all right with you? You hungry?"

Chloe lifted her head, surprised. "Yes. Yes, I am."

And she *was*. Chloe was never hungry. In the hospital she'd sometimes been put on drips because she couldn't eat. Even now, she ate little and rarely felt hunger. Often her stomach clenched tightly closed in protest at the thought of food.

Now she was *ravenous*. Mike's kiss, the orgasm, holding a child in her arms who looked just like her—it had opened up a huge hole in her stomach and the thought of food upstairs, to be eaten with these happy, welcoming, magical people . . .

"Let's go, then." Harry started ushering them to the door.

Chloe looked down at the little girl in her arms. Gracie's translucent eyelids were almost completely closed. She gave a gusty little sigh and smiled again. Chloe would swear to it.

"Chloe?" Harry stood at the door, Ellen beside him. Mike was by her side.

"She's falling asleep," Chloe whispered. "I don't want to wake her."

"No," Ellen's eyes widened in horror, "don't wake her. Do you feel like carrying her up? It's just a few floors up in the elevator."

At any other moment in her life, Chloe would have recoiled at the thought of being responsible for a child in her arms. Walking, holding a baby. She had trouble keeping herself upright at times. She sometimes tripped unexpectedly. She was not in complete control of her body and carrying a tiny baby was not a good idea.

But she'd claw the eyes out of anyone who took this child from her arms. She was suddenly infused with a huge dose of physical confidence. She was absolutely convinced that she wouldn't trip with Gracie in her arms. She felt strong, connected to the earth with massive roots that dug deep, invincible, unbreakable.

And then there was Mike, who stuck right by her side.

She couldn't possibly fall, not with Mike beside her.

She felt the warm weight of Gracie in her arms, anchoring her to the earth, and smiled at Harry, her new brother, Ellen, her new sister-in-law, and at Mike, her new . . . whatever.

"Let's go, then," she said.

Chapter 7

Sam and Nicole's place was as warm and welcoming as ever. It was Mike's favorite place in the world, closely followed by Harry and Ellen's apartment. And it held his two favorite people in the world—Merry and Gracie.

Gracie was in Chloe's arms, as if she'd been born to be there. Mike would never forget how dazzled Chloe had looked when Ellen placed Gracie in her arms. She didn't even notice Harry's and Ellen's reactions when Gracie immediately stilled, then became content and drowsy.

Harry told him that Gracie had been crying for days, barely letting them sleep. One second with Chloe and she was content.

Man, did Mike ever sympathize. Chloe had this . . . this magic aura of warmth and gentleness and calm. He'd be feeling calm, too, if he wasn't so goddamned aroused.

He'd been on a hair trigger kissing her. Only an absolute lifetime of serious and copious fucking had given him the self-control he needed not to come in his pants, something that would have been seriously uncool, something he hadn't done since high school.

But man, it had been close. He'd felt Chloe's orgasm in her

mouth, against her belly, throughout her entire body. And when she told him it was her first—whoa. Mind-blowing.

Sam and Nicole walked into the living room to greet them, Sam carrying Merry. She squealed when she saw him, turned to her father and ordered imperiously, "Down, Daddy."

Sam was hard-wired to obey Merry, something Nicole worked on constantly. She said she was having another child simply so Sam could spread his spoiling between two children instead of one.

Sam placed Merry gently on the ground and Merry ran toward Mike like a homing missile, because she knew Mike was even more weak-kneed when it came to her and Gracie.

"Unca Mike!" she squealed, and launched herself from two feet away, an old game. Mike caught her and whirled with her while she laughed. "Unca Mike, look!"

She caught his face between her two small hands to turn his head to her, just in case she didn't have his full attention. Merry had the princess gene in full.

"Yeah, pumpkin?" he asked.

She pointed at her feet. "Look, Unca Mike. New shoes!" She shot a small foot out so he could admire them. "They're *red*," she said in a hushed, worshipful tone, face solemn. "And *shiny*."

Nicole rolled her eyes. "She's been pestering me for those shoes since she saw them a couple of weeks ago." She shot an ironic glance at her husband. "I don't know who campaigned harder for those shoes—Merry or Sam."

Sam looked abashed for a moment. He'd try to get her the moon if she wanted it.

"They're beautiful shoes, Merry," Mike said solemnly, biting his lips. Bright shiny new shoes—*red* shoes—were indeed something to be taken seriously. No smiling.

She nodded her agreement, black ponytail bobbing.

"I want to introduce you to someone, Merry. You have a new aunt."

Merry's eyes widened, mostly because, for her, *aunt* meant presents and dancing when her aunt Ellen sang. "Aunt" was a pretty neat concept in Merry's world. One more aunt meant more loot and fun.

Mike turned to Chloe, Merry resting on one arm, Chloe holding Gracie in her arms. The moment, the picture, the idea—it was all so perfect, him introducing Merry to her new aunt.

"Merry, honey, this is your new aunt Chloe. Say how do you do."

"Down, Unca Mike," she ordered. She walked over to Chloe, held out a small hand and said, "How do?"

Merry was nothing if not well-behaved, which was all Nicole's doing. If it were for Sam's paternal discipline, Merry would behave as if raised by wolves. As it was, she was a perfect little lady.

Chloe reached down a hand, smiling. "How do you do, Merry? It's very nice to meet you."

Merry studied Chloe's face, then did something unusual. She leaned up against Chloe's leg and held on to her, looking up. "Aunt Chloe," she said.

It was quite a picture, so beautiful Mike took a snapshot in his head, knowing he'd be taking it out often. A beautiful young woman, with a beautiful blonde baby in her arms and a beautiful dark-haired child holding on to her.

Everyone felt it, felt the power of it. Certainly Mike did, like a blow to the heart. Harry and Ellen and Gracie, Sam and Nicole and Merry—they now had, forever more, someone else in their circle to love.

Merry had been studying Chloe's face, a small frown scrunching her face. She looked at him, then back at Chloe. "Aunt Chloe, are you Unca Mike's wife?"

I wish. The words nearly came out of his mouth, he felt it so powerfully. Because for an instant he could see it, he could feel it.

Chloe, his wife. Surrounded by their children.

She smiled down at Merry. "No, darling, I'm Uncle Harry's

sister." She smoothed her hand over Merry's ponytail. "And now your aunt."

"Well," Nicole said shakily. Her eyes glistened. "I think it's time to eat. Chloe—do you need help?" Considering she was holding one child and another child was holding her.

"No." Chloe smiled. "I'm good."

Mike walked into the big dining room with her, Merry still clinging to her. He understood Merry completely, he wished he could lean up against Chloe, absorb some of that serenity.

"Oh!" Chloe stopped at the threshold to the dining room. Manuela had done them proud. Sam and Nicole's dining table was enormous, a shiny mahogany polished so brightly the lit candles were perfectly reflected upside down. "How beautiful."

It was. There were candles in tall silver holders and small vases of cut flowers among about a thousand serving trays of food, steaming hot and smelling delicious.

Nicole clapped her hands. "Okay, Chloe, you sit here, Ellen here—"

"Mommy!" Merry's voice rang out. "Me next to Aunt Chloe!"

Nicole blinked because Merry always wanted to sit next to daddy, who never corrected her table manners.

"Me, too," Mike said quickly, before the seats next to Chloe ran out. No way was he sitting across the table from her. "I want to sit next to her, too."

"Here." Ellen turned to Chloe, arms out. "Let me take Gracie. I'm used to eating with her in my arms."

"Sure." Chloe held a blanket-wrapped Gracie out to her mother. Gracie woke up with a little snuffle, and after a few false starts, cranked up the engine and started wailing. Ellen rocked her gently, crooning a soft lullaby.

The wails grew louder.

"Honey." Harry put a hand on his wife's shoulder. "Let me try."

"Okay." Looking worried, Ellen gently handed Gracie over to

her husband. The wails grew louder, positively heartbreaking.

Chloe bit her lips, opened her mouth, closed it.

Gracie turned her head away from the pacifier, the wails as loud as a siren.

"Could I—" Chloe looked at Harry and Ellen. "Could I try to calm her down?"

Puzzled, Harry said, "Sure," and gently transferred the bundle back to Chloe.

Gracie stopped crying as if a switch had been thrown.

"Wow," Mike said.

"Yeah." Harry shook his head. "Man, am I glad you're going to be staying with us. You're going to stay a long, long time."

"Until all Gracie's teeth come in, at least," Ellen added fervently. "Maybe till college."

Chloe leaned to one side as Manuela heaped food on her plate. Seconds and thirds included. Manuela belonged to the More Is Better school of cooking.

"I only packed for a few days," Chloe said, smiling. "Be hard to stay here until Gracie goes to college."

"So buy new clothes," Nicole said, slicing into a sausage and onion omelette. "It'll be fun. I'll take you shopping." She slanted her eyes at Merry, leaning against Chloe, looking up in adoration. "Merry can come. She loves shopping. I think she's fallen in love with you."

"Shopping," Merry said with almost religious fervor. "With Aunt Chloe."

Harry laughed. He was seated across the table from her and leaned forward. "Honey . . ." He stopped, hesitated. Mike looked at him surprised. Harry wasn't the kind of man who hesitated. "If you need money, that is absolutely not a problem."

"Oh, not at all!" Ellen chimed in. "Whatever you want, whatever you need—"

Chloe held up a hand, looking dismayed. "No, no, I don't need money. As a matter of fact—" Sitting next to her, Mike could see her hands trembling. She drew in a deep breath. "As a matter of fact, that was the main reason I tried to track you down, Harry. My parents—my adoptive parents—left me money. A lot of it. And it's only fair that half of it go to you. We can make an appointment with a lawyer while I'm here and I can transfer half the estate to you."

Silence. All eyes turned to Harry, who was shaking his head.

"Chloe," he said gently. "I don't want your money. Not a penny of it. Our company is doing very well and even if the company went belly-up"—he shot a smile at Ellen—"if I were to go bankrupt tomorrow, Ellen here earns so much she can keep me in the style to which I've become accustomed. Not to mention the fact that she's so good with the damned stuff that she doubles the value of our investments every six months. You went through hell, Chloe. Keep all the money and enjoy it. Just as long as you enjoy it here in San Diego. With us."

Tears shimmered in Chloe's eyes.

Mike leaned in close to her. "Told you," he murmured. She turned to him with a choked laugh. "So it's dinner at the Del. Tomorrow night."

Oh yeah. Tomorrow night, the night after, the night after that. What Mike felt was right there in his face and she blushed when she looked at him.

Oh man. Life was really looking up. Last night he was fucking a whack job, and less than twenty-four hours later, here he was with the most delectable woman he'd ever set eyes on, and he wasn't going to let her go.

"Okay," she said softly, and he did a mental fist pump. Tomorrow night. Dinner in the Crown Room. Soft candlelight that would make her skin glow more than it did already. A great meal, a walk along the beach afterwards . . .

His cell phone rang.

He pulled it out to turn it off. *Nope, sorry, whoever you are.* Not in. Not now, maybe not ever again. Everyone he cared about in the world was right here in this room with him. The rest of the world could just fuck off.

Oh shit. Bill Kelly. A good guy from SDPD and, most of all, a former Marine. Being a Marine was the closest thing to a religion Mike had. Though he wasn't on active duty in the Corps, Mike was still a Marine. All Marines were his brothers. The second half of the famous motto. *Semper fi,* yeah. But above all, *semper fraternis.* Always brothers. Mike had Sam and Harry, his blood brothers. But he also had the whole Corps. Every Marine was in a sense his brother.

And Bill Kelly was one of the best. A hard-ass but a real good guy. Mike couldn't blow him off, not even tonight when he might have found the woman of his dreams.

So, with a sigh, he flipped open his cell. "Yo. Bill. Now's not a really good time, but—"

"You home?" Bill's gravelly voice was flat.

"Nope." Mike frowned. "I'm at Sam's, but—"

"Be there in two," Bill growled, and the screen went dead.

Mike held his phone for a second, staring at it. For Bill to be here in two meant that he was at Mike's door five stories down.

What the fuck?

It didn't take Bill two minutes, it took one. Nicole went to answer the door and Mike heard Bill's low rumble in the front hall as he greeted Nicole, then followed Nicole into the dining room.

Bill was no dummy. He saw he was interrupting something. He ducked his head. "Ladies. Reston, Bolt." He stuck his thumb over his shoulder. "Keillor, you're with me."

This was wrong. Everything about it was wrong. Bill had an old-fashioned sense of propriety. He would never interrupt a family party like this on a casual visit. So this was business.

But Mike wasn't a member of the SDPD anymore. He wasn't

under Bill's command. If Bill was going to ask for a favor, he was going about it the wrong way.

And, dammit, whatever it was, it could wait. Mike was having a real good time and he didn't want to leave Chloe's side.

"Can it wait, Bill?" Mike didn't even bother disguising the impatience in his voice.

Bill frowned. "No. It can't. And I'm about ten minutes ahead of an arrest warrant. This is a favor I'm doing you, Keillor, dammit, so you can get your ass on out there, right now."

Bill never swore in front of ladies, never. He must be under massive stress.

Then Mike focused on what he said. *"Arrest warrant?"*

"Yeah."

Sam and Harry were on their feet, chairs shoved back, suddenly bristling with aggression. Nicole and Ellen and Chloe looked shocked.

Aware that something was wrong with the adults, Merry ran to her mom and threw her little arms around Nicole's expanding waist. Gracie woke up and started crying. Chloe tried to hush her but it wasn't working. She transferred the little bundle into Ellen's arms.

The entire table was beautifully set, the food steaming, up until a minute ago immensely inviting. A table of celebration. Now the sharp smells of food rose in his nostrils like a fog and made him nauseous. The celebration was ruined.

What the fuck?

"Now, Keillor." Bill's voice was flat, command in it.

Mike didn't obey because this was a command situation—for the first time in his life he had no command structure at all, and he found he liked it that way—but because this shit was fucking with one of the best days of his life. He wanted this—whatever *this* was—over, now.

Some kind of mistake had been made and he wanted it straightened out, fast.

With an exclamation of impatience, Mike strode into Sam's living room, indicated that Bill should take one of Sam's big comfortable armchairs, and he sat down on the edge of the sofa, at a right angle.

A moment later, Sam sat next to him on the sofa and Harry on the armchair next to Bill's.

Bill raised his eyebrows. "You okay with this?" he asked Mike.

What a dumb-ass question. "Yeah. They're my brothers. I don't have anything to hide from them."

Kelly nodded, pulled out a notebook. He was the last holdout among the detectives, most of whom took notes on laptops or iPads.

Kelly flipped back a few pages, looked up at Mike. "Where were you last night?"

Mike froze. Christ, *last night?* Sam and Harry looked at each other, then at him. "Ah, I went out."

Kelly's jaw muscles jumped, gray eyes cold and frosty. He let the silence hang there. Mike knew better than to give that answer, he was a former cop, after all. But all of a sudden, for one of the few times in his life, he was ashamed of his tomcatting ways. Sam and Harry had been at home with their wives and daughters while he'd been in a dive, drinking too much and picking up a crazy.

He was too old for that, he suddenly realized. No more barhopping. It was a depressing way to drown his problems, and anyway the problems were right there with him, the next morning. Together with a hangover and a burning desire to get far away from the woman he'd been with.

Mike gave a heavy sigh. "Okay. I went out around eleven, drove down to Logan Heights, drank a few shots in a couple of bars."

Kelly had his notebook open on his knee, but he didn't look down. "Ending up at The Cave?"

"I don't remember," Mike began, when suddenly he did. He flashed on the big, broken neon sign over the filthy window, THE AVE. "Yeah," he sighed. "The Cave."

"You picked up a woman."

What the fuck business was it of Kelly's. What—he'd suddenly become the sex police? "I don't see what business that is of yours."

"What was her name?" Kelly's voice became even colder.

Jesus. Her name? If Mike were capable of blushing, he'd blush. If she'd told him her name he didn't remember it. He'd been way too drunk.

He shrugged.

"Real love affair, huh." Kelly's voice was icy.

Mike's teeth ground.

"The name Mila Koravich mean anything to you?"

Mila—Mike closed his eyes, tried to envision the woman's apartment. Filth, disorder, rank smells. All he remembered was the stench and the sick feeling of drunkenness. Had her name been on anything? He scanned his memory behind his closed eyelids. Nope.

Mike's eyes opened. "Sorry. I don't remember her name. So what's it matter to you?"

"You got rough with her, didn't you?"

Shame flooded his system in a hot rush. Harry and Sam sat silently, watching him. In the drunken haze that was last night, the memory of holding her down, of seeing her red, slightly swollen wrists with the white marks of his hands circling them, stood out.

"A—a little. Nothing serious."

"Yeah?" Kelly had been writing in his notebook but at Mike's words he looked up, face clenched like a fist. "I don't know what your definition of 'a little rough' is, Keillor, but it's not mine."

He reached into an envelope and pulled out some glossy 8 x 10s and tossed them down onto the coffee table. Mike leaned forward, trying to make sense of what he was seeing. Red and black, mis-shapen flesh . . . then the image resolved itself into the shocking images of a badly beaten woman.

He narrowed his eyes. Something about the badly beaten face was familiar . . . Oh God. The woman he'd fucked last night.

Shocked, he looked up into Kelly's angry eyes.

"Shattered jaw, concussion, broken forearm, three broken ribs, internal hemorrhaging it took surgery to stop, and a crushed spleen. That's not what I call 'a little roughness,' Keillor."

"Christ. I didn't do that to her." Mike stood, unable to sit still. "I couldn't do that to any woman. The only thing I did was hold her down when she asked for it." And well, fuck her harder. But she'd asked for that, too.

Kelly made an angry gesture at the spill of horrific photographs. "That looks like someone who was just held down? She was beaten half to death."

"Christ, Bill." A sudden shudder of fear struck Mike. He wasn't used to fear, but this was a new type of fear he'd never encountered before. If Bill Kelly, who knew him, thought he was capable of doing this, what about other officers in the Violent Crimes Squad? All his dealings had been mainly in SWAT. But the SDPD was big. There were plenty of officers who didn't know him and weren't willing to take anyone's word that Mike simply wasn't capable of this kind of violence against a woman.

Against an enemy who attacked him, sure. But a woman? Never.

It was beginning to sink in that he was going to have to convince skeptical officers he wasn't the one. And the D.A. And—God—maybe eventually a jury.

Kelly gave him a hard look. "So you're telling me you didn't have sex with this woman? And be careful what you say because we found a used condom in the bathroom." He snorted. "Used, not filled. You didn't even come, you poor bastard. So—what's the DNA test gonna show? And remember your DNA is on file."

Every police officer had donated DNA via a cheek swab to establish a data file.

"Yeah, okay, we had sex."

"Uh-huh," Kelly said. "And?"

"And . . . I didn't come. She was . . . asking me to be rough with her. Couldn't do it."

Now Kelly looked at him in pity. Kelly was a straight and narrow kind of guy who probably only got laid on St. Patrick's Day. Mike used to feel sorry for him but he suddenly realized the truth. Kelly was right and he was wrong. Fucking around was not good.

Kelly sighed. "The, um, lady in question used crack. We found it everywhere. You're a former police officer. Former Marine. Marines and crack. That's not a good mix, Keillor. You should have kept it in your pants."

Mike closed his eyes. Kelly was right. He should have kept it in his pants.

"So . . . what's your version? Tell me what went down."

Mike clenched his jaw. Christ, he didn't want to talk about it. Any of it.

Silence. Mike could hear his own teeth grinding.

Kelly sighed and stood. "Okay, if you're not talking, we need to take it downtown, Keillor."

Sam and Harry rose together.

Mike unclenched his jaw. It took effort. "Stand down, guys. Sit back down." Man, he wished his brothers weren't here, but they were and they weren't leaving. For the first time since he'd walked into Old Man Hughes' house of horror and discovered that he'd landed in another shithole of a foster home, but that there were two other boys who immediately had his back, Mike wished Sam and Harry were less loyal. What he wanted was to quietly clear this up with Kelly and not have his brothers involved.

But Sam and Harry were hard-wired for loyalty. They weren't about to let him face this alone.

Shit.

"Down, everyone," he repeated, and Sam and Harry sat back down, on the edges of the couch. Kelly stood for another long moment, grim-faced, then finally sat back down. He pulled out a notebook and waited.

"Okay," Mike said. He closed his eyes for a moment, almost tasting the cold steel in his mouth as he bit the bullet. "I was feeling restless last night. Went out around eleven. I wasn't in the mood for trendy bars, martinis, picking up investment bankers." No, he'd felt like going to a place as shitty as he felt. But he couldn't say that in front of Sam and Harry because they'd beat themselves up over not recognizing that he felt shitty and busting their asses to make him feel better.

Sometimes Mike wished his brothers weren't such stand-up guys. Wished they were worse friends. Wished they didn't care so much about him.

"I, ah, tooled around a little. Ended up in Logan Heights, in a place called The Cave."

Kelly held up a hand, spoke quietly in his cell, flipped it closed. Bent back over his notebook. "Okay. Get on with it."

"I . . . drank. A lot." Mike looked over at Sam and Harry. Both had poker faces. When Harry came back a human wreck from Afghanistan, essentially wanting to die, he'd tried the drinking-himself-to-death thing for a while, night after night. Mike and Sam had let him, because it's not easy to drink yourself to death, though God knows Harry tried. Mike and Sam had taken away his guns, wouldn't let him swim out to where he couldn't come back, and for a very bad month there had put up unbreakable screens around Harry's balcony.

But they let him try to drink himself to death because it was really hard to do and Harry wasn't managing it.

Mike had his drinking moments, too, only not with Harry's good reasons. It had been touch-and-go whether Harry would ever walk again, ever spend a minute of his life without excruciating pain, would ever have anything resembling a normal life.

And Mike's excuse? Nothing. Which was precisely what he felt sometimes—absolutely nothing inside.

It shamed him, but there it was. He didn't even have Sam and Harry's tragic childhoods as an excuse. He'd been securely wrapped in the strong embrace of a loving family until scumbags shot his mother and father and two brothers in a botched robbery and his childhood ended. That was on the twelfth of March twenty-five years ago when Michael Patrick Keillor was ten years old. On the thirteenth of March of that year, he was already an old man of ten, broken in two by grief.

But until that day, his life had been charmed.

And he drank to forget his life from that March 13 on.

"Get shit-faced?" Kelly asked.

It was sort of a technical term. Drunkenness had its own taxonomy and "shit-faced" was what he'd been.

"Yeah," Mike answered quietly.

Kelly sat and looked at him, pen hovering over paper. "And?"

"I picked up this—" This what? Girl wasn't the right term. Lady wasn't right, either. "Woman."

Actually, she'd picked him up.

"Name?" Kelly was staring at his notebook and Mike had a sudden flash that Kelly didn't want to watch his face as he recounted something depressing.

Mike didn't answer, and Kelly finally looked up.

"I told you. Don't know her name," Mike said quietly, and the three men winced. Man, not getting a chick's name was bad. He'd fucked her, at least partially, but he didn't know her name. There was really no excuse and he didn't offer one.

Kelly was staring at him now, as if trying to get inside his head. Kelly was an alpha male, too, and Mike didn't ordinarily let men stare at him. He'd have bristled except he knew that Kelly was only doing his job. Mike had forfeited his right to indignation.

"I gave you a name," Kelly finally said. "Mila Koravich. Ring a bell?"

Mike shook his head. He doubted they'd exchanged ten words together.

"Working girl?" Kelly asked casually, and this time Mike winced.

"No." Though she might have been. Cokehead, filthy hovel of a place. She might have been. "Not that I knew of, anyway. She didn't ask for money." If she had, he'd have refused. Part of his no-go list. No married ladies, no addicts—though he'd sandbagged on that one—no working girls.

No, siree. Mike Keillor had standards. High ones, too.

Another long silence. Mike couldn't meet Sam's and Harry's eyes. You wouldn't catch them puking the bourbon out of their guts at 2 A.M. in a miserable hole. No, at 2 A.M. they were with their wives, where you could find them every night of their lives they weren't on the road for work. And both of them made real efforts to come home as quickly as possible because what waited for them at home was something pretty damned wonderful.

"So," Kelly said the words in a level voice, one by one, without any inflection, "you got rough."

Mike stared at the floor.

"Real rough." Something in Kelly's voice made Mike raise his head and frown.

He was nauseated at the memory. "I, ah, I held her down. My hands were, yeah, a—a little rough. She asked me to hold her down, do her hard. But I hated that. Her wrists were a little red when I lifted my hands."

"And?" Kelly asked, his voice harsh.

Mike shrugged. "It wasn't *that* bad."

Kelly leaned forward, got in his face. "I don't know what your definition of bad is, Keillor. But mine includes the kind of violence that was done to that woman. No one deserves that kind of treatment. She was under the knife for four hours."

Mike's head snapped up. "Whoa. I held her wrists, that's it. They were red and a little swollen when I lifted my hands, I told you. But that was absolutely it. There wasn't anything that would require—God!—surgery. Nothing even remotely like that."

"Let me remind you." Kelly flipped back to the beginning of his notebook but he had it all memorized. He barely glanced at his own notes. "The woman was brought into the hospital with a shattered jaw, concussion, broken bones, crushed spleen."

"No, man." Just hearing the list made him sick. "That wasn't me. Jesus, I could never do that to a woman. Listen, this is what went down. I picked up this woman at a bar, The Cave. We went to her house and had sex. Some sex, anyway. She wanted me to get rough with her and it just turned me off. I went into her bathroom and took off my condom, which won't have sperm DNA, and puked in her toilet. I left her mad at me and screaming, so if anyone reported noise, that was it. I thought I might still have alcohol in my system and I needed air and exercise, so I left my vehicle there and ran to the ferry, ran down to Coronado Shores."

"What time did you get home?"

"I don't—wait. I got home around five. Yeah. When I got out of the shower my digital alarm clock read 5:17. I stood on my balcony and watched the sun come up and went in to work."

Kelly's jaw muscles worked as he stared at Mike, eyes cold.

"Well, let me tell you what we've got, Keillor. We've got a 911 call clocked at 4:02. Screaming and the sounds of a violent beating in room 321 at 445 Alameda Street, the home of one Mila Koravich. The cops found her unconscious and EMS took her to E and A, where she was in surgery by 5:15. We dusted for prints, found some good ones on the iron bedstead and on the tiles over the toilet."

God. Mike flashed on a vision of pumping into the woman while holding on to the bedstead because he'd suddenly had an aversion to touching her anywhere except with his cock. He'd held her down only when she insisted. And he remembered bracing himself against the wall over the toilet while puking.

"We ran the prints." Kelly huffed out air through his nose like an enraged bull. "Prints pinged with a lot of lowlifes, but all of us were astonished when your prints came up. Fresh prints. We ran it twice."

Mike had been in the armed services and had been a law enforcement officer. Of course his prints were on file. He had a sick feeling in his stomach.

"So we took your SDPD ID to all the bars in the area, and at The Cave we struck gold. You left with Mila Koravich, who by the way has had two arrests for prostitution and possession, at a quarter past midnight. The bartender confirmed the ID. He said he saw you leave with Koravich. This morning at eight, when she came out of anesthesia, Koravich ID'd you as the man who beat her up."

Sam and Harry rose again as one unit, big tough men, presenting a united front. "That's ridiculous," Sam growled. "You heard Mike, he was home by five A.M."

The four men stared at one another. Mike could feel the aggression bristling from Sam and Harry but Kelly stood his ground. He wasn't the kind of man to be intimidated. He'd been a Marine, he was now a very good cop. Not the kind of man who bent when pressure was applied.

Kelly ignored Sam and Harry and fixed Mike with a glare.

If he looked carefully, though, Mike could see pain behind the cold gray stare. He didn't like suspecting Mike. And he didn't like investigating him. But it was his duty, so he was going to do it.

Like that old SEAL saying. You don't have to like it, you just have to do it.

Kelly stuck his notebook in the saggy pocket of his jacket, which looked like he'd slept in it for the past month. "Gonna have to take this downtown, Keillor. No other way around it." He held up a big hand, palm out, when Sam and Harry took a step forward. "Guys. We can do this the easy way or the hard way. Your choice."

Mike felt old, all of a sudden. Old and ashamed. He hadn't beaten up the woman. He knew he hadn't and he trusted Kelly to be a good enough cop to follow the evidence. He'd be exonerated. Eventually.

But it might come to some nasty things before the situation got resolved. He might have to put up bail. RBK was doing real well but they were in the process of making major investments and taking a good chunk out of that would hurt his brothers. Mike knew that Kelly would instinctively try to shield him from the press but if word got out that Michael Keillor of RBK had been arrested for assault, it would be a huge blow to the good name of the company they'd all worked so hard to build.

It was very possible that Mike was going to watch his brothers, his company, get covered in mud. Not to mention costing money at exactly the wrong time.

He had no one to blame but himself for this, no one.

He hadn't beaten up this woman. He wasn't guilty of that, but he was guilty of everything else. He was guilty of not being able to spend one night alone, at the age of thirty-five. He was guilty of getting drunk and picking up a woman he knew nothing about and, which two seconds' worth of thought in his head, as opposed to doing his thinking with his dick, would have told him was bad news, the worst.

He was guilty of dishonoring his company, his brothers. He was guilty of shaming his brothers' wives, two women he loved and respected.

"D.A.'s waiting," Kelly said and Mike closed his eyes. Yeah, the D.A.'d be waiting and since he was ex-SDPD, they'd throw the book at him on principle. No one could afford to appear to favor a former cop. Kelly'd gone way out on a limb here for him, and he would pay.

If the press got a whiff of special treatment, Kelly'd be in deepest shit. The tabloids and political websites would bay for blood.

"We're coming with Mike." Sam's voice was flat. It wasn't a question. Kelly hesitated. He was a tough guy but getting into a pissing contest with Sam and Harry presenting a united front wasn't anyone's idea of fun.

Christ, *no*. Mike didn't want his brothers anywhere near this.

Mike would have given anything at that moment to have less loyal brothers. He didn't want them to troop downtown and watch him being treated like a potential felon. There'd be newbies at HQ, men who didn't know Mike and who for the rest of their days would know him as the ex-cop accused of assaulting a cokehead after sex. Mike's disastrous misjudgments would be right there, out in the open for all to see and snigger over.

His brothers would see that. Would suffer for that.

Mike wanted his brothers safely in their homes, with their families, where they belonged. They deserved that. They didn't deserve what was about to go down.

Thank God Merry and Gracie weren't old enough to understand anything at all about this sordid clusterfuck. Mike couldn't live with himself if he had to watch the confusion and pain in his nieces' eyes as they realized that their Unca Mike was accused of something so horrendous.

Mike turned to pick up his jacket to follow Kelly when he stopped in horror. It was like the entire world paused as he swooped right down into a deeper level of hell. All his previous regrets meant nothing because there was Chloe. Standing in the doorway, staring at him with sadness in her golden eyes.

Chloe. White-faced, stricken. She'd been there all along, listening. So she'd had an earful of what Mike Keillor was all about. She didn't know him in any meaningful way. What she did know about him was what she'd learned over the past half hour, and all of it was horrible and all of it was true.

Mike hadn't beaten up the woman, of course, but everything else—guilty. He'd drunk too much. As a matter of fact, getting shit-faced on a regular basis was beginning to become a habit with him.

The one night he was on his own, he got shit-faced and picked up the first woman who came on to him. A woman who turned out to be an addict and was borderline insane.

Didn't make any difference. Mike had heard someone back in the SWAT team locker room joke that if it had a vagina, Mike would poke it.

True.

He'd been using sex and alcohol for a long, long time as a way to drown out his thoughts. It never worked and he never stopped trying. The very definition of insanity. Doing the same thing over and over again expecting a different outcome.

That was the Mike Keillor Chloe was seeing. A guy who drank too much, fucked addicts, slapped around the women he fucked.

That's not me, he wanted to scream. He'd been a good Marine, a good cop. He worked hard in his company. He loved his brothers, their wives, and above all his little nieces.

He helped abused women disappear. He fucking gave to fucking charity.

The man she'd heard described just wasn't him.

Except—it *was*. He hadn't beat up the woman. But except for that, it was all true. He was a borderline alcoholic and a sex addict and he wasn't fit for decent women. And he had to come to that conclusion the day a woman rocked his world.

Chloe Mason had knocked him off his feet. In the few hours he'd spent with her he'd had this totally weird, totally new feeling in his chest. He couldn't breathe around the tightness in his chest, while at the same time he felt like he was pulling in pure oxygen.

He recognized it now as happiness—something clean and fresh and beautiful in his world. And he'd ripped it out of his life with his own hands.

They trooped out in a sad little procession, first Kelly, then Mike, then Sam and Harry bringing up the rear. Instead of spending the day together with his extended family, getting to know quiet, mysterious, beautiful Chloe Mason better, he was dragging his brothers away from their families to deal with squalor. And every step took him away from Chloe.

That kiss with Chloe at the Del had been the most exciting thing he'd ever experienced, a universe away from the sex he'd been having all his life. Mike had seen a door open and something mysterious and enticing beckoning to him from the other side.

That door had slammed shut. He'd slammed it shut with his own fucking hands.

Chloe watched them walk past, her eyes on him. Mike couldn't meet her eyes. Simply couldn't. Shame and regret were like acid eating him alive from the inside. He walked past her, eyes straight ahead, face grim.

Ellen and Nicole watched, too, eyes sad. Ellen had one of her pretty musician's hands over her mouth and Nicole was cupping her belly where her second daughter nestled.

Mike couldn't wait to get away. Away from them and their sad, loving gaze. He knew how much they cared for him. Both women had opened their homes and their hearts to him and how did he repay them? By bringing squalor and filth inside their homes.

He couldn't even look at his brothers. They flanked him silently in a sign of support as they marched down the corridor, but they looked straight ahead. No one spoke a word as they rode down in the elevator.

There were no words to say.

Chapter 8

"He didn't do it," Ellen said quietly but firmly.

"Absolutely not." Nicole was just as firm.

Chloe looked at them. They meant every word. There was nothing ambiguous in their body language or voices.

Something eased in her heart, a slight lightening of the oppressive heaviness that had weighed her down as she listened to the police lieutenant interrogating Mike.

She knew nothing about him, really. And what did she know about men, anyway? Practically nothing. Did she think that just because he'd given her her first orgasm, he was a good guy? Sex and decency were not linked together. She was old enough to know that.

But still . . . Something inside her resisted the notion that he was capable of hurting that woman the way the lieutenant had said. When he'd touched her in the hotel room, his huge, strong hands had been incredibly tender. She was in uncharted territory with only her admittedly weak knowledge of men and sex to go on, but she just couldn't see Mike hurting a woman like that.

She didn't know Mike at all, but Ellen and Nicole did.

"If there's one thing Mike is incapable of, it's hurting a woman," Ellen said, rocking Gracie in her arms.

Nicole rubbed her belly. "Absolutely," she said. "He's one of the nicest guys in the world."

Their words were directed at *her*. Chloe had no idea why. She had nothing to do with this. "I'm sure you're right," Chloe said gently. "For what it's worth, I don't think he beat that poor woman up, either."

Latent violence had its clear markers. She had an instinctive feel for it. It was why she shied away from her "father" all those years. When her P.I. Amanda uncovered what had happened to her at the age of five, she understood her unconscious obsession.

After Amanda lifted the rock and found her biological family, Chloe realized that her entire life had been marked by the uncontrolled violence of her mother's boyfriend. "I don't think Mike is the type, so you don't have to convince me," she offered.

Nicole and Ellen looked at each other.

"Yes," Nicole said, "we do." She opened her hand in invitation. "Come on. Let's go in the living room. I don't think anyone has any appetite for food anymore."

No. Chloe's stomach was as tightly closed as a fist.

In the vast living room, without seeming to, Nicole and Ellen boxed Chloe in between them. Chloe liked them both but she didn't like being manipulated.

Once they were seated, Nicole and Ellen shared another look in which it was silently decided Nicole would take the lead.

"Chloe, my dear. You really must believe us when we say Mike is absolutely innocent of the charges. He—"

"Oh, I believe you," Chloe said, looking from one tense face to the other. "Not that my opinion means anything."

"Yes it does," Ellen said softly. "It really does."

"Mike likes you." Nicole touched Chloe's hand. "I know you got an image in there of a guy who sleeps around a lot and I can't say that's not true. Unfortunately it is. You know that old saying about looking for love in the wrong places? That's Mike. But Mike has never once brought a woman around for us to meet. And both Sam and Harry say he's never had a stable relationship. We have never seen him act the way he has around you. He couldn't take his eyes off you. We think he's very taken with you and maybe"—her hand tightened around Chloe's—"maybe you're not indifferent?"

Chloe flashed on the hotel room, Mike's mouth on hers, his heavy weight against her, thick penis rubbing against the lips of her sex . . . her body simply lit up at the memory.

Curse her fair skin. Chloe didn't need to look in the mirror to know her face was stoplight red. She saw no reason to lie when her very skin was flashing the truth. "No," she confessed quietly. "I'm not."

Ellen smiled gently. "I didn't think so." She shot another glance at Nicole. "*We* didn't think so. And the reason why we're being so nosy and probably annoying you by butting into your affairs is that we want Mike to find some happiness. He deserves it."

Nicole leaned forward. "He saved our lives. Both our lives. We'll tell you the stories some other time, but the truth of it, the thing you have to know, is that when our lives were in danger, Mike didn't hesitate. Sam and Harry, well, they were in love. It was a given they'd put their lives on the line. Mike did what he did out of devotion to his brothers, but also because, for all his tomcatting around, he's like an old-fashioned knight. We're worried for him. Worried that he's been framed for something he didn't do. That he's in a mess he can't get out of."

"And we're worried that at the moment he's found a woman he can care for, he's going to lose his chance, together with his freedom," Ellen said bluntly. She squeezed Chloe's hand. "Please tell me this won't spoil anything. Please tell me you'll give Mike a chance. I've never seen him look as happy as he did today. He couldn't keep his eyes off you. He so deserves a chance at love. Don't take that away from him."

Both women were looking at her with hope in their eyes.

Chloe suddenly stood, crossing the room to her purse. They desperately wanted to help Mike and, God help her, so did she. There was one woman in the world she trusted to get to the truth of the matter. It was the one number she had on speed dial.

Nicole and Ellen were watching her, vibes of hope and worry all but quivering around them. "Okay. You want to help Mike? So do I." She smiled at the voice that answered. "Amanda? This is Chloe. Yes, in San Diego. Amanda, I need your help." She looked at the two women watching her and, for the first time in her life, felt the sharp, warm bite of family. "*We* need your help."

"Let's go over it again," Kelly said in the interrogation room, and Mike stifled a groan. They'd gone over it and over it and over it.

The bare, ugly room smelled of male tension and despair. Probably what a prison cell smelled like. Mike hoped to God he'd never find out, but it didn't look good.

Mike couldn't blame Kelly. Mila had ID'd him as the man who'd attacked her the minute she woke up from surgery. Defending the real son of a bitch who'd put her in the hospital. Mike understood the police thought they had an airtight case. They didn't. But they did have enough evidence to keep him in jail until a trial date could be set.

His brothers wouldn't allow that. They'd meet any bail the D.A. set, which made Mike angry because it just so happened that this was a tight moment for money. They'd just bought ten thousand acres of land in Baja to use as a law enforcement training center and shooting range for Mexican police trainees who were fighting a vicious drug war. It had been Ellen's idea and it was a good one but the cost of the huge tract of land and creating ranges and shooting houses had drained them. RBK would have to borrow the money to make his bail. Then his brothers would borrow even more to get him a high-priced criminal lawyer.

RBK would go into the hole because of him. The two families would have to tighten their belts because of him. Because he'd behaved like a hormonal teenager instead of a responsible adult.

The thought made him sick.

He was innocent. His brothers should just let him rot here until evidence proving him innocent came up or until the case went to trial. Sam and Harry wouldn't allow that, but he wished they would. Just leave him here and let the truth wind its way to him.

Mike didn't want to go home, anyway. He didn't want to face Ellen and Nicole and above all, he didn't want to face Chloe. The look on her face when she'd heard what he'd done . . . Mike didn't have anywhere to go with the burning shame inside him. That sense of hope he'd had since he'd set eyes on her, the glowing warmth in her eyes when she looked at him, those hot tender kisses promising much more—all gone.

Mike couldn't stand the thought of the disappointment she must be feeling, how confused and hurt she must be.

Fuck.

He'd faced gunfire and mortars without flinching, but the idea of watching a pale Chloe avert her gaze when she saw him— couldn't do it. He simply couldn't do it.

He deserved to rot in jail. Not because he'd done what they were accusing him of, but because he'd spent twenty years rolling out of beds he shouldn't have been in, having fucked women he didn't care about.

What did that make him?

"I went to a bar called The Cave," he began again, voice calm and remote. "I got there at around eleven. I met a woman there. We talked briefly—"

There was a knock at the door that surprised both Mike and Kelly. You don't interrupt an interrogation, that was an iron rule.

Kelly's jaw clenched and Mike felt sorry for the rookie who didn't know better on the other side of the door.

To his surprise, it wasn't a rookie. It was a detective Mike knew well from his SWAT days, Jerry Klein, and—Jesus. Harry and Sam, right behind him.

Kelly rose, furious. He was right. What the fuck were Harry and Sam thinking? This wasn't an expression of solidarity with a friend, this was interference with due process. There were legal implications to stopping a law enforcement officer from carrying out his duties.

Before Kelly could open his mouth to blast Jerry for allowing civilians into the interrogation room, Jerry put a laptop on the interrogation table.

"Sorry, boss, but I thought you needed to see this. These two, ah, civilians brought it to my notice." Jerry stood at attention, flicking Mike a gaze he couldn't interpret. Then, amazingly, Jerry winked at him.

What the fuck?

Jerry powered up the laptop and stepped back to give Harry access to the keyboard.

Harry was a wizard at computers, much better than Mike. Everyone leaned forward to watch him do his thing, but his thing turned out to simply be him opening his email.

He moved the mouse around.

"Ellen contacted me with some news. Chloe called this hotshot private investigator in Boston and damned if she didn't come up with something. Something really important." The email had a series of attachments. Harry clicked on the first one. It opened and the screen filled with grainy black-and-white footage shot at night. The camera had a slight wide-angle lens, enough to show about ten yards without too great a distortion. Everyone watched as a woman came up, punching in something below the bottom of the screen. It was footage from an ATM. No one spoke as four people walked up and withdrew money. White letters on the bottom right-hand side of the screen showed the time and date: JAN 4, 3:02 A.M. At 3:07 A.M. the screen was blank, then a figure appeared at the extreme right-hand side and streaked across the screen.

Harry's fingers danced over the keyboard as the four men watched. Harry slowed the film down on a slider, pressed a key and froze the frame with the figure dead center. It was Mike, running. His body was blurred but the camera had caught him as he turned his head and his features were clear.

"That was taken at 3:07:45 A.M., from an ATM on Griffin, about four blocks from Alameda. We can follow Mike's path as he runs down to the shore, ending up at the ferry at 3:48 A.M."

They watched a series of footage clips from security cameras along his route, fourteen attachments in all. Whoever Chloe contacted was *good*. She obviously had excellent facial recognition software and in a short span of time had canvassed almost all the security cameras in a broad sweep from Alameda to the ferry landing. That took smarts and serious crunching power.

The screen was showing the broad apron in front of the ferry where Mike was jogging in place. Steam from his breath wreathed his face but he was recognizable. He barely remembered the jog home, though he did remember waiting a while for the ferry, on a reduced schedule from midnight to 6 A.M.

The camera switched briefly to a view of the ocean, and the ferry slowly approaching the landing, then switched back to the passenger side, where four people were waiting with Mike, still hopping up and down.

They watched as five people boarded the ferry, including Mike. The time at the bottom of the footage read 4:10 A.M.

The final attachment was footage of Mike jogging down to their apartment complex on Coronado Shores, into the condo, exchanging a word with the night watchman.

Mike had said he'd come home at five, which their condo's security cams would have caught. It would have been to beat Mila Kosavich up at 4 A.M. and drive home by five. But Mike had jogged his way home and they had it on film.

"My understanding," Harry said to Kelly with a hard look, "is that the 911 call came in at 4:02 A.M. The ferry landing is 14.7 miles from Alameda. Mike couldn't possibly have been at the woman's apartment."

All eyes turned to Kelly. He stood mulling it over, then put his notebook carefully down on the table next to the computer.

He turned to Mike. "Case dismissed," he said quietly, then gave a half smile. "Glad I don't have to arrest you, Keillor."

"Ditto, man." Mike let out a huge breath, realizing what had just happened.

Chloe had set him free.

Sam and Harry clapped both Mike and Kelly on the back and the tension in the room disappeared.

Mike held out his hand to Kelly. Kelly was a good guy. He'd only been doing his duty. "Good luck with finding the bastard who put that woman in the hospital."

"Yeah." Kelly's clasp was warm and hard and brief. "We have word there was a boyfriend who liked pounding on her. We'll look at him. You stay out of trouble, you hear?"

Oh yeah. Mike had learned a really big lesson tonight. Even though he was terrified it was too late for Chloe.

Sam clapped him on the shoulder. "Let's get going. We still have to celebrate. Our women are waiting."

Our women. For Sam and Harry that was literally true. They had great wives and two lovely daughters waiting for them. In another world, the world where Mike hadn't fucked his way through a battalion of women, that other world where he hadn't met sweet, utterly enticing Chloe Mason after screwing a cokehead who couldn't get him to beat her up, so she called in someone else to finish the job, he'd go back to his woman, too.

In this other world, he and Chloe would have a clean slate, able to start this new fresh thing they had.

Whereas in *this* world, they'd hardly begun and she'd already learned the very worst about him.

He'd come on to her hard. He rarely came on to women like he had with Chloe. Maybe because he looked for women in low places, they came on to him.

But with Chloe, he'd been instantly drawn in, instantly attracted. And he'd—he'd courted her. Focused on her, happy just to be in the same room with her. Knowing something important was happening.

For just a second there, he thought he was living Sam and Harry's dream. They'd both been instantly smitten by their women and look how that had turned out. They were both insanely happy, both settled, both wildly in love with their wives and daughters.

And Mike—idiot that he was—thought he'd found what he hadn't been looking for. Found something real and true and lasting. Clean and bright. And he'd crushed it with his own hands the moment he'd found it.

He'd never know. Right now a part of him wanted Chloe close to him like he wanted air and water. And another part of him wanted to keep her at a distance. She'd had a rough life and she deserved better than him.

Because who was he kidding? If they got together, she'd find a woman he'd fucked around every corner. His past was like a tar pit. He would never be free, he could only taint her with it.

Harry was quiet as they rode down in the elevator. Sam didn't even notice. He was exhilarated, happy Mike was out of trouble, looking forward to picking up the celebrations where they'd left off.

And, knowing Sam, very happy to be getting back to Nicole and Merry.

As the elevator doors opened, Harry stuck out an arm, blocking

Mike. Harry was strong. Mike was stronger. He could wipe the floor with Harry. But Harry had something to say to him and he couldn't pound his brother. He loved him too much.

Harry spoke to Sam quietly. "Sam, Mike and I have something to discuss. Get the van started and we'll be there in five."

Harry's face was naturally grave and right now he looked as if his best friend had died and then his dog. Sam looked at him, at Mike, and nodded.

Harry waited until Sam was out of earshot, then turned to Mike, placing a big hand on Mike's shoulder.

"Congratulations. I'm glad this got cleared up." His face was absolutely expressionless. The words were good but his face was closed to Mike.

Wary, Mike answered. "Yeah, me, too. I have Chloe to thank for it. I never would have thought of canvassing the security cameras along my run." It was true. And he had no real memory of what route he'd taken. If Chloe's friend hadn't had the right software, he'd still be in PD headquarters, maybe in jail.

"Yes, you do. She's a good woman. She was the best little girl you could imagine. Loving and sweet and gentle." He fixed Mike with a hard glare. "Chloe's been through hell and back, Mike. I saw the way you were looking at her and I know what you're like with women. I'm sorry to say this but I have to. Go fuck someone else, somewhere else. I don't want you near my little sister. She deserves better than you. I want you to give me your word you won't touch her. Because if you do, I'll beat the crap out of you. Or try. You might even win, but she'd be even more disgusted with you than she already is."

Yeah. Mike would possibly win because he fought dirty, always. He'd win the battle and lose the war.

He didn't want to fight Harry. He understood exactly where Harry was coming from. If their roles were reversed, Mike would do the exact same thing. He'd want to protect his little sister from someone like Mike, who'd spent more than half his life fucking anything that would hold still long enough.

There wasn't anything Mike could do except take it. Because, fuck it, Harry was right.

He was bad news for Chloe. The worst.

Harry's hand dug into his shoulder. Harry had big strong hands, but Mike's shoulder muscles were like steel. Still, he welcomed the tiny bite of pain Harry was causing.

Harry's jaw muscles jumped. "I love you, Mike. You know that. But there's—there's just something broken in you, something off, and I don't want that touching Chloe." Harry shook him. "Do I make myself clear? Chloe is off limits to you. I can't ask you to stay away from her because we all see too much of one another, but I can ask you not to come on to her. You're bad news for women, Mike, and you're bad news for Chloe. Do her a favor and leave her alone."

Every muscle Mike had was clenched. Harry shook him harder. "Did you hear me? Talk, damn you."

"Yes." Mike said the one-syllable word as if coughing up a stone lodged in his throat and stopped. He couldn't say another word.

"Yes, what?"

Mike forced himself to relax a little, to allow some air into his lungs. Everything in him burned and hurt. "Yes, I won't touch Chloe."

Harry's hand bit deeper. "Do I have your word?"

Harry knew what he was asking. Mike might fuck around but he never broke his word.

Mike drew in a deep breath and it felt like knives were carving his chest open from the inside. "I promise. You have my word. I won't touch Chloe. Ever again."

Chapter 9

Six months later

On board the Svetlana
Twenty kilometers south of Petropavlovsk
Kamchatka Peninsula
Russian Federation

They came from all over the country, mainly from small towns. Two girls had been culled from an orphanage just outside the ring road of Moscow and one came from Ekaterinburg, but the rest came from small orphanages in small towns, cash-strapped, isolated. The kind of place where for a ridiculously small sum of cash, the recruiters could take their time, choose carefully, get the best.

It was important that the girls be utterly and completely alone in the world. There could be no vodka-soaked father, or poor aunt or jobless cousin out there somewhere who'd had to park the girl in the orphanage until times improved. The father might dry up, the aunt land on better times, the cousin find a job, and then they'd come back to the orphanage only to find the girl gone.

And start asking questions.

That wouldn't do. Everything had to run smoothly and seamlessly without any hanging threads.

These girls were completely alone. No one would come looking for them. Ever.

The whole world was in recession, but Russia, throughout her incarnations as a czardom, the Soviet Union and now the Russian Federation, had always been poor. The Motherland had always been a place where poor young girls fell through the cracks in the floor. Unwanted, unloved, alone.

Only now, through the magic of modern industrial organization and logistics, the girls had a use, became a commodity, could earn money.

So the recruiters made the rounds of the small, out-of-the-way orphanages, checking to make sure no stray relatives were around, and had their pick of the prettiest in each school.

It had been hard to tell what the girls really looked like. They all shared a look—emaciated, lank, greasy hair, dead eyes. But the recruiters had a good eye for bone structure and checked to see that the underlying health was good. A little food, soap and shampoo and tiny dollops of affection carefully doled out did wonders. The recruiters were good at their job and any mistakes . . . well, no one was going to miss any of the girls.

The girls now filing onto the ship, escorted by professional nurses, already looked infinitely better than they had only a few weeks ago, a testament to the eye of the recruiters who had seen the potential beneath the grime and misery. They'd been kept in a warehouse a few miles south of the city, fifty girls waiting for the last arrivals, waiting for this moment, for shipment.

Their time together in the warehouse had been the best time of their young lives.

The warehouse had been heated because even in June, the Kamchatka Peninsula was cold. They'd been fed and allowed to bathe.

They'd had access to a TV with DVDs—mainly cheap pirated versions of ancient U.S. films, but the girls had been so starved of entertainment they were riveted to the screen for hours—and books. Some girls hadn't been taught to read, some could read only laboriously. Some of the girls dove into the books and barely came up for air.

The warehouse had been abandoned decades ago, but workmen had come in the week before to install a generator, fix up crude lights hanging from the ceiling, set up portable toilets and an efficient space heating system.

The minor investment was worth it, because this was a trial run. If all worked according to plan, there would be regular shipments, using the warehouse as a staging area.

So the girls were rested and clean and well-fed when the buses came to pick them up in the warehouse way station for the first stage of a journey. If this transaction went well, as it surely must, the warehouse way station would be used many many more times.

This was the start of what everyone expected to be a lucrative supply line of fresh blonde meat.

There were eight million orphans in Russia alone, without even counting Belarus, Ukraine and all the other former Soviet republics.

When the first consignment was complete, a bus came to pick the girls up and drive them to the ship moored at a small pier that had been built the week before in a natural harbor ten miles away. No one noticed, or cared. It was a deserted land, a peninsula attached to the largest desert in the world, Siberia.

The business consortium running the logistical side of the operation had bought supplies in the city to the north, but Petropavlovsk was one of those cities where people minded their own business. The only people on the streets were the drunks and the desperate. Still, the heads of the conglomerate felt it was best to be discreet, so the transshipment point had been located outside the city.

It was also why boarding and landing were done by night. The satellites overhead did not have IR capability. That much their financiers, who had access to Russian secret services and who basically *owned* the Russian government, had told them. Spy satellites were intensely focused on latitudes much further south. This latitude covered the Scandinavian countries, Canada, Siberia. Not much terrorism going on there, which was all the *Amerikanski* cared about these days.

There was minimal risk that the eyes in the sky would watch, take note, investigate. Still, it was best to minimize that risk by loading at night, even though nobody really cared too much. After all, they weren't carrying fissionable material or drugs or arms.

Just girls.

The girls were obedient, biddable. They walked themselves aboard, they didn't even need herding like cattle. There were only two nurses on board to accompany the fifty girls. The rest were crew members who knew very well the punishment if they touched a hair on the girls' heads. Death would be infinitely preferable to what would happen to them.

The girls were guaranteed a safe passage. They were valuable commodities and were expected to be ferried across the ocean and landed in excellent condition.

There was a spreadsheet available to the top members of the organization, which was an excellent cost-benefit analysis. Allowing for wastage, and allowing for a work life of fifteen years—after which the average girl found a creative way to kill herself—each girl represented, in exchange for a negligible investment, an overall profit of thirty million dollars. Thirty-five to forty million if used hard, though then the length of useful life became quite short.

The girls filed obediently on board, four bunk beds to each cell. Space was tight but no one complained. There were clean sheets on the bed, they knew by now that they would have plenty of hot food. The nurses were dispassionate but not cruel. This was the best situation they'd ever known.

They would be ferried safely and comfortably to the other side of the ocean, to their final destination.

To market.

San Diego
Meteor Club

"More champagne, sir?" A beautiful young woman held a tray of crystal flutes in front of him. Franklin Sands accepted one, hefting the flute, admiring the way it gleamed like a beacon in the light. It sparkled, just like his life.

He loved this, loved everything about it. The large rooms full of designer furniture, the superb catering, the luxurious armchairs, the smell of expensive leather, the prosperity the rich men in the room exuded, the young beauties ready and willing to fulfill their every desire.

The young woman bending down to offer him champagne was almost beyond beautiful—a stunning brunette in a Valentino gown that showed off just enough of her glorious breasts. No one needed to sneak a peek. Every man in the room knew he could see them naked anytime he wanted. For the right price.

The tray was solid silver and polished once a week, the flutes were Baccarat crystal and the champagne itself was an '88 Veuve Clicquot. His supplier had purchased eight cases the week before.

He was sitting on an extremely comfortable Poltrona Frau sofa with a Philippe Starck coffee table in front of him. The room was enormous but broken up into elegant, intimate spaces by the furniture, all by top designers. Soft music played in the background. Sands chose his tracks depending on the age of the customers. The average age tonight was around sixty so the music was a mix of classical music and unobtrusive covers of hits from the seventies, when these men had been in their vital prime.

Now many of them needed stimuli Sands was only too happy to provide, for a fee.

"Sir?" The beautiful young woman who went by the *nom de lit* of Skye turned to his brand-new partner, Anatoly Nikitin. Nikitin waved her away irritably. Few men turned down anything Skye had to offer, but the Russian did.

She was one of his better investments, beautiful, willing and talented at her job. His accountant told him she grossed him a million and a half dollars per annum. Her deflowering alone had brought him a hundred thousand dollars. Tax-free of course.

How could the Russian be so immune to her charms? His new partner refused more or less everything in the Meteor Club, which had been designed to offer a man every possible pleasure, save drugs. No drugs in the Meteor, except for the legal ones. He had every variety of prescription upper and downer and a whole range of Viagra-like pills. All legal. Not to mention the finest wines and an infinite selection of choice spirits.

You could indulge every pleasure your mind could conceive of legally here at the Meteor, and no police officer could touch you.

There were plenty of street rats plying illegal drugs. It was a dangerous, violent, filthy business that the state punished severely, and quite rightly so. Only fools entered it, and they died young and badly.

The business of women, the business of elegant pleasures—ah, that was another thing entirely. Immensely lucrative, nonviolent. Or at least it was at the high end of the business where he had situated himself.

Everything in the Meteor Club was guaranteed to stimulate a man's pleasure centers. Thanks to an infusion of Russian capital from the investors Nikitin represented, the Meteor Club had undergone a radical restructuring and upgrading. Now it was a perfect place to relax, have an exquisite meal prepared by one of

France's best chefs accompanied by wine from the club's superb cellar. There was even a smokers' room with humidors filled with the finest Cuban cigars.

In the back were rooms where the men could find their pleasure with the finest blossoms Sands could pluck, up until now mainly from Mexico. But soon there would be a new influx of beauties from Russia. To cater to all tastes. Dark and light.

Soon they would cater to those who liked their pleasures . . . fresher. This would be a brand-new business. If you liked them young and were willing to pay the price, why the Meteor Club would guarantee excellence and discretion.

This, in contrast to the main business, was of course illegal. And so of course a hefty premium would be charged.

The Russians had started setting up a new system, a more dangerous, yet much more lucrative system. It required more careful organization, of course, which cost money. But the rich men who wanted certain things—they were willing to pay.

In the back were soundproofed rooms for men who liked their pleasures darker. For a suitable fee, Sands and his investors in the new Meteor Club would provide anything, anything at all.

Membership at the Meteor Club, for standard fare, started at $250,000 a year. Extras cost more. The new, younger line would cost considerably more.

Even in an economic recession, it was a seller's market. No one offered the kind of goods the Meteor Club did, in such an elegant setting, disease-free, discretion guaranteed.

His new partner seemed immune to the many delights of the club, though. It seemed odd to Sands, to turn pleasure down. Sands understood indulgence down to the bone. He had no understanding of abstinence at all.

He and Nikitin had been working together for almost a year ever since Nikitin, who Sands suspected had a military background, had contacted him. Nikitin represented certain Russian interests looking to invest in America and they had money to burn. Money on a scale Sands had never seen before. Indeed, the influx of capital had taken the Meteor Club to an entirely different level, to the point where it was in all likelihood the finest men's club in the country, offering absolutely anything a man could want as long as he could pay for it.

Though they'd often gone over business plans until well into the night, Sands had never seen Nikitin partake of the club's wares. He never ate or drank here and he never took a woman to the back rooms, though Sands had invited him to do so often. If for nothing else so he could gauge the quality of the merchandise for himself.

Nikitin never gave any indication of playing for the other team, either. No, when he arrived, he just sat, a still figure in a corner where the light never reached, and simply observed. Within a week, he had a complete handle on the business and had estimated the club's yearly earnings to within ten thousand dollars. And offered to increase those earnings tenfold.

He had a plan, too. With huge infusions of cash and a new supply chain. Fresher, cheaper goods. A river of it.

Irresistible.

Sands leaned forward and picked up a toast point with true Beluga caviar spread on it, washing it down with champagne. He pushed the plate over to Nikitin, who ignored it. Sands suppressed a sigh. Really, this would be much more pleasant if Nikitin were a friendlier person.

There was a woman's cry, the sound of a slap, a man's voice raised.

Trouble.

Beside him, he felt Nikitin stiffen.

Sands gestured to one of the bodyguards who unobtrusively mingled among the club members. They weren't obvious muscle. They weren't beefy and huge with enormous lumps under their arms. He chose his security carefully, both for their martial arts skills and their discretion. And, well, decorative value. They were attractive and graceful. He gave them an enormous dress allowance.

You only discovered they were security when there was trouble. Like now.

Consuelo. Again.

Really, Sands thought. Maybe she was more trouble than she was worth. A spectacularly beautiful woman, yes, even more beautiful than Skye, but lately quite . . . recalcitrant. And after all that he'd done for her. She'd been born Rosa Pérez and she was one of Sands' favorite personal discoveries. He'd groomed her from the age of ten when he'd found her cowering in a corner on the backstreets of Tijuana. She'd been almost feral, barely human. He'd taught her to read and write, to dress, to speak perfect English— she'd almost forgotten her Spanish—to move with grace and to please men in every way.

It had taken all his skill to see beneath the grime and filth. He'd effected a remarkable transformation. She'd been a superb investment, but maybe her origins were starting to show through.

The club never punished in ways that showed. But perhaps being locked up, given to the male staff to use at will . . . maybe that would bring her around.

His men whisked Consuelo away and the member who'd been insulted by Consuelo was offered a bottle of Cristal and a free pass for a week.

Keep your customers happy.

This was *not* the moment for displays of insubordination. The deal with Nikitin and his backers was just beginning, not yet fully established. It was important that the Russians have the sense of a well-oiled machine, bright and smooth and profitable, ready to be taken to the next level.

Not to mention the fact that in his deepest heart, Sands was just a tiny bit afraid of his new partners. All that money, yet so far away, and the money's emissary was frightening, beyond the temptations and weaknesses of the men in Sands' world. As if he were dealing with an alien species he didn't fully understand.

Nikitin turned his head, and for a moment Sands felt like he was looking into the eyes of an alien species. Cold, brilliant blue marbles, unearthly and inhuman.

"Mr. Sands," Nikitin said, the Russian accent strong in his deep low voice, "I have watched this woman react badly three times now. You have a problem. Either you take care of it or I will."

The room became chill, the champagne curdled sourly in Sands' stomach. There was only one possible answer. "Yes, yes. Don't worry. I'll take care of it."

The cold blue marbles held his gaze for a long moment, then Nikitin looked away and Sands gasped in a breath.

And admitted for the first time how very much Nikitin terrified him.

Anatoly Nikitin watched the American turn pale at his gaze. He turned his back. A gesture of contempt, not that the American would understand it. He found Americans almost incapable of understanding the nuances of threat.

Anatoly himself was a master. He'd grown up the son of a colonel in the KGB and he himself had spent ten years in its successor, the FSB. He knew the music of threat and violence inside out. Knew its tones and harmonies, understood them in his soul.

But then, he'd grown up in harsh surroundings. He understood full well the way the world worked. You were either strong or weak. Master or serf. Like here, the place the American pretended was a very posh and expensive "club," but was a brothel. The American would shy away from the term. He liked to think that the men who came here belonged to some kind of fraternity of the powerful and tasteful, having found a superior way to slake their appetites.

The truth was their money bought them high-grade sex. Instead of going out into the street, where it was public and dirty, they came here, where it was private and clean. For those who wanted complete privacy, there was a separate entrance and a suite. They could get a fabulous meal and exactly the kind of sex they wanted for $10,000. Cheap at the price.

The advantages of being an oligarch. America seemed to be full of oligarchs, which was why Nikitin was here.

It was a good business and promised to become better when they could start bringing younger merchandise online, as per numerous requests.

Nikitin had studied the photographs of the goods now crossing the Pacific and was satisfied that they would suit any man's tastes, which ran to young girls.

Nikitin frowned at the foreign sound of a commotion in this smoothest of places.

The beautiful one, Consuelo, raised her voice again, accusing her client of pinching her. The girls here were trained not to respond to pain.

However valuable a commodity she was, Consuelo was becoming a liability. It was exactly as if she had a disease. It needed to be contained before it spread to the other girls. There was no place for insubordination here, where men paid a premium price for instant and abject obedience. They got quite enough insubordination in the outside world.

The American was talking to one of his "security guards."

Nikitin nearly snorted. The only thing those guards knew how to do was look good in a tuxedo. No, his own men knew how to deal with problems. Directly and forcefully.

He opened his cell phone and dialed a number. Nikitin had to keep his men in a separate area because the American thought they spoiled the tone of the club. But when trouble came, his men knew what to do. Nikitin spoke with the head of his men, Ivan.

Tough and reliable. Ivan had fought in Chechnya. He knew how the world worked.

The American was still talking to his "security."

Ivan appeared with no fanfare. He was dressed in black combat boots, black jeans, black T-shirt and jacket covering his shoulder rig with the GSh-18.

"Consuelo, the girl in the red dress. Find out why she's being difficult and take care of it."

Ivan nodded. Unlike the American's security guards, his own men didn't sample the wares, just like he didn't. They operated under military discipline until the entire business machine was set up and running smoothly. Then they could relax. Nikitin would give his men ten of the girls to do with as they pleased when this was over. The girls would be useless afterwards, but his men knew what to do with bodies.

Ivan liked pain, and if this Consuelo woman was still around and not at the bottom of San Diego harbor, he'd throw her, too, to Ivan and his men for exclusive use as a bonus. No matter what she earned the club, sacrifices had to be made for the sake of discipline. "I heard she's been talking to some outsider," Ivan said in a low voice in Russian. "Some woman at a center. I think this outsider is stirring up trouble."

Nikitin nodded. His masters were coming to America to oversee the first shipment and to get a firsthand look at their investment. Everything had to be perfect for the *vory*. Anything else was unthinkable. "We don't need this, not now. Find out what's going on and put a stop to it. Teach the woman a lesson."

Ivan inclined his head and turned away. Nikitin could count on him. He and his men were promised a percentage of the increased business if everything went smoothly, on top of generous salaries.

"Oh, and Ivan—"

Ivan obediently turned around, big and tough and hard. Nikitin had every confidence he'd take care of this.

"Make sure this woman stays away. Don't kill because we don't want to deal with the authorities here, but short of that, do what it takes."

Ivan nodded and walked off.

Nikitin looked over at where Consuelo was listening to Sands, head down, a rebellious expression on her face.

She truly was a beautiful woman, Nikitin thought dispassionately. Such a waste.

Duschka, Nikitin thought, *your friend will learn a harsh lesson, then it will be your turn.*

Chapter 10

Hopewell Shelter for Women and Children
San Diego
July 5

This is ridiculous, Chloe thought. Just ask him. *What do you want from me, Mike?*

How hard could it be?

She finished folding the stack of donated clothes. Many of the women who came to the shelter arrived with only the clothes on their backs. They needed everything. Clothes, food, money. Safety, above all.

Chloe remembered that. Remembered clearly not feeling safe. She'd spent her entire life with the low drumbeat of danger in her head, not knowing where it came from.

Chloe's life now was perfect. She was totally ensconced in the warm embrace of a loving extended family. Harry was the finest brother a woman could possibly have. And Ellen and Nicole were more like sisters than sisters-in-law. Best of all, she got to have Gracie and Merry in her life. The idea that she could watch those two beautiful little girls grow up, be part of their daily lives, was an enormous joy.

San Diego was fabulous, beautiful and sunny. She'd bought an apartment in Harry's condo and had access to an immense white beach, right outside her door. To all intents and purposes, she lived in a resort. Sam was even teaching her how to swim. Her swim instructor was a former Navy SEAL. How cool was that?

She volunteered at the shelter three days a week. The work was so important and satisfying she was seriously thinking of going back to school in the fall and getting a degree in psychology and doing this full-time. Everything was perfect except for one thing.

Mike.

That first day felt like a lifetime ago and in a way it was. Her life had changed so much. That magical day she'd thought that maybe she'd found . . . well, a new love sounded foolish. It was the first day they'd ever met, after all. But she thought that maybe she'd found someone who could penetrate her wall of loneliness.

Mike had been blatant in his desire. And that kiss at the Del. . . . And the *orgasm!*

How stupid of her to confess that it had been her first orgasm. Women don't let men have information like that. It made them vulnerable, and if there was one thing Chloe was an expert on, it was vulnerability.

The memory of that episode at the Del still made her bloom with heat six months after the fact. How pathetic was that? How sad that she still blushed when she thought of a kiss six months ago from a man who hadn't touched her since. At the very most he would extend a hand that hovered when he thought she might fall.

Well, she wasn't falling these days. Mike had taken her in hand, so to speak—without ever touching her—and subjected her to his own bodybuilding program, pushing her and pushing her and pushing her to become strong. It appeared that Mike felt there wasn't a problem on earth that couldn't be solved by lifting weights.

And, well, he was right.

Chloe had had every form of physical rehab possible in her life, but it only served to put her on her feet, more or less.

Mike insisted on a strict regimen of weightlifting. Morning, noon and night. His theory was that she needed to strengthen the muscles wrapped around the bones and he made her train like mad.

Chloe had seen all those films where a nasty Marine shouted in the faces of the recruits, scaring them to death. Mike took the opposite tack—he cajoled her. Daily. Relentlessly. Without ever touching her.

And it worked! When she flexed her arm to make a muscle, *she made a muscle.* You could crack walnuts off her quadriceps.

She walked easily and well. A month ago she actually *ran!* To her knowledge, Chloe had never run in her life. She would have been too terrified. Once afternoon Gracie had wandered off on the beach and she found herself running after her. When she realized what she was doing, she laughed. And Mike laughed with her, sharing in her delight.

And that was the thing. Because though Mike's rejection of her as a woman was complete and total, insulting in its thoroughness, every time she turned around, it seemed, there he was. He moved in all her new furniture, set up all her shelves, fixed everything in sight. He drove her to the shelter, picked her up after work, took out her garbage, carried in her groceries.

Her little family ate together at most meals and Mike was always right next to her, passing her things, cajoling her to eat more.

And in all that, he never touched her, not once.

He was driving her insane.

Nicole and Ellen were no help. They didn't understand it, either. Mike had stopped, cold turkey, what Ellen delicately called his "fooling around" and Nicole crudely called his "fucking on an industrial level."

Both of them thought he was in love with her, but by the same token were totally unable to process the fact that he never touched her. Maybe because their own husbands couldn't keep their hands off them. For the Mike they knew, formerly known as the "man-slut," this behavior was incomprehensible.

He now led the life of a monk.

He rarely left her side.

He never touched her.

It was driving her *crazy*.

How could she get Mike out of her mind, how could she get over him, how could she move on, when he was always *around*?

And then of course there was the delicate issue of maybe dating someone else, though she found it impossible to drum up interest in the bank manager, the building superintendent, the orthopedic surgeon and the journalist for the *Union-Tribune*—all of whom had asked her out at least once.

It would be nice to want to go out with someone. But how could that happen when the sexiest, strongest, most vital man in the world was always in her face? Right next to her?

And—in the case of the journalist—glowering so menacingly the man had backed away, palms up.

Though Chloe wasn't confrontational by nature, maybe the best thing to do would be to just say it. Tell him to stay away from her because the truth was, he was breaking her heart. Having him so close, every day, there every time she turned around, but so far away emotionally . . . well, it was almost unbearable.

He'd snared her heart that first day and he wasn't letting it go.

The door that opened to an inner courtyard opened and she whirled, grateful for a distraction from her thoughts of Mike, stuck in her head like a burr. Maybe it was the director of the shelter, Marion. Kind, gray-haired, no-nonsense. Or maybe Consuelo, her favorite of the women who showed up for informal group therapy. She was stunningly beautiful and had a kind heart. And was being ground into dust by her job as a high-class prostitute.

But it was neither. Two big men pushed their way into the room. Very big men.

Chloe's heart rate picked up immediately, started beating wildly, a primordial response she was trying to learn to control. Not every big man was a source of danger. Look at Sam and Harry and Mike. She had to stop this instant panic every time a larger-than-normal man stepped across her path.

She'd seen a mug shot of Rodney Lewis, the man who'd killed her mother and had sent her to the hospital for ten years. He'd weighed more than 300 pounds and he was the origin of her panic. Knowing what caused it didn't make it abate, however.

Chloe schooled her face to blandness, wiped her suddenly wet palms down her linen shift. She had to stop reacting to big men like this.

The closer the two men came, though, the more her Alarm-o-meter dinged red. They carried themselves well, like athletes. Both blond, not badly dressed, not well-dressed. What terrified her were the eyes. Light blue and as remote as the eyes of dolls. Their body language was neutral, the only menace their utter and complete fitness. She watched them as they crossed the room to her.

Chloe planted her feet firmly and straightened. *Grow a backbone, Chloe.* She couldn't be a slave to her past all her life.

The two men weren't supposed to be here and she'd tell them that, after which they'd leave. A normal human transaction, the kind she'd been having for only the past six months, since reuniting with Harry. This needed to become permanent—this ability to speak to large men who weren't Harry or Mike or Sam without being terrified.

"Miss Chloe Mason?" the taller of the two asked. He had a guttural voice and foreign accent. Only a foreigner would call a twenty-eight-year-old woman "miss."

Chloe's heart was thudding hard against her rib cage. Her body was sending her signals she tried to ignore.

"Yes? May I help you? Though I have to tell you that men aren't allowed here in the shelter. The door on the wall to my left will take you directly out into the parking lot."

The only men allowed into the shelter were Mike and Harry and Sam, since RBK was such a big supporter. Not to mention the fact that they helped women who were in immediate danger disappear.

"We'll leave soon," the other man said. He was slightly shorter, stockier, with the same dead light blue eyes. He, too, had an accent. "Just as soon as we clear a few things up. We have something to say to you and you better listen."

They moved closer, right into her space. Chloe backed up and they followed. Classic aggressive behavior.

It was then that Chloe understood her body had been right all along. She was in trouble.

This was the administrative wing of the building and it was after hours. No one was around. If they knew the setup here at the shelter, they were banking on the fact that she was isolated.

"We need for you to listen to us," Tall Guy said. His face was blank and terrifying in its lack of emotion. Chloe could smell them—a nauseating mix of unwashed male and heavy cologne. They looked wrong, they acted wrong, they smelled wrong.

Chloe sidestepped and Tall Guy grabbed her upper arm in a strong, unbreakable grip, pulling her toward him.

She was instantly paralyzed, seized by a fear so great she couldn't breathe. Her oldest nightmare now made flesh.

There was a metallic click and suddenly a sharp blade was brandished under her nose, the wickedly sharp point right under her left eye. It was long, a lusterless black, razor-sharp and terrifying.

"We need for you to pay attention to what we're going to say. Are you paying attention?"

Terror gripped her lungs. She couldn't speak, she couldn't breathe. Tall Guy shook her, put his face right next to hers, so close she could see the broken blood vessels in his eyes, so close she could see glints of gold where his shaver had missed sections of beard. Above all, so close she could smell the terrifying cold, steely scent of violence.

His voice lowered, became even more frightening. "I said—are you paying attention?" His shake hurt, his grip around her arm cutting off circulation.

She couldn't speak. Her throat was paralyzed. She nodded.

The other man had circled around to her other side. His right hand snaked out and, shockingly, cupped her breast. "Pretty," he said, pinching her hard. He looked at his partner, a quick reptilian glance. "Maybe she needs help in staying awake while you talk to her, eh?"

The tall man's painful grip tightened even more as he lifted her up. She stood on tiptoe to ease the pain. She'd broken that arm twice. The shorter man's big hand left her breast, but before she could even breathe a sigh of relief, with his forearm he cleared the desktop of the clothes she'd been folding and the tall man threw her down onto the desktop, driving all the air out of her lungs.

They spoke to each other in a language she didn't understand, short sharp words. Finally, the taller man gave a gesture of irritation—*Okay, have it your way*—and stood to one side.

The shorter man unbuckled his belt and opened his pants, hands working fast. A huge, dark red erect penis jutted out from the dark blond hair of his groin.

Panic sang in Chloe's head as she gasped for breath, legs uselessly kicking at him.

"Pretty," he repeated with a grin, sliding big hands up under her dress, stepping between her legs. Oh God, this was happening so fast! Every move she made was countered by one man or the other. They were so strong, there was nothing she could do. She tried to bring her knee up to kick the man standing between her legs and he laughed, exchanging a narrow-eyed glance of amusement at his partner.

She couldn't breathe yet. Mewling sounds came out of her throat, the strangled sounds of panic and pain.

They were enjoying this. Loving it. Loving her attempts to defend herself, knowing she could never, ever win.

A flush of rage flashed through her, like a nuclear blast, clearing her lungs. She drew in a full breath that broke the bonds of her panic and screamed as loud as she could, the sound echoing in the room.

She'd startled them. The shorter man between her legs loosened his grip on her thighs and she landed a foot straight in his crotch, reveling in the feel of his testicles crunching beneath her shoe. He doubled over in pain and she screamed again, loud and constant.

She wasn't submitting without a fight.

The tall man shouted something, raised his fist, then turned his head with a frown.

Wood shattered and something large, moving fast, tackled the man assaulting her. They disappeared from view, dropping to the floor with a heavy shudder.

Terrible animal sounds came from the floor as the two men grappled, thudding against the desk, shaking her. Chloe scrambled upright, she had to move, she had to get to—

Suddenly a massive blow struck her and she flew across the room, bouncing off a pillar and landing painfully on the floor. A man, face bloodied, stood with a terrible roar and jumped the taller man. She had an electric moment of awareness—*Mike!*—and lost consciousness.

Fuck this, Mike thought, hand hovering over the wood-panel door at the shelter where Chloe volunteered.

Men really weren't supposed to be here. It was a law of the shelter and he understood it, completely. Everyone in this building, including Chloe, especially Chloe, had suffered at the hands of a violent man. For the women in this building, men were the enemy. A different race from them, sworn to destroy them.

Many of the women would never recover their self-confidence after what had been done to them. Would never breathe easy in the same room with a man. Would never have a relationship with a man again.

Chloe had been young enough that she could function in the world, though she still had problems.

He shouldn't be here, he should be out in the parking lot, waiting for her outside the building, as he always did. He knew that.

What the fuck was he doing here, then? Why come here to talk to Chloe when he'd be driving her home, or would be seeing her at Harry's for supper tonight? Or tomorrow morning in the building's gym where he'd run her through her weights cycle? Or at lunch tomorrow when she'd come in to consult with Marisa about one of the Lost Ones whose disappearance RBK was engineering?

He was here because he couldn't stand it anymore. Not for one fucking second more. The situation was driving him batshit crazy, and he was almost unable to function.

He couldn't eat. Just couldn't do it. Food tasted like wool in his mouth.

He was forgetting things on the job, which was unheard of. Mike was intensely detail-oriented. He didn't forget things, just didn't happen. Until now, because the situation with Chloe was eating up his hard disk.

This morning he had a contract with a bank to go over and yet he'd spent two hours staring at a picture of Chloe, taken at a family barbecue a couple of weeks ago. He hadn't even noticed the time passing. He just stared at the fucking picture and there had been wetness in his eyes. Not tears, Mike didn't do tears, but there'd been definite wetness. That's when he knew he had to see her.

Right now.

He needed to see Chloe *right fucking now.*

He'd butted his head against the iron wall of his word to Harry and it was breaking him. It was either Harry or his heart, and after holding out for six fucking months, his heart won out. He'd spent the past freaking six months in a hell of penance and enough was enough.

The first thing was to ask Chloe out for that date they were sup-posed to have had at the Del before his shit hit the fan. They were going out on a date like normal people and Harry could go jump in the fucking lake. Or the Pacific, which was right outside his door.

And then maybe Mike could start eating and sleeping like normal people did. Maybe this raw buzzing in his head would stop. Maybe this burning pain in his chest would go away.

First Chloe, then he'd bite the bullet and talk to Harry. He'd . . . what? Ask Harry permission to date his sister? Not just permission to be around her and carry her groceries in, and be her personal trainer, but be with her, date her. Because surely six long nookie-less months were enough to earn him points with Harry?

He'd tell Chloe everything, how he felt about her, how he couldn't even conceive of being with anyone but her, even though that still astounded him.

If you'd asked him six months ago if he could go six months without sex, he'd have laughed in your face. Mike Keillor didn't do abstinence. Mike Keillor needed no one, let alone a woman.

And here he might as well have been living in the seminary for all the sex he'd had these last six months. Even without the sex, he'd walk barefoot across hot coals to watch Chloe walk, talk, hell, even breathe.

Other women? He couldn't do it. Couldn't go to other women. He'd tried a couple of times and it just . . . didn't work. In the sense his dick simply wouldn't respond, like some contrary member of the board vetoing some proposal. When he tried, when some woman in a bar came on to him, he'd felt a form of repulsion, his cock a piece of dead meat between his legs. Once he'd actually felt his dick shrink in disgust.

If it wasn't for the fact that he had to hide his hard-on or will it back down whenever Chloe was near and that he woke up hard as a rock after dreaming of her, he'd have thought he'd suddenly turned impotent. A eunuch. Game over.

It was pathetic. He'd rather spend the evening with Chloe helping babysit Gracie and Merry, watching the three thousandth rerun of *The Little Mermaid*, than go out and finally get laid.

More than pathetic. Lame.

And not only that. Every fucking time he saw her, his heart did this . . . thing in his chest. Like a heart attack, only not.

Every morning he'd tell himself sternly, enough is enough. He was driving himself crazy honoring his promise to Harry. Even though Harry was one hundred percent right. There *was* something wrong with him, inside. He could recognize that now.

Mike functioned just fine in other areas of his life. He'd been a great Marine, made Force Recon, had headed up the local SWAT team, was a good businessman. In those areas he was okay, more than okay. But in everything else he was damaged goods.

Maybe success as a soldier, cop and businessman was all he'd be allowed in life, because sure as hell he wasn't good at human relations. Particularly relations with women. It was only now, when his goddamned feelings for Chloe threatened to slosh over and drown him, that he realized he'd never had any relationship at all with any of the women he'd fucked. Never. How terrible was that?

He'd perfected the art of the quick in-and-out fuck. In after sundown, out before dawn. One woman used to call him "the Bat."

He found himself incapable of staying away from Chloe. And even though he'd always had the Irishman's silver tongue with other women, he turned tongue-tied around her. Awkward. Jesus.

Chloe was grace itself. Calm and serene and fucking golden.

Harry was wrong to make him promise not to touch her, but he was right, too. Mike was not what she needed.

That was why he'd dedicated himself to doing what he did best with her.

Mike was good with gear. He didn't know how to open up to her, his brain seized up when he tried to talk to her about anything but externals, but goddammit he knew how to assemble her shelves and keep her car in running order and make sure she knew how to use the weightlifting equipment.

He could have gone on forever like this, shadowing Chloe like some stalker, happy just to be near her, except lately he'd been . . . what? Restless. Erratic. Jittery. Emotions all over the goddamned place. Unable to concentrate on work. Unable to eat. Unable to sleep.

He needed to talk to her. He started to knock, then stopped, his fist an inch from the door.

So . . . suppose he dumped all of this on Chloe. And then— Jesus!—just suppose she didn't feel about him the way he felt about her? What then? Chloe was gentle with everyone. Everyone loved her. Not as much as he did, that would be impossible, but still. But suppose she liked him but didn't want to go any further than that with him, ever?

Suppose he had to live with these . . . things slicing him open inside every minute, every day for the rest of his life?

What then?

Mike wasn't a coward, not in any way. He'd been in battle and been decorated for it. He'd taken point in a big SWAT takedown of a warehouse full of meth addicts armed to the teeth. He'd been born strong and made sure he stayed strong and he'd back down from no man.

But the thought of losing Chloe . . . it brought him to his knees.

So here he was, the Cool Dude with the Guns, standing outside a door with his hand raised like a dork, afraid to knock.

What the fuck?

He heard Chloe's voice behind the door, soft and gentle, and smiled. And then he heard the rumble of another voice. Low, deep, unmistakably male, and he froze.

Oh shit.

That hadn't occurred to him. Not really. Not seriously. That Chloe might be seeing someone else. Not possible. He'd made that journalist dude back away fast, and because he'd kept a close watch, no other guy was sniffing around her. He'd have taken a bet on it.

He was around her almost 24/7, after all. When the fuck was she supposed to meet other men?

But that deep voice was a man and he must be a really good friend if she allowed him into the shelter against all the rules.

Fuck. Mike dropped the hand about to knock and gently rested his forehead against the door, listening to the rumble of male . . . voices? Two of them?

She had two boyfriends?

And then he heard something else, something that stopped his heart. Something that galvanized him as nothing else could.

Chloe, screaming.

Pure instinct took over.

He smashed through the door, had a glimpse of Chloe struggling on the desktop, one fucker between her legs, cock out, the other standing by. He didn't even feel his feet as he rushed at them and brought the man assaulting Chloe down with a flying tackle.

The guy was big and strong but Mike was stronger and he had a berserker's rage inside him. He didn't even feel the blows as the man punched him over and over in the side. They grappled, wrestled, rolled around the room, shattering tables and chairs, grunting in a no-holds-barred struggle. There were rules to combat, but not now. Mike instantly realized it was a fight to the death.

The man had some moves in him, had been trained. Later, with hindsight, Mike would pin his style down to SAMBO, the martial arts specialty of Russian Special Forces. SAMBO was essentially ground fighting.

The man had him in a leg lock on the ground, almost immobilized. While Mike was on the ground with this bozo, he could see Chloe pulling her dress down, turning to fight the other man in the room, a tall strong son of a bitch. He backhanded her, hard. She flew across the room, bouncing against the wall, landing on the floor like a broken doll, deadly pale and still.

The idea that she might be grievously injured or—God!—dead gave Mike superhuman powers. He had to get to Chloe and the man holding him was keeping him from her. Mike had enormous strength in his arms, but to get to Chloe, he'd punch his way through steel if he had to. This had to finish, fast.

He flexed his arm and drove the point of his elbow into the man's windpipe with all the power of his upper body and heard bone crunch.

Instantly he was free. The smell of feces filled the room as the man's bowels loosened in death.

Mike didn't even look back as he scrambled to his feet and launched himself at the other man who was bending to pick Chloe up, hoping to get her away while Mike and the other guy were fighting.

Over my dead body, fucker, he thought savagely.

The guy didn't stand a chance. He saw Mike coming at him and dropped Chloe to free his hands but it was too late. Mike punched him in the stomach and then a straight punch to the center of the face, crushing teeth and cartilage. The man dropped like a felled bull, moaning, bubbles of air coming out of the mashed red wreck of his face.

Mike didn't even look at him. He just kicked the fuckhead out of his way as he dropped to his knees and gathered Chloe up, so terrified he couldn't feel his hands as he touched her.

"Chloe," he said, his voice raw. "Chloe, honey. Talk to me." She was soft in his arms. Still and boneless.

He pulled her to him, lifting her to his chest, and rocked. There was a keening sound in the air and it took him a second or two to realize it was him, that awful sound coming from his throat.

His head snapped up at a sound across the room. More assailants? If there were, good. He ached to punch, to maim, to kill.

Instead, there was a bunch of sad-eyed women at the door, one holding her hand in front of her mouth. The one who'd let the sob escape, which was the sound he'd heard. He must have looked crazy, because they all took a step back when his head lifted.

"Chloe," the woman who'd sobbed whispered. "Is she—is she dead?"

There wasn't much hope in the woman's voice. There hadn't been much hope in their lives, either. They all loved Chloe, but took it as a given that she could be taken away from them by violence.

No. Mike rejected even the thought of it with every cell in his body. He hunched over her even more, pulling her into him, as if he could transfuse energy from his body to hers.

"Call 911, medical emergency," he said, his words barely comprehensible as he shouted around the boulder in his chest. "And call the cops."

They stood there, staring at him, a phalanx of white faces.

"Now!" he shouted, and they scattered like birds at the sound of a shot.

A pressure on his arm, a shifting of the body he was holding so tightly. "Mike," Chloe murmured.

She was alive! Oh God!

Mike wiped at his eyes, which for some reason were wet.

"Chloe, honey. You've been hurt. Don't move. Medics are on the way."

Even as he said *Don't move* she did, shifting slightly so she could sit up. She looked down at herself, then up at him, placing a small hand on the side of his face.

"Don't look like that, Mike," she said softly. "I just passed out. But I'm okay." She frowned, touching her left forearm, discolored and slightly swollen. "I hope that's not broken, just sprained. It's been broken twice already." She touched her head, a slight frown between ash eyebrows. "What—what happened? Two men—" She stiffened in his arms, alarm in her eyes. "Two men, Mike! They came in and—"

A shift of her gaze and she saw them. One unmistakably dead, the other slumped against the wall, face a red mess, wheezing to get breath, blood burbling around his smashed nose and mouth.

"Don't worry about them, honey. They're never going to hurt you again." Mike's head fell to her shoulder. "Oh God, Chloe. I thought you were—I thought you were . . ." He couldn't even say the word. Couldn't form the thought. Could only remember the cold emptiness when he thought she'd gone from this world, leaving him behind.

Her skin was the color of ice, pupils dilated, entire body shivering from the aftermath of shock. He held her close and kissed her forehead gently, a mere brush of his lips because she seemed like glass, ready to shatter at any moment.

"No." Her voice was a whisper as she reached up a shaking hand to wipe wetness from under his eyes. "I'm still here. Thanks to you." A hard shudder ran through her. "What did they want? Do you know? Besides, um, raping me?"

Jesus. It hadn't even occurred to him to try to keep them alive to get intel. One of the fuckers was still alive only because he was distracted by Chloe. Because what if this wasn't a random act of violence? What if it was directed specifically at Chloe? What if she was *still* in danger?

He couldn't stand the thought, literally couldn't stand it. He couldn't go anywhere with it, was incapable of processing it. He shook with terror.

This wasn't like him.

He kept his cool during combat, always had. He was a fucking *sniper*, one of the very best. Snipers don't do terror. His heart rate had been tested at a cool, calm sixty beats per minute even under live-fire training. He knew how to use violence precisely, like a surgeon wields a scalpel. He knew how to measure his violence out into precise amounts, applied at specific times. He knew how to hold his fire, how to wait.

And yet he'd smashed into the room with no thought of strategy or tactics, none at all, just a wild bloodlust in his head drowning out all thought. And maybe his lack of control had endangered Chloe.

Still holding Chloe with one arm, Mike reached out to the guy slumped against the wall and bunched his shirt in his fist, lifting him up and away from the wall. "Hey, fuckhead. What are you doing here? What's your mission?"

Because even through the bloodlust, the wild singing desire to hurt and kill, he recognized one thing. He was dealing with trained men. Soldiers. Their moves, their demeanor. These weren't punks off the street who'd maybe seen a beautiful woman and followed her inside. No, they'd kept their cool even when he hadn't. The combat moves had been expert.

In a normal situation, it wasn't likely Mike could have prevailed over two highly trained men, but in this case, to defend Chloe, he'd have taken on a hundred men and won. He'd have taken on an entire fucking army.

But the inescapable fact was—these guys were pros. They'd been on some kind of a mission.

Mike shook the man, hard. His head lolled. Mike backhanded him, the sound of the slap loud and shocking in the room. "Hey!"

he shouted, to get through to the semi-unconscious man. "What are you doing here?"

The man's eyes opened to a slit, pale blue and aware. His mouth moved, but nothing came out but red bubbles and drool.

"Talk!" Mike shouted.

In the distance, sirens sounded, louder with each passing second. Good news and bad news. Good news because Chloe would get the medical attention she needed. Bad news because the cops wouldn't let him beat the shit out of the live one to shake some intel out of him.

The sirens grew to a wailing crescendo, then cut off. A couple of seconds later, boots pounded down hallways. "In here!" he shouted. Two EMTs came running into the room, followed by two cops in uniform.

The women at the door separated for them, then gathered again, wide-eyed, frightened, silent.

One of the EMTs approached him. Mike hated to do it, hated it, but he let go of Chloe.

"She blacked out for a minute or two." His heart pounded as one of the medics shone a light in Chloe's eyes. Had she sustained major trauma? Was she going to be all right? She'd been slammed across the room by a big, strong man. His heart had stopped as he watched her flying, bouncing off the wall.

Chloe's eyes opened wide at the light and she coughed at the medic's request. Her head turned to him, face paper white. "Mike?"

"It's okay, honey," Mike said, but he knew it wasn't.

She looked at him and shuddered. God only knew what his expression was. Deadly and enraged, probably, though there wasn't anything he could do to contain or hide it, not with the two fuckers who'd attacked Chloe in the same room. She pointed at her mouth and he didn't understand what she was trying to say until he caught on and wiped his own mouth. It came away bloody. "It's okay," he repeated helplessly.

"Okay, Ms.—" the medic treating her said, pulling back a little after examining her pupils and taking her pulse and BP.

"Mason." Second by second, Chloe was looking better.

"Okay, Ms. Mason. How many fingers?" He held up two fingers, palm out.

Chloe looked at the shocked, pale women gathered in the doorway and smiled at them. It was shaky and it broke Mike's heart. She was trying to make light of what had happened, to reassure the women in the doorway.

"I'm all right, Cassie. Ann. It's all okay." She turned to the medic. "Turn your hand around, and in England it would mean *up yours*. Two fingers. To answer your question—you're holding up two fingers." A choked laugh came from the doorway.

Her voice was weak, but she was making a valiant attempt to defuse the situation. She knew that every woman in that doorway had been violently attacked. She knew how scared they were and that they all looked to her for strength. Chloe was rising above her own fear and pain to reassure them.

At that moment Mike was struck by a wave of love so strong it would have brought him to his knees if he hadn't already been kneeling.

The other medic bent down to the dead guy, putting two gloved fingers to the side of his neck. "This one's gone." He crouched down beside the other one, who was breathing erratically, bubbles of blood coming out of his mouth.

"These fuckers were beating her up, one ready to rape her." Mike barely recognized his voice, raspy and low and deadly.

The attempted rape was clear. The dead fuck's pants were unzipped, dick lying limp on one thigh. Seeing that, knowing what the man had wanted to do to Chloe, knowing what he'd *done* to

Chloe, made Mike shake with rage. Jesus, he wished he could kill the fuck all over again.

The medic stood up. "Ma'am? What are you feeling? Do you feel dizzy or faint?"

"No." Chloe's voice was stronger. She sat up straighter and winced. Mike put his hand on her back, providing support. Chloe held her slightly swollen arm out. "Except for this. I don't know if the bone is broken. It might be just a sprain."

"We'll x-ray it when we get to the hospital." The tech who'd shone the light in her eyes nodded. He had a badge with his name on his uniform. Steve. "Do you want the gurney, ma'am?"

Chloe waited a second. "No," she said finally. "I'd rather walk." She braced her good hand on the floor to try to get up. Mike scrambled up, took her by her good hand and lifted her up.

Was this a good idea? Maybe she was concussed. Maybe she'd do permanent damage to herself if she walked. Jesus, what the fuck did he know?

Mike turned to the medic, Steve, and was about to protest when Chloe put a finger across his lips. "I'm okay, Mike. Let me walk out under my own steam. It's important." She looked across at the women in the doorway, then back at him. Expecting him to get it.

Damn.

He got it. He did.

But letting her walk out under her own steam, because it was important to her to be strong for the poor broken women of the shelter, clashed violently with his desire to either carry her out or have her taken out on a gurney, on the off chance that there might be some internal damage.

Chloe watched him as he worked it out, jaws gnashing. She trusted him to understand and he did, oh yeah.

But . . . *fuck!*

"Okay." It was a wonder the word came out at all, his jaws were clenched so tightly against saying *no way.*

While he was working it out in his head Chloe called out to the group of women on the threshold. "It's all right. I'm fine. Don't worry about anything. I'll see you all tomorrow."

By chance, Mike was looking around the room while she spoke to "her" women, trying to figure out the best way to usher her out without her bumping into anything. He happened to be looking at the wounded man when Chloe spoke and the man's eyes flickered. Pale blue, ice cold. There was intelligence there and a reaction to the news that Chloe would be here tomorrow.

He left Chloe's side for a moment and bent down to pull the fucker back up with his fist bunched in his shirt.

The man was badly wounded. He'd lost teeth, his nose was shattered, almost flat against his face, he had to breathe through his bleeding mouth. He was in excruciating pain. And yet, his expression didn't change when Mike brought him up face-to-face.

Oh yeah. This was a soldier. A well-trained one. He knew how to maintain discipline, knew how to work through pain. Knew how to give nothing away.

Mike leaned into him, nose an inch from his. Or where the fuck's nose had been. Crazily, through his serious injuries, the man started laughing, a grotesque wheezing sound.

"What?" Mike growled, his voice so low only the wounded man could hear him. The man was badly wounded, defeated. Cops were coming to take him away. What the fuck did he have to laugh about?

Garbled sounds came out of the wounded mouth, almost indistinguishable. But Mike had been in battle. He could follow what a wounded man was trying to say.

And what the man said chilled Mike to the bone.

"We'll be back," he said through torn lips.

Chapter 11

"Does it hurt?" the kindly but exhausted-looking emergency room doctor said as he finished wrapping an Ace bandage around her forearm. Which was sprained, thank God, not broken. The doctors had warned her against a third fracture.

"No," she replied, which was a lie. Of course it hurt. But Chloe didn't dare say anything because Mike looked so wild-eyed she was afraid he'd attack the doctor at the slightest provocation.

Mike stood by her side, every muscle tense, on the balls of his feet as if ready to spring to action any second. He looked like a force of nature.

He'd saved her life. In the ambulance, she'd tried to thank him but he'd waved it off, hovering over her with his wide shoulders as if space aliens might claw their way through to her from the roof of the ambulance van. And if they did, by God he'd be ready.

The doctor hadn't even tried to throw him out. He looked as if he'd welcome a fight.

It was, in a strange way, reassuring. He was so vigilant, she didn't have to be. Back in the shelter, with Cassie and Ann and Joanne and Emily and one young girl so traumatized they hadn't yet learned her name looking on, she'd had to be strong. Chloe didn't dare let her fear and pain show. Her shock at the near-rape and the brutal assault. The women looked to her for reassurance and hope and Chloe would rather die than let them down.

So she'd squeezed Cassie's hand as she walked past them under her own steam, down the hall and into the waiting ambulance, leaning heavily on Mike without showing it, because Cassie was just starting to recover from a husband who'd taken a knife to her. The shelter was putting these women back together again and Chloe didn't want to do anything at all to jeopardize that.

But later, knowing that no one who was vulnerable was looking, she leaned on Mike, who was a rock.

"Maybe we should keep you overnight for observation," the doctor mused, writing down a prescription for painkillers.

As soon as he spoke the words, Chloe rapped out a loud "No!" so sharp the doctor raised bushy blond eyebrows and looked at her over his glasses.

She'd had panic in her voice. Chloe tried to swallow, throat dry. "No." She tried to make her voice sound normal when a scream was rising from her gut. Tried to keep the shaking out of her voice. "I don't need to stay overnight. I feel fine. No problem. I'd rather go home. Please."

God, she sounded like a madwoman, and she probably was. The very idea of spending a night in a hospital, when she'd been held like a prisoner in hospitals for most of her childhood and adolescence, was terrifying. She'd have a heart attack. At the very least a panic attack, of the kind she hadn't had in fifteen years.

She looked over at her new family, a plea in her eyes. They were all there. Of course they were. The hospital staff hadn't even tried to keep them out of the treatment room, either. It helped that RBK had donated half a million dollars toward the establishment of a Women's Wellness Center.

Harry, Ellen, Sam, Nicole. If there was one thing Chloe had

learned over the past six months, it was that they were loyal. They acted as a unit with unquestioning love and support, starting from her wonderful brother Harry.

"Honey," he began, opening his hands in a cajoling gesture, "maybe the doctor is right. Maybe you should stay just for one night."

"No," Chloe said, and closed her mouth because her throat was too tight for another word.

"No," Mike echoed, putting his arm around her shoulder. Oh God, did that feel good, to have his heavy arm around her, strong and sure. "Hospitals scare her. And anyway the doctor said it would be a precaution, right, doc?" He swiveled to direct his fierce scary gaze at the doctor, who looked startled.

"Ah, yes. I saw no signs of concussion, but to be certain, it would be best if she were not left alone."

"Oh, of course!" Ellen cried. "She'll be staying with—"

"Me. With me." Mike dropped the little bomb in the room and scanned everyone in it—Harry, Ellen, Sam, Nicole, the doctor—narrow-eyed and defiant. "She's staying with me."

Utter silence. Deep, uncomfortable silence.

"Now listen here—" Harry began.

The doctor cleared his throat. "I think, ah, I have other patients. Yes. Um." He left in a hurry, white coat fluttering behind him.

"What the fuck—" Harry began again.

"Listen to me." Mike directed his gaze between Harry and her. Each time he looked her way, she had the feeling he was somehow reassuring himself that she was okay. "Those two guys came looking for *Chloe*. It wasn't some random rape attempt. And one of them told me that they'd be back."

Chloe jolted under his arm, mind racing to understand the implications of this. It had been bad enough thinking she'd been the victim of a random attack by two violent men. Horrible, but unfortunately something that happened in this violent and unstable world.

But they'd been after *her* specifically? It was almost impossible to process. There was no way she could grasp this.

"Why me?" she whispered, dry-mouthed. Chloe tried to be brave, but the truth was she was terrified. Those two men had been unstoppable. Only Mike had saved her from rape and a violent beating. "What could they possibly want from me?"

"I don't know, honey. And until we do, you're staying with me." Mike's big arm tightened around her shoulder. He turned to stare at Harry. "Those two guys were ex-military, I'd swear to it. I guess we're lucky they weren't armed. I wasn't, either, out of respect for the shelter, but that's not gonna happen again. No, sir. Next time I'll be carrying, count on it."

A shudder went through her. Next time . . .

Soldiers, Mike had said.

"They had foreign accents. I don't know if that helps," Chloe offered.

The three men focused their attention on her.

"What kind of accents, honey?" Harry's voice was gentle.

Chloe closed her eyes, eliminated her emotions. She'd been so shocked, it was hard to remember even what they'd said. But there was something . . .

We need for you to listen to us, the tall guy had said. What about that sentence resonated?

Like many introverts, Chloe really listened to people. She listened to their words, she observed their body language, she watched their eyes.

She liked to play a game and guess where people came from. She often failed with Americans since she'd had few contacts with people in what she called the Hospital Years and had spent so many years in England after that. But she was pretty good with foreign accents since there were so many foreign girls at Sacred Heart. Her best friend there, Lydia . . .

Why was she thinking of this? Because Lydia had a catchphrase—*You need to listen*, with a swooping sound in *listen*. Lydia's family had come from Moscow.

"Russian," she said decisively. She turned to Mike. "They had Russian accents. Or maybe East European."

"Okay." He nodded sharply. "That makes sense. They used SAMBO moves. One of the guys got me to the ground immediately. And I think the knife he threatened Chloe with"—he gave her a look so fierce she almost expected to see beams coming out of his eyes—"that knife looked like a Kizlyar. We'll have to ask Kelly. So, we've got Russians after Chloe, for some reason. We'll get to the bottom of this, but until we do, she's in danger, every minute of every day."

"I'll take care of her," Harry growled. "She's my sister." Harry's face was tight and pale with tension. "I'm not going to let anything else happen to her. She's my responsibility."

Ellen looked up at her husband and then at Chloe, face sad. She'd told Chloe how losing his baby sister had tormented him all his life.

"Look at you," Mike said. "You've got a wife and a child. And you—Sam." Sam had his arm around a hugely pregnant Nicole, due any day now. "You're going to become a father again in a few days. You guys have divided responsibilities. Your attention's going to be split at all times between caring for your wives and children and protecting Chloe. I don't have that. My full attention will be on Chloe. I don't have divided loyalties. Right now there is nothing more important in my world than keeping Chloe safe and she'll have one hundred percent of my attention until we figure out what's going on and we can be sure the danger is gone. However long it takes, whatever it takes, I'm on it. 24/7." He tightened his arm even more and kissed the top of her head.

Harry looked at Sam, then Ellen and Nicole.

"He's right, Harry," Ellen said. "I know you like to think you can do it all, but I think he's right."

Harry's mouth worked. "Chloe?"

Everyone turned to her. She looked up into Mike's face. He wasn't trying in any way to convince her with gentle words. His features were drawn tightly in harsh lines.

There was only one possible answer. "I'll be with Mike," she said softly, "until this mess is cleared up."

Nikitin sat in the very comfortable armchair in the very elegant room Sands had given him to operate in. It was almost too lush, this place. Made men weak, dependent. He'd spent years living in an unheated tent outside Grozny trying to crush the rebels, who were living under better conditions than he was.

He sat back and waited, watching his satphone on the coffee table in front of him, programmed to vibrate, not ring. Ivan was supposed to check in at 1600 hours. Ivan was utterly reliable. He'd been sent with Lyov to rough up one woman. How hard could that be? It wasn't the kind of mission Ivan could possibly fail.

Ivan had been his *serzhant*—his sergeant—in many battles. He was tough and efficient and dependable. And when this first shipment came in, he was promised a $50,000 bonus.

So why the hell wasn't he reporting in?

At 1800 hours, Nikitin picked up his satphone and dialed Ivan's number, on the off chance Ivan had lost his cell phone or—impossible!—had it taken from him. He listened, impotent, to the endless ringing. Nikitin's thumb pressed the OFF button as his jaw clenched. *Chert!* Ivan had *failed?*

This was beyond bad news. His masters, the *vory*, expected everything to run smoothly. They were investing a lot of money, and looking to invest even more in the future. They had big plans and were unforgiving when it came to messes.

Having two of his enforcers unaccounted for was an example of gross mismanagement. Or so the *vory* would think. Somehow, Nikitin had stuck his hand inside a wasp's nest, when he'd only wanted to take care of minor insubordination, before it ballooned out of control.

And here it was, out of control.

This wouldn't do. This mess had to be taken care of immediately.

At least he could be sure of one thing. His satphone ran on Thuraya, making his phone untraceable. The police could have no idea where he was or who he was. For all they could tell, he could be on the moon. His men had gone in clean, with nothing traceable. Ivan wouldn't talk. Neither would Lyov. Whatever happened, they would keep their mouths shut.

Maybe this disaster could be contained, he thought. If not, heads would roll. Starting with his own.

"Let's run through it again, Chloe," Lieutenant Bill Kelly said gently. When Mike tensed by her side, Chloe put a hand on his forearm. Normally hard as steel anyway, he was so tense she could see the individual muscles in his arm.

"It's okay, Mike." His jaw muscles were so clenched it was surprising enamel wasn't shooting out his ears. He almost quivered with stress under her hand.

She'd been pampered, been plied with endless cups of tea, had received hugs and kisses from Merry and Gracie, who had only been told that Aunt Chloe had a headache. Ellen and Nicole had all but rubbed her feet for her.

No one had thought to comfort Mike, who'd been in battle, had killed a man for her.

"She's freaked. She's scared. She's been through hell," Mike told the lieutenant, biting off each word. "She's gone over this a thousand times."

"I understand that. But we need for Chloe to remember everything, because the guy we've got in custody isn't talking. I think he's considering himself some kind of political prisoner. So our only clue is Chloe."

Mike's jaw muscles jumped. "Did you do what I said?"

Lieutenant Kelly must have the patience of a saint because he didn't roll his eyes or bristle at Mike's tone. "Yes. The body in the morgue is under a different name and the guy in the hospital isn't registered at all. We took out the footage at the shelter. If those guys were sent by someone, the guy running the op won't have a clue what happened to them. He won't even know if they made it to the shelter."

"The vehicle they came in?"

The lieutenant sighed. "Rental. Paid for by corporate credit card made out to Joseph Merck. Who doesn't exist. The corporation is a shell. We're still investigating. Now can I continue talking to Chloe?"

Mike nodded jerkily.

The lieutenant opened his notebook and gave her a kind look. "So, Chloe, let's run through it just one more time, then I'll be out of your hair."

Chloe tried to smile for him. She'd gotten to know him well in the six months since that terrible night Mike had been accused of assaulting a woman.

He was almost a member of the family, someone who dropped by unannounced to watch a ball game with Harry and Sam and Mike and stayed for dinner. He was tough, kind under his cynical cop veneer, overworked. A good guy.

It was clear to Chloe that he was interrogating her here in Harry's apartment, and not in police headquarters, as a courtesy to her and to Mike, who'd been a colleague and was a friend. As were Harry and Sam.

"You don't have any more information about the two men?" she asked.

"No, ma'am. The dead man—" He fixed Mike with a hard stare and Mike stared right back. If there was one thing about Mike she knew, it was that he couldn't be intimidated. "The dead man had nothing on his person that could identify him. No wallet, no cell phone, no ID at all. The tags had been cut off his clothes. I was told informally by the coroner's assistant that he had gold fillings that weren't done in this country, but that's about it. AFIS results show his fingerprints not on file anywhere in the U.S. We're still waiting for IAEG results."

"International fingerprint database," Mike explained.

"But Russia's not a party to IAEG." The lieutenant huffed out an exasperated breath. "So if they are Russian, he won't be in their system, either. I heard that the other guy's cell rang. Turns out the caller is untraceable. We're still figuring out how that can happen. So, Chloe. Starting from the beginning. How did they know where you were?"

"I don't know," Chloe said slowly, starting to feel woozy. Mike's hand covered hers, warm and strong and safe. She definitely wanted to answer questions but delayed shock was catching up with her. "I was in the supply room, which not many people know about. The door they came in isn't used much, either. Most people enter the room by the door all of you used, which opens onto a small terrace and then out onto the parking lot. You'd have to be familiar with the shelter's layout to know to use that door."

Bill looked up. "Are the blueprints on file anywhere?"

Chloe's mind went blank. She had no idea.

"We can check that," said Mike. "I've got a friend in the Land Registry Office. I'll text him now."

"So. You're in this supply room."

Chloe nodded. "Folding clothes."

"Is that something you do normally?"

"Donations of clothes are made in various points in the city and are collected and brought to the shelter on Wednesday afternoons.

So, yes, in answer to your question, I'm often folding and sorting clothes on Wednesday afternoons."

"And who knows this?"

Chloe lifted her shoulders. "Almost everyone at the shelter, I should think. It's not a secret."

"So the men came in through the door and what? What did you think?"

"I tried to talk myself out of it, but I was instantly terrified," Chloe confessed. "There was something about the way they moved, something in their eyes . . ." She shivered.

"Here, honey." Mike reached behind them for a small blanket Ellen kept on the couch in case Gracie got cold. He wrapped it around her shoulders, kissed her temple.

Absolutely no one reacted. Not Harry or Sam or Ellen or Nicole. Not even Bill Kelly. It was as if Mike hugging her and kissing her had become the new norm.

"I told you they moved like soldiers." Mike's jaw tightened. "Possibly Russian soldiers. The Russian Federation treats its soldiers brutally and the soldiers are brutal in return."

Bill nodded, mouth downturned. "What did they say to you, Chloe?"

She rubbed her forehead in frustration. "Well, that's the thing. They didn't say much at all, really. Just that I was supposed to pay attention to them. They said that over and over. And pulled out a long black knife to sort of drive that concept home. They put the knife under my eye."

Mike turned his head slowly. His eyes met Bill's. "Keep that guy under lock and key." He made a noise in his throat that sounded scarily like a growl.

"Yeah. He's not going anywhere and you're not coming near him. We picked the knife up. It's a Kizlyar. You pegged it, Mike."

"Russian combat knife. Used by their Army and Special Forces. Christ." Harry rubbed his forehead.

A Russian combat knife. Chloe tucked that away among the many terrifying and absolutely puzzling details of what had happened today.

Bill wrote something in his notebook. "So, Chloe. You were supposed to pay attention. To what?"

"They never said. They got . . . sidetracked."

By attempted rape. The words quivered in the air. Mike's breathing was audible, as if he were pushing some great weight.

"Is there any reason why two men, possibly soldiers, possibly Russian, would want to target you?"

She'd barely thought of anything else on the ride to the hospital and the ride back home. "I've thought and thought, but I pull a complete blank."

"No enemies?"

"No. I sometimes help RBK with—um—some special projects." Chloe looked at Mike and Harry and Sam, not knowing how much she could say.

"He knows," Mike interjected. "Several cops know what we do."

"Could this be revenge? From some bozo whose wife you helped get away?" Bill asked.

Chloe thought about it carefully. "In theory. But the last woman who came to us at RBK, her husband killed himself a week after she escaped. The kind of man you're talking about has impulse-control issues. He's going to want his revenge right away. He's not going to wait and coolly plan it."

Bill nodded his agreement. "And in the shelter? Those women come from volatile situations. Violent situations. The shelter offers them protection. Surely you've made some enemies?"

Chloe sighed. "I'm just a volunteer. I don't have any administrative responsibilities. I'm not in any way the official face of the shelter and my name isn't anywhere as a staff member. I just give a hand three times a week. Lately, we've started a very mild form of group therapy. Quite a few women come by occasionally, drop-ins from the street, we talk, and it seems to help them. But the women living there, almost by definition, have made a decision to leave their spouses. I didn't convince anyone to run away, if that's what you're thinking."

"And the Russian connection, if there is one?" He looked at Mike, then Sam and Harry. "Do you have any Russian connections? Any reason why Russians, or men who'd trained in Eastern Europe, might be after you? Have you protected any Russian women lately?"

"No." Chloe opened her hands helplessly. "I have no idea why Russian men would attack me."

She shuddered, something deep inside her icy cold and scared. The attack had plunged her straight into nightmares she thought were behind her, straight into a hell beyond her conscious memories. The world she'd trod so lightly on, afraid to leave any kind of imprint, had suddenly cracked beneath her feet. An abyss had opened up, inside a yawning, cruel darkness.

Mike looked at her narrow-eyed, perceiving something. It was reassuring and also frightening that he saw her so clearly. Reassuring because she was no longer invisible. Frightening because a curtain had been pulled back on a world in which she had no defenses at all.

Chloe shrugged helplessly. "Sorry I can't be of more assistance."

Bill looked down at his notebook, flipped it closed, heaved a huge sigh and rose. He was almost as tall as Sam. Chloe had to crane her neck to meet his eyes. "Okay then. Well, we'll try to interrogate this guy as soon as he can talk some, or at least write down info." He shot Mike a hard-eyed look, which Mike shot right back. "But I told you I'm not holding out hope. If we're talking Russian Mafiya, he'll be as hard as nails. He'll never talk because whatever we do to him will be less terrifying than what his bosses will do to him. In the meantime, keep an eye on Chloe."

"On it." Mike squeezed her shoulders again as Harry and Sam muttered, "Oh yeah."

"And Chloe, keep your eyes peeled and if you remember anything, anything at all, call me. We don't know whether they wanted to intimidate you, kidnap you or, eventually, kill you. So be careful. And be careful who you're with."

It occurred to Chloe for the first time that though she wasn't alone in facing the danger, she was dragging not only Harry and Sam into her problems, but Ellen and Nicole. And, worse, *Gracie and Merry.*

She loved those two little girls with all her heart. If anything happened to them because of her . . .

"We'll see you out, Bill," Ellen said, with a nod to Nicole. Nicole stood up a little awkwardly, with the help of her husband's huge hand. They were walking Bill out, but they were also leaving the men to make their arrangements.

"She's with me," Mike said in a hard voice to his two brothers. "I hope I made that clear. And I'll be on it 24/7."

"You have to work, Mike," Chloe said gently. She was touched to the core by his willingness to put his life completely on the line. Whatever those two men—Russian or not—were, whatever they wanted, they represented a nebulous threat that had no ending in sight. "You can't put your whole life on hold."

"I can," he said fiercely. "And I will. If you have to go out and I absolutely can't be with you, I'm seconding Barney. He's good. No one's going to get past him."

Barney had Harry and Sam's approval. They both nodded. Then they got into a long, involved discussion of shifts and vehicle inspection rotations, carjacking deterrents . . . Chloe tuned out. She was exhausted. Her arm hurt and she had bruises all over.

Nothing to be hospitalized over, but the pain that had been like a background noise suddenly pinged to life.

Right in the middle of the discussions, Mike rose, went into Harry's kitchen and came back out with a glass of water and two pills in his huge hand.

"Here, honey."

He continued where he'd left off with his brothers.

Chloe gratefully took the pills. Fifteen minutes later, the pain had eased off and she was in a mild haze that felt just great. The men's deep voices were a far-off hum.

"Okay." Mike clapped his hands and her eyes popped open. An hour had passed. "We're clear. Harry's going to brief Barney. Bill's going to continue trying to trace the vehicle the two men left and will keep us in the loop. Chloe, honey? Time to go."

Mike took her hand, stood and helped her up.

Chloe stood, too, and looked at her brother and at Sam. Sam kept his face expressionless. Harry looked at her with love and worry in his eyes. "Chloe? Sweetheart?"

Mike was steamrolling her, no doubt about that. His stance was aggressive as he faced his two brothers, arm around her shoulders, holding her tightly to him.

He was clearly perfectly prepared to fight to be the one who was her prime protector. Harry and Sam were there, willing and able, but Mike was right. They had other responsibilities, to their wives, to their children. Sam's wife was going to give birth any day now. Her previous delivery had been hard and she'd bled a lot. He wouldn't want to leave her side.

Quite right.

Chloe shook a little. However it had happened, she'd re-entered the dark world of male violence once again.

She had no doubt that she needed a protector. Pretending otherwise was foolish beyond words. She had no tools and no weapons against men like those who had come after her.

Mike was right when he said he didn't have divided loyalties. But there was something else. He'd defended her without hesitation, without any sense of danger to himself. He'd faced two deadly men head-on. He'd risked his life for her.

In the most primordial way possible, he'd fought for her, and in the most primitive way possible, she was his. There was also one more factor in this, one she kept close to her heart.

She loved him.

Chloe reached up to squeeze Mike's hand and looked at her brother Harry and at Sam. "I'm with Mike," she said.

Chapter 12

The Meteor Club

The man grunted heavily, fingers digging painfully into her hips, and slumped on top of her. Consuelo didn't dare push at his shoulders to get him off her—he'd paid for it, after all—trying to pull in breath even though her lungs were compressed.

Please, God, don't let him fall asleep.

After a few minutes, when Consuelo started seeing spots in front of her eyes, the man groaned, pulled out of her and rolled away onto his back, forearms across his eyes.

From this moment on, she was invisible. As they said, this was what prostitutes were paid to do. Leave.

She got out of bed quietly, breathing shallowly. He'd imprinted her skin with the smell of his rancid sweat with an overlay of Armani for Men. Her groin smelled of his semen. Sex without a condom paid much better, and under the new Russian management, whatever paid better was definitely preferred.

Some of the older women were given to men who liked to hurt. There were special soundproofed rooms in the other wing for that.

The Russian made it clear that there was no limits to what could be done, as long as the men paid enough.

Two women had disappeared in the last month.

Consuelo looked down at the man who'd hurt her, trying to push away the spurt of red-hot rage that raced through her.

"John," he'd said his name was, and she refrained from smiling at the name that was also a description. Yeah. John.

His real name was Larry Cameron and he ran a huge used car dealership in Chula Vista. His face was all over late-night TV.

Consuelo didn't care. She didn't care about much, actually. More and more lately, while the men grunted over her, using her body, she'd fly right out of it. She'd come reluctantly back in the middle of it this time because "John" had been hurting her so much it had been impossible to ignore. Ramming into her, digging his fingers hard into her hips, biting her breasts.

Before, Franklin would have had a quiet word with him. Between gentlemen, of course. Care for the merchandise and all. But since the arrival of the Russians, many of the customers had sniffed the new regime, like animals scenting freedom, and become violent, out of control. The girls started sporting bruises that took more and more makeup to cover up. A couple had needed medical care.

It was as if a new, evil spirit roamed the club. The Russians had come and somehow their rough presence had unleashed something. Something bad.

In Consuelo's opinion, men were very close to the animal kingdom. Like horses could sense the appearance of a lion among them and grow agitated, so the customers had sensed the appearance of a crueler race of man among them, a presence that lifted inhibitions, gave the men silent permission to let themselves give in to their darker impulses.

Because, after all, they'd paid for it and who was going to complain?

Consuelo could see in their eyes if they'd been infected with this new plague. Sometimes she flew out of her body the instant the door closed behind them and she was ordered to strip, because she could sense that they'd been infected. Even the many blue-eyes—their eyes grew cold and dark. She was sweaty and smelly and bruised.

Each luxurious room had its own bathroom, but she couldn't stand the thought of showering naked while the man was passed out on the bed. She had her own room in a separate annex with the other girls and longed for the quiet of her room, longed to take an hour-long shower under the hottest spray she could stand, knowing it wouldn't wash away anything.

Consuelo picked up her clothes, noting without interest the ripped panties and torn bra. "John" was one of those who got very excited for sex two seconds after the door closed behind them and they were alone in the room.

The panties and bra had been pretty, she mused. Pale lavender silk with lace around the edges. They were ruined now.

Consuelo-outside-Consuelo looked down from the ceiling as the young woman below her slid the silky, torn underwear through her hands. The young woman let the panties drift lightly to the floor and fisted her hands in the ends of the bra and pulled tight.

The silk was delicate but strong, like a soft rope.

Consuelo looked down at the naked young woman, flexing the rope-bra, pulling it over and over, testing its strength. Consuelo on the ceiling felt absolutely nothing. She watched with the very faintest of interest as the young naked woman walked slowly over to the bed and looked down at the man making a huge dent in the mattress.

He was big, heavy, hairy. His gleaming penis was slick with semen and K-Y jelly. The young woman down below had surreptitiously coated herself with it because she was so dry. Even with the jelly, it had hurt.

His penis lay spent along his thigh.

The labored breathing turned to snoring, great heavy snorts like a hibernating bear. So ugly. So useless.

Consuelo watched the young woman put a knee to the mattress, bend down toward the man, the silky rope-bra stretched between her fists, bringing the silk closer to the man's throat . . .

A sudden spurt of alarm and Consuelo shot down, back into the young woman's body just as the man's eyes opened wide, light blue and bloodshot.

"What—what are you doing?" he slurred, seeing her bending down, voice rising in alarm. "What the fuck? *What the hell are you doing?*"

Killing you. The words filled her head, together with a rage that came from nowhere like an immense wind rising in the desert. Where before Consuelo had felt nothing, now she felt too much. Rage pulsed in her like blood, washing over her in waves. A fury so total and complete it shook her bones.

The man tried to lift himself up on his elbows but slipped. Too drunk on whiskey and sex to keep himself upright. But the clouds were disappearing from his blue eyes, awareness seeping in.

Consuelo looked with longing at his throat. She could see where the rope-bra would go, right over the Adam's apple. She'd twist it around the back of his neck, twist it tight, hold it there . . .

She'd hold fast as he thrashed on the bed, all his beefy strength useless. She'd watch as he turned dark red, as his eyes bulged, as his hairy legs kicked.

In the orphanage, many years ago, she'd seen someone strangled to death and she'd never forgotten it.

She'd tighten and tighten until the man stilled, black tongue lolling out of his mouth.

"Get away from me!" Eyes fixed on hers, his legs scrabbled awkwardly as he tried to scramble away, and Consuelo hated every cell in his huge, puffy body and knew her rage was visible on her face.

Careful, Consuelo. Be careful not to let your anger overwhelm you. Because you are very very angry, and you don't know it yet.

The voice in her head was soft and reasonable. Chloe. Her lifeline. A woman who somehow understood her, utterly and completely, without judging her. Chloe, elegant and cultivated and rich, who nonetheless treated her as a complete equal and a friend.

It was Chloe in her head now, Chloe who smoothed out her features, turned her into the sex kitten that was her mask. Chloe who made her lower her voice into a husky growl when what she really wanted to do was scream.

"Ah, John," Consuelo purred, laying the rope-bra across his shoulders, slowly sliding it down his chest. She stopped at his nipples and flicked them with her fingernails, smiling narrow-eyed at his jolt of pleasure.

Chloe-in-her-head was saving her life. Consuelo realized she wouldn't have had the strength to strangle this man. He'd have overpowered her easily, called in security—*real* security, the Russian monsters—and her life would be over.

The girls of the club whispered about what happened to those who rebelled. They were given to men who loved the darkest of dark pleasures and were never seen again.

Chloe's voice in her head had stopped her.

"It was so wonderful before," she whispered, wondering at herself, at how she could lie so easily. She opened her thighs wide, knowing he could see her sex, lips puffy from where he'd plowed her for an hour. "*So* wonderful. I want more. More, more, more."

Consuelo straddled him, wrapped the silk cup of the bra around his penis and pulled. He could feel the soft silk and her hand milking him around it.

"Ah, baby," he groaned, head flopping back on the pillow, "why didn't you say so?" He grinned, waving his hand at his stiffening member. "It's all yours, baby. Get to work."

Afterwards, wiping her mouth with a shaking hand, Consuelo

got dressed and quietly closed the door of the room behind her, wondering what to do, where to go. Her next session was in an hour but the threads of self-control were fraying dangerously.

Her legs were shaking, she could hardly breathe. Her body felt battered. She hated her body, hated herself.

Hated the johns, all of them.

No. No more, no more today. She'd come dangerously close to trying to kill a man today, and ending her own life. She'd lock herself in her room in the dark and plead a massive headache. A migraine. Say she couldn't perform because she'd get dizzy and vomit all over the client.

That had worked before.

And then tomorrow she'd go back and talk to Chloe. Calm, understanding Chloe. Chloe, who'd talk her down from her murderous thoughts. Chloe, who'd teach her how to stay in her own body.

Her best friend, Elena, was coming down the hall. Elena was the first person to talk to Chloe, happening on the shelter in a moment of desperation. She'd been locked in a dark, soundproofed room for four days without food or water after biting a client. She'd been released only because Franklin had interceded with the Russian. Everyone thought the Russian would simply keep her there until she died. Elena had thought that, too.

Though Chloe never gave advice, never passed judgment, just listened, Elena always said she felt better afterwards. So Consuelo had dropped by, too. Once a month, at first. Like a compelling sweet, dangerous to consume. Then twice a month and now once a week.

Consuelo was thinking of running away and just living in the shelter, forever.

Except the Russian would find her. Drag her back.

Consuelo frowned. Elena was weaving, looking shocked.

"Consuelo," Elena whispered, grabbing her arm, looking left

and right. Since the Russians, they'd taken to talking in whispers. "Did you hear what happened?"

"No." What could have happened? It would take a lot to shock Elena, who'd seen it all. Did someone die? It wouldn't be the first time.

"Chloe. The Russians attacked Chloe. For talking to us."

Consuelo's heart stopped in her chest. *Chloe*. Chloe, hurt for trying to help them. For trying to help *her*.

Chloe, who helped her to live.

This time the rage was black, strong and bitter and overwhelming.

And there was no Chloe in her head to make it go away.

"You're worried about Chloe," Ellen said gently, watching her husband pace up and down the bedroom, love and concern in her eyes. Her wonderful husband, with that supermacho tough-guy exterior masking such a tender heart. "I'm worried, too. But you and Mike and Sam will figure out what's going on and all of you will protect her. And Mike . . . well, he's crazy about her. That's pretty clear. I can't imagine anyone getting past Mike."

"Yeah." Harry ran a big hand through his dark blond hair, a gesture she'd seen him do a thousand times. It meant stress and frustration and she understood them both. His sister was in danger and it was driving him crazy.

No one knew better than her the immense pain Harry had carried all his life thinking he hadn't been able to protect his baby sister.

And no one knew better than Ellen how ecstatic Harry had been on finding his baby sister again, and how much he loved her.

Ellen loved Chloe, too. It was so easy to love Chloe, it didn't take any effort at all. She was gentle and smart and kind. The girls, Gracie and Merry, adored her. Chloe was a blessing in all their lives.

But Mike . . . Mike loved her in an entirely different way.

"I could never figure out why Mike backed away from Chloe all this time when he's so crazy about her. A blind man could see that he was smitten and yet he just followed her around without making his move, the dork. And this is *Mike*, the man-slut. Mike, the man who'd nail anything that moved. Though, mind you, it's hard to think of him that way watching him follow Chloe around like an adopted mongrel for six months. He's even willing to watch princess videos forever with the girls as long as Chloe's there. What he feels is right out there for everyone to see. That's what's so strange. He backed away from Chloe but stuck so close. Nicole and I can't figure it out. Chloe, too. Drove her insane. If nothing else, this mess has forced Mike to make a move. He spent all these months practically stalking her and never touching her. How weird is . . . *Harry?*" Ellen shot up in bed. "Harry Bolt. What do you know about this? If you know something, spit it out right now, because it's been driving us crazy."

There was something wrong here. Ellen knew every single one of Harry's expressions, and this one was sheepish-guilty.

"Harry?"

With a sigh, her husband sat on the edge of the bed and took her hand. "You know that day when Chloe showed up and we were all just blown away?"

"Oh yes." Ellen smiled and reached out a hand to push back a stray lock of his hair.

Harry rubbed the back of his neck, something else he did under stress. "I can't tell you the impression she made when she first walked into our office. She moved so very carefully and slowly, not like now—"

"Well, Mike's been making her work out for the past six months. She's strong as a horse now. Mike saw to that."

Harry cleared his throat. "Yeah. That's true." He bit his lip, Harryspeak for intense unease. Ellen sat up straighter against the headboard. Harry was normally the most controlled of men. He was having a real emotional moment. "Anyway, that day all I could see was this fragile woman. Uncertain and afraid. She looked like a strong wind could blow her away. And her story—Jesus. Ten years in the hospital. A father who was not her father trying to rape her. And don't forget, I knew what had come before that. Living in terror in the home of a violent methhead who near as dammit killed her. Who I thought *had* killed her. Chloe seemed so terribly vulnerable, this young woman who hadn't had any breaks in life. When I saw Mike coming on to her so strong, I just—it just blew my mind. He broke hearts left, right and center. And then when he was taken in for questioning . . . I mean I knew he'd never hurt that woman. I knew he couldn't. But he did fu—have sex with her. Some crazy cokehead he'd just met. Because he'd have sex with anything that breathed and had the right equipment. Like he was seventeen instead of a grown man. The whole thing was so sordid. I just didn't want any of that to touch Chloe. I didn't want her to have her heart broken. So—"

He stopped, his jaws working.

"So?" Ellen asked softly.

Harry worked at getting it out, the words coming reluctantly. "So . . . when Chloe pulled that smart trick with her P.I. and exonerated him when he was looking at possible jail time, I thought . . . she's going to fall for him. Maybe she already has. They all do. And she'll get her heart broken. And I just couldn't stand the thought. So I made him promise that he wouldn't touch Chloe."

Ellen blinked. "In those words? Those exact words? Don't touch Chloe?"

"Yeah." Harry hung his head. "I don't know what I was thinking. I guess you're pretty mad."

Ellen laughed and Harry's head snapped up. "What?"

"Oh, my dear darling husband." Ellen held out her hand and smiled when his hand curled around hers. Her hand felt so wonderful in his. Always had, always would. She knew, without a shadow of a doubt, that if she died first, he would be by her side and she would pass from this life to the next with her hand in his.

Ellen tugged and Harry obediently came to her. He buried his face in her hair and breathed out a deep sigh. "You're not mad at me?"

"Oh, my love." Ellen pulled away to smile into that beloved, worried face. "How could I be mad at you when you single-handedly brought two of my favorite people together?"

Harry looked around the room, then back at her, as if seeking understanding from the walls. "I did?"

"Mm." She twined her arms around his neck, loving the feeling of the strength under her hands, knowing it was both physical and psychological strength. "It would have been a disaster if they'd hooked up immediately. Chloe was so uncertain of herself, so lonely. So damned vulnerable. You were right about that. And Mike—he was conditioned to having easy, emotionless affairs. He's never had to work for a woman. He's never really gotten to know his women, in any true sense of the term. It was really smart of you to force him to keep it in his pants. So, when were you thinking of lifting your ban?"

"Ah . . . Never?"

Ellen blinked. "Never? Wow. That would have been hard to work around, because as you saw, Mike took you at your word. I wish I knew this beforehand and could have told Nicole. We went bananas trying to figure out what was going on. He rarely left her side but he wasn't making any moves. Drove us nuts."

"The two of you could have simply minded your own business," Harry pointed out.

As if. "Not an option. So I guess soon Chloe's going to be my sister-in-law in all senses."

Harry jerked. "Whoa. No, absolutely not." He frowned. "Aren't you going a little fast?"

"No, not at all." Ellen kissed her husband. A peck, then a little deeper. "He's crazy about her and she's head over heels. And instead of having a disastrous affair at the beginning, where he'd dump her abruptly because he couldn't deal with his feelings and she'd be overwhelmed and bewildered and hurt, they're in a really good place right now. Except of course for Russians gunning for her. But aside from that, they're really on track. You did good work, Bolt. Very good work."

"That wasn't my intention. My intention was to cut Mike off for life, but I'll certainly take the credit."

Holding his gaze, smiling, Ellen shimmied her shoulders in a move she wouldn't have been remotely capable of two years ago. The straps of her nightgown fell from her shoulders, the entire nightgown now resting on the tops of her breasts. She stood up by the bed, shimmied again, and the nightgown pooled in a silky heap on the floor. In her brand-new sultry and sexy voice she said, "I think good deeds require a reward, don't you?"

She reached down and placed her hand on his groin, in complete and utter faith she'd find him hot and hard as steel. Bingo. Did she know her man or what?

A quick pump of her hand had him hissing in a breath. "I do deserve a reward, don't I?" he asked, his voice low and rough. "Being so astute and all. So smart at planning this out."

He pulled her back down on the bed, coming down on top of her. Though he was much taller than she was, they fit perfectly. They always had. They always would.

She felt him pressing against her mound. A wave of heat rose from her groin and she pressed upward, loving the feel of him. He lengthened and thickened against her.

She loved this. Loved that she knew his body so well and he knew hers. Far from becoming stale, it made their lovemaking infinitely rich and complex. She'd pitied Mike that in his bed-hopping fervor, he'd never know this.

Maybe now he would.

Harry bit her behind the ear, knowing she would break out in goose bumps. She smiled into his shoulder, brought his big hand to her belly.

She bit his earlobe and smiled again at his shudder. She whispered directly into his ear. "I think you deserve another reward, too. An extra-special one."

"Yeah?" he whispered back, interested. "Better than sex? This sounds good. I can't wait."

"You'll have to wait, because it'll take time." Ellen pressed her hand over Harry's lying on her belly. "You'll get your present sometime around St. Valentine's Day. In about eight months."

Harry's big body jerked on top of hers as if an electric shock had been applied. He lifted himself up on his forearms, looking her deep in the eyes.

"*Ellen.*" She nearly cried at the raw emotion in his voice, at what she saw in his eyes. "Another child? Oh God. Another child?"

She knew what it meant to him. The same that it meant to her. They were without family, had been alone in the world for a very long time. They'd found each other and made Gracie, who filled their lives with joy. Then Chloe had been found. Now another child.

It was almost too much happiness.

Harry collapsed on top of her as if his arms suddenly couldn't support his weight. His shoulders shook and she held him tightly, tightly, kissing his ear, his neck, his face. Anything her mouth could touch. She embraced him with her arms and legs, trying to wrap herself around him, and as they kissed, he slipped inside her and they rocked gently together, Harry, Ellen and the child she was carrying.

Chapter 13

Mike wheeled in Chloe's suitcase and parked it against the wall. They'd stopped by her apartment so she could get some things. She could go back anytime she wanted for things she might need, as long as he was with her. Or Barney. And only for about ten minutes.

Otherwise she was going to stay in his apartment until they figured out what was going on.

Because his apartment had a steel-reinforced door with steel panels extending either side and security cams outside.

His gun locker had two Glock 19s, two Glock 23s, a Colt 1911A1, a Browning Hi-Power, a Sig Sauer P226, an HK USP Compact Tactical .40, a Colt AR-15A Carbine, two M4 rifles exactly like the ones he carried in the Marines, an enormous Mossberg 590 Combat shotgun, good for killing anything including bears, a Remington 700, a Barrett M92, a Barrett M95, and his baby, a Barrett MRAD, which could probably take down a bad guy on the moon. And fifty thousand rounds of ammo.

Two scopes, combat helmets and night-vision goggles that fit over the helmets, two sets of specially made body armor tailored

for his extra-wide frame. All his weapons were spotless and oiled.
A hundred feet of cable, four grapples of varying sizes. Ten flash
bangs. Fourteen ounces of perfectly illegal C4 with a mile of det
cord. Five pairs of combat boots. Two combat vests. Five prepared
syringes of an animal anesthetic, guaranteed to put a man down
in seconds.

And knives. He loved knives. He had a black titanium SOG
Aegis, a Zaccara bowie, a Garrison Fighting Knife, a Gerber Fast,
a Balisong and a kerambit.

So if the zombie apocalypse ever came? Mike was so prepared.

Chloe stood on the threshold of his door, looking at the ground.
In these past six months in which Mike had been her shadow,
she'd been in his place exactly twice, for two minutes each time.
That was probably because there wasn't much there.

He'd lived here almost five years and it wasn't as welcoming as
Chloe's place a week after she moved into her apartment.

His place was an upscale bachelor pad with a place to sleep, a
place to eat and a place to watch TV. That was it. In six months
Chloe had made her small apartment up on the same floor as Harry's apartment a little haven, the kind of place where you heaved
a sigh of pleasure just as soon as you crossed the threshold. Everything there was soft and colorful and smelled great.

Maybe with Mike's place you could heave a sigh of relief that
you'd be safe against just about anything except an RPG launched
from a boat on the ocean, but no points for softness or color coor-
dination or even nice smells.

His Moldovan cleaning lady was a big believer in zapping germs
with Lysol. No wimpy lemon polish for her. His place had no
germs. They'd be too terrified of Alina to thrive.

No warmth, either.

Once the door closed behind them, Chloe looked around carefully, as if she'd never seen the place before. Just as carefully not
looking at him.

Mike should offer her . . . something. What? He had plenty of beer and chips. Full array of liquor, including every whiskey known to man. Frozen fries and pizza. Frozen steaks. Nachos and cheese. Some chorizo.

Christ. No milk or tea. Come to think of it, no vegetables or fruit or even bread and jam, either. Nothing that could even remotely be considered comfort food or drink.

What was there for Chloe here? Nothing.

They looked at each other, then looked away.

Man, this was so not how Mike had planned it. Because plenty of nights, awake, with a massive hard-on and nowhere to go with it, he came up with a lot of different scenarios.

First, of course, he had to somehow get Harry to lift the Curse. He had no idea how that could work so in his daydreams and even night dreams, it just happened, like magic. Whoosh, curse gone.

Then, he'd charm her.

Except Mike had no fucking charm in him at all.

His daydreams didn't go very far. Usually, he skipped the entire beginning with the complicated negotiations with Harry and just shot straight to imagining Chloe naked in his bed. That was always his starting point.

Now there was a real starting point and words just died in this throat.

"I'd, ah, offer tea, except I don't have any."

That made Chloe smile. Jesus, he liked seeing her smile. Her face just glowed, even when it was a small smile, like now.

She rummaged in one of the side pockets of the suitcase and came up with a number of small packets. "Well, I must have sensed that, because I took along a selection of teas from my flat."

She might be looking lost, but man, she also looked so fucking beautiful. Worn and weary, with a bandage on her arm, all her makeup worn off, she outshone any woman Mike had ever set eyes on, including Nicole, which was saying a lot.

There was just something so . . . so golden about her. The soft gold hair, the gold eyes, that beautiful pale skin now suntanned the lightest of golds. She simply stood there, looking at him, taking her cue from him. And he was just standing there, staring at her.

Willing his hard-on down.

Okay. Well, hard as it was to understand and hard as it was to do, Mike was going to go against every single instinct he had and be a perfect gentleman. Harry might have tacitly lifted the Curse on touching Chloe, but the fact was she'd been through violence and had been sexually assaulted.

Jesus, every time he thought of that he wanted to go to the morgue and revive the guy he'd killed and whack him all over again. Then go to SDPD where the other fucker was, and whack him, too.

He was used to violence. He thrived on violence. You could say he was a violence expert, always had been, as of five minutes after his family was slaughtered. He'd made it his life's work to understand it and to master it.

Violence was a language, the only language bad guys understood, and Mike was really fluent in it.

But the kind of violence Mike believed in had a purpose. To protect people like Chloe, who weren't supposed to be touched by it.

And yet, Chloe had been touched by it all her life.

He'd trained since boyhood for violence and he *still* couldn't wrap his head around it. How Chloe's mom's boyfriend could take a little girl, break her arm and slam her violently against the wall. How her adoptive father could break that same arm and want to rape her. And how those two Russian fuckers could try to rape her and then throw her across a room.

How could men *do* that? How could any man do that to Chloe? *Just look at her,* he thought, standing quietly in the room, sad-eyed and nervous, unspeakably beautiful, a spirit so gentle you instantly felt better the minute you saw her.

Everyone felt better when she was around. Gracie and Merry, with the sure animal instinct of the very young, gravitated to Chloe like plants to sunshine. Everyone loved her.

Including him.

Jesus.

He rubbed his chest.

Get this back on the ground, you understand. Get her into your bed.

But instead of one of his usual smooth lines, what came out was . . . "So, you want some of that tea you brought?"

She was looking more and more lost. "Yes. Please."

He didn't move. Neither did she.

Something had happened to Mike's brain. It had ground itself into a new gear he didn't recognize.

Over the years, he'd perfected his seduction patter. He had whole bits of dialogue memorized, little logic trees he followed like a bot. If she said this, he said that. But if she said *that*, then he'd say this.

He also had it timed perfectly, and within half an hour, tops, he could get any woman he wanted naked and into his bed. Or hers. Actually he preferred hers, so he could leave as soon as it was over.

Often it took only a few minutes to close the sale. It was all so familiar it had worn a huge groove in his brain, so he didn't have to actually think about anything.

Put the mechanism into gear and it rolled along all by itself, while he was thinking of where to leave his clothes and where was the exit, for after.

None of this was any help with Chloe. There was no script here, none at all, because, well . . . because this was *Chloe*.

Mike knew he should be heading for the kitchen because she wanted—what did she want? He couldn't remember. Didn't make any difference, because he didn't want to leave a room she was in.

Say something.

"And, uh. We'll get you settled in my room. Just dump my stuff out of the drawers and there's plenty of room in the closet. Towels and . . . ah, stuff are . . ."

Fuck. Where did he keep his towels? The cleaning lady took them away from the bathroom, did something with them, and brought them back to the bathroom. He never saw any of it.

"In the closet in the hallway," Chloe finished for him. "That's where Alina keeps them."

Oh. Okay.

Mike felt awful. Awkward. Hands and feet and tongue too big. He couldn't move, could barely speak.

"So . . . I guess I'll just bunk down on the sofa. No problem. I've slept on a lot worse, believe me."

Chloe took a step toward him, then stopped. Her eyes searched his, looking for something. "Is that what you want, Mike?" Her voice was low, barely above a whisper. "To sleep on the couch?"

Hell no!

The words were on his tongue, the tongue that wasn't working. He opened his hands helplessly, unable to speak.

Chloe took another step forward, and another. She was so close he could smell her now. Seeing her like this, so beautiful and soft and golden, feeling her body heat, smelling her . . . it was sensory overload. He couldn't take it and closed his eyes.

A gentle hand landed on his shoulder. "Mike? You didn't answer my question. Do you want to sleep on the couch?"

Mike's eyes popped open to find her face so close to his he could see each individual eyelash. The question wasn't teasing. She wasn't being coy or playing games. It wasn't an idle question. She was dead serious.

She really wanted to know whether he'd rather sleep on his

couch than—God!—with her. How could she wonder about that?

And then something strange happened. Mike drifted outside himself for the first time in his life. He wasn't looking at a situation entirely from his point of view.

Mike saw Chloe, really saw her, looking past himself. Saw how scared she was, how brave she was. Saw what she felt for him right there in her eyes. Saw that whatever his answer, she'd accept it.

Pale, bruised, Chloe was asking whether he wanted her. And even as he looked, he could see her bracing herself for rejection.

"No." The word came out raw, rough, as if he hadn't spoken in days. "No, I don't want to sleep on the damned couch."

Mike reached out a hand, looked at the bandage on her arm, stopped himself. His arm dropped back to his side. "You're wounded."

Man, just the thought of hurting her . . . it made him nauseous. Mike was rough in his sex. He never really thought about it. Most times his brain just switched off and his body took over.

When he thought about it, which wasn't often, he realized he fucked the right kind of women, ones who got off on him, and a good thing, too, because he didn't work too hard for their pleasure.

In taking care of his own, they got theirs. Win-win.

Right now, he was crazy excited, hard as a club. Muscles tight with sexual tension. This was familiar ground, this was right about the time when his mind switched off and his cock took over.

But . . . suppose—just suppose he forgot himself and hurt Chloe's arm, or was rough where she had bruises? It could happen, if he wasn't paying attention. He felt slick hot bile rise up in his throat at the thought.

The picture of Chloe in pain because of him bloomed bright and clear in his mind, cool and precise. Hearing her cry out in pain, pain he'd caused . . . oh Jesus. Fuck no. He'd rather tear out his own heart.

Because he could. If he went with fucking-as-usual, he'd be

entirely concentrated on his own dick inside Chloe, and experience told him he wouldn't be thinking at all.

And he could hurt her.

"I can't do this, Chloe," he whispered, the words almost physically grating against his throat. "I just can't."

She stepped back sharply. Her face closed up completely and now she looked like a little doll—porcelain and perfect and lifeless. Somehow she was far away from him, out of reach of his touch though she was only a foot away. She was utterly closed to him.

"No problem," she said smoothly. "I need a shower and then I'll go to bed. I don't need tea. I'll just, um, go into the, um, bedroom. Right now." Her voice started shaking, breaking up. She turned around fast, but not fast enough for him to miss the pain on her face, and he nearly burned up with rage at himself.

He didn't want to hurt her? *How about right now, slick?* You're goddamned hurting her right now.

This was a woman who'd had violence done to her *three times*. More than any woman should have to bear. And each goddamned time she'd been left completely alone. Including right now.

Right now he was sending her to his room without even a hug. And why? Because he was a coward. The whole hurting her thing was true but was also bullshit of the highest order.

He didn't flail around while fucking. He didn't bite or twist limbs. He could control himself enough not to physically hurt her. That was all a line of crap.

The truth was he was scared shitless. There was nothing here he even remotely recognized as familiar, except his hard-on. And even that felt somehow different. It wasn't a normal hard-on, the kind he had when an available woman was around. No, it was a Chloe woodie, through and through. Impossible to deal with, impossible to get rid of.

He buzzed with crazy energy.

He felt raw and unsure, like he was about to fall into some huge black hole, never to find his way back again. He was terrified this was going to change him in some unknown way, and instinctively, he was taking the coward's way out by rejecting her. Never mind that Chloe was being hurt in the process, just as long as ol' Mike's butt was covered.

Those fuckers had hurt her physically but Mike, man, he was a real champ because he wasn't hurting her body, which would heal, he was hurting her heart, which wouldn't. At the very moment she needed him, he was turning his back on her.

And even realizing this, even knowing Chloe was heading back to his bedroom to deal with her fear and trauma on her own, as she always had, he hesitated, frozen like a statue. Unable to move forward, unable to move at all.

Because this was a huge moment for him and his life was going to divide into two, right here, right now.

She was disappearing into his room, and in a second it would be too late. He'd stay forever on this side of the divide, alone and hurting.

"Chloe," he said quietly. "Stop."

She stopped, back to him, head low.

And then Mike said three words he had never said to any human being before. Three words he never thought he could say, three words he'd worked his whole life not to have to say.

"Chloe." His voice was hoarse, the words painful to get out. "I need you."

She turned around and he winced at the sight of her face. Ice white, hurting, without hope.

If she wanted to rant at him, scream at him, she'd have every right. Mike wouldn't have treated any woman who'd suffered violence this callously. So why was he doing this to Chloe?

Looking deep into his heart, something he was extremely uncomfortable doing and did as little as possible, he understood why.

It was because he cared too much for Chloe, but how could she know that?

He sure as shit had never told her what he felt. Not in all these six months in which he'd been her shadow. He'd fixed things in her house, driven her around, carried in her groceries, kept her company when she babysat, made sure she did her weight reps right. All those good-guy things that cost him nothing but that meant he could be near her. Because getting up in the morning, knowing he was going to drive Chloe to RBK or to the shelter or spotting her in the condo gym three mornings a week, well, that made his day.

Not one word about what she meant to him. Ever. Not one fucking word.

No wonder she wasn't expecting anything from him, not even now, when she needed him.

She was looking at him, eyes wide, mouth open. Shocked. "What did you say?"

He was shocked himself. The hand he held out to her trembled. A sniper's hand that trembled. His hand never trembled, but it did now.

He stepped over that chasm sharply dividing *before* and *after* and took her uninjured hand, brought it to his mouth. Her skin was smooth and icy cold. The cold of shock. Well, of course.

She'd been attacked, brutally and violently. Her worst nightmare, come to life. Again.

Mike hated to see her like this, the old Chloe, the Chloe who'd showed up at RBK on a wild quest, frightened and uncertain. She was even moving like the old Chloe, slow, hesitant, shaky.

That old Chloe had all but disappeared these past six months, wrapped into the folds of a loving extended family, deeply loved by two little girls and with Mike—well, with Mike around *a lot*. If nothing else, building up her muscles.

She walked well and fast now, laughed often, was a quiet

charmer. Had been pretty before and was now extraordinarily beautiful.

How it hurt him to see her back to the damaged woman who'd arrived in San Diego, hoping but not expecting to find a family.

"How do you need me? What do you mean?" she asked finally. She was so shocked it took her a couple of beats to answer him. "I don't understand."

Mike kept holding her hand, trying to warm it up. But also because it just felt so good in his. He reached up his other hand to touch her cheek. She flinched instinctively and his heart gave a huge thud in his chest.

Men had hurt her all her life. Though Chloe knew in her head he could never hurt her, he hadn't given her any reason to turn to him, to think of him as a refuge. She was feeling raw and alone, hunkered down into herself, surrounded by her loneliness like a force field. He wanted to break that force field down, shatter it.

She controlled her wince and let him stroke his fingers down her cheek, run the back of his fingers down her neck. Skin so smooth, so soft, so chilled. "I need you every way there is, Chloe. I'm not good with words the way you are, so I can't explain it, but I sure as hell can show you."

He stepped closer still, bent slightly, lifted her in his arms and carried her into the bedroom.

Mike carried her into his bedroom.

Chloe had never been carried as an adult woman. She'd been carried as a child, sick in the hospital. In all the thousands of romance novels she'd read, she always loved it when the man carried the woman somewhere. It just seemed to feed right into some primordial female lobe that was stubbornly resistant to modern notions of female equality.

Chloe sighed at the scenes she read, never believing in a million years that something like this would ever happen to her. And yet, here she was, in a man's strong arms, being carried somewhere. To the bedroom, actually.

Mike carried her easily, without watching where he was going. The only thing he watched was her eyes.

He was preternaturally strong and showed no sign whatsoever of making any kind of effort. He could just as easily have been carrying a glass of water, not a full-grown woman. And she'd even packed on fifteen pounds of pure muscle these past six months. Mike had seen to that.

To keep her balance, Chloe had to put her arms around his neck, loving the play of Mike's shoulder muscles along the inside of her arms. Sheer, unadulterated male power.

He walked slowly and directly into his bedroom, which she'd never seen. Her heart thumped painfully as they crossed the threshold.

Moonlight shining outside the big picture windows cast a soft glow over an enormous bed with a curved wood headboard, a big chest of drawers, a light-colored rug and an armchair.

He walked right by the bed to a door set in the left-hand wall. Dipping slightly with her in his arms, he opened the door and flipped the switch to the bathroom. Chloe narrowed her eyes at the flare of light.

"Wow." He put her down carefully, not letting her go until he was sure she was steady on her feet. He shook his arms as if he'd carried an almost unbearable weight and huffed dramatically. A man who'd just finished a hard, daunting task. He whooshed out a last breath, putting fervor and drama behind it. "Man. You really packed on those pounds, Chloe. I barely made it here."

She looked, startled, into his bright blue eyes, like looking into blue searchlights. His lips pursed, fighting a grin.

He was flirting with her!

She'd been underweight all her life. Once, when she was twelve, after three operations in four months, she'd lost so much weight her kidney had slipped.

Now she weighed something close to normal, and a lot of that weight was muscle. She narrowed her eyes at him. "Watch your step, Keillor. Or I'll clean your clock."

The grin broke loose. She smiled back, so glad of the light moment, switching off the darkness for a second. Then the darkness and the memories returned.

She shivered involuntarily and Mike stilled. His eyes searched hers, face grim. "I can't guarantee that nothing bad will ever happen to you again, honey. I can't. No one can. I can't guarantee that a shingle won't fall off a roof and bean you. I can't swear some drunk asshole won't plow into your car. But look at me, Chloe." He took her chin in his strong hand. "One thing I can guarantee? Those two or anyone else they send will never touch you again, not while I live. I hope that makes you feel better."

Mike's face was set, slightly pale. Light-years away from the good-time guy face he presented to the world. Good old Mike. Good for a beer and a laugh.

This wasn't that Mike. He wasn't even in the same universe as that Mike. This Mike was a force of nature, strength and will in every line of his body.

She nodded as a heavy pall lifted. No, no one could guarantee her nothing bad would ever happen again. That wasn't possible for anyone. But she was absolutely certain that right now she was utterly safe, and if the hot glow in Mike's eyes was any indication, something very good might happen very soon.

The bathroom had a huge tub and a big glass-enclosed shower cabin.

"I imagine you want to clean up," Mike said. "Or do you want something to eat first?" His arm was still around her. He was very close, so close she could see the line of demarcation between his heavy five o'clock shadow and the clear, tanned skin of his neck. Blue eyes stared into hers.

"Clean! Oh yes, please!" The idea of washing off the horrible experience, of washing away the violence and horror, trumped food or sleep.

Mike smiled a little. "Thought so. Bath or shower?"

Normally, bath. Soaking in warm water was nature's way of healing many things, including bruises. But she wanted water washing over her, washing away the violence, sluicing down her body and gurgling down the drain, together with the memory of the two men attacking her.

"Shower."

He nodded, his blue eyes never leaving hers. He watched her carefully as he walked her in and reached behind her, keeping his hand flat against the upper part of her back, his huge hand nearly covering it. The hand was warm and heavy and he kept it there, at the top of the zipper, awaiting permission.

She nodded jerkily.

He pulled at the tab, a slow long glide down her back, opening the two panels. Cooler air washed over her bare back. She was watching him carefully and noted the exact instant he realized she wasn't wearing a bra.

Her breasts weren't large or heavy. She didn't really need a bra. In the winter she wore silk camisoles and in the summer nothing, liking the feel of silk or cotton or linen against her bare skin.

His skin tightened over his high cheekbones as the back of his fingers ran down her without encountering anything but skin. His hand rested on the bare skin of the small of her back, a hot, exciting weight.

Heat radiated from his hand throughout her body, banishing cold and even the thought of cold. Chloe was essentially in his embrace. She stood quietly, relishing every single sensation, simply soaking it up. The expectant hush, the soft sound of his breath, the heat of his hand, the aura of strength and sex that pulsed around his person.

Mike had studiously refrained from touching her these past six months, so this massive sense of power and heat was new. Welcome, disconcerting, exciting.

They were standing chest to chest, Mike's hand on her lower back in the quiet bathroom He reached out without looking and turned a tap. A rush of water broke the silence. He kept his hand under the stream, never breaking his gaze.

"How hot do you want it?"

"Hot, but not boiling."

Both his hands were on her now. He gently brought the panels forward, sliding them off her arms, being particularly careful with her bandaged arm. Holding her gaze, he swiped at the dress and it fell to her feet.

She was dressed in panties and sandals.

Face tight, Mike stepped back a little and looked her over. Everywhere he looked her skin heated, as if he'd touched her with his hands.

Bringing his gaze back up, he whispered, "You're so beautiful, Chloe."

The way he was looking at her, she could have been Grace Kelly and Angelina Jolie and even Nicole Kidman all rolled into one, only shorter.

"Thank you." She lowered her voice as he did, as if they were exchanging confidences.

He stepped even closer. Then, without warning, dropped to one knee, as a knight would to his queen.

Startled, Chloe looked down at the top of his head. He had beautiful, glossy, thick chestnut hair that he kept short. But from here she could see that it would be unruly if it weren't cropped.

The bathroom light picked up a few blond highlights and some white hairs along the temple.

Her hand lifted, hovered over his head, unsure. Then—*to hell with it*—she placed the palm of her hand on his hair, ran her fingers through his scalp. The hair was warm and soft. A minty shampoo smell wafted up.

Something came out of Mike's throat, a sound like a big cat purring, and he moved his head under her hand, the invitation clear. He liked it when she touched his hair. She spread her fingers, curled them, letting the short strands tickle them.

Mike let out a whoosh of air. "I like that." His voice was deep, almost guttural.

"I'm glad," Chloe said simply.

He stayed kneeling before her another minute while she ran her hand through his hair, then reached up and slid her panties down her legs, lifting first one foot, then the other.

Chloe moved her hand from his head to his shoulder, for balance. His hair had felt pleasant under her fingers, but his shoulder . . . well, pleasant wasn't the word for it.

She'd held him in her arms six long months ago, and it had been wonderful. But it had been so fleeting, so brief. She barely remembered kissing him, except in her dreams.

But now—ah, bliss. Steely muscle, pure male power flowed up through her fingertips, almost like a transferal of force.

Mike slipped her sandals off, but didn't rise. Instead, he brought his head forward and nuzzled her belly. His face was warm against her belly. He had just a little beard stubble and it tickled against her skin.

He licked her, right next to her belly button, and the tickling sensation morphed into a rush of heat so intense it was like a door opening onto a bonfire. He licked again, opened his mouth against her skin and bit, just a little.

Chloe shuddered. Heat was blazing inside her. He nipped again, just a little bite that sent electric sparks through her. When he licked the tiny bite mark, her vagina pulled, muscles clenching around an invisible penis. The pull was so strong her stomach muscles moved.

Mike blew out a breath against her belly and leaned his head back to look at her face. He'd seen—he'd probably *felt*—what he did to her. But he didn't have that smug male look of a man who'd turned a woman on. His face was pulled down in lines that looked almost like pain.

He blew out another breath and rose stiffly, as if his muscles ached. A glance down and Chloe could see why. Mike didn't have his usual jeans on. He had on tan chinos and she could see him outlined against the lightweight material.

Wow.

"I turn you on." She couldn't believe she'd said those words. She almost looked around the bathroom to see if anyone else was there. But there was only Mike.

He winced. "You have no idea, Chloe."

"Then why—" This was so *hard*. She wasn't used to expressing her desires. This would be embarrassing if she didn't need to know like she needed to breathe. It hadn't made any sense to her then and it still didn't. All she knew was that his distance these past six months had been so painful, like a sharp barb stuck in her heart.

"Why did you stay away? I mean, you didn't stay away, you were around, but—" The words stuck in her throat but she had to get them out. No more swallowing what needed to be said. So she looked him straight in the eyes and opened herself up.

What could be the worst thing that could happen? Well, he could rip her to shreds . . . no, never mind. Even if he ripped her to shreds, she'd survived worse.

"You kissed me that day, at the Del Coronado. You remember, don't you?"

Silence. Only the sound of the water hissing as came out of the showerhead, splashing onto the tiles. Mike's jaw muscles jumped. "Oh yeah, I remember. Until the day I die, Chloe, I'll remember."

He sounded so sincere. And yet—"So *why*, Mike? It hurt me so much." The words came out harsh and raw, against the closed muscles of her throat.

She remembered it so clearly, that day. The magic kiss, as she now thought of it. Something enchanted, golden. Gone. Like a dream, long ago. When Amanda's work proved beyond a shadow of a doubt that Mike couldn't have beaten up that poor woman, Chloe had been waiting with Ellen and Nicole. Both had jumped up to join their husbands, embrace them.

Chloe had jumped up, too, to run to Mike.

And he had taken a step back, eyes shuttered and blank, and broken her heart. Arms that had been outstretched to hold him fell back down to her sides.

He had stood there stiffly, eyes on the ground, thanked her formally, and disappeared. Chloe had stood there, shocked, unable to move.

The others had looked at her, the women with pity in their eyes. Harry had put his arm around her shoulder and squeezed. "Thank you, honey, for what you did," he'd said, and she had nodded, unable to speak. Because if she spoke, tears would have burst out of her.

The rest of the evening had been a blur as they sat back down at the table, without Mike, and finished the food. Chloe had much experience with feeling out of place, so she'd choked a little food down, spreading the rest around her plate, counting the seconds until she could say she was tired and would like to go to bed.

Where she cried herself to sleep.

And then Mike showed up the next morning, having called up the condo manager and found her a flat on Harry's floor. He accompanied her to every furniture store in San Diego, or so it felt, worked alongside the delivery guys bringing in the furniture and, where necessary, assembled it, and had her set up in less than three days. She'd seen him every day since, and he never touched her again.

"Why?" she whispered.

He shook his head, eyes never leaving hers. "That's not important now, Chloe. What's important is that things have changed. It's not like that anymore. Here." He kissed her forehead. "Let's get you cleaned up."

In the shower, he gently placed her injured arm on his shoulder. "There you go. We need to keep it dry."

Chloe had been washed before, of course. Plenty of times, in the hospital. Hospitals. But never like this.

Mike pumped some minty-smelling soap onto a washcloth and ran it over every inch of her body, followed by warm water and then his mouth. Long, sensuous strokes of the cloth followed by long, sensuous strokes of his tongue. Her neck, her shoulders. The warm cloth went lower, circled her breasts while he watched her so very carefully.

Chloe could see the skin move over her left breast, in time with her heart. Did he understand the effect he was having on her?

She looked up to find him watching her carefully, face tight, eyes like blue fire locked onto hers.

Oh yeah. He understood.

He bent her slightly over his left arm and with his right washed her belly. Chloe felt unbalanced, in every way there was, unsure of her footing. But Mike had her. She wasn't going to fall down.

He nuzzled the underside of her left breast, the one that was pounding, lips brushing lightly over her skin while taking light little tastes. A flush went through her at each touch of his lips, stroke of his tongue. And then—oh God!—he was suckling her nipple, long, hard pulls of his mouth echoed in her vagina, internal muscles tightening with each tug of his mouth. Her breathing became ragged and if she didn't have his strong arm holding her up, she'd slide down to the tiles, unable to stand.

Her hands slid from his shoulders to his head, holding him as he suckled her. His mouth pulled back, he gave her nipple a last lick, which she felt down to her toes, and straightened.

She didn't have to look down to know he was aroused. His nostrils were flaring as he breathed in and out heavily, underneath his dark tan he was flushed and his lips were red, engorged.

His eyes suddenly widened.

"What?" Chloe asked.

Mike gave a half laugh, which sounded as if he were choking. "I can't believe this. I have not been without a condom in my pocket since I was fifteen years old. Ever." He closed his eyes in pain, then opened them again, blue and fierce. "And now I am without a condom. Totally. Don't even have one in the house. Haven't needed one these past six months. Fuck." He blew out a big breath. "What are we going to do? I can't make it to the drugstore. Closest one's about a mile and a half away. Just can't do it. Can't ask Harry or Sam, either. And don't ask me to pull out because I don't think I can. Once I get in you, I'm not leaving for a good, long while."

Chloe stroked his shoulder, then ran a fingernail along the top muscle, hard and bulging, slowly going from the ball of his shoulder up his neck to behind his ear. She wasn't hurting him but he could feel the bite of it.

It excited him. His breathing speeded up and his lips grew even darker. "This is torture, right? You're going to torture me because we can't make love. But even if we can't, you're going to keep me in this state. There are rules, Chloe. There's even a Convention. The Geneva one."

She laughed. Leaned forward and bit him gently on the jaw. He shook. Looking down, she could actually see his erect penis move inside his pants.

He was completely at her mercy. A plaything. This powerful man was in *her* power now.

There were things she needed to tell him, but not now. Now was not the moment for darkness, now was the moment for heat, and light.

She leaned forward again, kissed him gently. Pulled away a fraction of an inch; he would feel the puff of her breath against him. "It's not a problem, Mike. Make love to me now."

His face changed, grew darker. Gazing into her eyes, he undressed. Threw his shirt open, the ping of the buttons off the tiles loud enough to be heard over the roar of the shower, unbuttoned his pants, dropped them and his briefs, stepped out of them, stepped out of his shoes, toed off his socks, all without wavering his gaze.

He stepped into the cabin, right under the showerhead, the water turning his hair dark, sluicing down his chest, straightening out his chest hairs so they arrowed down, as if to showcase that huge penis.

He backed her up against the tile wall and placed a huge hand on her chest. She was sure he could feel her heart pounding against the palm of his hand. Watching her carefully, he ran his hand down the center of her body, slowly, the calluses on the palm of his hand raising goose bumps.

At her hips, he turned his hand around, moved lower, cupped her. Every sense she had was concentrated there, where his hand was. He held it there, warm, pressed against her, then stroked her gently, running a finger around her labia.

At the touch of her, the skin tightened around his eyes and over his high cheekbones. He didn't need to ask if she was aroused. He could feel it against his hand.

The finger dipped inside, moving slowly up inside her. Her legs started trembling.

"Mike." Her voice was a whisper, not out of sexiness, but because she couldn't draw in enough breath to speak normally. "We need to get to a bed because I don't think my legs can hold me."

His jaw muscles jumped. "No?" His fingers opened, spreading her. "I like it fine here."

Now all of her was trembling. All her breath left her body as he fit his penis to her and slid inside, slowly, completely. He was huge, but she was ready. In a very real sense, she'd been waiting all her life for this moment.

He moved his big hands to her hips, then around to her buttocks, and lifted her until her legs went around his hips. He leaned heavily into her, so deep inside her now it was as if he reached her heart.

She felt everything. His dark chest hairs against her breasts, rough and prickly, the hard defined muscles of his abdomen against her belly, the rough mat of his pubic hairs against the sensitive skin of her sex.

She could feel the beat of his heart in his penis, buried deeply inside her. Her sex contracted sharply and he moved inside her, becoming somehow larger, thicker. It made her contract again.

"God," he muttered.

They were staring at each other. Chloe had never watched another person's face from so close up before. Everything that happened—every time she tightened around him, every time she shuddered, every time her fingers clutched his arms, her legs tightened—she could see the effect on him.

"If I move, I'm going to come," he said, his voice strained.

She huffed out a laugh and his penis surged in her as she moved. "If we stay here, we drown."

"Stalemate," he whispered.

"Not quite," she whispered back, and tightened around him deliberately, milking him while rising against him, pushing him even deeper inside her.

Mike threw back his head, groaned, swelled inside her and finally moved, short, hard, fast strokes, the friction creating immense heat, heat that was going to make her explode.

It was Mike who exploded first, though, one hard deep thrust, gritting his teeth against a shout while jetting inside her, the strokes and the jets of semen somehow exactly in time with the pulses of her sex, and it went on and on, each stroke, each contraction feeding the pleasure.

The back of Chloe's head thudded against the tile wall as hot water sluiced down over her upturned face and her head disappeared as her body simply took over, rubbing against the wall in time with Mike's thrusts until it all became one big blur, her body contracting, Mike coming, the water falling, heat exploding inside her in a fireball of sensations. She forgot who she was and became a creature of instinct and of sensations.

Finally, Mike stopped moving, his head nestled against her neck, huge shoulders heaving as he pulled in breaths as if he'd run a four-minute mile.

Mike opened his hands and she stood on shaking legs.

He kissed her neck and slowly pulled out of her, still hard.

"I think we need that bed now," he said.

Chapter 14

The Meteor Club

The prostitute screamed, struggled. Coughed, screamed again. Struggled.

Stupid cow.

What did she think she was going to gain? She was fastened to the board and her hands were in police restraints. Unbreakable restraints.

And yet the human will to live was strong, no one knew that better than Nikitin. He'd done this hundreds of times. And even when the man on the inclined board knew it was going to end badly, he struggled.

Dmitri continued pouring water over the three layers of cloth covering the woman's face and looked over at him.

Nikitin waited, taking another long puff on a Marlboro. American cigarettes were excellent. How stupid of the Americans to put all those warning signs on the packages. Of course cigarettes killed. What didn't kill? Life itself killed.

The cloth was sucked in as the woman instinctively tried to

breathe. But the cloth was soaked in water and the only effect was a trickle of water coming into the nose and mouth. The body considered this an imminent threat, as invasive as a gunshot wound, and reacted accordingly. The bucking and writhing increased. In silence, though, as there was no breath to make a noise.

Nikitin hated it when they made noises.

Nikitin breathed out the smoke, counted. *Thirteen, fourteen, fifteen.* He nodded. Dmitri immediately stopped pouring water over the cloth and lifted it.

The naked woman was writhing crazily. She was young and strong, kept herself in shape. Lean sleek muscles moved beneath that deep honey-colored skin.

She wasn't going to break her bonds—they'd been tested on battle-hardened soldiers, after all—but she could do herself an injury. Pull or strain a muscle. Nikitin had known men who'd broken their own bones in anguish, trying to get away from the water.

There were soft cloths between the restraints on her wrists and ankles and her skin.

The whole point of waterboarding this *prostitutka* was to avoid marring her. Avoid leaving any tangible signs of torture. She was an expensive commodity. Nikitin knew how much she earned the club. His masters, the *vory*, would be over here soon and would make inquiries if they saw a drop in income.

Nikitin blew another plume of smoke out of the side of his mouth, got up from the stool where he'd been watching the proceedings, and walked over to the woman. Her forehead was strapped to the board so she couldn't turn her head, so she did the only thing she could do. She closed her eyes.

"Look at me." Nikitin didn't bother putting menace in his voice. He wanted this over and done with as soon as possible. He needed information and as soon as he had it, he wanted to get away from this woman, fast.

She didn't open her eyes.

"Dmitri," Nikitin said quietly, and his second-in-command placed the cloth over her face again and slowly poured more water onto it.

She held her breath for as long as she could, but the breathing reflex is the most powerful reflex of all. Primordial. There are many ways to use the body to kill itself. You can bash your head against the wall until you fall bloody and unconscious. You can cut your arteries at the neck or the wrist. You can even swallow your own tongue. But you cannot hold your breath until you die. Your body won't let you.

After a minute the cloth bulged inward as she breathed in water and writhed madly.

Nikitin waited a second, two, judging. Lifted his finger. Dmitri stopped immediately. Removed the cloth. "Look at me," Nikitin said again, no change in his tone. "We can do this all day and all night."

Her eyes popped open. *Da.* This was more like it.

Defiance was written all over her face. Clearly, Sands treated his women too well. If this woman only knew what Nikitin could do to her . . . He wouldn't because she was still a money-earner, but he was tempted.

"Hijo de puta! Pendejo!" she spat.

Interesting. Nikitin knew her background, knew she was born on the streets of Tijuana. She'd educated herself out of that. Her English was, as far as he could tell, accentless and perfect. She'd turned herself into an American whore.

But under stress, her origins showed.

The board was inclined, feet up, head down. Nikitin dragged his stool over, sat next to her head at the bottom of the board. He leaned over, knowing his face covered her entire field of vision. Good. Right now, he needed to fill her world. He was her God and she had to appease him.

She stopped wrenching at her restraints and lay there, breathing hard. Nikitin looked at her carefully, going from her face slowly up the board to her feet.

She was naked for a reason. Being naked thrust you back into defenseless childhood, stripped you of all dignity. Not that a whore would know much of dignity.

She was an extraordinarily beautiful woman, head to toe, though Nikitin was immune to her charms. Was immune to all women. But he could easily see that she had the kind of body and face men would pay a great deal to rent for a while. Very few men had something like this at home.

Intelligently, Sands made sure his whores ate well, slept enough, exercised in the club's downstairs gym; he also had a strict no-drugs rule which was enforced with pain.

The merchandise was protected and treated to last more than most in the field. Nikitin had once seen a whore on the streets of Odessa who looked forty but whose papers showed she was six-teen. Life on the street was measured in dog years. Each year on the street was like seven. Except at the club, where the goods were pampered and had a much longer shelf life.

His gaze drifted back from her feet to her face, the message clear. *I own you. All of you.*

He hitched his stool closer, bent down to her until their noses touched.

"Two of my men are missing," he said, voice cold and clear.

The woman blinked, taken aback. This wasn't what she was expecting. A frown appeared between her eyebrows. "You think I did something to them?"

"Yes."

"To your . . . men?" She looked down at herself, then back up to him. If she'd said the words aloud, the message couldn't have been clearer. What could one woman do to two of his men, former Spetsnaz?

Fuck.

For the first time, it occurred to Nikitin that she might not actually have any information.

If so, he was in deepest deepest shit. He'd come with only three men. How hard, how dangerous could it be to invest in a brothel? The mission had been more economic than military and Nikitin had chosen his men accordingly.

He hadn't brought his entire A team. Most of them were involved in protecting a diamond route in Sierra Leone. Stupid, stupid. Because this investment here might prove to be even more lucrative than diamonds. Particularly diamonds that had to be mined a thousand miles from civilization and then accompanied to market.

He'd underestimated this, thinking there would be no opposition. They were flying right under the radar of the authorities and Sands had assured him that one of the mayor's assistants and two D.A.s were members of the club and they'd be protected.

And yet, there were enemies of the club out there, had to be, otherwise his men would be here now.

Two men—two good, smart soldiers—couldn't simply disappear from the face of earth, could they?

They had gone to give a lesson to an *Amerikanskaya* who was a minor annoyance, like a piece of grit in a shoe. Creating disharmony among the women. Nikitin had even debated sending one man for such an easy task, but in the end decided on sending two. Ivan was harder but Lyov had better English.

Nothing to it. Have a talk with the woman who was disrupting their business, convince her to stop, call in mission completed. They never called in. They had dropped off the face of the earth.

Ivan and Lyov's cell phones were offline and they weren't contacting him.

This woman had to know something. She went to the shelter

often. Sands was just now waking up to the fact that he'd allowed insubordination to seep into his stable of women.

"Where are my men?" he asked again. He kept his voice low, even. He didn't have to scream to make his point. His point was clear. She was trussed like an animal and he held the power of life and death over her.

She tried to shake her head and forgot that it was bound. A sound like steam escaped her lips.

This was getting them nowhere. Nikitin looked up at Dmitri, flicking his finger. *Get ready for another round.*

Dmitri poured water from a large pitcher into a smaller one, so the trickle of water could be better controlled.

"My men went to the shelter, where that woman indoctrinated you. They were going to talk to the woman, tell her how she was making a mistake with the whores of the Meteor and had to stop."

Consuelo panted, black eyes shiny with hatred. Had Nikitin been the kind of man to care, it might have bothered him. But he'd been hated by the best. One whore's hatred didn't mean anything at all.

"You *hurt* her!" she screamed, spittle flying.

Nikitin averted his head, pulled back from the spittle, full of distaste. "The fact is," he continued, as if she hadn't spoken, "my men never came home. I have no idea what happened to them. I need to know from you where they are."

Nikitin was aware of the fact that Consuelo might have no idea what had happened to Ivan and Lyov. But women, like primitive tribes, had some kind of jungle system of information, which spread among them like a virus.

He had no alternatives. He was alone here, in this strange world. Dmitri was muscle. Decent muscle, true, and he'd been well-trained, but his English was minimal and he had limited use outside enforcement.

So Nikitin was reduced to waterboarding whores.

Nikitin drummed his fingers on his thigh, the only expression of frustration he could allow himself.

He had no resources here in this country, none.

He had resources back home. *Pirat*, the best hacker in Russia. Nikitin had no idea where he lived or even what his name was. It made no difference. Pirat was a genius and always came back with an answer.

Except now. Pirat had hacked into all the hospitals, all the police stations, all the news feeds, even the morgues, because surely two men could not just disappear into nothing? And yet they had.

Nikitin desperately needed to keep this news from the *vory* back home. Lots of money was involved and the *vory* did not want even a hint of trouble.

Losing two men into the void was the very definition of trouble. *Chert!*

This whore had to know something. "Again," he said.

Dmitri placed the cloth on her face.

The whore started keening with terror, which was exactly what he wanted. He watched dispassionately as the water was poured, the cloth sucked into her mouth as she tried to breathe. He judged the right moment, just before drowning . . . ah. He lifted his finger and Dmitri lifted the cloth.

Tears were streaming down the whore's face, she was choking for air, trembling all over. She was screaming, but had very little breath, so it came out more a gurgle than a scream. She was terrified.

And she wasn't talking.

Dmitri moved to place the cloth over her face again but Nikitin held up a hand. Dmitri stopped, obediently.

Nikitin inched his stool closer. "Tell me everything about this woman who is spreading discontent among you. Her name is Chloe. Chloe what?"

Even bound, she was able to shrug one shoulder. "Mason. I think." He opened his mouth to tell Dmitri to start again when she spoke. "No one uses last names at the shelter. It's forbidden. So I don't know her last name for sure and no one else would. I just saw an envelope in her purse once. It said 'For Chloe Mason.' That's all I know."

"She's a volunteer?"

The whore nodded. "They all are."

Nikitin didn't truly understand that. Volunteer to work with whores? For *free*? What would she get out of it? But he had long since resigned himself to the stupidity of humankind. Volunteering to work with whores was right up there with the men he'd seen who'd destroyed themselves over the love of a woman. Or what they thought was love.

Nikitin didn't understand that, either.

No matter, there were plenty of other things he understood just fine.

"What else?" Because there was something else, he could tell. "What else do you know about this woman?"

The prostitute's throat worked, the sign of words not wanting to come out. "Again," he said quietly to Dmitri.

"No!" The prostitute screamed. The skin over her left breast was trembling with the rapid beating of her heart. "There's something else, the only thing I know."

Nikitin didn't answer. He simply waited. She could see Dmitri holding the cloth. He didn't have to talk.

"There's—there's a man. He comes for her almost every day she's there. He's like her shadow." She coughed, a paroxysm that lasted several minutes.

Yes! Nikitin didn't move a muscle. Merely asked, quietly, "Who is he?"

"I don't know," she wheezed. "But he's a big man. Not tall, but big. Like a weightlifter."

"What did he drive?"

A frown appeared between her eyebrows. She coughed again. "I don't know. One of those big gringo cars."

"An SUV?"

She nodded. "Tell me the model."

She shook her head. Nikitin restrained himself from slapping her hard. It wouldn't help. She didn't know. The whores didn't drive. Weren't allowed to learn. A driver's license in the hands of a whore could be very dangerous.

"And where does this Chloe live?"

She shook her head but her eyes flickered. She knew. The bitch knew. Nikitin leaned right over her, gazing directly into her eyes. Out of her line of sight, he signaled to Dmitri. He dropped a cloth over her face and started pouring. She didn't have time to prepare herself and breathed in sharply. The only effect was to tighten the grip of the cloth over her face. She started choking immediately, kicking madly against the restraints, mewling sounds coming from under the cloth.

If he took a blood sample right now, the carbon dioxide level would be extremely high.

Thirteen, fourteen, fifteen. He looked at Dmitri, who lifted the cloth.

Her eyes were wild, unfocused. She'd been convinced that she was going to die. Nikitin had once seen a Special Forces soldier, an *Amerikanski*, resist hours of waterboarding, but he'd been trained. He hadn't talked but he had been reduced to an animal and had been shot later, almost as an act of pity.

Her eyes were rolling around in her head like an animal's. Nikitin clasped her jaw tightly, painfully, and turned her head to him. "Listen to me." He waited until her eyes focused on him. She was breathing in short, ragged breaths, her entire body shuddering.

Good.

"Where. Does. Chloe. Live."

Nikitin deliberately looked up at Dmitri, who stood ready. She saw that and shuddered. The whore's body would be telling her she wouldn't survive another round. She would, but she wouldn't understand that. There would be very little reasoning bouncing around in her head, just dark primal fears.

The whore opened her mouth but only wheezing sounds came out of her throat, the sounds of sheer terror. Nikitin waited. No use punishing her when her body wouldn't let her talk. He waited, watching her eyes carefully. He recognized the exact moment in which she came back into herself.

"Where?" he repeated.

There was no resistance in her. None. Her body had almost died and had come back, the most primal experience a living being can have. Next to that, there was nothing she could do.

"Coronado Shores," the whore gasped. "That's what I heard some of the other girls say. *La Torre*." She wheezed, her body trying to pull in air.

Nikitin didn't press. He had a vague idea of where—and above all what—Coronado Shores was. A place for the rich. *La Torre*. He tucked that name away for later. He merely nodded, as if confirming what he already knew.

"What else?" he asked, keeping his tone low and bored. As if what she was saying were of little significance. "What else do you know about her?"

Now she was looking confused. She gazed right into his eyes, something a *chernye*, a whore, should never do. And they didn't. The women at the club were trained not to look a man in the eyes until they were having sex.

This one was looking straight at him, training forgotten, terrified. "Nothing. I know nothing else." Her voice was low, shock still in the tones. And truth in every syllable.

Nikitin knew truth and he knew lies. He'd broken enough men to know the difference. The woman had no more information to give. She didn't know where his men were. If she had any information at all, she'd have given it. She was useless to him.

"Three more times," he growled to Dmitri in Russian.

Three more would break her. The bitch deserved it. If she hadn't started acting up, he would never have had to send his men on a mission that had inexplicably swallowed them whole, leaving him with one man in a foreign country, with the *vory* back home expecting everything to be ready for the arrival of the first shipment very soon.

He stood and looked down at the woman who was so much trouble. If she hadn't been worth money to his backers, he'd have had her killed, and not slowly.

"Three more," he said again, and left the room, closing the soundproofed door behind him.

Consuelo came to her senses slowly. She was cold. Terribly cold, down to her bones, in a way she'd never been before. Born in Tijuana, living in San Diego, she'd never experienced true cold, had never seen snow. Now, it was as if she were encased in ice.

She opened her eyes, at first not recognizing what she was seeing. A flat expanse, a reflecting surface. She stared for a long time until she finally understood. Water. Water all over and her own vomit.

She blinked and things started to come into focus. She was lying on the floor, naked, in a pool of water. She shivered convulsively, mind blank.

She had no idea how long she lay there, shivering and shaking on the cold tile floor, moving only her eyes. Nothing made sense. She was used to being naked—that was how she worked, after all—but not like this. She felt more than naked, she felt stripped bare of everything, even her humanity.

It was coming back in slow, painful stages. The cruelty of the Russian's eyes, the endless questions, the near-drownings.

She couldn't remember how many times that horrible cloth had been put over her face but she did remember that desperate shock of knowing that she was drowning, being on the verge of death, then brought back to life at the last possible second, gasping and shaking, numb with fear.

And the Russian, carefully watching her, with no expression on his face. It was almost worse than some of her customers who secretly liked inflicting pain. They had a sly smile as they sneaked in a hard pinch, pulled her hair too hard. There was always a secretive smile, because they were doing what they liked best—hurting.

This was nothing like that. The Russian didn't like what he was doing to her. He didn't dislike it, either. He was totally indifferent. There was no doubt that if he felt it helped him in any way, he'd have ordered his man to keep pouring water over the cloth until she drowned for real. But she still earned the Meteor Club good money, so she wasn't killed.

None of it meant anything to him.

Of course, Consuelo had never meant anything to the men who bought her, she knew that. But this was one level down from the horror of the Meteor Club. And they were all going to stay deep down at this level, since the Russians were here to stay. Word had it that they were pumping so much money into the club, they could kill her and her friends and use the skins for coats, for all Sands could care.

She rose shakily, hand slipping in the water, landing facedown on the floor again. Getting up seemed impossible, something beyond her.

She was broken inside.

Often after sex sessions, she was left hurting in some way. Most men went to prostitutes because they could treat a woman exactly as they pleased. A wife, a girlfriend expected certain attentions, which some men found difficult to give. Something built up inside them they had to release during sex for pay.

Consuelo was used to feeling used and thrown away, brought low by lust and coldness. But this was something else again. This was a level of darkness and cruelty she'd never even suspected existed. She knew she'd touched rock bottom. Any further down and she would die.

Consuelo had felt the dark wings of death brush her. The long-forgotten teachings of the nuns in the Tijuana slums when she was a tiny child, before her mother abandoned her, suddenly rose in her mind. She had a soul, and it had just been touched by the Devil himself.

Consuelo knew, beyond a shadow of a doubt, that she had to get out. For her life. For her soul.

She couldn't stay one second longer.

The ground was slippery and she was shaking, weak. She had to get up, *get up now*. She had to get away from this place as fast as she could.

Sands treated the girls relatively well. Consuelo knew that. When he'd found her, an abandoned girl living on the streets, he'd saved her life. God knows he'd told her often enough.

And he'd waited until she was fifteen to turn her over to the life. She recognized now that it wasn't his goodness of heart, but a cold-eyed business decision. First had come intensive English lessons, deportment, long talks with the older women. He'd turned her into an upscale prostitute who earned him much more money than she would have on the street.

She'd been so *grateful*. It shamed her to realize that she'd been a little in love with Sands all these years. She'd wake up having dreamed that they got married and had children. The dreams left a lingering warmth that lasted until the first trick of the day.

Fool. She was a fool. And if she didn't want to be a dead fool, she was going to have to move fast.

The core of chill was still there but her muscles felt stronger now. Able to bear her weight. Fear and dread and determination fueled her as she placed the palms of her hands on the slick floor.

She looked around for a second to see what she could cling to if her legs wouldn't bear her up, and that's when she saw it. A small metal object on the floor behind an armchair. If you weren't lying with your face on the floor you wouldn't see it. It belonged to *him*, to the *ruso*. She had an almost tactile memory of him carelessly flinging a dark leather jacket over the chair back, not paying attention because there was work to be done. A woman to torture.

She slithered through the water, pulling herself along by her elbows, reached out and picked it up. A small object with a removable cap. A thumb drive.

Nothing about the outside of the small metallic object gave any indication of what it was, what was contained within it. Consuelo only hoped it would be something that could harm the *ruso*.

She lay on the cold, wet floor for a while, panting, clutching the thumb drive in her fist until it warmed up, the only source of warmth in the entire world.

Finally, she pushed with her hands and sat up, head swimming, nauseous. After another minute she pulled herself to her feet with the help of the chair.

She looked down at herself, naked and shivering. There were faint red marks across her chest, her shins, wrists and ankles where the restraints had bitten her skin. Other than that her skin looked pale and colorless, with an underlying gray, like that of a dead person. As a child, she'd seen lots of dead people, shot in the streets like animals by the *narcotraficantes*. As a child, she'd thought death to be the most horrible thing that could happen to a person.

She'd been wrong.

She dressed. Just the bare minimum, panties and the linen shift dress she'd had on. The bra and shoes were beyond her. As she made her way to the door, she glanced at a mirror and stopped, shocked.

She looked like the living dead.

Consuelo brought a hand to her mouth and watched the woman in the mirror do the same thing. It was like watching someone else. Consuelo as she knew herself was dead. She peeked out the door, saw no one and slipped out.

The corridors were mainly empty. Life at the Meteor Club didn't really start until 10 P.M.

Consuelo knew she looked like a ghost as she made her way to her room, a wild-eyed ghost with messy hair and ruined makeup. The few girls she met looked downward as she passed and Consuelo realized how many times she'd seen the women of the Meteor looking abused since the arrival of *los rusos*. They'd all learned to let it go, avert their gaze, pretend nothing was wrong.

This was the beginning of a road that shot straight to hell.

In her room, Consuelo went to the closet and took out her one pair of jeans and a white shirt.

She stared for a moment with loathing at the clothes in her closet. Bright colors, plunging necklines, clothes meant to entice men, clothes easy to get out of so the men wouldn't have to work for their sex.

Her hand fisted in a blue satin gown that looked good on her. Made her skin glow, highlighted her breasts. She hated it. There was at least $50,000 worth of evening gowns and fine lingerie in her room and her hands shook with the desire to rip all that satin and silk and lace to ribbons. Slash it all, then burn it.

But she didn't dare. If she had any chance at all, it would be because nobody would sound the alarm until tomorrow evening. Her first client was at 9 P.M.

She would be far far away by the time the client, a famous attorney who had gotten out of control a few times lately, showed up.

So instead of ripping her clothes up or tossing them to the floor, she left the closet as it was, neat and organized.

All of this was so easy to walk away from.

Her hands started trembling again as she pulled a card out from a hidden pocket in the lining of her purse, since their rooms were routinely checked. Most of the girls had the number memorized and so did Consuelo, but she loved the card so much she kept it because it was so beautiful.

A normal visiting card, cream-colored, with only a number and a stylized bird in flight.

Freedom.

There was a rumor that one of the people at the other end of that number was Chloe's brother. If that was true, Consuelo could only hope he wouldn't blame her for the attack on Chloe. Whatever the man's decision, he was now her only hope.

She punched the numbers in and waited, trembling. When a quiet female voice answered she said, "I'm in trouble. Can you help me?"

Chapter 15

La Torre
Coronado Shores

"Are you hungry?" Mike asked. "I never fed you."

Chloe was in a sex coma. She barely understood what he was saying. More than hearing the words, she felt his deep voice reverberate in his chest and, since she was lying naked on top of him, reverberating against her chest, too.

"Are you?"

That luscious sound was words, presumably meaning something. She should be paying attention to them, instead of relishing those utterly male bass tones.

Mike rubbed his chin against her hair. He had the beginning of a five o'clock shadow and her hair caught in his beard, pulling a little. The tiny bite of pain brought her back to reality.

He'd said something . . . food!

Chloe was just about to answer that food was the last thing on her mind when her body spoke for her. Her stomach rumbled loudly.

He laughed and, after a second, so did she.

"Apparently, I am hungry." And she was—ravenous. Wow. All of a sudden. This explosion of entirely new feelings had masked it. She lifted her head from his chest and smiled into his eyes. "What's on offer?"

Was that voice coming out of her mouth really hers? It was sultry, husky. Mike smiled, took her hand and moved it over his groin.

His penis was still iron-hard, slicked with their juices. Chloe lifted her eyebrows. She was exhausted but he seemed to have this nonstop battery. She didn't want sex right now, but still . . . her hand curled around him instinctively. She felt him thicken even more, moving in her hand.

Like Prince Charming kissing Sleeping Beauty on the lips and bringing her to life. Only the other way round and using another part of the anatomy.

Mike's breath came in on a hiss and his eyes narrowed. The sound felt like pain, and a couple of hours ago, Chloe would have lifted her hand, startled, wondering if she'd hurt him.

But now she knew better. She wasn't hurting him.

Now her face creased in a knowing smile.

"You're not going to get fed anytime soon if you keep that up," he said, the corner of his mouth lifting.

"Men really are different from women," Chloe mused, looking down at her hand caressing his penis. She pumped her hand slowly, down, up, down, and felt blood coursing through it. It was dark red again, the enormous bulbous tip a plum color.

His penis was the most fascinating thing in the world. She'd been to the Tate, the Louvre and the Uffizi and nothing there could compare to this.

"Well . . . yeah." Mike arched his hips a little, to put himself more deeply into her hand. His tone was—*duh. Yes, men and women are different.*

"I mean, we aren't quite so . . . blatant in our desire. It's not so easy to tell that we're turned on. And, well, we have a turn-off switch, too. I'm not that experienced, but you don't seem to have that switch at all. I'm all tapped out and you're still raring to go. Sort of like the Energizer Bunny."

It was a feeble joke, but she did expect him to laugh. Instead, his face grew somber and his hips stopped moving. He placed his hand over hers, stopping her movements.

"I—" he began. "It's not—" He stopped, clenched his mouth tightly. Some strong emotion was working in him. His throat moved with unsaid words.

How Chloe understood that, needing to say something but not being able to. How many times she'd wanted to say things and choked them back down her throat? If human anatomy were like plumbing, her throat would be clogged with black, unsaid words.

She lifted her hand away. Mike wanted to say something and couldn't. It was cruel to distract him by sex.

She sat up and covered herself with the sheet. It wasn't modesty. Mike had feasted on her breasts, he knew every inch of her. But instinct told her that this was a moment for talk, not sex.

His throat clicked and she took pity on him. She picked up his hand, examined it. Actually his hand was almost as fascinating as his penis, and had been the source of almost as much delight. His hand was definitely a sex organ.

And beautiful.

Large, rough, calloused. Immensely strong, big veins popping on the backs. The epitome of male hands. Utterly different from hers.

She curled her fingers through his. A gesture of affection, rather than sex. Meant as support, not arousal. "There's something you want to say, Mike?" she asked gently.

He looked away, jaws clenched, then huffed out a breath and swiveled his head back to her.

"Yeah. There is." He stopped. His throat worked, muscles

moving. This was obviously hard for him. Chloe understood hard. She waited.

Another long breath whooshing out of him. His fingers tightened around hers. "I guess now's as good a time as ever to say this. It's hard because it's not pretty. I-I've slept around a lot, Chloe."

She smiled. His beautiful face was so solemn, so serious, as if imparting a state secret.

"I know, Mike. Ellen and Nicole told me, and, well, Harry, too. They, uh, they were quite clear that you . . . messed around. A lot."

Messing around. It was a delicate way to put it.

"But not in the last six months." He said it belligerently, as if she was going to deny it. "Not since the day I met you."

After that, he just shut down. The silence in the room grew heavy, then oppressive. He didn't say a word.

His body was speaking, though. Every muscle was in high relief, a body in complete lockdown. What he wanted to say was painful. It was entirely likely he didn't even have the words for it.

She laid her other hand on his chest, right over his heart. His thumping heart.

"You have something to say, Mike. I can tell. And it looks like it's hard for you. But I'm not in a hurry. Whatever it is, it can wait. Maybe tomorrow—"

"No!" He breathed in, said it more quietly. "No. I need to get this out." He looked down at his lap, at where his rigid penis reached almost to his belly button. So stiff you'd have to pry it away from that flat, muscular abdomen. "So here it is. I have a strong sex drive. Which most people think is a good thing. I'm male, relatively young, healthy. Strong sex drive kind of goes with the whole package, right?"

He was sweating. A drop of perspiration rolled down his cheek and dropped on his chest. There was such tension in him, like a tuning fork quivering. Chloe had no idea how to relieve him. Her only gift to him could be stillness, and attention.

She nodded.

"Wrong." The word came out through clenched jaws. "In all these years, it's never been good, never been clean, healthy fun. It—it didn't feel healthy, it felt sick. It was more than an itch I had to scratch. It was like—like on a regular basis some terrible poison accumulated in my body and I could only expel it through my dick. There was this tension that would build and build and I simply couldn't stay put. It was like being possessed. I'd just have to go out and do something about it. And without even planning it, I'd end up in some bar. Exactly the kind of bar a woman looking to hook up with someone goes to. I don't know . . . I think maybe I gave off some kind of special vibe or smell or dog whistle or something because five minutes in the bar and some dame comes up to me. Regular, like clockwork. Five minutes, ten, and a woman's drinking my beer and telling me her address. I learned a long time ago to recognize a working girl. Paying for it was going too far, even for me. But anyone else was fair game as long as she wasn't married or seeing someone else. That was another line I drew. But that leaves a lot of women in the game. I was like this grenade and someone had pulled a pin. So I'd grab the fuck du jour—" He stopped, fixed her in his intense light blue gaze. "Sorry, but that's exactly what it was. I can't whitewash it."

He was vibrating beneath her hands. She kept her voice quiet and low, exactly as if speaking to a distressed animal. "It's okay, Mike."

He shook his head sharply. "No, it's not okay. Not even close to being okay." He drew in a deep, shuddering breath. "So . . . I'd go off with the woman, mostly to her house because I didn't like anyone in my place. And we'd fuck. And fuck and fuck. I could keep it up for as long as I had to. Once, I heard we lost two guys I'd trained with. IED in Iraq. Went out, found myself three women and fucked for twenty-four hours straight. I was like in a daze. I'd had too much booze, yeah, but it wasn't that. It was like—like if I drank enough, if I fucked hard enough, long enough, I wouldn't—"

His throat clicked again. His entire body now was one huge stress signal. His eyes were red, breath wheezed in and out of that barrel chest.

"Die," Chloe said, and he jerked.

"What?"

"If you fucked hard enough, long enough, you wouldn't die."

It was the classic addiction story. God knows, she'd heard enough of them when volunteering on the hotline and at the shelter in London. The means changed but the mechanism never did. Drugs, alcohol, sex. Those were the classics but there were others, too. Some had foot fetishes, some had to spend money until they were bankrupt and still kept on, some cut themselves . . . she'd seen it all and she'd heard it all.

The story was always the same, when you dug down deeply enough. Addictions were like a wall between you and the void. Until you discovered that the addiction *was* the void.

Chloe's body couldn't handle alcohol well. Otherwise, she wondered whether she would have become an alcoholic, simply to fill the massive emptiness at the heart of her life.

Mike's case was so clear. He'd seen his family being slaughtered when he was just a young boy. They were dead and he was alive. He did what he could to keep from remembering that, every second of every day.

"No, of course not. That's not it at all." Agitated, Mike threw back the covers and stood up. Every muscle was tense. His veins stood out, as if his body was even now pumping blood to the extremities, readying himself for battle. "I fucked and drank so I wouldn't die?" He made a sound of disgust deep in his throat. "That's crazy. I'm not crazy." He pointed a trembling finger at her, eyes wild. "I'm *not* crazy!"

"No, of course you're not." Chloe pulled her legs up to her chest and put her arms around her knees. She understood the reaction.

She wasn't afraid of Mike, not in any way, but instinctively, her body was curling itself up in the presence of a strong, agitated male. "I didn't say that. You did."

Mike paced the room, long, fast strides. He pushed his hands through his hair, which was already mussed from their lovemaking. It stuck up in sweaty spikes. He was even more aroused than before. It seemed his entire body was in agitated movement except for his penis, lying like a rock against his flat abdomen.

He was buzzing, agitation almost visible on his skin.

Chloe watched him pace back and forth, wishing she could help, knowing that she couldn't. He had to work this out for himself. Everyone did. It was the one big lesson she'd taken away from her work in crisis centers and from her own therapy. You could be helped, but the real work—well, you had to do that yourself.

Mike was resisting.

"I wasn't afraid I was going to die if I didn't fuck. That's crazy talk. But there was something there, something really dark and uncontrollable. This . . . thing would build up in me and I'd just explode if I couldn't get it out. Except in battle. Dodging bullets took me right out of myself. In combat, I'm the Man. Cool as ice. Fucking Sniper-Man, with nerves of steel. I once hunkered down in a hide in my ghillie suit for three days to get a shot. I knew I'd have a window of about a minute in those three days, so I didn't eat, drank very little, always kept on eye on the scope, and didn't sleep. Didn't budge an inch. My heart rate slowed down. Didn't give my dick a thought. Came back Stateside and it went up and stayed up."

"I'm really sorry about your family, Mike," she said quietly, and he stopped with a jolt and swayed, as if shot in the heart.

Had she overstepped the bounds? For a second, she wondered. He looked like a wild man, with his hair sticking out all around his head, red eyes holding back tears, humming with tension.

"You know?" His voice was rough, hoarse.

She nodded.

Mike was frozen for a minute, two. Then he scrubbed his face briskly, as if just waking up. When he lifted his hands from his face, his cheeks were wet with tears.

"Oh God." He sat down abruptly on the side of the bed next to her. The mattress dipped with his weight. He pushed the heels of his hands against his eyes. "I see it. Almost every night. I see it, over and over again. Sometimes I just hate the thought of trying to sleep, because then I'll see it in my nightmares, you know?"

"Yes," Chloe whispered. "I know." Her hand lingered over his naked shoulder, then landed, lightly. She could feel him quivering under her hand, as if his very flesh couldn't stand to contain his thoughts. "Do you want to talk about it?"

Mike stared at the ground for so long she decided to get up, give him some space. His hand caught hers. "Don't go."

She settled back down, waited.

They sat there like that, Mike staring at the ground, for almost an hour. Chloe didn't mind. She was used to waiting. Sometimes it seemed that her entire life had been waiting. And, in a way, it had. She'd been waiting for this.

She could wait for as long as it took.

Finally, the tension left his body in an enormous sigh. "I never talk about it. Never. Sam and Harry just know the bare bones. When we first got together at Old Man Hughes', I was a wild child. I'd been kicked out of four foster homes. I couldn't talk about it at all. Just didn't have the words. And even if I wanted to, Sam and Harry wouldn't have understood, not really. Sam's mom threw him away in a Dumpster when he was just a baby. Harry's mom? She was an addict with a thing for druggie scumbags."

He stopped suddenly, looking at her. Realizing. "Oh God, it was your mom, too, honey. I'm so sorry."

Chloe nodded. However unpalatable, it was the truth. What she knew of her biological mother was that she was a druggie with a thing for other druggies. Preferably violent ones.

"What could I say to them?" Mike shuddered. "The thing was, both of them grew up in squalor, completely unloved. How could I talk about my family? The family I'd lost? My dad and my mom, they were . . . they were the greatest. Just great parents. I didn't know that as a kid, of course. What do kids know? They think their world is the only world there is. So in my world, every husband loved his wife and every wife loved her husband. And they both loved their kids. Dad was an engineer with a company that designed avionics for Boeing. Mom taught high school. There were five of us. I had two brothers, both older than I was. Eddie and Jeff. Twelve and fourteen. I was the youngest, the runt. I was small for my age. Got teased a lot, but no one outside the family ever messed with me because Eddie and Jeff had my back, always. If I ever got picked on, Eddie and Jeff made sure it never happened again. The Keillors. Don't mess with them because you're gonna regret it." He gave a half laugh and shook his head. "I thought we were just this average family but we weren't. We were something rare and special. Five people who loved one another. That doesn't often happen in this world."

It didn't. Chloe tried to imagine it, imagine being in the loving embrace of a tight-knit family. She'd had a taste of it, albeit on the margins, these past six months and it was wonderful. But to have had this as a child, to know nothing else, and then have it taken away. That would mess with anyone's head.

Mike went back to staring at the ground.

"Do you want to tell me what happened?"

Her words seemed to shake him out of a reverie. He looked at her, just a quick sideways flash, like a blue bolt of lightning. Chloe kept her face blank, as she knew how to do. But it was hard not to react to the raw pain on his face.

"Okay. I'll tell you. I've never really told anyone the whole story." He blew out a shaky breath, stared at his knees. "March twelfth. I was ten. It's Saturday, and we're headed for the beach. Dad stops at a gas station. You know one of those places with a little mart attached?"

She nodded, though he wasn't looking at her.

"Mom forgot the volleyball at home. It was old anyway, she said. Might as well buy a new one. So we went in, bought the volleyball, bought a cheap beach Ping-Pong set and five Cokes. I wanted some Snickers bars but mom drew the line at that. She'd packed sandwiches and didn't like us eating junk food. I looked up at Eddie and Jeff, expecting them to make signs that they'd buy them without Mom knowing and sneak them to me afterwards. But nada. No Snickers bar for me. I threw a fit and stomped off while she was paying. I was the baby of the family and pretty spoiled. I don't know what I was thinking. Maybe I was thinking of shoplifting the Snickers, putting them in the pocket of my cutoffs, because I was a budding juvie. Whatever. I don't remember. Mom and Dad and my brothers were waiting for me. Mom called out, said it was time to go. I was at the other end of the store, eyeing the Snickers, when they—they came in."

His family's murderers. Chloe gripped his shoulder.

"There were two of them. I had a good view between the aisles. I stared because I'd never seen anyone like them before. Two guys, one tall, one short, both rail-thin. Dreadlocks, pants down to their crotches, unlaced sneakers. Back then, it was a new look, this was before it went mainstream and every kid tries to look like a convict. They were like aliens to me, red-faced, snot running from their noses. They giggled crazily, barely made sense when they talked. Eyes rolling around in their heads like ponies' eyes. Stoked to the gills. Couple of years ago, when I was still in SWAT, I accessed the files of the case. Perps were higher than a kite on coke. And both had BALs of more than 1.02 percent. It is entirely possible they had no idea what they were doing, operating purely on animal instinct."

He sat there on the side of the bed, knees open, hands clasped between them, head hung low. Watching the tragic past unfold.

"I read the transcript of the trial. One of the lawyers advanced the argument that Scumbag One was so mentally impaired by the drugs and alcohol he had no concept of what he was doing and was only following what Scumbag Two told him to do."

"Did it fly?" Chloe's heart already ached.

"No, thank God. Judge had a lot of sense. Put them away for forty years. Threw the book at them."

"Good," she said, and he gave a faint smile. "So these two delinquents walk into the mart. And?"

"And demand that the cashier open up the cash register. I figured this out later. Personally, I wrote them off as weirdos and went back to staring at the candy counter at the other end of the shop." His voice was dark, bitter. He spat the words out one by one as if they were made of poison. "My family was under threat and I was contemplating shoplifting two Snickers bars."

Chloe took a chance and rubbed between his shoulder blades. The tension felt bone-deep. It came off him in waves. "You were a young boy," she said gently. "And it wasn't your world."

Mike shook his head as if ridding it of dark thoughts. "The cashier was no dope. He emptied the register. There was $137.32. The price of my family. Not even a hundred forty bucks. About twenty-eight bucks a head for their lives, including the cashier. When they saw the amount, the scumbags went wild, started screaming. The tall one pulled out a pistol. The guy behind the cash register—a kid, really, nineteen years old. He looked twelve on the tape. This kid at the register is shaking, pulls out what's in his pockets. Not even ten bucks. Both scumbags scream even harder. By this time I figure something is up and I walk up the aisle toward where all the commotion is. My dad sees me and shakes his head, motions me away. The fuckhead—sorry." This with a narrow-eyed glance at her.

Chloe nodded. Fuckhead sounded about right.

"Scumbag with the gun is waving it in the air, partially covering my family. Dad's in front, arms out, Mom and Eddie and Jeff behind him."

Mike stopped, breathing heavily. Chloe continued to rest her hand against the deep, solid dip between his shoulder blades and waited.

"At the time it seemed to stretch out forever, everything in slow motion, but the clock on the security camera says the whole thing clocked in at two minutes forty seconds."

Two minutes forty seconds that changed his world forever. Mike didn't have to say it.

"The clerk reached under the counter to push the police call button and the scumbag with the gun—who was probably seeing double at the time—just opened fire. Blew his head apart. Again, my dad motioned me to stay put. It wasn't necessary. I couldn't have moved an inch. I was in a state of shock. Dad was trying to edge toward the door when the guy turned and started shooting. It was a semiautomatic and I remember watching the brass casings twirl in the light. He just . . . opened fire. Gunned them down like animals. They were left in a heap, Dad on top, arms still outstretched, still trying to protect them. The other scumbag slipped on the blood and fell, laughing like a loon."

Chloe could see it so clearly in her mind's eye—the felled family, the blood, the crazed gunman, the horrified little boy.

"I was really good at baseball, really good. Until this—this happened, I wanted to be a professional ballplayer when I grew up. I had a good, strong pitching hand. I grabbed cans of fruit salad and tomato sauce and threw them as hard as I could at the gunman first, then the guy howling with laughter on the floor. Nailed the shooter on the first throw, knocked him unconscious, nailed the other guy, too. I didn't stop at one, I hurled can after can at them, even when they were on the ground, head shots every one. Their heads were bloody, I broke their jawbones, cheekbones. I was screaming, hysterical. I only stopped when this big guy in a blue uniform gently took my arms and stopped me."

"The police," Chloe said.

He gave a short sharp nod. "Cops, yeah. I really don't remember the next part at all. They looked for relatives, but both my parents were only children, all four grandparents were dead. I was assigned a social worker who 'managed' my family's estate and ended up destroying it. I was put into a series of foster homes. I quickly got a rep as a troublemaker. Fought like hell at every one. Went down the list of acceptable homes until I landed on the last of the list, the only home that would accept me, as a 'problem' child, because the state paid more. The household was run by a sadistic monster named Hughes. But Sam and Harry were there and we had one another's back. Joined the Marines as soon as it was legally possible."

"I'm so sorry, Mike," Chloe said quietly. The words meant nothing but they came from the bottom of her heart. Because he'd just told the story of a little boy whose world was shattered on a single afternoon.

"It didn't have to happen," he said hoarsely.

"What?"

"Didn't have to happen. None of it. We could have been on our way to the beach when those scumbags came into the mart if I hadn't been a spoiled brat. My whole family was gunned down like dogs because I wanted a fucking—" He stopped talking and the clicks came again as his throat muscles worked. "Snickers bar. My mother and my father and my two brothers, dead because of me."

Chloe sucked in a breath, appalled.

"Oh no, Mike." She leaned forward to see his face, to try to look into his eyes. He wouldn't lift his head. She could see the tendons in his neck stand out, the grooves in his cheeks deep and drawn. "It wasn't your fault! Nothing in any of it was your fault. You can't possibly think that you could have stopped two drug addicts, one of whom was armed."

"We would have been out of there, on the road, if it wasn't for me."

"That's magical thinking. And you yourself said that everything happened very fast. Probably all five of you would have still been there and you would be dead, too."

He shuddered under her hand and Chloe had a startling flash of insight. He wished he'd died, too, together with his family. The fact that he'd survived wasn't a consolation, not for him. It was a curse. He still grieved for his lost family, still felt guilty. He had an iron mantle of guilt around his shoulders, weighing him down every minute of every day.

Chloe understood him profoundly. All through her childhood and until very recently, she blamed herself because her parents couldn't—wouldn't love her. They had never tried to express even a false kind of affection. And she'd blamed herself, every day. Wondered, every day, what she'd done to alienate them. Tried to be quiet and obedient on the rare occasions when her mother visited. She saw her father about once a year, and each year she did her very best to win him over, to have him show some emotion toward her. It never worked. Nothing she did worked. Ever.

How she'd scout her mother's face for some sign of . . . something. Something she could do to stir some warm feelings, something she could say, something she could be. It was this huge puzzle she never managed to figure out, and she kept circling back to the only thing that made sense. There was a fatal flaw that made her unlovable. There was something deeply wrong with her. It was all her fault.

Chloe understood down to her bones the acid drip of guilt dribbling like a corrosive in the bloodstream. Understood a child bearing a load too great for small, young shoulders.

Her heart ached for Mike. For having known a family's love and having lost it, and on top of that bearing this terrible burden of guilt almost all his life.

Those massive shoulders were shaking, his head was turned

away, but she could still see the red eyes, damp cheeks.

A wave of tenderness rose up in her, so vast she was surprised the earth didn't shake with it.

"Mike," she whispered, pushing at his shoulders to turn him around. He was so massively strong. She couldn't force him to turn to her, but he did. Her heart cracked open a little at the sight of his face, strength warring with suffering, and she leaned forward, pressing her cheek to his. The tears were cool but the skin underneath was burning hot. "Lay your burden down, darling. You've carried it for so long. Let it go. It's not yours to carry."

She was embracing him, arms unable to meet around that enormous chest. Against the inside of her arms and against the skin of her chest, she felt a deep trembling, a ripple of emotions.

"Let it go," she whispered again, and he shuddered, hard, as something powerful moved through him.

Chloe could almost *see* the iron burden of guilt leave Mike. He seemed almost to levitate for a moment, something dark passing through him and out, and then he turned with her in his arms and bore her down to the mattress.

Startled, Chloe made room for him, instinctively. Her body and her heart opened wide, arms and legs wrapping around him. He was shaking with emotion, so unusual for such a strong and highly controlled man. Chloe could feel the stress of the emotions being released, could feel it in her fingertips, under the palms of her hands, along the front of her body.

He kissed her, avidly, sucking, licking, as if her mouth held something vital to him. As if he couldn't live without her mouth.

He lifted his head for just a second, nose to nose, bright blue eyes blazing into hers. His hands tunneled through her hair and cupped her head. His hands were so huge they almost completely covered her head. He was holding her tightly, holding her still, as if she could somehow want to avoid his kiss.

When, of course, she craved it.

"I know you must be sore," he whispered. "And I know I just finished talking about using sex as a crutch. This isn't that." He shook his head sharply, a lock of dark hair falling like a comma on his forehead. "Though frankly I don't know what the fuck it is. It's just that I need this right now, more than I've ever needed anything in my life. I need this. I need *you*."

Chloe watched him. She'd never seen such intensity in a human face before. It was as if he were able to see behind her eyes, walk around inside her brain.

She nodded, throat dry.

Mike let out his breath in a whoosh, wide back moving against her arms.

"Open for me." The command was low, guttural.

She instinctively looked down, but all she saw was a broad chest, sharply defined pectorals covered with a thick brown pelt and part of his abdominal muscles.

"I'd put myself inside you, but I don't want to move my hands. Open your thighs wider. Let me in."

He lifted slightly higher and she saw his penis, so hard it looked waxen, so large it frightened her a little.

This was no time to be frightened, not even a little. Chloe felt she'd been frightened all her life, of things unseen, of things unsaid, of ghosts. She wasn't going to be frightened now. Not with her man to love.

She shifted her legs, opened herself with one hand and grasped him with the other. Mike let out a huff of air at the touch of her hand on him. He was utterly still, big hands around her head, staring intently into her eyes. He didn't move, hardly breathed. This powerful man was giving power to her.

And she wanted it. She wanted the power in him, she wanted *him*.

She pulled him down, positioned him at her opening, tilted her hips a little so he was already inside her. She lifted her head until her lips brushed his ear. "*Now*, Mike," she whispered, and bit his earlobe lightly.

With a growl that came up from his belly and gave her goose bumps, he thrust inside her. He filled her completely, almost but not quite to the edge of pain. Almost immediately she could feel her inner muscles start to accommodate him.

"Are you okay?" Mike asked roughly. A drop of sweat fell down his chin onto her breast.

Chloe tugged at his back until he was completely settled on her, bearing his full weight. Her bones stretched a little but it felt wonderful. She lifted her legs, tilting her hips so he moved even more deeply inside her. He had to feel her welcome. Every cell in her body was smiling, just for him.

"Oh yes," she sighed, grasping him even more tightly. "Love me, Mike."

He did. He went slowly at first, slow measured thrusts, completely in control. He touched her everywhere, inside and out, tongue echoing his thrusts. Their mouths and their genitals were making wet, sucking noises, the noises of total intimacy.

Chloe let herself go utterly, muscles lax, like water, Mike's thrusts like gentle oceans waves curling in toward shore, it felt like the very rhythm of life, on and on and on . . .

She was so relaxed, not thinking, just feeling, that the orgasm caught her entirely by surprise. One moment she was enjoying the warmth pulsing in waves throughout her body, verging into heat, enjoying the feel of Mike under her hands, against her chest and groin, feeling the rhythms of his thrusts, and then *wham!*

Her body shot into overdrive, just like that. From one second to the next.

No buildup, no increasing sense of warmth in her groin, no rising tension. Just a sudden electric shock so huge she thought it would short her brain and then her body began convulsing. Not just her vagina contracting in strong pulls, but her entire body convulsed, a prickling wash of heat suffusing her. She jerked, feeling completely out of control, like a puppet on strings.

Instinctively, she clutched Mike harder because he was the only stable thing in this red-hot world turned upside down. Her eyes were closed but the insides of her lids turned red, as if a bomb had gone off into the room.

Chloe gasped and Mike muttered, "Yeah." She was contracting hard around him, deep pulls of her vagina she could feel in her stomach while she went into free fall, holding tightly on to Mike because otherwise it felt like she could fall into some kind of abyss and never come out the other side.

Mike moved in her faster, harder, keeping the contractions going on and on. For a while—and later she would have no concept of how long it lasted—Chloe lost all sense of self, all notions of her being separate from Mike. For a while they were one organism, one body, moving tightly in unison, feeding pleasure to each other like a huge golden ball passing from one to the other.

"Oh God," Mike breathed. His voice sounded slightly shocked and shaky. A shudder went through him and passed through her.

Finally, some sense of consciousness made its way back into her head, the contractions started slowing, she started coming back into herself when *wham!* Mike started coming in huge hot jets she could feel against the walls of her vagina and she climaxed all over again, pulses of heat sparking through her entire body.

When it was over, she was completely wiped out.

Their bodies were covered in sweat. More his than hers, but still. She was wet around the groin, another his-and-her effort. They smelled, too—of sex. But it was an earthy, pleasing smell, the smell of two bodies that had just joined.

Mike's head was buried next to hers in the pillow. She turned her head slightly but he kept his face planted in the pillow. He was breathing heavily, panting almost, that big barrel chest bellowing in and out. He didn't move. He wasn't getting off her, but he wasn't looking at her, either.

A thin track of wetness trickled down his cheek.

Another wave of tenderness washed through her, more powerful than the orgasm. Mike had let himself go completely with her. She had no idea how he made love ordinarily, but she couldn't believe that the powerful thing they'd shared was something he could experience every night with a different sex partner. It just didn't work that way.

He was as affected as she was, and it came on the heels of telling the story of his family's slaughter and the terrible shame he'd carried around with him ever since.

He didn't want to look at her. It was possible he *couldn't* look at her.

That was fine. Chloe understood very well. His emotions were too much for him and she knew precisely how that felt. She tightened her arms around his shoulders, feeling the absolute strength of him, knowing that now he was as defenseless as a child.

She'd watch over him, protect his feelings. No one but her would ever know these vulnerabilities. She'd watch over them, too, guard them fiercely.

He'd protected her. By God, she would protect him.

Her hand ran through his hair, spiky with sweat, and she cupped his head.

"Sleep, my love," she whispered. Mike's breath left him in a whoosh that was taking some of his tension with it.

Chloe thought she would stand guard over him but her own exhaustion and stress caught up with her.

Inside of five minutes, she fell into a deep sleep with a ton of man on top of her.

Chapter 16

Consuelo clutched the thumb drive in her damp hand and checked for the tenth time the address she'd scribbled on a scrap of paper and the address on the big brass plaque next to the ornate doorway of the elegant building in downtown San Diego.

She'd never ventured into this part of town. She had no reason to. It was mostly made up of office buildings. The people streaming in and out of the huge glass doors were as remote to her as Martians.

None of them, she was sure, sold their bodies for a living.

She lifted her head, suddenly very determined. That part of her life was over. The people in the office she'd called helped women disappear. They'd helped two women in the shelter disappear, that's how she got the visiting card.

Consuelo would either be able to convince them to help a whore or she would disappear herself, though she had no tools for that. The only thing she had was the twenty thousand dollars she'd taken from her hiding hole and the thumb drive. She had no documents, none.

She was in the United States illegally, always had been illegal.

Even if she could get back across the border, which she couldn't, she had no documentation in Mexico, either. And no place to go. She was allowed no documents, no passports, no driver's license, no home to go back to, nothing.

All in all, they'd be crazy to help her. She was going to be more trouble than she was worth.

On the other hand, maybe what she held in her fist might be worth something to them. Something she could barter with for her life.

Sweat trickled down her back, as it often did when she was scared. When she was smilingly escorting a trick back to the room he'd paid for together with the rent of her body, and he looked like he might be violent. Might enjoy hurting. There always was one and the house rule was if no blood was spilled, no harm was done.

That client would simply be charged more the next time.

So Consuelo did now what she did whenever she was scared— pasted a smooth smile on her face and walked through the door, not knowing what was on the other side.

Mike had been a soldier for much of his adult life. Soldiers do not open their eyes slowly, confident that the world is a wonderful place. They snap awake, instantly alert, ready for action, knowing the world is full of murderous motherfuckers who can't wait to smoke them.

Soldiering is a Darwinian occupation. Those who can't shoot from deep sleep to alertness in a second are winnowed out pretty fast. Usually from the end of a barrel.

Old habits die hard, particularly when they are the kind to foster survival. He wasn't a soldier anymore, but Mike still woke up in a flash, usually trying to figure out how to get out of having to spend time with the woman he'd fucked the night before.

He usually woke up to a flat, exhausted, melancholy feeling, itchy to jump out of whatever bed he was in and get home. Where he'd feel flat, exhausted and melancholy.

Oh man. Not now. No, siree. He felt *great*, though he definitely did not want to jump out of bed and get going. Nope. He had no strength in his muscles at all. Man, he didn't want to go *anywhere*, not with Chloe's sleek, soft little body half on, half off his.

Sometimes he had to remember who the babe in the bed was, but not now. Because it wasn't a babe, it was *Chloe*.

It was a sunny day. He could tell because the inside of his lids were painted golden. And there was a warm breeze coming in off the ocean, fluttering the curtains.

He felt clean. Purified. Purged of some ancient black bile that had been poisoning his system since forever. He couldn't remember the last time he'd felt so hopeful. The sex last night had almost burned him alive. It had reduced the old Mike to cinders and here was the new version, ready to face a new day with a cheerful smile.

Mike couldn't remember the last time he'd thought to face a new day with a cheerful smile. Maybe never.

He felt . . . he felt like a virgin must feel after sex for the very first time. He didn't actually remember much about his very first time, except that it had been standing up in a doorway, because he'd been wasted at the time. But if he'd had a different life, if he hadn't been so fucking *angry* all the time, he could imagine his first time feeling like this. Like he'd personally discovered an entire new realm of pleasure.

Except instead of discovering sex with some nice bland high schooler at seventeen, he was discovering it with Chloe, who was anything but bland.

She was so wise and so loving.

And so fucking hot.

Man, he was a lucky guy.

"Mike?" Chloe pushed at his shoulder.

"Hmm?"

She wriggled out from under his arm while he groaned at the loss of her slight weight and warmth. He could stop her, anytime. No question. Except, whoa, he didn't seem to have any control over his body. His muscles had been replaced by cotton. He tried to hold on to her but his hand flopped right back down to the mattress.

"Mike Keillor," she chided, "you promised twice to feed me last night and yet here I am, still hungry. You should be ashamed of yourself. A girl could starve to death here."

The words were a light, gentle buzzing sound somewhere off on the horizon. He didn't pay them much attention. He just liked the sound of Chloe's voice.

A rustle of sheets, the bed dipped lightly, and he could hear her padding about in bare feet.

Chloe had such pretty feet. His mind went off on a little meditative trance on Chloe's feet while the pleasant sounds of a shower filled the room with white noise.

"Okay," she said, back in the bedroom, "I guess I'm going to have to cook something myself. We'll see what you have. I hope there's something to work with."

He could hear her padding off.

A frown formed on his forehead. Chloe. Kitchen.

The buzzing grew louder, darker.

This does not compute.

His eyes snapped open. Chloe in the kitchen. No, no, no!

Galvanized, he rolled out of bed and pulled on a robe. Chloe and kitchens was not a good combo. Chloe in the kitchen was a disaster in the making. The woman had no feel for cooking at all, but was interested in learning. After one bite of her experiments, no matter how much everyone loved her, they couldn't choke down the rest. Not even Merry, who adored her, could eat more than a bite or two.

Chloe in the kitchen was not a good thing.

He ran to the kitchen, then stopped in the doorway, watching her moving around in the warm morning sunshine. True, she couldn't cook. But then again, she was just so fucking pretty.

She had on one of his tees which hung to her knees, billowing around her arms. She was barefoot, one pretty foot over the other as she concentrated on burning the toast. She'd turned the radio on the counter to a classic rock station and swayed that pretty behind to "Hotel California."

She was like a little fairy princess come down from heaven to burn his coffee and make scrambled eggs with shell bits.

He hadn't said a thing but she suddenly put down the wooden spoon she was using to push a stringy mass of eggs around his pan and turned.

The counter was a mess and the food smelled awful. But she smiled at him and his heart simply turned over in his chest.

Chloe.

Fuck it. He'd hire a cook.

"Here." Her smile was blinding. How the hell was a man supposed to resist? She held out a mug. "I made us breakfast."

"That's nice, honey." He took the mug, trying not to gag at the smell of burned rubber, and took a sip. It wasn't so bad, if you didn't mind the taste. At least it was hot.

"Sit," she ordered, and placed a smoking pan on his kitchen table. Burnt toast followed on a dish. But she'd done the table up nicely, scavenging in his cupboards for presentable plates, coming up with tea towels to use as place mats. It looked nice. Mike was glad he'd finally broken down and gone to IKEA to buy every kind of glass there was after Ellen laughed at the jelly jars he used as glasses.

The table looked really pretty. It looked even better when Chloe sat down. Mike gamely scraped some black off his toast and buttered it, slathering it with jam to cover the charcoal taste.

Chloe was cheating. She was sipping a cup of tea—no way to

burn tea—and delicately chopping the head off a soft-boiled egg. Mike helped himself to the scrambled eggs, ignoring the shells. When he bit into one, he just swallowed. Hell, it was protein.

It was a gorgeous morning. The sun was rising behind the building but a warm gentle glow off the ocean shimmered from the open French door that gave out onto a little balcony. The sky was that glorious blue only Southern California seemed able to produce, and the sea was calm, with only a few wavelets looking like lacy ruffles.

Mike felt an enormous sense of peace settle over him. He smiled at Chloe and she smiled back. Then schooled her face to a disapproving frown. "You didn't give me much to work with," she said, and shot him a reproving look. "I think I used up everything in your fridge. We need to go on a food run, don't you think?"

Mike froze, the happiness he'd been feeling just a second ago fizzing out of him like air out of a leaky balloon. The world and all its problems, the events of the day before, rushed back into his head on a black tide.

He took her hand and chose his words carefully. "Honey—" He breathed in deeply, bracing himself. Might as well get it over with. "Honey, I don't like the thought of you out and about right now." That was putting it mildly. The thought of Chloe out, a target for these unknown scumbags, drove him a little insane. "We don't have a handle yet on who attacked you yesterday. Until then, I'd be happier if you just . . . stayed here."

A little line appeared between her eyebrows. "Stay here? In the house? Without ever going out even if I'm with you? Until when?"

Mike clenched his jaws. "Until we know more about who attacked you."

"But—one is dead and one is in the hospital, apparently not talking. Am I correct?"

He clenched his jaws even harder. He had to focus to unlock them. "Yeah."

The line between her brows deepened. "But . . . does that mean you think I should stay in here indefinitely?"

This was the hard part, the part that was driving him crazy. If he knew anything about women—and he did—she was not going to like being ordered about. Though to his mind, Chloe was now definitely his, his to protect and to care for, Mike realized he hadn't actually said the Words. And females liked the Words. Or at least he thought so, because here he was treading in unfamiliar waters. Nothing more than the occasional "honey" in bed when he couldn't remember the woman's name had ever passed his lips.

The fact was that Mike felt bound to Chloe by bands of steel, immutable and unbreakable. She was his family now. He'd lost one, and he was not going to lose her. No way.

How to say any of that to her? To propose that she be locked up in his house 24/7 until he was sure it was safe to come out? And who knew when that would be?

Chloe liked moving around, quite natural for someone who'd spent her childhood years basically in a hospital bed. She enjoyed her daily walks along the beach, she enjoyed coming into the office, she liked shopping and going to bookstores and tea shops.

She also liked soft, welcoming surroundings. Her apartment was a delight to be in, as opposed to Mike's place, which was functional and bare.

He winced as he looked out the kitchen door into the living room area. Spare, unwelcoming, with one huge sofa, one huge coffee table and a humongous TV. Nothing else, not even a rug on the floor. This was so not Chloe, and yet he was proposing to lock her up in here.

She was going to rebel and he was going to put his foot down and he *hated* the thought. Just hated it. As far as he was concerned, Chloe was It. He wanted to love her and pamper her. He wanted to give her whatever she wanted. He wanted to shower her with presents, do what she wanted to do, go where she wanted to go.

He wanted to make her happy. And one day into their being a couple—and that might be entirely in his own head—he was proposing locking her up for an unknown period of time.

Because there was no question. There was no way he was letting her out while there was even a suspicion of a fucking Russian gangster targeting her. No way.

If she got mad at him, screamed at him, he'd take it because *no way* was she stepping into danger.

He might lose her by keeping her safe.

The thought of it—the thought of losing Chloe . . . well, it was unthinkable. Not going to happen.

"Mike?" she repeated softly. "You want me to stay here indefinitely?"

His jaws hurt, he was clenching them so hard. He could actually feel a gritty shard of enamel breaking off. "Yeah." His voice came out guttural and hard. "That's what I think."

He was vibrating with tension, ready to do battle, ready to do what it takes, but sick in his heart at the thought.

"You think I'll be safer here than elsewhere?"

"Fuck yeah!" The words shot out of him. "Yeah," he repeated, forcing his voice to be a little less insane-sounding.

He and his brothers had done a few modifications to their apartments. He had a door that wouldn't be too shabby in a bank vault, to be opened only by a keypad. He'd lined the walls next to the door with steel panels, then covered them with drywall and painted them over. All the windows were ISO 9001, ten layers of Mylar-coated glass. Essentially, you'd need an RPG to get in.

There was no real platform for a sniper to get them. A sniper on the ground wouldn't have a shot. Too acute an angle, too high up. And a sniper on a boat would have a very long shot on a moving platform.

He was a sniper himself and he'd gamed it all. He'd even gone out on a boat to see if a sniper could make the shot. He couldn't.

He had motion sensors on the balcony just in case some insane fuckhead got it into his head to lower himself from the roof, and to do so he'd have to overcome the spiked covering he'd placed over the balcony.

No, this place was safe. Now he just had to keep Chloe in it.

He was sweating and could hear his own heavy breathing in the room, like a bull's.

This was not going well and he had no clue how to make it better.

Chloe was watching his face carefully, her own face completely blank. She could do that. He couldn't. He knew that right now, his own face reflected every ounce of the tension he was feeling.

And then, to his astonishment, Chloe placed her hand over his and squeezed gently.

"If that's what you want, Mike, okay." She searched his eyes. "You wouldn't feel comfortable with me out and about until you figure out what's going on. Am I correct?"

His throat was stopped up, gripped in an unbreakable vise. He nodded his head jerkily.

Her voice was soft, gentle. "I spent a lot of my childhood locked up. Staying here while you clear things up won't kill me. If it gives you peace of mind, Mike, I'll gladly stay here."

Oh *God!* He felt like falling to his knees. She wasn't going to put her foot down on principle. She wasn't going to make him be the bad guy, the villain of the piece, because he'd do it if he had to, but man, he didn't want to.

Though he'd never encountered this in his dealings with women, he recognized it instantly. This was teamwork, like in the Marines. Like in SWAT. Like with Sam or Harry. Do the hard thing for your buddy. Make a sacrifice if necessary.

She didn't want to stay indoors but she would, if it gave him peace of mind.

They were a team. He had his own team, now.

Mike turned away horrified, blinking away a spurt of tears. What the fuck? He never cried. Ever. He hadn't even cried at the funeral of his family he'd been so angry. Here he'd cried last night and damned if he wasn't leaking water right now.

It baffled him. He had all these raging . . . things inside him he didn't have a clue how to handle.

"Mike." Chloe touched his hand softly again and he looked up at her. She was smiling. "Let's go out on the balcony and get a little fresh air. Because you're probably going to want me inside when you're not here."

"Yeah, absolutely." Okay. Now *that* he knew how to handle. He wiped his face and rose. "Let me check first."

He went out onto the balcony. Almost every room in the place had a balcony that looked out over the ocean. It was what had sealed the deal for him, not counting the fact that his two brothers, Sam and Harry, already owned apartments in the condo.

The kitchen balcony was narrow but deep, big enough to hold a small table for two so they could eat outdoors. Something he'd never even thought of doing up until now. When all of this was over and Chloe was living with him and, presumably, he'd decorated a little so it wouldn't be like living on the space station, that was something he'd do. Set up a little table out here on the kitchen balcony so they could eat outside.

Not Chloe's food, of course. He'd have Sam's cook, Manuela, send something down. Or order in.

He leaned on the balcony railing and looked out carefully. Like a soldier would, dividing the area into four quadrants. One quadrant, blink to black, two, blink to black, three, four. The entire horizon was blank. Nothing out there, not even fishing boats. Nobody walking on the beach, either. A completely empty landscape.

"Come on out, honey. It's clear."

Mike stepped back so Chloe could lean against the railing. She

lifted her face, smiling, and took in a deep breath, then placed her
elbows on the railing. "It smells so wonderful. And the colors are
so intense. You're so lucky to have this view, Mike. I love my view
over the bay but this is something else."

He stood behind her, hands next to hers on the railing, making
a cage of his body. She'd be living here soon enough if he had anything to say about it. She could watch the ocean all she liked then.

"Glad you like it."

Her face turned and she smiled at him and he smiled back, all
nerves gone. Completely relaxed.

Well, except for one part of him. That part wasn't relaxed at all
and was getting tenser by the second.

She was looking back out over the ocean. He lifted her hair, the
soft waves falling over his hand, and placed his lips on the nape
of her neck. She shivered. He was so attuned to her, he felt her
pleasure against his lips, like a swell of honey transferring itself
from her to him.

Oh yeah.

He opened his robe and moved closer, pushing against her. She
couldn't help but feel his hard-on. She turned her head slightly
and he could see the faint smile. He pushed against her bottom
and felt her pushing slightly back.

He hummed a little in his throat as he pushed his T-shirt up,
looking down at the expanse of smooth light-gold skin on her
narrow back and slender waist. He placed his hand on the small
of her back, almost covering it, then smoothed the palm of his
hand over her back. Her skin felt like warm silk flowing beneath
his hand, brand-new muscles sleek and tight. A light kiss right
where her hair made a little curlicue against her slender neck, and
she shivered again. He could feel her breathing change. Becoming
deeper, slower.

His lips moved up and down, tongue behind her ear, where
she shivered once again. Though Mike had a beautiful ocean view

right in front of him, he had eyes only for the woman before him. The sound of her sighs, the soft movements, the arching of her back when he caressed her sides, they were like some addictive substance he could never get enough of.

He was hard as a rock. She was right. Anyone could tell he was raring to go, but what about Chloe? Was she ready? Only one way to find out.

Mike smoothed his hand over her bottom and down, down into her silky depths. She wanted him, oh yeah. When he slid a finger into her she clamped tightly around him like a tight wet fist. She whimpered and he kissed her shoulder, feeling like whimpering himself.

Oh man, this was so exciting. Though he couldn't count the number of women he'd fucked, this felt so new, as if he'd never done this before. And he hadn't. Certainly not like this.

He was glad he'd had a phobia about bringing women home because this made it all new and fresh with Chloe.

He nipped her shoulder, just a little, though the way he was feeling it could have been a sharper bite, and felt her little start of surprise. Moving his lips slowly, slowly from her shoulder, up her slender neck, to her ear, he said, "Open your legs for me, Chloe." He could hardly recognize his own voice, hoarse and low.

She slid her legs apart and he nearly fell to his knees. Oh yeah, right down on his knees, turn her gently around and just lap her up. Kiss her right there just like he did her mouth. A vibrating sound rose in his chest just at the thought and he could see it, clear as day. Chloe, knees wide apart, shaking as he loved her with his mouth.

But that scenario worked best in bed and was going to switch from theory to practice just as soon as he could manage it, but not right now. Because the railing was just low enough that if Chloe arched backwards she could conceivably fall four stories down and he didn't even want one molecule of that possibility in his head.

There'd be time enough—the rest of their lives in fact—for him to lay her out on the bed like this scrumptious vanilla ice cream cone he'd just lap up.

But for now . . . he circled her with one arm and anchored his other arm on the railing. Chloe would not fall down. If it rained fire from heaven he wouldn't let her fall. He'd never let her fall.

With a long sigh he slid into her, into all that heat. He could feel how her body welcomed his, how with every inch, she made way for him. He started moving slowly, hunched over her. He placed his palm on her belly, holding her still for him, and was rewarded when he felt her internal muscles pull on his cock, the movement so strong he could feel it against the skin of the palm of his hand.

He could stay like this forever, moving in her like the ocean tide, in and out, slowly, like an eternal force made just for this. Made exclusively to love Chloe.

Another pull from her little cunt and he moved even closer, thrust more deeply. She moaned and her legs shook. Christ, this was going too fast. He wanted to spend the entire morning on this balcony, making love with Chloe, with the smell of the ocean and burnt toast in his nostrils, but it wasn't going to happen.

"Mike," she whispered shakily, head down, small fists on the railing. Her hair swayed back and forth with his thrusts. She arched back against him, fully open to him, and he stepped even closer, movements short and quick now as he felt a hot liquid line run down his spine. He was sweating, panting, movements quick and hard.

Chloe let out a keening sound that rose high in the morning air and began coming, hot liquid pulls that were impossible to resist. Mike set his feet and pounded in her until something sweet and hot rushed through him and out his dick, strong hard pulses that seemed to echo the beat of his heart.

Mike stayed wrapped around Chloe for long minutes after-wards, coming slowly back into himself. With a sigh, she relaxed, moved her head back to rest against his shoulder. Mike kissed her hair. They were so close it was hard to tell where he stopped and she started.

He nuzzled her, his breath and heart rate slowing. He was still in her, but if he moved, he'd slip out. He wanted to stay exactly like this for the rest of his life. His arms tightened. "I love you," he whispered.

"I know," she whispered back.

They stood there, Chloe in Mike's embrace, watching out to sea, perfectly content. Mike swore when he heard his cell phone ring.

"Gotta take it, honey."

She turned to smile at him.

Goddamn. Whoever was calling, it better be good or he'd fucking rip them a new one.

He pulled out of her, his dick hating the cold after the warmth of Chloe, picked up the cell, checking the display. Harry.

"Yeah?"

Harry's voice was low, serious. "Mike, you've got to come in. We've got a lead on who attacked Chloe."

Chapter 17

Amerikanski, Nikitin thought with disgust as he watched the two fornicating on the balcony through camouflaged binoculars. Almost as bad as the Russians.

He'd found a photograph of Chloe Mason on Facebook. Amazing, the Americans, how stupid they were. But now he knew what she looked like and that bitch up there fucking someone was Chloe Mason, his best chance at finding out what happened to his men. He was here, hidden in the lush bushes forming a barrier between the buildings and the sea, reconnoitering her apartment, which had its curtains drawn, when there she was, one floor down, fucking some unknown man.

He'd parked down at the beginning of the strip known as Coronado Shores, which he'd reconnoitered on Google Earth. He'd seen right away that there was a good observation post right about fifty meters from the building, across the road that ran along the peninsula. This area—this Coronado Shores—was rich man's territory. Nikitin served the *vory* and he knew how the rich liked to live.

But no Russian *vor* worth his salt would allow a thickly landscaped strip separating the road from the beach to exist. Or if it existed, it would be patrolled day and night by guards.

Foolish Americans, so trusting.

He watched this Chloe Mason's face as she was being fucked from behind, observing her every move, every expression. Trying to figure out what kind of a woman she was, how she could cost him two good men.

The man fucking her. That had to be it. Nikitin watched to get a glimpse of his face, but for the moment, his face was buried in Chloe Mason's shoulder. But he was strong, unusually broad-shouldered, thickly muscled, though not tall.

Like the prostitute's description.

Was this the man who had cost him two good men?

Nikitin pulled out his iPad from his backpack. The Americans were so lousy at so many things but they were superb at high-tech. Still, whenever brainpower was needed, you had to look to Russia.

Nikitin entered his login and password, took a picture of his thumbprint on his iPhone 3GS and sent it all off.

Forty-seven seconds later, Pirat was online. Nikitin had an open account with him. Just talking to Pirat was $10,000 an hour. He'd like to keep it down to a quarter of an hour.

What do you need?

Schematics of a building in Coronado Shores, San Diego, California. La Torre. Names of owners. Particularly owner of third apartment from left fourth floor.

After a minute and a half, he had the schematics and the names of all the owners of record. The owner of the apartment who was at this moment fucking Chloe Mason—Nikitin lifted his binoculars to check. The man had stamina. The owner of the apartment was one Michael Keillor.

A photograph filled the screen. Dark brown hair, light blue eyes. A hard, even brutal face.

Nikitin started to type in a request for intel, but facts were already scrolling down.

Michael Keillor. A former Marine, Force Recon. It was a huge slap to the face. A warning that a formidable enemy had just crossed his path. A tiger instead of a cat. Americans were, yes, a soft people. But not its soldiers. Force Recon was Special Forces. Spetsnaz.

Yes, this man could certainly have taken Ivan and Lyov down, if he had weapons and the element of surprise.

The data scroll continued. After leaving the Marines Michael Keillor joined the San Diego Police Department as a member of the SWAT team. Nikitin knew they were the tactical officers of the police department.

And now he was a partner in a security company, RBK Security Inc.

Ex-soldier, former policeman, now co-owner of a security company. Nikitin felt his senses sharpen, exactly as if this were the moment before going into battle.

But no soldier goes into battle blind.

Intel on Chloe Mason, owner of a property in the same building.

While he waited for Pirat to search his databases, Nikitin lifted the binoculars to his eyes once more. The couple were straining, clearly at the end of sex. Did people not realize how ridiculous they looked in the throes of sex? The woman's mouth was open, eyes closed. Both their bodies were bathed in sweat, visible from here.

It was disgusting.

The display changed and he put down the binoculars and looked at the screen.

> *Chloe Mason, age 28, adopted at age of 5 by Rebecca and George Mason of Boston. Attended Catholic boarding school in London from the age of 15 to 18. Degree in English literature from University College London. Sister of Harry Bolt, partner in RBK Security Inc.*

Once was coincidence, twice was a pattern.

RBK Security.

He reached into his pocket to write down the address and froze. *Nyet!*

He scrabbled in his leather jacket, desperately trying to find a hole in the lining because . . . because this was impossible. Maybe in the other pocket. No.

He ripped off his jacket as if it were on fire, ran his hands through the two outside pockets again, the inside pocket, over and over again. Carefully inching his fingers along the lining just in case, all the while knowing that it wasn't there.

The thumb drive. The thumb drive with the entire auction data—photos, statistics, measurements. Doctors' certificates. And above all, the names of those admitted to auction. Doctors, lawyers, CEOs, all in a blind auction bidding to buy prepubescent girls.

That thumb drive contained dynamite, and if he lost it, his life was over. And the ending would not be pretty. The *vory* were not known for their mercy.

He kept that drive on him at all times. Where—

And suddenly, he knew. The whore Consuelo had it. He'd taken his jacket off for the interrogation, no use getting the leather wet. Somehow the thumb drive had fallen and she undoubtedly had it.

He'd left her lying on the floor in her own vomit. She'd have seen it, picked it up.

All the information in the drive was encrypted but there was no way he could be without it when the ship landed with the girls. The data was necessary to set up the auction. There was at least five million dollars' worth of intel on that drive, maybe more, depending on how the auction went. It was to be an anonymous online auction, but they couldn't organize it without the data on that fucking thumb drive.

The girls at the Meteor, at his insistence, had been injected with a tiny RFID transmitter, under the guise of vaccinations against STDs. There was a way he could track them all on his cell phone but it would be time-consuming to download the data and then scroll through to find Consuelo.

Pirat charged in quarter-hour segments. Nikitin still had seven minutes. He uploaded the code for the RFIDs, the login and passwords and asked for him to check for Consuelo.

Pirat was fast. Inside a minute, he had an answer.

He was expecting her to be at the Meteor but instead he got the message:

RFID tag #3701 at 1147 Birch Street. Morrison Building.

Where in building? he typed.

He stared at the answer in shock.

Company called RBK Security.

It all went smoothly, much more than she expected. Consuelo had stared at the blank wall in front of her with the plaque stating RBK Security next to it for long moments, starting to panic, when it whooshed open and a smiling, kindly woman in an elegant suit and cropped gray hair stood on the other side.

"Call me Marisa," she said in a slightly accented voice, and Consuelo felt immediately better.

It was a busy place, a rich place, where rich successful people did whatever it is they did. Consuelo had no concept of the outside world. She'd been an abandoned child and then a whore all her life.

She'd never seen much of the outside world. When she walked in, it was as if walking into another universe, a better one.

One where women weren't half-naked and on display like meat at a butcher's shop. And where the men weren't glassy-eyed with alcohol and lust, almost subhuman in their desires, like animals with money.

That was her daily life and she realized how impossibly deficient of everything that made life meaningful it was. The only saving grace was solidarity with the other girls, but since the Russians had come with their harsh new regime, they avoided one another. They couldn't help one another. Nobody could help them now.

Everyone knew what had happened to Consuelo. No one could have helped her, so they avoided her. She'd walked out of the Meteor this morning without meeting anyone's eyes.

Here it was so different. Everyone was busy with something that mattered, valued for what they were, what they knew. She eyed everything greedily, simply absorbed into her pores the cool, calm atmosphere where no one was buying anyone else.

This was going to be her new world. It was either that or die.

Marisa walked her across this enormous lobby that smelled fresh and clean, and not of perfume and alcohol, down a corridor, and stopped in front of another blank wall.

A green light flashed on a camera above the door and it whooshed open. "Come in," a deep voice said.

Consuelo froze for a moment. This was it. This was her last refuge and her last hope.

She looked across another large space at two very large men, standing. For a second, she wondered why they were standing and then it hit her like a blow.

They were standing for her.

As if she were a lady.

She stopped, heart pounding, knees suddenly weak, fighting back tears.

Everyone waited patiently. Marisa by her side, the two large men in front of her. She drew in a deep breath and continued walking until she stopped right in front of the big shiny desk.

Both men watched her, faces blank, eyes on hers. Neither of them eyed her breasts or her legs, they looked her straight in the eyes. It gave her permission to look right back.

One of the men looked familiar, though she knew she'd never seen him before. Dark blond hair, light brown eyes, almost golden in color, skin a light gold.

"You're Chloe's brother." It wasn't a question. It was there, in his face.

He dipped his head. "Yes, I am. My name is Harry Bolt and I am Chloe's brother though we don't share a name." He tilted his head to his right. "And this is Barney Carter. Happy to meet you."

And then he did something so unusual Consuelo didn't recognize it. He offered his hand. For a second, she thought maybe he was showing her something and looked at his hand to see what it was. But the hand wasn't palm up, it was simply outstretched. Outstretched for *her*.

She looked at it for a moment, then up at him. His face was so like Chloe's, yet utterly male while hers was so feminine. It puzzled her. She had no family and none of the other girls at the Meteor had families. She'd never seen family resemblances before.

Hesitantly, because she couldn't remember the last time she'd shaken anyone's hand, she reached out. His grip was warm, strong, brief.

"Ma'am," a bass voice said, and she turned to the other man. Where Harry Bolt looked like a successful businessman who worked outdoors sometimes—as opposed to the lawyers and CEOs she had sex with—this man looked dangerous. Someone you'd cross the road to avoid. Even taller and broader than Harry Bolt, he was huge, rough, biceps bulging out of a T-shirt.

He, too, took her hand and squeezed it even more briefly than Harry Bolt had, but with great gentleness. He could crush her hand on a whim, but everything about him spoke of enormous strength under enormous control.

Harry Bolt nodded. "Sit down, please, Ms. . . ."

"Just Consuelo," she said. She'd almost forgotten her last name, she said it so seldom.

"Consuelo, please take a seat." Harry Bolt indicated a comfortable chair, walked back around his big desk and sat down. The dangerous one, Barney, sat in a chair next to her.

Both men looked at her with expressions she couldn't figure out until it hit her. They didn't know she was a prostitute. She was dressed in jeans and a white blouse, with no makeup. They didn't know.

Oh God.

For a second, she just sat there with two men she didn't know and who didn't know what she was. Who looked at her and treated her as if she was a normal woman.

She had spent most of her life inside the Meteor. She couldn't remember the last time a man didn't treat her like a whore.

She breathed this in and breathed this out. If everything went well, there was a possibility of a life where this would happen every day. Leave it all behind.

Please.

"So." Harry Bolt folded his hands on his desk. He wanted her to say why she was here but there was no pressure on her, none. It was a busy, successful company, that was clear from everything she'd seen, but he was giving her his time. "You're a friend of my sister's?"

Another breath. Just one more second of being normal.

She lowered her eyes, raised them. "Yes. It's my fault Chloe was hurt. My fault and the fault of a few of my—my friends."

Nothing changed in his expression. Consuelo turned her head slightly to look at the other man. Barney. No expression there, either.

"How so, Consuelo?" Bolt asked gently.

"She talked to us, encouraged us. Gave us a little courage. Some of us started to talk back. Rebel a little. They couldn't stand it and they sent the Russians."

He straightened suddenly, shooting a glance at the other man.

"The Russians? What Russians?"

Another deep breath. It had been such a brief moment.

She lowered her eyes again, spoke to her knees. "The Russians at the Meteor Club, where I work. Three men and their leader. A man called Nikitin. They've been there for about a year. They've put money into the club, a lot of it. There's something coming, they're preparing for something. Something big is about to happen."

She finally raised her eyes, expecting to see scorn and disgust. Instead Harry Bolt looked thoughtful. He met the other man's eyes again, tapping the desk with a pen. Both of them turned to her again but she saw absolutely nothing in their gaze to show they'd understood her. Nothing.

How could that be?

"Do you know what the Meteor Club is?" she blurted out.

"Yes, of course," Bolt answered, mind obviously elsewhere. "So two of those Russians were the ones who attacked Chloe?"

Amazing. She had just told these two men she was a prostitute and they simply ignored it. She'd stoically thrown away her pleasure at being treated like a lady when she told them where she worked. Her chest had become tight, her breath shallow, but at their reactions, the tightness eased.

"Yes. Their names are Lyov and Ivan. They are thugs. Violent men. They beat up two of my friends at the Meteor. One had to be hospitalized. She was taken across the border for medical care. We never saw her again."

"Hold on." Harry Bolt never took his eyes off her as he picked up a cell phone and pressed just a couple of buttons. "Yeah," he said suddenly as someone picked up at the other end. "Something has happened. We've got a lead on the men who attacked Chloe. Russians, she was right." He listened. "Uh-huh. As soon as you can. Hurry."

He switched off. "So why is it that they attacked my sister?"

"These Russians. They're making some big investment, as I said. Something big is coming. The owner of the Meteor, Franklin Sands, is always trying to make a good impression on the Russians, wanting everything to be perfect. Chloe—she talked to us. Listened to us. Made us feel better. She has a special way, you know?"

Bolt nodded grimly. "Yes, she does."

Consuelo wanted to rub her damp palms together, wanted to look at the floor again, but she did neither. She straightened her shoulders and looked Chloe's brother right in the eyes.

"Chloe held group sessions. I don't think it was really therapy, but I wouldn't know. She listened, mostly. But all of us felt better afterwards. Felt better, felt cleaner. And then we had to go back. Back to the Meteor." Her voice became hoarse. She coughed to clear it. "Each time, it was harder. And I guess we started rebelling a little. It wasn't Chloe's fault. She didn't say anything to us about what we should do, how we should behave, but it was just—some of us couldn't go on. Our boss, he was furious with us. He's trying to make a good impression on the Russians. He doesn't want any problems at all. Susie—one of us—said she was going to quit, that Chloe wanted her to quit. It wasn't true. Chloe never said anything like that at all. She never gave us advice, never pushed in any direction, she just listened. But what Susie said was enough to make the Russians mad."

"So that was it?" Bolt asked. "The reason why they attacked her?"

Consuelo nodded. "To get her to back off. Stop making waves."

"Son of a bitch." The man's face grew even grimmer, white brackets appearing around his mouth. He looked briefly at the other man, who looked as if he wanted to hit someone, too. "Those men are going down. The top Russian, too."

Her moment!

"This might help." Consuelo dug the thumb drive out of her purse and slid it across the large, shiny desk. "I took it off the head Russian, this Nikitin. I don't know his first name. It must contain something valuable. He kept it in his jacket pocket."

"Intel, eh?" Bolt carefully examined the device. "Russian manufacture. I guess that's not surprising." He turned, plugged the thumb drive into his computer and watched the screen carefully. He manipulated some keys. Consuelo knew nothing about computers. It was forbidden for the girls to have computers.

Bolt made a sound of frustration. "It's encrypted. Looks like a 216-bit encryption, too. That's a pretty strong degree of protection. Take some doing to crack."

Consuelo barely understood him. All she really grasped was that maybe what she'd brought wasn't useful. She'd paid such a steep price for it. She blinked back tears. "You can't read it?"

Oh God, she'd been counting on this. Counting that because of the thumb drive, they'd help her disappear. She'd left the Meteor forever, there was no going back. But if there was no going forward, either, what was going to happen to her?

"No, not without some work. And we'd need to find a cracker who speaks Russian." Bolt spoke absently, then looked at her. Though Consuelo was used to hiding her emotions—all whores learned that or they couldn't work—she found she couldn't right now. What she was feeling was right there on her face.

She couldn't breathe, she couldn't think.

"What's wrong?" That deep voice was suddenly gentle.

She twisted her hands, then stilled them. She looked down at herself and was horrified to see that the modest white cotton blouse was fluttering over her left breast as her heart pounded with panic.

She looked at Bolt and at the rough-looking man, Barney.

"I can't go back," she whispered. "I brought that to you as—as payment, because they say you help women disappear. I thought that if the Russian had information, it must be valuable. I can't go back. I can't—" Her voice broke and she stopped talking, breathing shallowly in her panic. "I can't go back. I can't go through that again. The Russian—he put a cloth over my face, poured water over the cloth and—"

The other man, Barney, all of a sudden stood up. "You were fucking *waterboarded?*" he roared, and Consuelo shrank back.

She'd long learned to recognize men's moods, she had an animal instinct for it. And this man had turned dangerous.

She stiffened, turned her face blank.

"Can it, Barney," Bolt said. "You're not helping. You're scaring the lady." He nodded at her. "Sorry about that. Barney's not angry at you, he's angry at a man who could waterboard a woman. So you'll have to excuse him, ma'am."

She kept her back straight, turned to Bolt, then to the other man, this Barney, then back to Bolt. It had been nice being called a lady and addressed as "ma'am," but though it made her feel dead inside, it had to be said.

"I'm not a lady, Mr. Bolt. If you know what the Meteor is, and you know that I work—worked—there, then you know what I am."

"A beautiful woman," Barney growled, and she turned back to him, startled. He'd had bad acne as a youngster. His sallow skin was pockmarked. His rough ugly face was flushed. "That's what you are. Doing what my mom did, because she had three kids to feed and that was the only way to do it. There's no shame. There's plenty of shame for the motherfu—"

"Barney!" Bolt barked.

The man's jaws worked back and forth. "Sorry, boss," he said finally.

Consuelo hung her head, letting her hair fall down around her face, hiding it. Hiding her. A tear dropped on her thigh, making a tiny wet spot on her jeans.

Barney's rough bass voice became soft. "The shame is not yours. It's all on men who would do that to a woman."

Consuelo continued staring at her knees. She couldn't lift her face, she couldn't talk, she couldn't move, she could hardly breathe.

Bolt was talking softly into an intercom system. Nobody moved until the door opened. Consuelo didn't turn around. It was probably someone else from the company.

Maybe to throw her out because she'd brought something completely useless.

It wasn't a man, it was a woman. An extremely beautiful woman, tall, black-haired with intense blue eyes. For a moment, Consuelo thought, *She'd make them a fortune at the Meteor*, then was ashamed of herself.

This was a woman who was loved. She was followed by a big man, hand held to her back because she was hugely pregnant. Hovering over her, watching her like a hawk.

Girls at the Meteor didn't get pregnant. Those that did were made unpregnant very fast. Consuelo hadn't really ever experienced a couple that was expecting a child together. It was a novel thought. People had kids all the time, of course. It's just that she hadn't seen it. Her world and children did not mix.

Harry and Barney stood as the woman moved slowly but gracefully notwithstanding that huge belly. Barney pulled a chair over next to the desk and the woman sat down in it with a huge sigh. Her man—lover? husband?—stood behind her, huge hands on her shoulders.

Harry frowned at her. "What are you doing in the office when you're going to pop the kid any second?"

She sighed again. "Yes, but I'm just finishing up a huge job and I wanted to clear the decks so I can take a couple of weeks off after the birth."

"Couple of *months*," the man behind her growled. It was protective, and endearing, even though he was scowling and looked quite frightening, almost as frightening as Barney, but the woman just laughed. "Weeks. I can do some work from home in the beginning, Sam."

The man behind her—Sam?—huffed out a breath of exasperation through his nostrils, like a bull. The woman laughed again.

Sam looked at Bolt. "So what do we have here? Why'd you call Nicole?"

Ah. The beautiful woman's name was Nicole.

"As long as Nicole's here, I thought maybe she could help us." Bolt handed her the thumb drive.

She looked at it curiously. "What's on it?"

"I don't know. It's Russian, encrypted. And the files inside are probably Russian. You know Russian, don't you?"

"A little. Enough to get the gist of a text."

"And you told me you have this Russian computer whiz on your list of collaborators. Does technical translations. Do you think—"

"Oh yes." Nicole smiled and Consuelo blinked. How could any woman a hundred months pregnant be so very beautiful? "Yes indeed. I think he's just the man for the job. Is it urgent?"

"There might be information on the drive about the men who attacked Chloe."

There was an electric silence.

Nicole held her hand out as if knowing that her husband's hand would find it, and it did. He lifted her out of the chair.

"Then we'll find out what's on this drive just as fast as humanly possible," Nicole declared, holding her hand out for the small drive. Her face had turned serious. "Harry, I'm confiscating your other computer."

He nodded as Nicole sat down before a sleek laptop. She opened it, and with a beep it started up, the glow of the screen reflected on Nicole's face. In a second, she was gone.

Nicole was deep into whatever she was doing, staring intently at the monitor, typing quickly, stopping, then starting again.

"Okay," she said, sitting back, rubbing her belly. "I sent it off to my crazy cracker Russian friend Rudy. He never sleeps. He took a look and said it shouldn't take long. He called it 'Mafiya' encryption, he's used to it. Do you have a clue as to what's in it?"

"It's got something important in it, that's for sure," Bolt replied. He nodded to Consuelo. "She took it off the guy who ordered the attack on Chloe. The guy who waterboarded her."

"Waterboarded?" Nicole straightened, wincing. She held out her hand and her husband took it, gently helped her out of the chair.

Nicole walked over to her and put her hand on her shoulder. "You're not going back to those horrible men."

"That's for damned sure," her husband said. Bolt and Barney nodded.

Consuelo's throat was tight, raw. She couldn't speak, shook her head. "No." Her voice came out like the sound a wounded animal would make. "Never."

This was her opportunity. This is what she came for. But she couldn't get the words out. All four of them watched her, three men, one woman, waiting with blank expressions for her to speak.

Consuelo had been trained in a hard school to repress her feelings, otherwise she couldn't function in the Meteor. Some nights she repressed them so far down she thought they'd disappeared.

They hadn't.

They'd compressed into a hard, black ball that was choking her.

The four continued watching her, waiting.

She had to do this. She had to, because there was no going back. She'd rather die.

"I—I hope there is something useful in that flash drive," she said finally, voice thick and strained. "I hope there is something that will hurt the Russian, put him away. Because he is the one after Chloe. I brought it as payment. Partial payment. Because they say—they say you can help women go away. Disappear. And never be found." *Please*, she prayed to the God she no longer believed in. "And I have money, too." She hid the shaking in her hands as she pulled out a fat manila envelope. She watched Bolt's eyes as she slid it across his desk. He was watching her, not the money. "Twenty thousand dollars," she whispered. "To take me away."

Was it enough? She had no idea. All she knew was that she might as well have pushed her beating heart across the table.

Harry Bolt placed one big hand on the envelope and paused. Did he want more? Could she get more? Not by working at the Meteor, of course. Maybe she could waitress, but where? Anywhere in San Diego and Nikitin and Sands and their men would find her.

Her heart nearly stopped when Bolt moved his hand with the envelope underneath it back across the desk to her. "We can't take your money, Consuelo."

But of course, how could he accept the money of a *puta*? He was a respectable man in a respectable business. Rich and powerful, even. What had she been thinking? She'd been around rich men long enough. Her life savings was probably what he spent for Christmas presents for his wife, if he had one. Of course he had no use for her tainted money.

He'd just condemned her to death.

She should get up and walk out and go . . . where? Her legs wouldn't hold her, she knew that. What could she do, where would she go? She couldn't even think beyond the panic in her mind, flashing nightmare scenes of drowning.

Consuelo wheezed in a breath.

Bolt was saying something but she couldn't hear anything over the noise in her head. "What?"

He repeated patiently. "We don't take money from the women and children we help. Disappearing takes some time and preparation. For the next few days we'll put you in a very safe place while we prepare some documents for you, for your new life. You'll be safe, I promise. Barney will look out for you. Nobody will hurt you."

Her eyes shot to Barney. He held her gaze and nodded his head, as if to confirm what Bolt had said.

No one will hurt you.

"Where would you like to go?"

A blank. A complete blank. She hadn't even considered *choosing* a place. She just thought she'd run, like a piece of tumbleweed rolling in the wind, and stop when the wind stopped.

She could *choose?*

"Miami." The word came from nowhere, but the instant it left her mouth, it felt good. Right. "I'd like to go to Miami."

"Good choice. Lots of Hispanic Americans. Big cities are good to hide in. We'll prepare new documents for you and a background story. Keep a low profile and after a year or two you'll start to feel like this new person."

Please.

"We'll open a bank account for you in Miami under your new name and put another ten thousand in it for you. With what you have, it should be enough for a while. Wait a few months and then you can look for a job. Waitressing, or shop assistant. Nothing too fancy."

Consuelo was almost beyond words. She shook her head numbly. No, nothing too fancy.

The Meteor was fancy. She wanted to be as far away from fancy as possible. Far away from the false luxury and sharp smells of expensive perfumes and liquors. She wanted a small, spare apartment that was just for her, normal clothes, she wanted to take long walks in the park and watch TV and sleep alone at night. She wanted that so much she shook with it.

And the people in this room were going to give it to her.

"Thank you," she said. She blinked, and the tears began. "Thank you so much. You've given me my life back."

Nicole rose, with the help of the rough-looking man who never left her side, and walked toward her. This beautiful, elegant woman. A lady.

She put her hand on Consuelo's shoulder. "You thank yourself, Consuelo. You got yourself out of this situation. We're just helping. Follow the instructions you'll receive from Harry and from Barney and you will be fine. We all wish you well in your new life."

Consuelo placed her hand over Nicole's without thinking, then, appalled at herself, tried to pull it back. But Nicole had grasped it, and wouldn't let go.

"Good luck," she said, bending down to whisper in Consuelo's ear, and it was like a benediction.

Barney was at a side door, holding it open.

"Ma'am," he said, his voice so deep it reverberated in her stomach. Or maybe it was the word. So insignificant. So important.

Consuelo rose and walked out the door.

The man who'd been fucking Chloe Mason on the balcony drove away. Nikitin watched the vehicle drive up from the underground parking lot. The side windows were smoked but the front windshield was clear and gave him an excellent view of the man's face, which he'd last seen sweating as he humped the woman.

Chloe Mason was alone. And Chloe Mason was going to get him his thumb drive back.

He was going to need his trunk, and he was going to need Dmitri. But first he emailed Pirat.

> Find coordinates of flat empty landscape around San Diego.

The answer came immediately.

> Exceeded retainer.

Pizdets! Fuck!

Nikitin kept Pirat on retainer. And yes, he'd exceeded it. Gritting his teeth, he transferred $10,000 from his Bahamian account to Pirat's account in Goa.

Happy now? he thought sourly. But he didn't text it.

Three minutes later he had a set of coordinates, satellite photographs from 10,000 meters altitude, 5,000, 1,000, 500, 100, and so close he could read license plate numbers if there were cars around. There were none. It was a desert. Anza-Borrego Desert was written in white script along the bottom of the 1,000-meter resolution photo. Though his iPhone screen was small, Pirat had provided extensive maps and Nikitin spent ten minutes scrolling through them. Pirat had also provided a map with a course set in a blue line leading to the desert.

He made calculations in his head. If he drove fast, he could make it to the desert in forty minutes. It would give him time to set up the handover.

He called Dmitri, gave him the coordinates of where he was, told him to bring the trunk and to park two condo buildings down from La Torre.

While he waited, he watched the apartment on the fourth floor.

The curtains in one room—the bedroom?—were drawn, but the rest of the apartment, which stretched out over five rooms, all connected by one balcony, with a small, separate balcony where the two had fucked, was open. He could see the woman moving around occasionally.

His jaw was aching and his fingers clenched the binoculars so hard it was a surprise he wasn't denting the metal. Sweat trickled down his back.

Nikitin was a soldier, and a good one. He'd been Spetsnaz for fourteen years, in the Vympel, the best of the best.

He'd been in combat, fought numerous firefights in Africa and Chechnya. But going into combat, if you were good—and he was—you had a chance of survival.

Not here. If he was not able to produce the thumb drive when the *vory* came over for the auction, he was a dead man. And his death would be long and lingering.

It wouldn't even be personal. The *vory* knew they'd have to make a lesson out of him for others who might be careless with several million dollars' worth of information. The lesson would be a death with an epic amount of pain, every minute filmed, as an object lesson.

He was developing a plan on the fly with very little intel, in a foreign country, with one operative. All because of that bitch up there in her fancy condo, talking rebellion to the prostitutes.

Nikitin kept a close control on his emotions at all times. He had moved in dangerous circles all his life. His father had been shot for sedition when he refused to take his men in on a suicide mission in Afghanistan.

Nikitin knew how dangerous the world was, knew it in his bones and his blood. That he now found himself on the knife's edge of a horrible death because of the meddling of some fucking woman made him shake with rage.

If it were up to him, he'd fucking walk into that apartment

and blow her head apart, and for a second, for one uncontrollable second, he wanted to do that so badly he trembled with it.

But then a lifetime of discipline descended upon him once more, enclosing him in its hard embrace. It was like his brain had had static for a moment, bad reception, but now was back in tune.

He saw clearly what had to be done and how he would do it and saw that if he did it clean and fast there might be a way out of this. With some luck, which had to begin turning his way again, the *vory* would never know what had happened.

He could, perhaps, explain away the disappearance of the two men assigned him by reporting the loss of a considerable sum of cash. The two men had embezzled the money and disappeared, probably south to Tijuana. Nikitin could promise the *vory* that as soon as the new transaction was over he'd track them down and get the money back.

But for now, he had to get his hands on Chloe Mason.

Dmitri was parking about 500 meters away. Nikitin carefully scanned the horizon, 360 degrees. There was no one observing him, no one on the balconies of the luxury condo, no one out for a walk. This was a residential neighborhood and most of the inhabitants were at work.

The binoculars went into his backpack, then he rose and strolled up to the sidewalk, just a man taking a morning break and getting some exercise.

He walked past Dmitri, watching carefully for onlookers, then doubled back, knocking on the driver's side window. It buzzed down.

"Did you get everything?" Nikitin asked, voice low. In answer, Dmitri unlocked the back of the vehicle.

Nikitin made a quick inventory. He prepared two backpacks, for him and Dmitri. GSh-18s with suppressors, three magazines each. No rifles, not now, that would come later. Two gas masks, a canister with fitted tube, high-speed drill, small amount of C4 with det cord.

He tucked the pistol in the small of his back, the rest fit into his backpack. He hefted it and signaled to Dmitri.

Dmitri closed the trunk and fell into step beside him. Nikitin gave him his backpack. "Easy," Nikitin murmured. "Nice and slow."

They ambled toward the end of the peninsula, two men in sports clothes, out for a walk. Without hesitating, they walked through the huge two-story glass doors of La Torre.

His luck was holding, Nikitin thought. About time. They had encountered no one, not one car was on the road. The huge atrium was deserted except for one guard behind a U-shaped console.

Nikitin looked around with a faint smile on his lips, a connoisseur appreciating a well-designed building. Four security cameras in the corners, angled to cover the entire footage of the atrium. And two more vid cams over the elevators.

"Help you folks?" The security guard had a polite smile on his face, but he was young, fit and alert. He rose as Nikitin and Dmitri approached, one hand on the counter, the other loose at his side, right next to the Beretta in a holster.

An array of high-resolution monitors glowed on a shelf below the countertop.

Nikitin leaned on the chest-high counter with a smile, making sure he didn't touch anything with his hands. The guard couldn't see him reaching behind his back. "Yes," he said, shaking his head ruefully, "I'm looking for a Mr. Darren Smith. He said he lived in Coronado Shores, in the La Torre condominium. Am I in the right place?"

"Yes, sir, you are," the guard replied. "But I'm afraid we don't have anyone living here by that—"

In a smooth practiced move, Nikitin brought the GSh up, firing point-blank at the bridge of the nose, straight through the neocortex. Pink and gray spray shot out behind his head and the guard slumped boneless to the floor, already dead.

"Name," Nikitin finished the sentence.

They didn't need to talk. Both of them donned latex gloves that were in Dmitri's backpack. Nikitin disconnected the monitors while Dmitri disposed of the body beneath the shelf. There was some blood spatter on the floor but you'd have to come right up to the security desk to see it. Nikitin nodded at Dmitri who walked briskly across the huge atrium, boot heels echoing on the marble floor. He threaded plastic restraints around the inside door handles and tightened them. The restraints were almost invisible from the outside. It would take 500 pounds of pressure to break them. The building would be cut off from the outside world for the short time it would take them to snatch Chloe Mason.

Anyone visiting or returning to the condo would see a missing security guard and locked doors and assume there'd been trouble and probably call 112.

No, this was America, he reminded himself. 911.

He studied the security camera system for a minute while Dmitri was taking care of the front doors. He was familiar with most security systems. This one was particularly upscale.

But not invulnerable.

He flipped a switch and raised his eyes to the four corners of the atrium. The LED lights next to the cameras were off.

Okay, the building was sealed and blind.

Phase two.

The Mason woman had been on the fourth floor, third apartment from the left. Ordinarily, he would have ascended to several floors above the apartment, then come down the stairwell, but time was tight. The security system was off but he had no idea whether there were two guards on duty. That was the problem with improvisation—no intel and no proper planning. So they just took the elevator up.

Outside the door of the apartment, Nikitin held out his hand and Dmitri placed an infrared scanner in it. Nikitin switched it on, then looked, frowning, at the screen. There was nothing. Absolutely nothing.

He walked quickly down the hallway, aiming the scanner, and found two people behind the doors and the walls of the apartments. One two doors down to the right, and the other behind the door of the last apartment to the left.

The heat signatures were small. Women or very small men. Housewives or cleaning ladies, most likely.

He walked back fast to the apartment where Chloe was. Nothing.

The door was featureless, obviously a sliding door operated by a keypad to the right. The door was impenetrable to infrared. So were the walls to either side of the door.

Shit! This Mike Keillor was very security-conscious. Nikitin met Dmitri's eyes. He indicated the next apartment over and Dmitri nodded.

They moved to the next door in complete silence. Dmitri had been well-trained. Nikitin didn't have to give orders.

He aimed the infrared at the door of the apartment right next to where Mason was staying. Wood, no barrier at all to infrared.

He walked the length of the corridor corresponding to the apartment and saw no heat signatures at all. Perfect. Whoever owned this place was out, probably at work. If they were out shopping, they'd regret it because Nikitin would shoot to kill if they returned.

His weapons were beyond traceable reach of U.S. law enforcement authorities. The security cameras were down. If he had to kill, they'd never trace it back to him. They were being very careful, but even if they left some DNA behind, neither he nor Dmitri would be in their system.

Nikitin eyed the lock. It was pickable, but it would take time. He nodded to Dmitri and stepped back. The shot was barely audible standing right next to the gun. It sounded like a can of beer being opened.

With a slight push of the door, they entered. Nikitin immediately turned right, aiming his scanner at the walls while Dmitri went from room to room, weapon up.

By the time Dmitri came back giving the all-clear hand signal, Nikitin had found Chloe, sitting in a room directly next to this apartment's living room. He studied the scanner's monitor.

A slight figure sitting on a chair, hand curled around something hot, the only other heat source what looked like a microwave, cooling rapidly.

She was sitting drinking tea or coffee. Perfect.

On October 23, 2002, Nikitin had been a young lieutenant in the elite Vityaz counterterrorism unit under the FSB. He'd been seconded to Moscow from Grozny for a three-month course in NBC terrorism when the call came in at 9:20 P.M. Fifty terrorists had taken more than nine hundred people hostage at a theater during the presentation of a popular musical. The terrorists were armed to the teeth and wore explosive vests. A few hostages who had been backstage escaped out the back and briefed the Special Forces who were staged around the theater. The terrorists moved among the hostages, essentially walking bombs.

It was impossible to storm the theater—the casualties would be horrific. Unsustainable for a government elected on an antiterrorism ticket.

Negotiations sputtered into a stalemate that lasted four days. At 5 A.M. on the twenty-sixth, Russian forces streamed fentanyl, a powerful anesthetic, into the theater, knocking out hostages and hostage-takers alike.

Fentanyl was a hundred times stronger than morphine and could fell a bear in five seconds. One small human female was going to be a snap.

Nikitin placed the infrared scanner on the floor, turned the monitor up and took a high-speed drill out of his backpack. He had to act quickly. If the Mason woman left the kitchen to go into a room with no common wall, his only other alternative was to break through the wall immediately, but that would give her time to call 911.

No, he needed her unconscious, right now.

He knelt next to the join between wall and floor and applied the drill. It emitted a soft whine, which made him frown. It was minor, but noticeable in a quiet room.

He looked up at Dmitri and mouthed *shum*. Noise. Dmitri nodded and a few moments later loud rock music came from the living room. Perfect. It blocked the noise of the drill.

The drill was small but powerful. It bit through the apartment wall, through the insulation and Sheetrock, and, finally, through the wall on the other side. He immediately switched off the drill.

Nikitin kept his eye on the monitor. The woman was still sitting in her chair. Her thermal signature was the same, but the cup's temperature had dropped.

Nikitin fit one end of a small rubber tube over the spout of the canister and threaded the other end carefully through the hole on this side of the wall and the other side. He stopped when he gauged that the tube exited one inch from the hole.

It was a calculated risk. Nothing indicated that this Mason woman was an operator. She was a civilian, an *American* civilian, and was as dumb to surrounding perils as a rock. It was highly unlikely she would notice a tiny piece of flesh-colored rubber and very soon she would be knocked unconscious.

Nikitin fit a gas mask over his face, tossing Dmitri his. Once they'd checked that they worked, Nikitin flipped a lever, picked the scanner up and stood.

At first nothing happened. Then, the flame-colored woman on the other side of the wall sat up straighter, lifting her head. Weaponized fentanyl was odorless, but it was possible there was a slight hiss as it filled the small room.

The woman stood up, and for a horrible moment Nikitin thought the fentanyl wasn't working. She lurched suddenly, hands braced on the table, then slid bonelessly to the floor.

Phase two, complete.

Nikitin packed everything away while Dmitri placed small charges along a virtual rectangle a meter and a half high and two meters wide. When he finished, Dmitri turned the music to its highest setting and they exited the room, waiting to the side of the living room door while Dmitri pushed the detonator.

The explosion was audible, but less loud than the music. Nikitin and Dmitri rushed to the wall dividing the two apartments, the gas masks protecting them from the drywall dust and from the fentanyl.

They put their shoulders to the wall, ripping and punching their way into the other apartment. Nikitin bent, handed Dmitri his backpack and pulled the unconscious woman up and over his shoulder.

A quick glance at the front door showed that there was another keypad, which doubtless was linked to some kind of signal to the owner that the front door had been breached.

No problem. They exited through the hole blown in the wall and out through the front door of the apartment owned by less paranoid people.

Their luck held. The elevator took them down to the garage level. Nikitin stood in the shadows while Dmitri went to get the SUV. While waiting, Nikitin checked the security cameras. Out, every single one.

Dmitri rolled down the ramp, turned around and backed up. Nikitin placed the Mason woman down in the back, checking her eyes and pulse. She was completely unconscious. Fentanyl was a dangerous substance. Nikitin hadn't dosed it and didn't even know what the lethal dose was. At the Nord-Ost siege, 170 people had died from the gas.

Chloe Mason was definitely going to die, but not before he got his thumb drive back. No one was going to trade something valuable in for a cadaver.

He put plastic restraints around her wrists. Then he pulled out a syringe and plunged it into her thigh. M5050, an antidote. She had to be able to walk in about an hour.

He climbed into the passenger seat, dialed in the GPS coordinates into the sat nav system and signed Dmitri to drive off.

Phase three complete, ready for phase four.

Chapter 18

Mike walked into Harry's office, taking in the situation at a glance. Harry, looking like he wanted to chew someone's head off, Nicole sitting back in an armchair, feet up on the coffee table, fingers linked over huge belly, eyes closed. Sam, standing behind her like some huge guard dog, hands on her shoulders.

"Sitrep," Mike said, as soon as the door closed behind him. Nicole's eyes opened for a second, then closed again.

"Okay, we have the name of the man who ordered the attack on Chloe," Harry said, and Mike froze. Every cell, every muscle on lockdown.

"Who? And where?" He managed to unlock his throat enough to get the words out.

The man who'd ordered the attack on Chloe. The man who had only a few hours to live.

"Whoa," Sam said when Mike headed without a word for the gun locker.

"Yeah, hold it," Harry said, holding up his hands when Mike snarled at him. "Listen, she's my sister. You think I don't want to get back at this fucker? At least as much as you do? But we need more intel."

Back home, Mike had been so relaxed he felt boneless. Now he felt as if the top of his head was about ready to blow. He didn't want more intel, he didn't need it. If they had a name, they had an address, and he wanted to be there *now*.

He could barely reason through the buzzing in his head. Barely think of steps to take, how to plan it through, because his head was so full of images of a broken and hurt Chloe. "Where's the intel coming from?"

"Same place the name came from. A woman Chloe helped. She works at the Meteor Club. Chloe did some talk sessions with her and some of the other women, they all started rebelling, and this guy sent his goons to teach Chloe a lesson."

"Name?" *To teach Chloe a lesson*. That some man would hurt Chloe, send men to beat her up because she befriended some of the poor women who worked at the Meteor . . . Christ, that was a dead man walking. When Mike heard who he was, the hair on his body stood on end.

"Anatoly Nikitin. Former FSB, Special Forces. Now works for one of the big Russian mafiya conglomerates as an enforcer." Harry shot an annoyed look at Nicole, resting in the armchair. "Nicole found that out. She beat me to it."

A faint smile appeared on Nicole's mouth. Without opening her eyes, she wriggled her fingers in a hello gesture.

"According to the woman who came to us, this Russian is the vanguard of a major investment Russians are making in the Meteor, and they've got something big planned. The Russian came over with three other goons, two of which are out of commission thanks to you."

My pleasure, Mike thought sourly. Man, was he sorry he hadn't whacked both of them.

"We got this intel from a woman, as I said. The Russian is blind over here and doesn't know what happened to his men. That was a good call to keep the info anonymous. The Russian—this

Nikitin—waterboarded the woman for more information."

Mike turned his head slowly, carefully toward Harry, trying to make sure his head didn't explode. "He *what?*"

Harry blew out a breath, grim lines in his face. "You heard me. Fucker waterboarded this woman for intel on Chloe. She didn't have anything to give him so he did it three more times. Just to show her who's boss."

Mike felt nauseous for a moment. SERE training was part of Force Recon training, and Mike had undergone it at the Remote Training Site in Warner Springs. Survival, Evasion, Resistance and Escape. That more or less said it for what they trained them to face if they ever got caught by the enemy.

The Marines were right to subject applicants to the worst things that could be thrown at them because, by God, the enemy had even worse things in store. He'd undergone R2I—Resistance to Interrogation—where he'd been subjected to everything short of life-threatening physical torture. Of all the tests Mike had survived, waterboarding had been the absolute worst.

There had been something so very dark about it—reducing you to an animal state of panic. It got results, because it broke men down fast. Mike had survived two bouts by the skin of his teeth, but it had taken him days to recover and he still had nightmares. Used against enemies sworn to destroy his country, he could sort of justify its use.

But a woman being waterboarded for information on another woman? And when she didn't have anything to offer, being waterboarded three times more as punishment? That was the kind of man after Chloe? Man, he was going down.

Chloe. Without thinking, his cell was in his hand, the first number on his speed dial list ringing.

"Hello?" Mike let out an exhale at hearing her voice. Harry relaxed just a bit, too.

"Hi, honey, just checking. Everything okay?"

He listened carefully to her tone. "Mike, you left about half an hour ago, what could possibly happen in half an hour? I'm fine. I'm sitting in your kitchen, sipping tea. Pretty soon I'm going to go looking for something to read that isn't gun magazines and every novel Stephen Hunter ever wrote. I left my Kindle in my place and I need something to read."

He smiled. She sounded just fine. Maybe a little bored. Bored was fine. Bored was great, actually.

"There's a Kindle in the bedroom. Order yourself some books from Amazon. On my credit card, password 'remington.'"

"Figures." Chloe laughed. "Okay, I think I will. So, I guess I'll see you later?"

You bet. "Yeah, honey, just as soon as I can make it. Don't go anywhere and don't open to anyone except me or one of us. Check the security cam outside before you open the door." He switched the cell phone off and looked at Harry. "She's okay."

"Yeah, I heard. And good luck to anyone trying to break into your place. Just a little while longer and I think we'll get a handle on this thing. Just as soon as we crack what's on that thumb drive, we can retaliate. With any luck, we can take it to Kelly and he'll have this Russian, Nikitin, and the other guy deported so fast their heads will swim."

Mike narrowed his eyes. Having them deported wasn't permanent enough for him. He wanted to—

Harry narrowed his own eyes. "And that's it, Mike. We have to bring him to justice. No funny business that will just come back and bite us in the ass. Is that clear? I want Chloe safe just as much as you do, but I also don't want you spending thirty years in the brig. Chloe would be really pissed off at that, big-time."

Mike opened his mouth to answer when the side door opened and Barney walked in frowning, a small, frilly woman's purse hanging incongruously from one big, hairy paw, a scanner in the other. Right behind him came a gorgeous dark-haired woman, clearly frightened, tear tracks drying on her cheeks.

Before Mike or Harry could ask what Barney had done to make the woman cry, Barney threw the purse on Harry's desk in disgust. The woman was barely holding it together, arms crossed over her midriff, shaking like a leaf.

"What's this, Barney?" Harry frowned.

"Bad news, boss. I asked Ms. Consuelo here"—he jerked a huge thumb at the woman—"whether she was being tagged. She said she turned her cell phone off before coming here. But then I turned on the scan and it's picking up on a transponder somewhere, and we can't find it. I don't think it's in the purse." He switched the scanner on. A small LED light lit up and it emitted a faint whine. Unfortunately the audio level of the scanner wasn't correlated with distance. It could only tell that there was a transponder within a radius of five feet, not where it was.

"Let's find out," Harry said. He picked up the purse, which looked almost as ridiculous in his hand as it had in Barney's, and pressed a button. Marisa appeared almost immediately in the doorway. She looked at the crying, shivering woman and immediately looked daggers at every man in the room. "What have you men done to that woman?"

Barney held up his huge hands. "Nothing, Marisa, I swear."

The woman, Consuelo, had stopped crying and was looking astonished. "No, no, ma'am. No one hurt me. Nothing like that at all. I'm afraid I might have hurt *them*."

Harry handed the frilly purse to Marisa. "I need for you to take this into the lobby for a few minutes please, Marisa. We need to understand if there is a bug transmitting Consuelo's location in it."

Marisa's face cleared immediately. She was intimately familiar with all the tricks men could use to track down women they wanted to hurt. Harry didn't need to explain any further.

"I'll take it into the lobby and then into the outside hallway, just so you can be sure." She looked at Consuelo. "No one but me will touch it, I guarantee it."

Consuelo waved her away, swiping at her face with the heels of her hands. "I don't care. All I care about is that maybe I have something on me that will let him follow me here."

Marisa disappeared. The door whooshed behind her.

The LED light was still on, unchanged. Whatever was setting off the signal wasn't in the purse.

Barney was standing in front of Consuelo, a dull red on his cheekbones. "Ma'am?" he rumbled. "It's on your person. It has to be." He looked helplessly at Harry and Mike, the blush turning stoplight red.

Barney was a certified sharpshooter, a sixth dan, and the company mechanic. He kept the RBK fleet of vehicles in perfect running order. He was a master at close-quarter combat and had an amazing collection of blues LPs.

He also had difficulty dealing with women, particularly in the saying-no department. Nicole, Ellen and Chloe ran roughshod over him.

Mike disappeared behind a door that he firmly closed behind him. In front of him was a panel with a keypad. He punched in a long string of alphanumeric digits and the panel opened. Behind it was a very large locker room filled with weapons, mostly Mike's, and gear for every possible need. There was several hundred thousand dollars' worth of stuff in there, every item catalogued.

Mike had no need to look around. The locker had been organized by him and he was definitely OCD when it came to weaponry and gear. He knew exactly what to get and where it was. He pulled it out, reset the code and alarm, and walked back into the room.

This scanner was the latest model, both the audio signal and light signal sensitive to proximity.

Mike approached the woman, one hand open in the universal sign of peace, the other with a short titanium stick with a display just above the handle, looking a little like Harry Potter's wand.

"May I?" he asked, and she nodded, looking a little less freaked out.

Nicole opened her eyes suddenly. She was prone to tiny little naps during the course of the day and everyone let her rest. She took in the scene at a glance and held her hand out to Sam. Sam didn't help her up so much as lift her up. Bless her, Nicole had realized that the woman might be uncomfortable, so she went to her and placed a reassuring hand on the woman's shoulder.

The woman tried to smile, though anxiety was etched on her face. The closer Mike got, the louder the audio from the scanner. Something was on her, all right.

Mike started at the head and didn't make it beyond the neck. The light pulsed and the audio signal grew to an annoying whine. The shirt?

"Nicole?"

Nicole smiled and touched Consuelo's white shirt, fingering the collar. "May I?"

The woman nodded.

Nicole gently brushed the woman's glossy chestnut hair to one side to check the collar and froze. She ran her finger up the woman's slender neck. "Uh, guys? I think we have something here."

Nicole lifted the hair up in a ponytail and pointed at a small red spot. "Consuelo, what's that?"

Consuelo's hand went up to touch her neck, her face blank. She blinked. "Oh, I completely forgot that. It's a shot of some kind. some vaccine. All of us got one. Against STDs. And also birth control."

Mike wanded her neck and the scanner practically jumped up and screamed *There it is!*

"I don't think you got a vaccine jab, ma'am. I think you got tagged with a bug so they could know your whereabouts."

The woman's head whipped up so fast Nicole dropped her hair. It swirled around her shoulders. She was white-faced, shocked. "I have something *inside* me that tells them where I am? Oh my God, oh my God!" She twirled, frantic, trying to escape something that was in her body. "Get it out of me, get it out of me, *get it out of me!*" She was screaming and jumping up and down. "He'll find me, he knows where I am right now, he's going to come get me and take me back, oh my God, help me! He's coming, he's coming! *Help me!*"

A man of stone would be unable to withstand such levels of panic and none of them were made of stone.

"Quiet, ma'am, it's okay. We'll get you to a doctor—"

"No!" she screamed. "Get it out of me now! Oh God, please get it out of me!" She was hopping up and down in a panic.

Harry stood still for a moment looking perplexed, very un-Harry-like. He always knew what to do. Mike was at a loss, too. They had to get the bug out of her, but if she didn't want to go to a doctor, what were they supposed to do?

Barney was entirely red-faced now. "Uh, ma'am? Would you trust me to get it out of you? I've trained as a medic." He held his huge hands up. "I can be delicate, I promise."

She didn't even hesitate. "Oh God, yes! Get that thing out of me now!"

Barney looked at Mike. "I'll need our medic kit."

Mike knew exactly where it was. Inside a minute, he was handing Barney their kit specially made for them by a team of doctors, modeled after a field trauma kit. It contained almost everything necessary to deal with wounds that didn't require major surgery.

Consuelo sat holding her hair to one side while Barney sprayed an anesthetic on the spot Nicole had found, swabbed it, took a scalpel and carefully made a small incision, pulling a tiny electronic device out with tweezers. The wound barely bled and only required two butterfly bandages.

He held up the tweezers.

Consuelo was white-faced, hands shaking. "Get rid of it, now! Nikitin knows I'm here, he'll be coming for me!"

Mike pushed a button on Harry's desk.

"Nikitin is in for a big surprise." One of their men, Dan Ryan, poked his head in. "Come in, Dan. Barney, wrap that transmitter up in a piece of paper and give it to Dan." The tiny blood-flecked piece of silicon went into an envelope and into Dan's hands. "I want you and Lee to leave right now. Take one of our vehicles, cross the border into Tijuana, check into a room at a dive that offers surveillance possibilities front and back, pay for several days in advance, leave the envelope in a drawer and get right back out without being seen. Set up surveillance and wait for two Russians to find it. That's a transmitter being followed by some bad guys, so execute security protocols. You know what to do."

"On it, boss." Dan executed an ironic salute and left.

Consuelo had stopped crying. She let out a huge exhale. "Thank you," she said shakily.

Harry nodded. "Barney, go to the safe house with Consuelo. I'll have someone bring you some new ID for her. Then take Consuelo north. Drive around for a couple of days until you feel you've found the right place. Text me on my throwaway cell when you've landed. Have Consuelo find a place and open a bank account. We'll transfer some money there as soon as you do. Consuelo, don't look for a job right away. Stay under the radar. When we take Nikitin down, we'll let you know and you can go to Miami. You'll be safe."

"Safe," she whispered. "Please."

There was complete silence in the room. Nicole put her arm around her and kissed her cheek. "Good luck, my dear," she said.

Harry waited until Consuelo and Barney were gone. "I wish we knew what these fuckers were up to, then we could go to Kelly. I wonder—"

His spare laptop gave a soft ping.

Nicole looked at the monitor and smiled. "Good old Rudy. He cracked the code. Let's see what we have here. Oh, he's on Skype."

Mike, Harry and Sam gathered around the monitor, looking at a small square in the upper half of the screen. The man was impossibly young-looking with huge blue eyes and a spotty ginger beard. He looked serious and spoke a few words in Russian. Nicole answered back slowly, choosing her words carefully.

Mike really admired that. She was basically trilingual, her French and Spanish as good as her English. And knew enough Russian and Arabic to get by. Mike himself barely knew English. He was much better with guns.

"What did he say?"

"He said . . . he said it's bad." Nicole's face was somber. "Let's take a look."

She sighed and shifted in the chair trying to find a comfortable position with about ten billion pounds strapped to her stomach. It had been that way with Merry, too. She'd been as big as a house and then Merry had come out, this tiny delicate little creature. What were the kids doing in there? Playing golf?

Nicole touched a key and the screen came to life. There were a series of photographs, full-face and full-figure, of young girls. All of them blond, and all of them very very pretty. The age range was from about six to ten. The photographs were very clear, professional quality, well-lit and well-staged. Next to each photograph was a series of words in Cyrillic script followed by numbers.

A male voice-over kept up a running commentary in Russian. Nicole leaned forward, concentrating, a frown between her eyebrows.

Suddenly she gasped, held out her hand. Sam's hand was right there for her. She looked up at her husband, face deathly pale.

"Oh my God, Sam," she whispered.

"What is it, honey? What's wrong?" He crouched in front of her, holding her hand. "What's the matter? Is it the baby?"

"Sam." Nicole looked up at Mike and Harry, tears tracking down her white face. "Mike, Harry. Oh my God!"

Sam was a tough guy, tough in battle and tough in the board-room. His only known weaknesses were Nicole and Merry. And the little girl on the way. If Nicole was hurting, Sam was frantic.

Mike's skin prickled. What was on that monitor was also a threat to Chloe. He leaned forward. "What is it, Nicole? What's he saying? What are those photographs?"

With a strangled sound, Nicole stood and took two shaky steps to the wastepaper basket near Harry's desk and vomited. A worried-looking Sam held her as she straightened trembling, wiping her mouth.

Tears were streaming down her face as she turned to her husband, holding on to his arms. "Sam," she said urgently, "we have to stop them! You've got to do something!"

Mike looked at Harry. Nicole was not a hysterical woman. There was something very nasty in those files.

A huge sob escaped her and she leaned over the wastepaper basket again, though only thin bile came up. She straightened, shaking.

"Those girls are on a boat, coming here. Those poor little girls. We have to do something! Stop it! It's an auction. They're going to sell those little girls to the highest bidder."

Another shudder and her water broke.

Chapter 19

Chloe woke up with a gasp, heart pounding. Her head pulsed with sharp pain, as if she were wearing a crown of spikes. "Good. You're awake." The voice, deep and accented, came from somewhere in front of her. "You're no good to me dead."

The words made no sense, none. It was noise, together with other noise, a low humming sound.

Her world was pain—sunlight directly in her eyes that was like a bright lance piercing her head. She could keep her eyes open only for a few seconds at a time. Her right side hurt, as if something hard had fallen on it. There was a sharper pain in her right biceps, tight and focused and burning. Her arms were tied together at the wrists. Finally she was able to twist around enough to look at where it hurt, but only for a moment. She stared at the bright red spot blankly. In the middle of the spot was a hole, a tiny puncture wound. She closed her eyes.

Had she been bitten by a venomous insect? Could that explain her reaction to light, the pounding headache, the lassitude? Maybe, but it didn't explain the low humming sound, like—like an engine.

A . . . car? Was she in a car?

Keeping her eyes open for more than a few seconds was impossible, it was like having a stage spotlight shine right in her eyes.

The tone of the humming noise changed and she rolled against something soft. The deep fog in her head lifted long enough for her to recognize that, yes, she was in a car that had just changed gears. She was lying on her side in the backseat and there was a plastic strip keeping her hands tied. She tried to pull her hands apart but it was hopeless. All she did was cut into the flesh of her wrists.

She couldn't fathom anything of this. Was she in a nightmare? Her last memory was sitting happily in Mike's kitchen, sipping tea. Had she gone back to bed and fallen asleep and now she was dreaming being held captive?

The metallic mechanical beeps of a cell phone. Not a number. Someone on speed dial.

"No, this is not Chloe, Mr. Bolt," that deep Russian-accented voice said. "Chloe is alive and your sister will stay that way as long as you do exactly what I say . . ."

Harry, who was almost as good at computers as Nicole, was sitting at the computer, scrolling through the files on the thumb drive.

Nicole and Sam were on their way to the hospital, Sam keeping them up to date. He sounded frantic and was breaking land speed records to get Nicole to the doctors so he wouldn't have to deliver their little girl.

Harry suddenly sat up. "Shit."

"What?" Mike walked over, frowning. There was something worse than little girls being sold at an auction?

He'd scrolled through the photographs, wishing he could throw up like Nicole. Pretty, innocent little girls. Most too thin, but clearly beauties. He didn't understand the Russian but he understood the numbers all right. The ages, which ran from six to ten and the bids, which all started at $50,000.

There was tons of other info, which was going straight to the FBI just as soon as Sam and Nicole's little girl was born. The FBI was going to want to talk to Sam, too, and there was no way Sam would leave Nicole's side. Not even a gun pointed to his head would do it. It was better all round if they just waited until Sam was free.

"Look at this." Harry pointed to the screen.

"I don't see—" And then Mike did. A list of names in Latin script, not Cyrillic. A list of names of potential customers, men who'd bid on those little girls.

It took a lot to shock Mike, but he was floored. There were people here he knew, people he recognized. Men he would never suspect could be filthy buyers of little girls.

The mayor's top aide, four district attorneys, five CEOs of major corporations, a famous journalist, the head of surgery at a major hospital . . . the list went on and on. Little girls being obviously a popular commodity.

He wanted to vomit like Nicole had and he wanted to punch a hole in the wall. Harry just stared grimly at the screen. "Those scumbags are going down."

It was a thought to warm the heart. "Oh yeah," Mike promised. "The FBI will be all over this." And he knew precisely whom to call. Special Agent Aaron Welles, who was a friend and whose mother had been beaten on a regular basis by his dad. He was a big help to RBK in helping battered women because he had an emotional stake in it.

And pedophilia—again, Mike had to suppress the gag reflex. All he had to do was think of his nieces and some fuckhead hurting them and he went a little crazy.

"Aaron's going to be all over these guys. When are the girls arriving?"

Harry peered into the monitor intently, as if the harder he

looked, the better he could understand Russian. He threw up his hands. "I can't tell," he growled, frustrated. "Goddammit. I hope it's not now. Those girls will be disappeared fast if they get a chance to land."

"Try cutting and pasting the info into Google Translate," Mike suggested. "What?" he said when Harry glared at him.

Harry was pouding at the keyboard. "I hate it when you have good computer ideas. That's my thing. You're good with weapons, I'm good with computers. That's the way it should be. Okay, here we go." He read the translation and sat back, relieved. "Got it. Ship's due in San Diego harbor two days from now. The Coast Guard can intercept them. Those guys won't know what hit them. We have to make sure no one warns them, otherwise they'll throw those poor girls overboard."

Harry's cell buzzed. He pulled it out, looked at Mike. "It's Chloe."

Mike frowned. Why was Chloe calling Harry and not him? He moved closer to Harry, shamelessly listening in. Did Chloe need something? If she did, by God Mike'd get it for her, not Harry.

"Yeah, honey," Harry said, then stiffened. He shot a glance at Mike and switched to speakerphone.

"—not Chloe, Mr. Bolt," a deep, strongly accented voice said. "Chloe is alive and your sister will stay that way as long as you do exactly what I say. You have something that belongs to me. I will give you your sister back in exchange for it."

Every hair on Mike's body was standing up in panic. A drop of sweat rolled down Harry's temple.

"Who is this?" he asked, though Harry knew as well as Mike who it was.

Nikitin. The Russian. The man who hadn't hesitated to water-board a woman. The man who had Chloe.

Chloe in his hands.

Mike shuddered. His body had a reaction it had never had before. He felt an electric shock throughout his body as he pumped out sweat in one stinking rush. His muscles were weak, he had to stiffen his legs to keep upright. His insides roiled painfully and he barely made it in time to the fancy designer wastebasket Nicole had used and which had just been cleaned by Marisa.

It was absolutely uncontrollable. Mike had had a vision of Chloe being waterboarded and his entire body had rejected the thought so hard his guts turned inside out.

Harry scowled at him, covering the microphone so the fuckhead at the other end of the line wouldn't hear him puking his guts out.

"—GPS coordinates," the man was saying. "You will follow those coordinates on your own. I will see if anyone follows you, believe me. Come alone and come with the thumb drive and we will all walk away from this and forget about it."

He disconnected.

"You almost gave yourself away," Harry complained. He sounded normal but his face was ice white.

"Couldn't help it," Mike mumbled, wiping his mouth.

Harry's scowl deepened. "Get it together, Mike," he snapped. "You're not going to help Chloe if you're out of control. Trust me on this."

"Does he have Chloe? How could he? My place is *secure*, goddammit. How could the fuckhead get in?"

Mike went to the program that controlled the video cams at their condo. The super knew nothing about it. He clicked onto the feed and got nothing but static. "Fuck," he whispered, punching out a number. He listened as the phone at the ground-floor security unit rang and rang. "Security's not picking up. José's on duty this morning. The guy's good. If he's not picking up, he's either knocked out or dead. Let me try one more thing." He dialed his own landline and listened as it rang, each ring like a gong that echoed through his body. No way would Chloe not answer.

Mike and Harry looked at each other. "He's got her," he said flatly. Harry nodded.

Fuck.

Mike tried to stabilize, tried to get his head back in the game, tried to find his icy calm, that cool, still place inside him that allowed him to function under the most terrible of circumstances.

It wasn't there.

It was gone.

He stood there, sweat pouring down his body, hands shaking, mind full of static, incapable of thinking, just seeing. Images of Chloe, broken and bleeding, in the hands of violent men.

He couldn't do it. He simply couldn't. He didn't have any mechanism inside him that could cope with this. He moved to the wastebasket and bent over, then reeled back from Harry's blow, nailing him right on the jaw.

"Fuck that!" Harry got right up into his face. "You're not going to get all panicky on me now, Mike. My sister's in the hands of a monster. I almost lost her to one once and I'm not going to lose her now. Come back, you son of a bitch, and help me here! If you don't pull your head out of your ass, we're going to lose her!"

He straightened, fingering his jaw, breath heaving in and out of his lungs. Harry still packed a punch.

Harry was terrified. But the thing was, if Chloe died, Harry would be devastated. He'd mourn forever. But his life would go on. He had a wife and a child and his family would remain.

If something happened to Chloe . . . Mike's mind skittered away from the thought, but he hung on to it grimly. He needed to understand this. If something happened to Chloe, if she died, Mike had nothing. It was as if he'd lived his life in a dank, dark cave and Chloe had opened the cave door and shown him a beautiful world of light. With Chloe gone, that door would shut forever.

He'd never have another shot at it because it was only Chloe who could open that door for him.

He had to fight for her life and for his.

He stood there, head down like a bull, ignoring the pain in his jaw. The cooling sweat on his body chilled him, but he'd stopped pumping out sweat like an animal. He looked at his hands. They were steady, as they'd always been.

His head was clear.

Chloe was not going to die. Not while he had a breath in his body.

"Where are the coordinates?" he asked sharply.

Harry slumped in relief. "Thank God you're back. I need you, Mike. I can't do this alone."

Their eyes met. "Nothing's going to happen to Chloe," Mike said, his voice steady. "We're bringing her home. If we can nail the scumbag, then that's icing on the cake, but bottom line? Chloe's coming home."

Harry was punching the keyboard. "The GPS coordinates are here." His finger rested on a map. "Here, near the Los Coyotes Indian Reservation."

Perfect. Near Warner Springs, where he'd undergone SERE training. Mike knew that area intimately. He'd been on the run from Marine "enemies" for two weeks. He'd sweated and bled and nearly died there.

"He chose it because there are flat stretches. He's planning a showdown, an exchange. He chose it from a map, or someone found it for him. Because that's a Navy special-ops training site, and he won't be familiar with it. I am, Harry. We're going to win this." Mike zoomed the map out and followed the route with his finger. "It's mostly freeway almost all the way there. The 163 to the 15 to the 78. Then we get into the hills over to where he wants us."

"He doesn't know I have you." Harry's heavy hand landed on

Mike's shoulder and he stared into Mike's eyes. He'd aged ten years in the past ten minutes. "We're going to get my sister back."

Mike briefly squeezed Harry's hand, then went to the gun locker.

"Fucking A, we are."

Chapter 20

"Coming up," Harry said quietly. He was driving the company's Transit van, which looked ordinary, even shabby, from the outside, the paint a little rusted in spots, dirty and caked with mud. It was equipped with enough horsepower to get them to the moon, had enough armor to stop anything but an RPG, and had as much communications gear as any combat platoon.

Mike moved around in the back of the van, steady and sure. The panic of earlier was gone, replaced by a deep calm.

A unarmed Predator B was circling overhead at 20,000 feet, completely invisible. Mike had no idea how many Pentagon arms Aaron had to twist to get it up there, and he didn't give a shit. All he cared about was that he was watching the combat area on his monitor and was able to zoom in and out.

Fact: two men were waiting in a Ford Taurus at a point almost two clicks from the texted GPS coordinates. Fact: Chloe was nowhere to be seen.

The terrain was easy to read for a sniper. Flat and featureless. They'd chosen it so they could be certain there would be no ambushes, but they couldn't know that Aaron and the SD SWAT team were deployed ten clicks away. Not near enough to save Chloe, but near enough to ensure that no matter what, the Russians weren't getting away.

Saving Chloe was Mike's job. And he had the right tool for it. On instinct, he'd chosen a Barrett MRAD with .338 Lapua rounds. It could shoot the balls off a fly and keep it alive, singing soprano.

It was a SEAL weapon of choice. Though SEALs weren't anywhere near as good as Force Recon Marines, as he often reminded Sam, they had damned good armorers. If the Barrett was good enough for the SEALs, it was good enough for Mike.

He'd spent the past hour going over possible scenarios in his head. He was ready.

"Braking," Harry said, and brought the van to a slewing halt. Right on the coordinates, Mike saw on the monitor.

His cell phone buzzed. A text, from Aaron.

Remember no kill shots.

The dust had barely settled around the Transit when Chloe's cell phone rang on the front seat. The Russian had called twice along the way to make sure they were coming.

The driver got out, holding a pair of binoculars in one hand, a cell phone with the other, a rifle slung across his back. He brought the cell phone to his ear.

Harry put the call on speakerphone.

"So. You are alone, yes?"

"Yes."

"Turn the vehicle around so the back is toward me, and open the doors."

Mike scrambled. The van had a fake panel behind the driver and passenger seats. His shoulders were too broad for a comfortable fit, but he managed it. They had powerful Sunagor binocs in the van. The lenses had a special nonreflective coating. A narrow opening showed him the scene two thousand yards away. The tan car, the blond man holding binoculars, rifle slung against his back. A man in the passenger seat. No sign of Chloe.

"Show me my sister first," Harry said.

The Russian, Nikitin, jerked his head. The man in the passenger seat got out and opened the back door of the car and started tugging.

Mike kept his breathing even, his mind calm. But somewhere deep inside him, hatred burned.

The second Russian pulled Chloe out so hard she fell headfirst into the dust. Mike watched as the Russian yanked her up with a powerful jerk. Chloe's mouth opened in a cry of pain he couldn't hear but he could see.

Mike moved the binoculars a fraction and took a good, long look at the man's face. It was seared into his mind.

"Mike?" Harry said quietly, barely moving his lips. He held his hand over the microphone. "Sitrep."

They both had a comms unit, almost undetectable.

Mike spoke into the mike. "Chloe looks basically unharmed. A little slow, maybe. I think they drugged her."

"Satisfied?" The Russian's voice came over the speakerphone. "Get that vehicle moving."

Without a word, Harry put the Transit in gear, turned it around so the back faced the Russians. He got out and opened the doors. Mike knew the Russian was seeing an essentially empty van through his binoculars. All their gear was stowed along the walls. The floor was bare.

They were in a shitload of trouble if the Russian insisted on leaving the Transit like this. Mike needed room to set up.

Harry closed the back doors and hurried back to the driver's seat. He positioned the van so that the long side was facing the Russians.

"What are you doing?" Nikitin roared.

"Oh. Just putting the van back in place." Harry stepped outside and walked forward, forestalling any objections. Mike couldn't hear the Russian any longer, just Harry.

"What do I do now?" Harry asked. He listened, placed the cell phone in its holster on his belt and started unbuttoning his shirt.

The Russian had asked to show he was unarmed. Harry took his shirt off, held his hands up and turned around. When he'd made a complete circle, he pulled up his pants legs, one at a time, to show he didn't have a backup weapon in an ankle holster.

He did, however, have a Glock 17 in a holster inside his waistband in the small of his back. They'd chosen the weapon together. Any long-range shooting would have to be Mike's lookout. Harry couldn't hide a rifle. Harry put his shirt back on, but left it unbuttoned.

"Okay," Harry said into the cell, and started walking forward slowly. The second Russian put a gun to Chloe's head and started walking forward, too.

Nikitin pulled his rifle with a couple of feet of scope to his shoulder. It was an SVD, the Dragunov. It was a good rifle. But Mike's was better. And however good a shot that fuckhead was, Mike was a better one. The Russian could be the best fucking shot in the world and Mike would still be better.

He could feel the cool deadly calm of the sniper coming over him. His heartbeat slowed down, his breathing, too, both becoming so regular they could be used as metronomes. He was cool, in control. Nothing could bother him. He had no thoughts, only the mission.

A tiny, tiny beat pulsed when he saw through the binoculars Chloe stumbling along, trails of dust following her feet, a gun at her head. A spurt of heat pulsed through his system until he reined it in.

Cool. Calm.

They'd strategized a number of scenarios and this was one. Nikitin was counting on his rifle trained on Chloe to keep Harry in line. Even if Harry managed to attack the Russian holding a gun to Chloe's head, Nikitin could shoot Chloe.

They would have a tiny window of opportunity and Mike started getting ready for it.

He pulled back the sunroof slowly. It was a special sunroof that allowed for operations out of the top of the vehicle. The Russian wouldn't be able to see that the entire top was now free and open to the sky.

The calculations began, complex and intricate and so familiar he fell into the numbers because the numbers would save him. Because being fast wasn't going to be enough.

The numbers were running in his head. Wind—none. Heat— 87 degrees. Humidity—low. Distance 1,782 meters. He calculated for bullet drop.

Harry was now fifty meters from the gunman and Chloe. Mike could see her face better now. She was terrified but seemed more aware, her head was up, she was focused on Harry.

Forty meters.

The Russian looked behind him and moved Chloe slightly to the left so that she was exactly in the line of sight for Harry. Mike couldn't get a shot at Nikitin without shooting Chloe. Harry used to have a hand signal for Chloe when she was little. A special signal that meant—*Get out of Rod's way*. He'd reminded her of it just a few evenings ago. She'd completely forgotten.

Harry was going to use that signal and Chloe was going to have to understand it, even through a drug haze.

Fuck.

Thirty meters.

Mike was watching through his scope now, a Schmidt & Bender 5-25x56 PMII with P4F Reticle, rated to 2,000 meters.

The Russian was saying something to Harry, who pulled the thumb drive out of his pocket and held it up.

Twenty meters.

Harry casually let his hand drop to his side.

Mike put a crate under the sunroof and stood on it, keeping his head below the roofline. He would have only fractions of a second to pop up.

The Boyd Loop. *Observe. Orient. Decide.*

Fifteen meters.

Harry's hand curled to one side and back as if scooping sand at the beach.

Chloe dropped like a stone.

The Russian had been holding on to her and was pulled out of alignment by Chloe's fall.

It was all Harry needed. His hand continued its movement and he pulled his Glock out and shot the Russian in the head, a neat round hole that turned into a pink mist haloing his head from the back.

Chloe was down. Mike had the shot.

Act.

In one smooth move, as if he'd rehearsed it a thousand times, Mike popped up, shouldered his rifle, sighted and squeezed the trigger, putting five thousand pounds of kinetic energy into Nikitin's head.

It exploded.

Mike remembered Aaron's injunction. *No kill shots.*

"Oops," he said, and threw the rifle down.

In a second he was running full tilt on the hard-packed sand, running as fast as he'd ever run in his life, running for his life, because there she was, picking herself up off the sand.

His life.

All that cool, calm control was gone, vanished. *Poof!* He was sweating and shaking, unable to take a deep breath from the tight bands that bound his chest.

He ran straight to Chloe and managed to skid to a stop before crashing into her, the sand kicking up in front of his boots.

"Chloe!" He managed to get the word out before his throat locked down.

Harry was looking down at the dead Russian at his feet. He hauled off and kicked him, a vicious slam of his boot that would have done real damage if the fucker hadn't already been dead.

"Chloe?" Mike tried again, his voice scratchy and raw, as if someone had rubbed it with sand.

She stood, slowly, smiled at him and held out her arms.

He snatched her up, trying not to crush her against him, trying not to pull her right into him, past his skin, straight to his heart, where she belonged.

His own heart was jackhammering, the sound so loud he couldn't even hear what she was saying, his whole body pulsing with the beat of his heart.

"Eh?"

Chloe laughed and pointed up at the helicopter flaring above them, FBI stenciled in white on the side.

Sand blew around them in hot, choking swirls.

"Cavalry arrived," Harry shouted, thumb angled up. "We'll spend hours at the station house."

"No," Mike shouted back. "Chloe and I are going to get married first. Right away."

Harry rolled his eyes. "Don't you think you should ask her first, smart-ass?" he shouted.

Mike turned to Chloe.

It would have been nice to lift her hair with his hand and whisper a gentle marriage proposal in her pretty ear, but her hair was being whipped into a froth by the rotors and she wouldn't hear a whisper.

"Chloe Mason," he screamed, "will you marry me?" *Nail it down*, he thought. "Right now?"

She laughed and kissed him. "Yes!" she screamed back.

Epilogue

They weren't expected. Mike and Chloe arrived around lunch-time two days early.

They both felt they had to rush back home with the news.

The two families were having lunch together, as they often did on Saturday. Merry, sharp as usual, was the first to see them. Or rather Chloe. When Chloe was around, Mike barely existed.

With a squeal, Merry ran into Chloe's arms, followed by Gracie, her sister Emma, and Laura, born the day Chloe almost died.

The four girls jumped around Chloe in a jumble of words and excitement, jostling for attention. Mike stepped sharply to one side, getting out of the way.

Nicole and Ellen were great. Sam and Harry were really lucky guys.

But Chloe was the catch and Mike had caught her. She couldn't cook and she wasn't any great whiz with money, but the kids loved her and that was more important than anything. Aunt Chloe was central to their lives. She was always there for them, and Nicole and Ellen knew, beyond a shadow of a doubt, that if they had to work and there was a sick girl, Chloe would be there and would love them and care for them like a mother.

It was the best gift of all.

Merry was jumping up and down, trying to see behind Chloe's back. "Aunt Chloe, Aunt Chloe, did you bring us presents?"

"Pwesents!" Laura echoed, clapping her hands. It was a ridiculous question, of course. Chloe was absolutely incapable of going somewhere without buying presents for the girls. Let alone go to London, which they'd been doing on a regular basis for the past two years. She could just as easily have sprouted wings and flown as come back empty-handed.

Every time Chloe hoped she could hand out the presents in an orderly fashion and every time fate laughed cruelly. The sounds of ripping paper and cries of joy started up behind them. Merry, Laura, Gracie and Emma were hopping up and down, in girl heaven.

Nicole got up from the table, smiling, followed by Ellen. "Well, this is a pleasant surprise. We were going to organize a little welcome home party for you, but you're early! So come on in, we were just about ready to sit down to lunch. Manuela made us a fabulous pot roast."

Ellen touched Chloe's hand. "How is Sister Mary Michael? And the girls?"

Mike helped Chloe take off her jacket, wondering how they could miss it. And yet there they were, Nicole and Ellen, two piranhas when it came to sniffing out news, totally clueless.

"Sister Mary Michael is fine. She sends her love. Ludmilla won first prize in an international piano competition. Everyone's really excited about that. And the girls were all really happy with their presents. I've got thank-you notes in my bag."

Nicole and Ellen beamed. Putting together packages for the

girls in London for Mike and Chloe to take over had become a big deal. A big, happy deal. They'd spent days trolling the shops for just the right things, and judging from the excited, happy faces, they got it right.

The ship had been stopped and boarded as soon as it crossed over into American waters. The huge scandal over the pedophile ring that was smashed made headlines for six months and the ripple effects were still felt.

Mike, Sam and Harry had followed each case with grim focus, rejoicing in each prison sentence.

In the meantime, no one knew what to do with the girls. The records of their existence had been destroyed. Some of the girls couldn't even name the town where they lived. All they knew was the orphanage, and they had been expunged from the records.

So Chloe called in Wonder Woman. Or at least that's how it felt at the time. Sister Mary Michael of Chloe's boarding school. A tiny woman, 100 pounds dripping wet, in a nun's habit, and she carried the authority of a general. Through negotiations that wouldn't have been out of place in a merger between Microsoft and General Motors, she managed to acquire custodianship over the young girls and ferry them back to London, where they were all growing into young, beautiful and happy young women.

Chloe always said she'd inherited way too much money, so she set up a $20 million trust fund for the girls, to help with the expenses at the Sacred Heart and for their university education.

Chloe and Mike visited often, and lately their trips to London had increased, but it wasn't just to see the girls.

There was a new, very efficient fertility clinic in Knightsbridge and they'd hit the jackpot.

"I have some news," Chloe said softly, and everyone stopped and looked at her. She was glowing, her eyes that golden color that still drove him crazy with desire. She reached out for his hand. "Mike and I have something to say. We, ah, we've been going to

London a lot these past six months, and I know you've been wondering why. We've been going to a center that specializes in a new IVF technique."

Sam and Harry looked blank. Nicole and Ellen drew in a sharp breath.

"We have good news. Mike and I—we're pregnant. With twins." Chloe blushed a fiery red, smiling with happiness.

Behind them the present frenzy had grown to crazy proportions, shreds of wrapping paper flying in the air. Mike thought of all the estrogen that was going to be floating around in a few years' time.

Well, his guys would take care of that.

"Boys," he said with satisfaction.

Sensual Books
by LISA MARIE RICE